THE

SECOND LIFE

of

SAMUEL TYNE

THE
SECOND LIFE
of
SAMUEL TYNE

A NOVEL

Esi Edugyan

Amistad

An Imprint of HarperCollins*Publishers*

HarperCollins books may be purchased for educational, business, or sales
promotional use. For information, please write: Special Markets Department,
HarperCollins Publishers Inc., 10 East 53rd Street,
New York, NY 10022.

Originally published in Canada in 2004 by Alfred A. Knopf Canada,
a division of Random House of Canada Limited, Toronto.
Reprinted by arrangement with Alfred A. Knopf Canada.

FIRST EDITION

Printed on acid-free paper

Library of Congress Cataloging-in-Publication Data

Edugyan, Esi.
   The second life of Samuel Tyne : a novel / Esi Edugyan—1st Amistad ed.
      p. cm.
   ISBN 0-06-073603-8
      1. Inheritance and succession—Fiction. 2. Fathers and daughters—Fiction.
3. Computer engineering—Fiction. 4. Ghanaians—Canada—Fiction.
5. Blacks—Canada—Fiction. 6. Community life—Fiction.
7. Inventors—Fiction. 8. Twins—Fiction. I. Title.

PR9199.4.E35S43 2004
813'.6dc22   2004046126

04 05 06 07 08 ❖ /RRD 10 9 8 7 6 5 4 3 2 1

For my mother
1942–1997

THE

SECOND LIFE

of

SAMUEL TYNE

chapter ONE

The house had always had a famished look to it. Even now when Samuel closed his eyes he could see it leaning, rickety and rain-worn, groaning in the wind. For though he'd never once visited it, he believed that strange old mansion must somehow resemble his uncle in its thinness, its severity, its cheerless decay. The house sat on the outskirts of Aster, a town noted for the old-fashioned fellowship between its men. Driving through, one might see a solemn group, patient and thoughtful, sharing a complicit cigarette as the sun set behind the houses. And for a man like Samuel, whose life lacked intimacy, the town seemed the return to the honest era he longed for. But he knew Maud would never move there, and the twins, for the sake of siding with her, would object in their quiet way.

News of the house had arrived in that spring of 1968, an age characterized by its atrocities: the surge of anti-Semitism throughout Poland; the black students killed in South Carolina at a still-segregated bowling alley; the slaughter of Vietnam. It was also an age of assassinations: that year witnessed the deaths of Martin Luther King Jr.

and Robert Kennedy, and those of less public men who gave their lives for ideas, or for causes, or for no good reason at all. But in Calgary, Alberta, in the far remove of the civil service, Samuel Tyne, a naturally apolitical man, worried only over his private crises. For his world held no future but quiet workdays, no past beyond youth and family life.

Sitting in the darkened shed in his backyard, Samuel examined the broken objects around him. Smoke from the solder filled his nose, his mouth tasting uncomfortably of blood. Snuffing the rod on a scorched pink sponge, he abandoned the antique clock and stood at the dusty window. He dreaded telling Maud about inheriting his uncle's house. She was prone to overreacting. Their marriage, plagued by the usual upsets of conjugal life, suffered added tensions, for across the sea, their tribes had been deeply scornful of each other for centuries.

Jacob's death had been the first shock, but Samuel deliberated longer over the second: his unexpected inheritance. The first call had come days ago, after dinner, during Samuel and Maud's only shared hour of the day. Already weary of each other's company, they settled down in the living room with the resignation of people fated to die together. Samuel took up his favorite oak rocker, Maud the beige shag chair, and the clicking of her knitting needles filled the room.

"They've always been withdrawn," she complained. "But this is madness. They won't even talk to me. Their world begins and ends with each other, without a care for anyone else."

Samuel sighed, scrutinizing his wife. She was thin as an iron filing, with a face straight out of a daguerreotype, an antiquated beauty inherited from her father. Her church friends so indulged her worries that Samuel, too, found he had to stomach her complaints good-naturedly. She took everything personally.

"Perhaps they did not hear you," he said.

Maud continued to knit in silence, thinking. The twins really had changed. Only Yvette spoke, and she wasted few words. Maud couldn't understand it. As babies they'd been so different she'd corrected the doctor's proclamation that they were identical. Now they'd grown so similar she couldn't always say with great authority who was who. But she suspected it was her own fault. The thought of being responsible unsteadied her hands, and the sound of her nervously working needles began to irritate Samuel.

He'd been lost in his own meditations, contemplating what to fix next so that he would not have to think of his stifling job. Officially, Samuel was a government-employed economic forecaster, but when asked lately how he made his living, he lacked the passion to explain. The civil service now seemed an arena for men who woke to find their hopes burnt out. Every day, he too grew disillusioned. Even his children had become a distant noise. Samuel was the oldest forty in the world.

Yet fear of quitting his job did not unnerve him—it seemed only practical that he should fear it. What humiliated him was that he failed to quit because he dreaded his wife's wrath.

Agitated, he'd begun to run through ways of asking Maud to stop knitting so loudly, when the phone rang. People rarely called the house, so Samuel and Maud paused for a moment in their chairs. Finally, Maud dropped her lapful of yarn to the carpet, saying, "I'll get it, just like everything else in this house."

Samuel stared at the empty armchair. From the kitchen her voice droned on; he could pick out only the higher words. But they were enough. His chair began to rock, unsummoned, in what seemed like a human, futile move to pacify him. His childhood came back to him, a bitter string of incidents more felt than remembered. And the memories seemed full of such delicate meaning that he might have been experiencing his own death. When he opened his eyes, his wife stood before him, uncomfortable.

"You've heard then," she said in a soft voice.

"Uncle Jacob," he said. He stilled his chair.

"It took this long for them to find our number. I guess he didn't mention he had family." The spite in her comment sounded crass even to Maud. She went quietly back to her chair. "I'm sorry," she said.

"When did he die?"

"Night before last. That's what they think, anyway. He was very stubborn about being left alone in that old house. A neighbor he'd been friendly with went to call on him for something, and the front door was open. Just like that. They found him collapsed in a chair. Said he couldn't have been gone more than an hour before they found him. It was God's grace, too, because the neighbor had only gone to say goodbye before leaving town for a week, and no one else called on Jacob much."

Samuel nodded. Jacob had been a private man. So private that he'd cut from his life the man he'd raised as his own son. Samuel looked at Maud's hands, a dark knot on her lap.

"Good night," he said.

Maud rose with deliberate slowness, giving him time to change his mind, to reach out to her. She stood quite uselessly in the doorway; then after a moment the hall lights went out and he heard her ascend the stairs.

At the brief funeral held just outside of Aster, Samuel wore the only gift his uncle had ever sent him—an elephantine suit that sulked off his joints and seemed to be doing the grieving for him. Samuel had eschewed a church ceremony, opting instead for a secular gathering in which his friend Halldór Bjornson, a retired speechwriter, mumbled a few lofty clichés over the already-covered grave. Samuel had put his full faith in Jacob's neighbor's judgment, choosing not to identify the body, and now he wondered if he'd done the wise thing. Maud saw his decision as an attempt to shield off more grief, but Samuel himself was less sure.

In truth, he was a man incapable of coping with sadness. Since the day Jacob had abandoned him for Aster, Samuel had unconsciously struggled to become his uncle. He thought often of Jacob's face, which despite a life of labor, or perhaps because of it, had the craggy, aristocratic look of a philosopher's. Jacob's speech had even sounded philosophical; praised for his practical wisdom, he'd had a hard time believing he wasn't always right. But Samuel only succeeded in imitating Jacob Tyne's stubbornness, which went no deeper than Samuel's face: he wore a look of mourning with the graveness of a sage, without irony, like an amateur stage actor.

His overt melancholy aggravated his boss, for it made Samuel hard to approach. Just a glance into Samuel's cubicle gave his co-workers much to gloat about. It seemed a wonder he was such an exacting employee, with the swift but pitiful stride that brought him, disillusioned, to the threshold of every meeting. Yet he was so indispensable in that ministry that his co-workers regretted every slur they flung at him, lest the slights drive him to suicide. For not only would the department collapse without his doting, steady logic to balance it, but it seemed at times that the entire Canadian economy depended on the reluctant, soft-wristed scribbling he did in his green ledger.

There Samuel sat each day, painfully tallying his data, his pencil poised like a scalpel in his hand, frowning at the gruesome but inevitable task ahead of him. Dwarfed by a monstrous blue suit, Samuel would finger the mournful, pre-war bowler that never left his head. And it was such an earnest sight, such an intimate window into a man whose nature seemed to be all windows—people wondered if he actually had a *public* self—that he might have been the only man in the world to claim vulnerability as his greatest asset.

The day after the funeral, Samuel returned to work to find a note from his bosses on his desk: *Come See Us.*

What could they possibly reprimand him for? He was a fast and diligent worker, with enough gumption to use a little imaginative reasoning when some economic nuisance called for it. He was punctual and tidy, not overly familiar with his co-workers; quite simply, the best employee they had. Rather than indignation, though, Samuel only felt fear. To buy himself time, he crumpled a few clean papers from his ledger, and walked the narrow aisles between cubicles to throw them in the hallway garbage bin.

He returned to find both bosses, Dombey and Son, as he'd nicknamed them, at his desk. Dombey's German sense of humor often failed to translate, at least to Samuel, who always overdid his laugh to mask confusion. Son, whose current prestige was pure nepotism, looked at Samuel with the coldness that cloaked all of his dealings, as if he knew he was inept and needed to compensate.

"Tyne," said Dombey, "we need to talk about the Olds account."

Samuel pinched the brim of his hat with his thumbs. "Ah, yes. Sorry, yes. I think, sir, I handed that in before I took day leave for my uncle's funeral."

"It contains a dreadful error," said Son, blinking violently behind his glasses. He jerked the report at Samuel.

There it was, plain as day, on page six. A miscalculation Samuel must have made while thinking about Jacob's death and the house. He stood there, hat in hand, aghast.

"We realize," continued Son, "that the job sometimes gets stressful. That, per se, there are times when one cannot always be as on-the-ball as is required. But this defies all. Not only is it not up to standard, it's downright misleading."

That was the way Son spoke, as though he hadn't mastered the bureaucratic language, wielding phrases such as "per se" and "not up to standard" like the residue of some management handbook. Even Dombey seemed perplexed by this at times.

The muscle in Samuel's cheek trembled. He nodded.

"We understand you've just suffered a big loss, Samuel," said Dombey, "but as you know this is a federal workplace. What would happen, say, if you made this kind of error daily? Now, we're certainly not saying you do. But what would happen? I'll tell you what would happen. You'd have ladies collapsing in ten-hour lines just to get a loaf of bread to feed their families. You'd have children skipping school because there aren't enough clothes to go around. Babies dying without milk. Old folks crumbling in their rockers. It'd be pandemonium with a capital P—depression. We *are* the economy. We answer to the prime minister. There is no room for error here." Dombey scratched his head and looked wistful. "Oh, for chrissakes, don't look so *glum*."

Again, Samuel nodded.

Son, fearing his role in the reprimand unnecessary, added, "We are, of course, deeply sorry for your loss, but you must remember our country is in your hands."

Dombey frowned at Son, and the two men walked off. When they left, Samuel heard through the divider the rude laughter of Sally Mather. His face burning, he sat at his desk, and picking up his green ledger, tried to make up for the ten minutes of lost time.

He didn't allow himself to think about the incident until lunch. He tried to suppress his rage by reasoning that, though he hadn't made a single mistake in his entire fifteen-year career, this one was so severe that it merited rebuke. And he was able again to forget his indignation until nighttime, when he retired to his shed after the obligatory hour of his wife's silent company. His work shed was a refuge, a hut where life couldn't find him. A place where only Samuel's verdict mattered, and the only place it *did* matter. Into the early hours he'd sit and tinker with the guts of a stubborn radio, or a futile clock, or some negligent object borrowed from Ella Bjornson without Maud's knowing it. Only after months of stealthy repairs did she start to wise up to his secrets, berating the flier boy for bringing *Northern Electronics Monthly*. How little credit she gave him. Never once did his stash of *National Radio Electronics*, prudently kept at work, occur to her, or the digital electronics certificate he was earning, his lessons also left at the office.

Initially, he'd had no noble ambitions for this new knowledge, but today's run-in with his bosses made him ache for a vocation, not a mere job. He sat on the dusty workbench, the imprint in his seat betraying his dedication. Just when thoughts of quitting his job had grown ominous, he forced himself to forget them. This was how Samuel dealt with things—by ignoring them. The tactic had given him forty sweet years, and he was convinced that if every man had such strength of will, there would be decidedly fewer wars.

In forty years there was a good deal of life to forget. He'd been born the privileged and only son of Francis Tyne, an august cocoa farmer in Gold Coast, whose sudden death at the playboy age of thirty-six had devastated the family fortune. Faced with having to quit school to keep his family from poverty, Samuel was saved by his estranged uncle Jacob, who worked the harvests while Samuel completed his schooling. Family legend had it that Jacob, whose unparalleled erudition had been a rumor of Samuel's childhood, had betrayed Francis in their youth. When, years later, Samuel was bold enough to go to the source, the old patriarch only said, "Rather than gouge old wounds, one's energy is better spent making amends."

For this reason, Jacob left the plantations and his chieftancy in the hands of two incompetent cousins to accompany Samuel to England, where Samuel, whom all had agreed had inherited Jacob's erudition, completed a college degree with first-class honors.

They moved to Canada on a wave of immigration. War brides, Holocaust survivors, refugees of every skin were seeking new lives in a quieter country. For a time things were awkward in Calgary, what with no work for a classically educated black man who refused menial chores. At twenty-five he lived off the backbreak of Jacob, a man more than twice his age. But Jacob maintained Samuel would waste himself in a toil job—what was the point of all that schooling? Within five months Samuel had found his position as economic forecaster, Jacob had abandoned him for the town of Aster, and like some cosmic consolation, Samuel met Maud Adu Darko, whom he married one month later at city hall. No dowry, no audience. The most liberated time of their lives.

Maud refused to speak anything but English, though Samuel knew the language of her tribe. And though she hated Gold Coast, she could never completely bleed its traditions from her life, for Samuel disliked Western food. When Gold Coast won independence in 1957, they ate a half-hearted feast of goat stew and fried plantain. And though rechristened "Ghana" after its once-glorious ruined kingdom, the country would always be "Gold Coast" for them; having lived so long away from it, in their minds, it was largely defined by its name.

Work changed for Samuel after his bosses' confrontation. He began to treat each excruciating day as his last. He couldn't forgive the Dombeys' crass disregard of his uncle's death. He began to discreetly box up his belongings, a simple urge that after hours of work became a definite decision to quit. But after a mug of strong coffee and an hour fearing his family's possible impoverishment, he'd resumed work. Samuel found himself waiting for a sign.

It came that Saturday morning, again with a phone call. The mood in the Tyne house was somber. Rain came in through the cracks, so that the household paper curled like lathe shavings and the bedrooms reeked of soil. Samuel lay in bed, tearless but with an undefined agony deep inside him, so ashamed of these episodes that he pretended they had to do with Maud's food, and glanced admonishingly at her every time she entered the room.

Drama exasperated Maud, who didn't understand grief, least of all in a man. "Will you be needing your corset and crinoline when you're finished, Miss Sorrow?" she'd say, though not without a pang of guilt.

And Samuel's sadness did seem theatrical, like something manufactured. Even he had trouble believing it, but he let himself go, seeing Jacob's death as a singular chance to get all his sadness out, to cure himself of the widower's look he carried through the world.

Almost as soon as Maud left the room, the phone rang. And for some reason, call it the intuition of the unfortunate, Samuel didn't answer and instead rolled over in bed. Soon enough there was the knock at the door, and then the hinge twisting in the jamb. His twin daughters, dressed in identical green jumpers with huge collars like palm fronds, gripped each other's hands with a naturalness that unsettled him. Even preoccupied, it was impossible not to notice their strangeness. They had the sleek, serious faces of greyhounds, with a confidence to their identical gestures that had upset other children in their daycare days. Each had a cold, shrewd look in her eyes, an exaggerated capacity for judgment in a twelve-year-old. Yvette spoke with a mocking sweetness.

"Telephone," she said in a falsetto.

"*Telephone,*" mocked Chloe. Neither laughed.

Samuel sat up in bed. "Thank you, girls." He waited for them to leave before taking the extension from the cradle.

The only words Samuel could make out sounded disjointed and senile, everything said in a moist voice so filled with contradictions that it was impossible to place its accent. Samuel banged the phone on his palm, and the caller's voice rose out of the static.

"Alberta government were going to make his house a heritage site, gone and drawn up the legal documents two, *two* days after I found him. Those crooks, they wait till a man leaves town, then—"

"I am sorry. With whom am I speaking?"

"Trying to rob a decent man from leaving something behind him, as if—"

"Excuse me, who are you?"

There was a deep silence, a crackling of static. "Porter. Name's Porter. I witnessed the will."

Samuel felt sick. "There was a will?" Suddenly he realized he'd been embittered by the fact that there hadn't been one, that Jacob hadn't bothered to spend the hour it would take to draft the papers, to think of him.

"Handwritten," said Porter. "Everything's yours."

"No."

"The house has a lot of land surrounding it. Two, three acres."

"*No.*" He couldn't believe it.

"I do horticulture. I have the will."

Samuel grew confused. "Yes?" There was another silence in which he thought he heard a woman hushing a child in the background.

"I'll be passing through Calgary tonight around seven. Meet me downtown by the Tower and I'll hand over the keys." Porter hung up.

Samuel lay back, unsettled. He turned on his side and tried to sleep. Three hours later he was still looking at the wall.

When the time arose for him to go, Samuel dressed with quiet deliberation, telling Maud he was going for a drive to clear his mind. When he reached downtown, it had grown dark. A young man in a tired baseball cap stood just outside the doors of the concrete tower, and sullenly, without any greeting, he began making arrangements with Samuel. Common sense told Samuel the man was too young to be the one who had phoned. But he said he was Porter, so Samuel decided he must be the man's son, accepting the keys forced into his hand. He drove home to find his own house dim; Maud, luckily, had gone to bed without him. Lying beside her, Samuel meditated over the strangeness of the meeting, but tried to put it out of his mind. He slept badly that night, and found himself obsessing over the house in his usually disciplined work hours.

Then on Monday, just before lunch, it happened. In old age, when asked what he'd made of his life, Samuel realized he could only say he'd made it to the end. This was the outcome of his gifted and cocky youth. He'd failed. For an hour he sat in a useless stupor, seeing the green lines on his ledger as if from a watery distance.

He was shocked from his thoughts by Dombey's Son, who'd been looking over his shoulder for some time. "Tyne, I've noticed that you've done nothing today. This is simply unacceptable," he said in a tremulous voice. Son's glasses sat askew on his face, and his shirt buttons danced against his chest, thumbed loose from months of nervousness. He flinched when Samuel turned to him, glancing around like a child lost in a store.

"The standards call for six point seven five work hours per diem, with the opportunity for a second break in the afternoons . . . with, with, a second afternoon break only sometimes. But, as you've been informed, we have specified the areas allotted for . . ." he stammered, as though trying to recall the appropriate phrasing, "allotted for . . ."

Without his father, Son's rhetoric seemed not only ridiculous, but pathetic. Samuel wondered that he had ever feared this man. With a feeling of utter self-assurance—invincibility, almost—Samuel began to pack up his belongings.

Looking alarmed, Son said, "Don't misunderstand me, Tyne. This is not a dismissal, only a reprimand."

Ignoring his coworkers' shocked silence and Son's weak pleas to "be reasonable, Tyne," Samuel walked out without a word.

The gray rag of a day, with its first snow of the year, was filled with the singing of thrush and that lucky feeling people have after mysteriously surviving an accident. He felt, in effect, the precocity of his youth, he felt like that teenager who'd bragged he would lead a country or win the Nobel Prize for economics one day. In short, Samuel Tyne was alive again.

Driving, he saw a goods stand pitched away from the roadside, the thin wood roof buckling under the snow. "Here is one like me," he said to himself, wanting to share his new joy with a fellow deadbeat. "A man of great potential wasting away under the tortures of meaningless work." In full empathy he pulled over, shaking hands with the fat Greek salesman and running the rules for barter over in his head. Seeing the pitiful merchandise, Samuel wondered if he'd been too hasty. It seemed the man had just emptied his attic, stacking his junk in the open air. Samuel hesitated, discomfited by the man's desperate look every time they made eye contact. Then he saw the dolls.

He was so reminded of his daughters that he knew at once the dolls were good luck. "Give me those!" he said, forgetting to talk down the price. Driving home, he knew he'd made a mistake. The dolls sat like livid children in the back seat, and Samuel couldn't help but glance at them in his rearview mirror. Their sharp red hair looked like rooster combs, and they had the lush, vulgar mouths of prostitutes. The stitching around their eyes was done so childishly that Samuel wondered if the Greek hadn't made them himself. He parked in an alley five houses away, then strode to the shed to throw the dolls in the ashcan. But some vulnerability about them, inanimate though they were, made him stuff them high on a shelf instead. Sitting down to the wires of Maud's prized clock, Samuel thought of his job, and of the inherited house in Aster. Maud knew nothing of either.

When the time came to fake his punctual return from work, Samuel found himself in such a good mood that, like all men who wake from the graveyard of an empty life, he assumed his joy was universal. Taking the dolls down from the shelf, he put them in his briefcase, which he walked into the humid kitchen swinging like the happy apparition of the boy he'd been.

Maud looked at him with suspicion. "Look who's won the lottery," she said. "Supper will be ready in ten minutes. Sit down."

He sat across from the twins, whose rigid unresponsiveness to his smiles hurt his mood a little. He thought of presenting his gift right then, but forced himself to wait until after dinner. He ate a lukewarm spinach stew with sweet fried plantain, and watching the twins, with their oblong faces leaning over their plates as though the whole of their fates could be found there, Samuel recalled their infancy, when they'd refused to eat in a sensible way. No sooner was baby Yvette fasting than baby Chloe grew gluttonous. The next day, with Yvette greedy from the previous day's starvation, there was barely enough time to clean up what Chloe threw up. It was maddening. Their erratic eating patterns had left Maud feeling lost. Helpless, Samuel could only console his wife.

Now his daughters ate by rote, chewing as though they resented meals for the time they had to spend in their parents' company. Maud asked them probing questions about school, and keeping her eyes on her plate Yvette barely raised her voice for the one-word answers. Samuel was discouraged. But, nevertheless, when the meal ended, he pulled his briefcase onto the table and, delighted with himself, presented the dolls.

Neither girl moved. Then, raising their heads, they looked in Samuel's direction with sharp eyes, more in assessment of him than of his gift.

Samuel cleared his throat. "They're rag dolls. Thought you girls might like them." He eyed Maud, who deliberately didn't look his way. Her face was a confusion of feelings; unnerved by her twins, she nevertheless felt vindicated. Samuel was just as useless a parent as she was.

Chloe wouldn't look at the dolls. Under her sister's direction, Yvette gave them a quick appraisal and signalled with her eyes that the dolls were not worth the pain of talking to their father. Or so things seemed to Samuel, who was more perplexed than hurt by their behavior.

"You could thank him," said Maud.

Chloe fixated on her plate.

Yvette raised her dark-lined, almond eyes, and in her mocking falsetto, she said, "*Thank* you."

The table fell silent. The longer no one said anything, the more embittered Samuel became. He left the table without speaking, but not before noticing that the twins had grasped each other's hands beneath the table. He went out to the shed.

But thoughts of the house he now owned, and of the easy way he'd abandoned his job, made him feel less rejected. He even smiled at the twins' precocity. They had a special knack for making Samuel feel like a hopeless child.

But then, the twins had always been brilliant.

chapter TWO

Years before, during the first devil's rainstorm of August, Maud Tyne turned from the rain at the window when she heard a baby say, "You don't have to name me. I am Annalia."

Maud felt a shadow pass over her. The voice was so precisely what one would expect of a six-day-old, if six-day-olds spoke, that it resounded like a bell. Maud scanned the spare room, its gaggle of toys clogging one corner, a tall Roman lamp with a jaunty orange shade, the blue table sagging with almost human exhaustion. Nothing. Not even a talking doll to take the blame. Maud glanced at the twins in their shared bassinet by the closet and, annoyed at her fear, strode over to draw back the blanket.

The girls were moist and sluggish, so that disturbing them felt like a kind of violation. The girl on the left yawned, and the yawn passed to the mouth of her sleeping sister, who shuddered. Within seconds they both dozed, and Maud walked back to the window. There had been no miracle. But instead of relief, Maud felt even more disturbed.

Outside, people rushed through the downpour, a sharp sun giving the light the quality of an eclipse. But Maud looked without truly seeing, so distracted that the sound of the doorbell startled her. She'd forgotten. She had been waiting since two o'clock for a day of tea and prophetic gossip with Ella Bjornson, now more than an hour late. Maud checked again on the sleeping twins, then descended the stairs.

Ella was soaked to the bone, her green bonnet flattened against her scalp. A church counselor, she advised those she called the "the wretched, disconsolate products of thoughtless love," namely the children of mixed marriages. Ella herself had married a gentle Scandinavian, the father of her two well-adjusted children. But she balked at that fact, saying it was only by chance they had turned out so splendid, and shattering her confidentiality oath, would list the names of twenty children who had not.

An expert gossip, Ella got her information by feigning sympathy, so that Maud always weighed her words during their conversations. And yet, despite Ella's ruthlessness, people still invited her for tea and entrusted her with their children, for she had a politician's charms.

"The hail out there is big enough to give you a concussion," said Ella. "Maud, what's wrong? You really look in pain." She shrugged out of her drenched overcoat and wrapped her arms around Maud. "Tell Ella."

Maud shrugged. "How about you, Ella? How are you doing?"

And it was as though Maud had flipped a switch, for forgetting Maud's problems entirely—that was another of Ella's quirks, that she had the attention span of the children she counseled—she began a critique of the Pratts, who made daytime love without the good sense to close the door. "Imagine a child seeing that," said Ella. "The damage!"

"Oh, don't be stupid," said Maud, leading Ella through the hall into a somber room in which the tea set sat prearranged like a chessboard. The storm light gave the furniture the dark quality of ruins, and a smell of mud and ferment saturated everything. Maud shut the windows and motioned Ella to the closest chair, which her friend collapsed into with a fanfare of sighs and rustling. Maud slid the rum from the bookshelf.

"Well, there's nothing wrong with your generosity," said Ella. "How are the twins? I've been dying to see them."

Without so much as a pause, Maud topped their toddies with a few drops of tea, though her pulse quickened. "It is easier to raise the dead than to get two bad-tempered babies back to sleep. Next time."

Ella so easily accepted Maud's authority that Maud wondered why she didn't try to be stern more often. She might have saved herself three years of humiliations. Not that Ella dared gossip about Maud (or so Maud hoped), but too often Maud found herself Ella's unwitting accomplice and, lacking the ingenuity to extricate herself, ended up shouldering the blame for slandering good people. When Ella had repeated to anyone with ears that old man Davis was a licentious cross-dresser, and that his wife's holidays were actually electroshock treatments in Ponoka, Maud, least interested and last to hear it, got caught bringing it up as known news at a church social. The Davises now despised the Tynes, refusing to invite them to their Christmas parties. Ella, on the other hand, still received her invitations yearly.

"You were so humiliated, I thought you'd kill me on the spot!" laughed Ella.

The sound of a baby crying dried the conversation. Ella looked expectantly at Maud, who sat calmly drinking her tea and trying to quiet her heartbeat. She simply could not bring herself to go and check on her children. It was a stupid, unfounded fear, but she felt paralyzed in her chair. It took her a while to realize that she hadn't completely ruled out the incredible idea of the babies speaking, and this troubled her. As the dry, plaintive cries resounded through the house, only to be magnified when the second twin began crying, Maud saw Ella smirk with the nervous delight of finding a new topic. For Ella was one of those women for whom it was never too late to betray old friends; great gossip was life to her, so that it was difficult to side with people when a decent story could be lost.

"Aren't you going to tend to them?" Ella sounded baffled, but somewhere in those words lay a challenge.

Maud settled her saucer on the table. "If you pick up a child every time it cries, you will be picking that child up for the rest of its life."

They drank without speaking as the cries intensified. Maud tried to talk casually, but it seemed absurd; they had to raise their voices to be heard, all the while pretending this was normal. Maud was so anxious to determine if she'd be hearing about herself on the street that she couldn't respond thoughtfully to anything Ella said. Ella rose to leave, and putting on her coat, she grew serious and gave Maud a grave, searching look.

"Tell Samuel to take the twins off your hands and get yourself a good night's rest," said Ella and left.

Maud was mortified. By the time she reached the bassinet the babies were dozing just as she'd left them half an hour ago, so that the eternal crying seemed like another hallucination. But Ella had heard it, too. Maud grew humiliated, knowing Ella thought childbirth had weakened her reason, and she despised herself for caring more about appearances than her children. But she had done it for the good of the family name, after all. She spent the last hours of the afternoon watching the twins sleep, and resolved not to mention a word of what had happened to Samuel.

Yet, when Samuel came in, his rain-logged blazer slung fussily over a forearm, the twins were the first subject on her tongue. Samuel grew nervous as she followed him to their bedroom and helped him out of his frail, bitter-smelling clothes, tossing them across the rack to dry. She sighed, then sat on their sensitive bed without making it move. Strangely, the weight of carrying twins had almost left her body, and in lapses that betrayed just how deeply this new country had altered her thought, she bragged about having "good genes." She was even thinner than before they had married, when just the sight of her awkward bones made him mournful for the destitute child she'd been. Now Samuel felt uneasy near that body. "What are you muttering about?" he asked.

Maud looked toilworn, as if she'd aged a year since morning. But her voice retained its vigor. "In less than a week you'll have to drag me off to a madhouse," she said. "You know I heard the twins talk today?"

Samuel placed his briefcase on the bed beside his wife. "It is much too early for such things."

"I'm just saying what I heard."

"What is it they said?"

"Only one spoke. She said her name was Annalia."

Samuel felt a pang of self-consciousness and walked behind the closet door to dress. "A child must have a name before she herself can say it. Your conscience is telling you it has been too long."

"It's not like naming a cat or a recipe. Even God took his time."

"He created the whole world in the time you have taken to choose a simple name."

A gust of rain sprayed the house, and looking at the window, Maud collapsed into the sagging pillows. "It's not like you've shown any genius in this business of names. Just use the Thursday name and 'Ata' for 'twin,' he says. A backyard ditch in a world of indoor plumbing."

Samuel stepped from behind the closet door, his pantwaist wallowing mid-thigh. "After my mother."

Maud continued to look out the window.

Samuel finished dressing, the rain making him melancholy. The noise of it hitting the foliage opened in him the memory of his uncle's laborers in Gold Coast, who came in from the downpour to share their only meal of the day with his family. He smiled sadly as he stepped from behind the closet door, buttoning down his collar. "So what will you call them, then? Annalia?"

Maud addressed the window. "They say a child's face will name itself, but . . . why did we complicate the world with names in the first place?"

But their angst over names was nothing when compared with their initial depression over Maud's pregnancy. Samuel's own father was virtually unknown to him, so he felt deeply perplexed by the role. Maud wandered the house repeating how impossible it was, absently patting her stomach. Her father's parting words had killed all her ambitions, so that pregnancy seemed as likely as winning the

Nobel Peace Prize. She had spent her childhood serving that father, who groomed his hatred like a favorite horse. Maud's mother had died giving birth to her, and in a joke that became a promise, her father vowed to break one of his daughter's bones for each year of his wife's life. This seemed utterly strange, for her father was the village's most accomplished polygamist, with a tedious hatred for the wife who'd just died. But he was also a man of his word, and Maud left school behind for ten bouts of bilious fever, two broken ribs, a fractured tailbone, a week-long blindness in one eye, and hands worked so raw they were nailless.

After months of praying for salvation, it finally came. Maud was granted a nanny position with a missionary family returning to their lives on the Canadian prairie. Keeping her escape a secret was no easy chore, for the people of her compound, dragged down by the monotony of life, made other people's business their household entertainment. But her luck held, and one day she gathered her meagre belongings into a fishnet and carried it to the dirt road. During the interminable wait she felt nostalgic for the home a few yards behind her. The air carried silt into her eyes, and when she set her bag down to rub them, her father stepped from the shadows of the compound where he'd been folding crude roots into his pipe and calmly walked over to pick it up.

"And where is it you are going?" he asked in their language. He took something from her bag. "And with this photograph of mother? Eih? You thieving? You thieving to sell this?"

Maud felt sick. If the escort car hadn't arrived, the missionary father calling from a lowered window, she might have returned to the compound. Her father, always dignified under the eye of foreign strangers, affixed a smile to his face while slipping the picture of Maud's mother into his robes. He handed Maud her bag with perverse decorum and, speaking under his breath, said, "Death comes soon to those who kill their parents. Abandon me and your mother's spirit will fell your husband and dry your insides to stone."

Distraught, she climbed into the car, watching her smiling father wave until he couldn't be seen from the road.

It takes no great empathy to see why she never returned, or to explain her utter failure as a nanny, without the first knowledge of children's needs or the instinct of love to compensate for her ignorance. Discharged within a few months, Maud received a sympathetic fistful of cash and was left to make a living in a country that had no need of her. Though plagued with menial jobs, and living in the basements of churches, during these years she learned to read, using homemaker magazines and a dog-eared copy of the New Testament. She sounded out the words, enunciating to shave her origins from her voice. By the time she met Samuel, only her tribal marks, still visible under face powder, gave her away.

When the pregnancy assailed them, Maud had already reached thirty-one, a distasteful age for a first child, both by Gold Coast and Western standards of the time. Her failure as a nanny also haunted her. So it devastated her when not one, but two babies arrived, and not even boys at that. Twins. Both Samuel and Maud were embarrassed to admit that not even an ocean could distance them from their superstitions. For twins were a kind of misfortune. Samuel's great uncles had been twins, and the advent of their birth had brought a maelstrom of controversy to the family. Primogeniture had been jeopardized—without knowing for certain who'd been born first, how could they name an heir? And twins, a freak occurrence, scared people. Only some awful wrongdoing could produce the same person twice. The mother's fidelity came into question; for no man on earth was so virile that he could do two at once. Only the prestige of the Tyne name saved their matriarch from suspicion. Samuel's ancestral experience was enough to put both him and Maud off.

On the seventh day they named their children. The firstborn was called Yvette, a name neither fully liked, a sullen compromise between Efua and Betty. The second-born Maud named Chloe, because she liked its European appeal. Wearied by the argument, Samuel allowed her names, though it took days of nagging for him to refer to his girls as anything but *them*. Even Annalia seemed more inventive to him. But Samuel, always a quick healer, recovered from his defeat as scarlessly as if he'd picked the names himself.

Maud was surprised at how easy it was to love the babies. She realized the ingredient lacking in her stint as a nanny was that the children had to be her own. Their stupidest behavior amused her, even their volatile eating patterns, which exhausted her with their inconstancy. But she was smitten. At their third birthday party, Maud's tea circle gathered to marvel at the cold concertos whistled with the sincerity of a flute. Two years later, the girls took to calling themselves Dracula (Yvette) and Ms. Diefenbachia (Chloe), which in the company of others became the single identity Ms. Diefendracula, or more simply, Drachia. Maud saw this as a clever allusion to the Diefenbaker government, and took pride in knowing the Tyne wit would not die out with her. By age seven they amazed Maud by performing Shakespeare, though still in the habit of sucking each other's thumbs. At nine, Maud caught them playing the Same Game, repeating each other's gestures like a delayed mirror, speaking pig Latin with the dexterity of a first language. Chloe even had such a strange magnetic makeup that watches ran backward on her wrist. Now, at twelve, they'd begun to pattern their own poetry after Lord Byron's. Genius, Maud liked to say, was obvious.

When their childish games degenerated into fights, Maud consoled herself that after the first outburst things would pass. One day Chloe chose the wrong outfit (for they dressed alike and despised looking like others), and Yvette boxed her ears. This was followed by Yvette's disastrous attempt to steal candy from Maud's nightstand: she and Chloe stuffed their mouths with the dried liniment balls used to soften Samuel's baths. After throwing up in the neighbor's flowerbeds, Chloe punched her sister, screaming, "You *poi*soned me!" Then came the day Chloe refused to answer to anything but Diefenbachia (retaliation: a kick in the leg); the day Yvette refused to whistle the sugar-beet song that would prolong Chloe's life by five minutes (retaliation: a dime-sized patch of baldness); the day Chloe ate Yvette's cassava (retaliation: a cherry pit hidden at the heart of Chloe's ice-cream dish, chipping her molar and, so she claimed, plaguing her with a lifetime of insensate tastebuds). The only time Maud intervened was when she caught them doing synchronized backflips off the roof, landing like rag dolls in the juniper. Yvette cried a single, isolated tear, while Chloe seemed invigorated by the fall, so that Samuel, seeing them unharmed, nicknamed them Young Tragedy and Comedy.

The day after Samuel's doll fiasco, Maud found the twins in the kitchen eating graham crackers and laughing. They lowered their voices when she entered.

"What do you call a Second World War vet, noarms, nolegs, floating in a pool?" said Chloe.

"Bob!" said Yvette. "What do you call a Second World War vet, noarms, nolegs, stretched out on a porch?"

"Matt!" said Chloe. "What do you call a Second World War vet, noarms, nolegs—"

"Yvette and Chloe, that is un-Christian and you will stop telling those jokes this instant," said Maud. She looked in dismay from one face to the other. Last year she'd had a meeting with the twins' school guidance counselor. The encounter had been less than pleasant. In the counselor's tidy, moist office, Maud had sat in a child's chair as a harassed, large-boned woman lectured her on the ills of her children from the vantage of her oak desk. It was not that the twins were poor students, the woman explained, but they were rude and insolent, and sometimes defied authority by falling completely silent. Painful as this was to Maud, she was fully prepared to comply with any of the school's solutions until the counselor spoke again: "And their speech is pretty sluggish, not very clear. Though I suppose we're just not used to the accent."

Maud set her jaw. "The twins were born here. In Canada."

The woman raised her brow in surprise, but made no further comments. Throughout her speech, Maud couldn't help but feel the whole thing was some subtly racist attempt to discredit her daughters. Promising nothing, Maud got up and left, telling neither Samuel nor the twins about the meeting.

chapter THREE

S amuel sat in the shed. It was a cold, vague day, with the dull feel of a hundred others, but for a time Samuel let himself be consoled by it. The weather seemed complicit with his mood. He pressed his feet to the electric heater under his workbench, rubbing his hands together.

Something was bothering him, but he could not say exactly what. Three days had passed since he'd walked off his job, and he'd so far managed to keep his secret from Maud, who spent most of her days immersed in cleaning or shopping in town. He cracked open the wooden case of a radio and fiddled with its innards in a distracted, unskilled way. His workbench touched two walls of the tiny shed, and was riddled with wires. Forced to be fastidiously tidy at the government office, Samuel often let his shed get messy. Drops of solder speckled the bench, and the dust he roused each time he moved gave him a vague pleasure. Despite this, he still felt painfully preoccupied. It surprised him that he could be unhappy in his new freedom.

Samuel's hackles rose when he heard the shed door's hinges rattling. He turned to see Yvette standing in the doorway, dwarfed in her mother's wool sweater. Her thin, chapped knees peeked overtop of a pair of his own rain boots. With her serious face, she looked like an old woman who'd shrunk. She let in the dry, metallic smell of winter.

Samuel singed his knuckle on the soldering iron. Flinching and tensing his fist, he tried to smile.

"What are you doing home from school?" he said after a moment.

"What are you doing home from work?"

The girl had always been bold, but not in any admirable way. Samuel shrugged and half rose from his bench, sitting abruptly when the gesture struck him as silly. He was terribly nervous. He cleared his throat. "Well, well," he said, as though delighted to have company. "Well, well."

Yvette kicked aside his clutter of paint cans, stripped wires, burnt fuses, soiled newspapers, rousing the smell of kerosene. She sat decisively on the floor and looked at him. Samuel hesitated, turning away when he discovered she had nothing to say. Finally, as though bored that her silence didn't bother him, she cocked her head to one side and said, "I woke up sick, and the thought of going to school only made me sicker."

Samuel giggled nervously. "Amen. You and I, we are two of a feather today." He assessed her long, docile face. The fact that she didn't scowl encouraged him to continue. "You know, when I was your age back in Gold Coast, I once despised a class so much that I asked permission to go to the bathroom and never returned." He laughed to himself, having not thought of the incident in years. "Oh, how my uncle beat me when he found out." He paused. "I was so precocious—like my uncle. Like you."

Yvette continued to look at him. Disquieted by her stiffness, he frowned and returned to his work. "Those were indeed the days."

They sat in silence, the iron smell of solder filling the little wooden room. It wasn't long before Samuel was so preoccupied he began to feel alone. He felt like the only man in the world to whom permanence still meant something. This gutted radio in front of him, this junk, was a trifle, a mere grain of the greater work these hands were capable of. He'd wasted his prime years as a trifler, and there was something intolerable in the thought that life would see him to the grave on such meagre achievements.

"Yvette, what would you think of a change of surroundings?" said Samuel.

"I don't know," she said.

He nodded, continuing to solder. He'd believed somehow that she would respond more enthusiastically, even given her reserved nature. Perhaps it was because he'd always sensed a similar discomfort in her, a feeling of being limited by these sad surroundings, this inert life. He recalled an afternoon when, returning from a particularly torturous workday, he'd heard the tinny noise of a radio he'd just fixed and followed the sounds to the living room. There, with Maud's tea towels fastened to their heads like veils and wearing scratched brown sunglasses, stood the twins, dancing. Clutching his work files and his broken umbrella, Samuel watched them jerk to the music. He fell against the jamb, laughing so athletically he thought he would strain himself.

"Young Tragedy and Comedy are discovering their likeness to sheiks," he declared.

"To shakes!" said Yvette, misunderstanding him. And they embellished their fits with a shake and shuffle that nearly suffocated Samuel in his laughter.

Only later did Maud tell him that their headscarves were really an attempt to duplicate the hair of their classmates, and that she'd eavesdropped on a conversation in which Yvette had said she "got tired of being black." Tired of the sugary way she had to behave to get people to play with her. Tired of being asked where she was *really* from, tired of being talked to as though she didn't speak English.

That saddened Samuel. He turned to where Yvette sat on the shed floor; she gazed back as indifferently as before. Put off by this, and lacking any real words of wisdom, Samuel returned to his work, only speaking again when she rose to leave.

"Please do not tell your mother that you saw me here."

Yvette's reaction surprised him: the request seemed to hurt her feelings. But she went out wordlessly.

At the precise time of 4:49, Samuel stood from his bench to shake the wrinkles from his pants. He smoothed out his jacket, put on his overcoat, looped his worn briefcase over his forearm. Spitting in his kerchief, he ran it across his face and, tucking it in his pocket, returned to the house.

Just outside the storm door, before boarding the stoop, he heard girlish voices. Surprised, he paused to listen for a minute.

". . . set your friends on us," hissed one of the twins.

"I didn't. I swear I didn't," said a nervous, quite striking voice. It was the voice of early womanhood, still childish, but with the base notes of a cello.

"We know who cracks the whip," said the ruddy voice so obviously Chloe's.

Ashamed of his daughters' behavior, Samuel walked in to put a stop to it. Yvette and Chloe sat staggered on the stairs leading to the bedrooms, their knees drawn up as though a fortress of bodies. On the very bottom step sat a tall, lithe girl of undeniable beauty. When the twins had made such a friend, or any friend at all for that matter, he couldn't fathom. She was the most charming girl Samuel had ever seen, with skin the color of oats and almond-shaped eyes of a nameless hue. Samuel unconsciously clasped his hands. He was aware that, despite the pristine lines in his suit and the elegant way he'd placed his bowler on his head, he smelled distinctly of solder. He laughed a little, and the girl frowned and wouldn't meet his eyes. He cleared his throat.

"Samuel Tyne," he said, offering his hand, in which she placed her shaking one.

"Ama Ouillet," she said.

"Ama?" said Samuel, giggling. "You do not at all look like you are from Gold Coast, is that right?"

Ama looked confused. "No. Yes. Ama is short for Amaryllis. My parents aren't from Gold Coast."

He held her hand longer than was proper. Stepping away, he frowned at his twins. "What seems to be the problem here, girls? What is it you are arguing about?"

All three in unison said, "Nothing."

"All right," he said, distracted. "Allow me to change, and we will eat." He straightened his tie and, clearing his throat again, snatched the bowler from his head and lurched past the girls to go upstairs.

The twins' laughter intensified Ama's panic. She didn't like how long the twins' father had held her hand, and the fact that they, too, must have noticed it mortified her. In truth, the Tyne house was the last place she wanted to be. She'd only come because her father, having caught Ama's friends bullying the twins on the playground, sent her to the Tyne house to apologize on her friends' behalf. In the twins he saw an opportunity to teach Ama about mercy.

Catholicism was Ama's birthright. Her piety seemed to annoy the twins, who'd accused her of using her crosses, rosary and moral dignity to make herself a saint, like she "needed to believe she was better than other people." They called her "Godgirl" and "Asthma" (in fact, Ama seemed almost tubercular), and accused her of having set her friends on them.

On this last point, especially, they were misled. Ama disliked her friends as much as the twins did; they'd had the gall to make fun of her mother, whose MS worsened by the month. She only accepted their company because, blindly, her parents approved of them, the daughters of pious and moneyed families.

When Ama had rung the doorbell, Mrs. Tyne was so pleased to finally meet a friend of the twins that she invited her to stay to dinner.

Amid the clutter of knickknacks and other trifles, Mrs. Tyne had set a colorful table, with teal placemats and a narrow-throated vase of marigolds as a centerpiece. The food looked strange to Ama— scorched bananas, sludge with cubes of meat—but sitting to eat she found she liked it. The twins sat on either side of her, and their tension made for grudging conversation. To lighten things (though, Ama believed, also out of loneliness), Mrs. Tyne ran off at the mouth. The twins seemed mortified. But despite an aggressive happiness, Ama often caught the woman looking critically at her. She smiled when their eyes met, but not kindly.

When Mr. Tyne entered, grinning with the nervousness of a small child, he glanced at Ama, who stiffened in her chair. "Do not stop eating on my account," he said.

"Then don't be so vain to think it's on your account," said Mrs. Tyne, who'd risen to heap his plate with plantain and bean stew.

The dinner continued in silence. Samuel kept glancing at Ama, and seeing the girl was nervous, he surmised there must be some hidden reason for it. Trying to put her at ease, he began to look more earnestly at her, as if to say, *I, among everyone, am on your side.* The girl squirmed in her chair, and pleased she was uncomfortable, the twins glanced coyly at each other.

Seeing his daughters' strange eye movements, Samuel knew he had solved the riddle. "Girls!" he said. "Stop that tomfoolery with your eyes. Can you not see you are making your guest uncomfortable?"

Both twins let out a loud piercing laugh, one following the other. They resumed eating.

Yvette cleared her throat at the other side of the table. Samuel turned to see her looking mischievously at him. "Did you quit your job? Is that why you spend your whole day in the shed?"

Maud looked at him, aghast. "What nonsense is she talking, Samuel? Have you really quit your job?"

Samuel bowed his head. "I have indeed quit my job."

Maud's mouth twitched. "Of all the—What will we do now!"

So agitated he was shaking, Samuel rose from his chair and looked from face to face. "I have inherited Jacob's house in Aster. We will be moving there." He turned gravely to Ama. "Ama, you are invited to spend the summer with us in my uncle's mansion in Aster."

Mrs. Tyne spoke through her teeth. "You've gone mad."

"We are moving. That is final." Samuel's mouth tasted of rust, and in his restless stomach something was straining at its chains. He felt sick, but believed God had given him a crucial choice at that moment. Samuel could either continue the dog's life he'd already half abandoned, or he could do the job of a proper man and guide his family through this necessary, even prosperous, change. He threw his paper napkin on his plate and walked to the doorway. "That is final," he repeated, and left the room.

Crossing the dark slush to the shed, Samuel felt exalted. He didn't regret what he'd just done; in fact, he looked upon it as the truest gesture of his life. Had he been a man given to poetry, he might have said that something both stark and glorious had got hold of his future. That after fifteen years of the leash he'd finally seized it.

chapter FOUR

No one could refute that Stone Road was one of Aster's stranger beauties. And though the river it bordered was murky, an oily strip that boiled out its mulch every autumn, the stones remained dry. Myth told of the town's birth as the first black hamlet in Alberta, one not so welcome in those days. As more blacks migrated from Oklahoma to set up lives on the prairie, the locals, folk who had themselves migrated little earlier, took action. Everything from petitions to newspapers to name-calling was used to cure the province of its newcomers. To keep the general peace, the government decreed that no other foreigners of this class would be allowed into the country. These words, intended to hush the public, sounded like perverse cowardice. Certainly, no more would enter, they would see to that, but what to do with the ones who'd already claimed land? Not a single local paper didn't fatten with advice on how to cope with the strange pilgrims, this epidemic of filth and sloth that would soften Alberta's morals.

Public prediction rang true. During the next few months the surrounding homesteads lost their morals to the cold pleasure of sabotage. Never had they felt so futile as when the blacks accepted these offenses as just another facet of Canadian life, no more trying than dry fields or mean spruce roots. They were said to have set up a Watch; eighty-nine families met once a week and, after a brief vote, decided to pitch up their fear in the form of a wall. Discretion, they believed, was vital to such a plan, and so they used only those materials that would give the wall a modest look: pallid rock, cement caulking. As if, should what they built be pale enough, their neighbors might fail to notice any difference at all. If the benefits were to be shared, so was the effort. Each man took his hand in the construction, and before long every layer read like a patch in a stone quilt, with a detailed square from each family. No one knows the details of what came next, whether a war of sorts was started, or if the backbreaking nature of the work itself was enough to tame the project, but the wall remained ten inches high for several decades. The passing of years saw it kicked down, eroded by constant rain. Now it rises scarcely two inches, a skirt of parched rock at the river's edge. So the myth goes. Truth is, no one knows how Stone Road came to be. Too mathematically perfect to seem natural, its mystery is the theme of an annual town contest.

Though few people actually believed the myth, they had lived with its shadow at their doors. Literally. Another tale recounts the day the Jefferson girl lured all of Aster to the streets to see what no one would see again.

"A shadow! A shadow!"

People fell from their homes, not from the belief that there was a shadow on earth worth the intrigue, but because Galla Jefferson was a quiet, nervous girl who'd spoken less than ten words all summer. And here she was, screaming in the streets about a shadow. Women left their kitchens, babies began crying; even those few shiftless men always between business rose gamblingly from their hammocks, knowing once their feet hit grass they'd be back at a job, their wives slicing the tie-strings from the trees for good this time. These men tailed the crowd as though they might go unnoticed. And much of the same must have been happening on the other side, in the skirts, because high noon saw a mass of people lining each side of Stone Road, struck and amazed at the five-foot shadow tracing the proper side with no seen object to put it there. People took it for a sign, though by now one knows how differently both sides would take it. The shadow faded in the night, and with it most of the townsfolk's memory of the event, so that waking on a new day, Aster proper had founded a race of lost prophets. Such people claimed to remember the event. No one believed them.

Aster was so isolated and secretive, Albertans worried about an uprising. Within Aster, though, isolation meant community. Whole families congregated on their stoops, sipping orange juice from Mason jars and calling across to their neighbors the paraphrase of some curiously deft comment just spoken by the man of the house.

But among all this, one building retained its silence. That worn, splintered house was rumored to have hissed with all of Aster's secrets in its heyday. It cut a splendid figure against the town's purple dusk, and many believed that the weathervane, for all its ostentation and screeching (which woke even the deepest sleeper on windy nights), was used as a landmark to guide its residents home. For, since Aster's beginnings, the home had borne the misfortune of a boardinghouse. Not that it had officially been one; simply, one of the town widows had opened her home to those ready to pay two dollars in exchange for a month of shelter and meals that, even sweet, stung with cayenne. Her contemporaries didn't know what to make of her, and neither does history. It's been said that she housed mostly men, weary travelers in need of a night of peace. But was it a brothel or simply a sanctuary? No one ever knew. Only that after the May rains came, she appealed to the town council to sell her their surplus cement wholesale, so that she could wall off more rooms and boost profits. After three years in which the matter was passed from one hesitant official to the next, she was finally given the cement for free on the anniversary of her husband's death. Two teenage boys volunteered their help, and despite her praise for their altruism, they were amply paid by their own parents. Next spring the house was finished, though not without complications. Two hormonal boys and a construction guidebook aren't a likely mate for precision, and the extra walls looked like rows of cauliflower. Time has drawn all color from the details, but it's been said that the walls didn't last long, that the hasty layers, knuckling from under each other like nursing kittens, left only piles of rubble and a keen view of your neighbor's room. The house was sold not long after, its ruins passed from hand to hand until, generations later, it was cheaply sold to one Jacob Tyne.

By then the Second World War had changed the nature of the town, so that very few blacks remained. They left in favor of war service or city life; some returned to the United States. Jacob wasn't concerned with this. As soon as the purchase went through, he gutted the rooms and rebuilt proper walls. Even old age didn't slow him. Half-blind, he masked his lack of sight by aiming shy left of where he meant to go. His intuition was so exacting that even at his death no one was the wiser. Jacob was a man of little tolerance and his face wore the brunt of his nature. Roman-nosed and thin-lipped in a way unusual for those of his tribe, he cut a strict figure in Aster, where his repute grew as a man of morals, one to turn to when in need of advice. Myth has him sitting on a chair in his backyard, advising his few friends on the know-how of life; and having come from nothing, he'd deem he'd seen the worst of it. His brother's house in Gold Coast had grown poor after his sudden death, and Jacob was said to have renounced his chieftaincy to care for his prodigy nephew. He'd toiled the fields, his small reward his sister-in-law's hot meals between shifts. If these words didn't move his listeners, he'd go on to explain how he'd also put Samuel through high school in Legon, had seen him through his studies on scholarship in England and his now lively career as an economic forecaster. His belief in his nephew was so strong he'd ruined his back for it. His eyes, too, he wrote in his journals. The fields brought out the worst of a man's fastidiousness, and searching out the most futile buds in a dark cracking with mosquitoes, Jacob had strained his sight to his one-eyed blindness. He regretted nothing, though, given how far these efforts had taken Samuel.

But Samuel didn't know he was still spoken of, and miles away felt pained that Jacob had so easily disposed of him. Even a decade and a half later, as he loaded his reluctant family into the car to claim the Aster house, his feelings of abandonment had not healed.

In the final days before the move, the Tyne house was clogged with boxes. Crossing a room, you never knew what treasures you'd find in your hair. Often dust, the brine of old lamp oil, once, in the collar of Samuel's shirt, a crustened moth. He took them for what they literally were, signs of decay, and from these signs he drew his sense of luck.

Despite the usual irritations of a move, Samuel felt blessed in how smoothly his life was now going. He had quit his job free of the imagined horrors that had kept him from doing it all these years. He was a free man, and his freedom proved he was, after a decade of doubt, a man of action. And Maud, usually so obstinate, had simply watched him do it. Not a word had been said since Yvette had let it slip, and though Maud made her anger clear by overdoing her gestures, he took the lack of a lecture as a sign of her reluctant consent. Even the twins had stopped giving him those off-putting grim looks. So life continued; he ate, he slept, he soldered, while his life began to rise in sloppy piles around him.

After leaving a duplicate key with the Bjornsons (Mrs. Tyne, insisting the arrangement was temporary, demanded Samuel keep up the rent), Samuel checked the hitching on the trailer and, satisfied, climbed into the car with his family. He had not forgotten the Bjornsons' warnings about an arsonist in Aster, but it was a chance he was willing to take.

"My whole family was born by firelight," he said. "There is no reason to fear it now."

He had also suppressed his guilt for not holding the Forty Days Ceremony. It seemed to him that in these last forty days he'd thought less about Jacob than about the house. Jacob's life, his character, his passions, had been abstract to Samuel even when the men were supposedly close, so that to talk about them now would be an empty gesture. Also, who was there to gather in Jacob's home to remember him? A recluse these fifteen years, Jacob had given up the privilege of being remembered. And Samuel was not going to make himself uneasy by

dragging past traditions into his life when the man he would do it for
had willingly, in all but ink, tried to forget him.

Mrs. Tyne turned her stern look straight ahead. Samuel almost
laughed. His wife's anger might have made him second-guess himself
in the past; not so now. He drove the short distance to Ama's place,
where the child sat on her pale white steps, looking for the first time
untidy and a little hassled. André and Elizabeth Ouillet waited for
him at the curb, where they made small talk Mrs. Tyne felt obligated to join. She spoke quietly, as though it were all she could
manage under such forced circumstances, and André helped Samuel
coax Ama's things into the overfull trailer. They drove away.

Ama pressed her palms against the hot vinyl seat and refused to
look at the twins. She'd had to endure them every Saturday night since
that wretched dinner at their house. As it happened, Mr. Tyne had
called the Ouillets just an hour later, asking their permission for Ama
to spend the summer in Aster.

By some hateful coincidence ("Divine Providence," Mrs. Ouillet
had called it), the Ouillets wanted to visit a spa this summer, but could
not think of a single reliable relative to entrust with Ama.

"Usually you come with us," Ama's mother told her, "but this is a
different kind of trip. The rumor of Lourdes, France, is going around—
they say it's a miracle what it's done for people. We're using the last of
Grandpa Ouillet's inheritance." She clasped her hands, raised her
shoulders and laughed. "I might even walk."

Her flippancy appalled Ama, as though walking had the attraction
of a new water sport. "But you don't even *know* the Tynes," she'd said.

Her father paused. "Well, we'll get to know them, then."

And so, every Saturday the Tynes came over so that the families
might know each other better before the summer. These evenings
usually ended in a three-way round of jokes between her parents and
Mr. Tyne, at which the four left out looked on with bemused discomfort. The night was a useful one only in that it strengthened her
parents' conclusion that Mr. Tyne was a worthy man. Ama hated
slander of any kind, so she never spoke of how nervous he made her

feel. Not wanting to make her parents rethink their trip, she bore it stoically. What couldn't be understood, though, was how Mr. Tyne had managed to convince his wife to move.

Maud felt the question like a goad at her back, and kept her eyes on the pavement. How indeed had this meek man, this sponge-boned husband, gotten her to move to a house she hadn't seen? She'd wondered at it for weeks. Not that she hadn't tried to thwart him; she'd called him "Senile Sam" or ignored him so deftly that she'd worn herself out. But all in vain. When Samuel came upon her one spiteful night, as she longed for home, she gave in. A lengthy bout of dreaming of Gold Coast had the effect of a good Calgary winter: it left her dull and cold, in a frost that stalled all reason. In the end, she couldn't really say why she'd given in. Boredom with her current life? The need to own the property on which she lived? A fear of her husband's sudden will? No one reason seemed enough. Samuel had told her that the house wasn't really in Aster proper, that it sat unbiased on the line between its outskirts and the country. Besides, some of the wealthiest men in Alberta owned land near Aster, and Maud liked the thought of living close to high society. She fought off feelings of compromise and believed herself admirable for it. She couldn't account for her daughters, though, whose brooding she envied.

An hour passed in silence. They all realized it at the same time, and in this discovery made an unspoken pact to keep it that way. Only the engine's grief could be heard, and then the weather, when the drawn sky gave way to a terse hailstorm. The sun recovered itself, the trip ran on. Sprawls of beer-colored brush shot by. Bundles of threshed wheat lazed fatly in yellow fields. It was the quietest drive of Ama's life, and it set her on edge. She could feel the heat of Chloe's bare thigh beside hers, and tried to steady herself to spare them the doubly undesired touch. Outside the window, the green began. The windows misted, and Yvette lowered hers to let in a damp rush of wind. The car rocked over gravel, and one could see they'd reached some place so private that all roads leading in broke off. The gravel cracked like static underneath them, then suddenly became clean road. They rode down a heavily treed street on which well-dressed

people milled about at the pace of a Sunday afternoon. Almost everyone was white, with the occasional dark face among them. A stocky
man shook a carpet in the street, and a woman in checked pants
skipped out of the path of dust he created. Samuel slowed down as
the carful took in the scene. After a minute he asked Mrs. Tyne for a
map, which she searched for while reading the storefronts aloud:
Woolworth's, Eaton's, Hudson's Bay. Even the twins seemed impressed.
Goodwill filled the car, and they were even on the verge of speaking
to each other, when suddenly the road turned bad again. Mrs. Tyne
directed her husband through pretty but empty streets, toward a
river gilded in oil. Vast and flat, the Athabasca's green, fluent waters
smelled weakly of algae. Samuel slowed before moving on. Then the
foliage thickened again, as if they'd driven back to the bush. The car
stubbed its wheels against stubborn tree roots.

As suddenly as the woods had deepened, they began to clear, the
backlit leaves parting with a slow sort of awe. The streets now became
strips of hard, unpaved ground, with pale wood sidewalks on which
men in worn clothing strolled, pinching the smokes from their mouths.

"We tore through some hole in time right back into the thirties,"
said Maud, giving Samuel a look, for if her sense of direction was right
(as it was sure to be), they'd now driven to the heart of Aster proper.
She led them through a few more streets, some filled with catcalling
men, others with decaying handmade storefronts, none of which
changed her opinion of the place. She directed them past all this to
another grove, into which the car pitched with a dark gurgle. Samuel
motored it from the rut, and the car stumbled over holes and stumps,
greenery that breathed its bitter stench. Chloe leaned across Yvette and
closed her window. And even through the closed pane, even through
the anguished rattle of the car, a high-pitched whine rang out like the
coarsest voice in a choir.

"What's that?" said Chloe, putting fingers in her ears. "Sounds like
a whole field of dying cats."

It was not the first time the sound of the weathervane had been mistaken for something else. Driving up they made out its shape against the sky.

The house distinguished itself in the distance. The carload was speechless. But what could be said of such a house? Brown and ivory, it sat fat and pacified among the overgrown foliage. Thick, thorned vines veined its face. It had the white front stoop so classic of Aster culture, but flanked by colonial pillars, as if built by a Confederate. It was beautiful in a brooding sort of way. The railings, gnawed loose from the porch, drifted in toward each other like saloon doors. Every nook looked green with mildew and weeds. Nearby shrubbery shuddered with the panic of small animals. The ground shifted when the car drove over it.

Samuel parked on the house's east side, and with trembling hands leafed through the papers in his wallet to find the tiny envelope with the key the neighbor had given him They all climbed from the car, Maud with a meaningful slam of her door, and strode over the shifting, rank land toward their new home.

Had Samuel been asked, he might have admitted that his uncle's death, though large in itself, was outdone by the death it had brought to the order of the house. Bramble roamed the vacant halls on some unfelt draft. The dust-gray sills had collected the fat, petrified bodies of insects, scattered like droppings. In the front room, sheets, probably blown from the covered couches, sank in hog-ties around the furniture's ankles. There was a heavy odor in the air, an amber, nagging smell like that of towels left damp for too long. Samuel imagined the other rooms were in even worse mourning. Behind him, he heard Maud breathe. Even before she had spoken, his shoulders lowered in shame. Silence pervaded the house. And all this before the true decay would make itself known to them: sidewalks eaten by constant frosts, sinks piebald with rust, pipes choked on years of parings and hair, cracked windows, ceilings swaybacked with water, shot bulbs, wood softened by insects' eggs, and the chimney's fitful gray breaths that set them all to coughing no matter where they sat in the house.

Embarrassed for Mr. Tyne, Ama thought to say something to lighten the mood. But under the twins' heavy stare she managed only the grieved look that confirmed for Samuel his fault in this new unhappiness. He concealed his awkwardness as if confronted with a woman who'd lost her beauty; he decided to treat the rooms as if they wore the luminosity of their earlier days, and stepped from his shoes to admire the rest of the house.

Mrs. Tyne squinted, then turned a kind face to the children. "Get a good look around." She walked in the direction Samuel had taken. "Don't, however, get comfortable."

Ama felt grateful. The finality in Mrs. Tyne's words would easily end their stay before it began. Chloe and Yvette had begun their sly glances again, and uncomfortable, Ama looked away. She ran her eyes along the scraped ivory walls, the furniture that bore the burden of age despite rare and fussy use, and marveled that a house only recently left to its own upkeep could have rotted out so quickly. The twins made their way to another room, and not wanting to be left alone, Ama followed. It was then that the girls, grudgingly lurking together, discovered the house's strangest flaw. What had looked so monstrous from outside was as cloistered as a catacomb. The hallways were narrow and shadowed, and broke off into occasional rooms of the sort Ama imagined a monastery might have. This warmed her to them. One room well in back of the house, with sliding bay windows, opened onto a chin-high sea of grass. She watched it roil in the wind, until a voice behind her, whistling with disuse, asked, "Coming or not?"

It was the first she'd heard from the twins all day, and she was glad of the offering. She followed them to the front room, biting the tail of her braid as they all sat at the cold mouth of the fireplace. The drafts brought in bits of the Tynes' argument, and Ama could just make out Mrs. Tyne saying something about *duty*. After some bustle in the hallway Mrs. Tyne emerged, her husband nervous behind her.

Mrs. Tyne leaned against a white loveseat whose far leg levitated with the weight. She looked resolutely at them. "We've decided to let you girls choose if you'd like to *live* here." If she had struggled to keep from sounding severe, she'd failed. Ama knew the choice had already been made for them; the twins had only to confirm what her tone suggested.

There was a long pause before Chloe said, "We want to stay."

Samuel looked up in confusion.

"Are you sure?" Mrs. Tyne set dark eyes on her daughter.

Stepping forward, Yvette grabbed the bewildered Ama's hand. "We want to stay," she said. In the silence the weathervane screeched above the distant rooms.

chapter FIVE

After a week lost to clutter and dust, Maud committed an act that set the whole house on edge: she began to clean up. Her solemn pleasure in scraping the rust from the hinges proved decidedly that they were staying. Samuel spent his victory in the front yard, ripping weeds from where they'd burst in black veins through the pavement. A full afternoon passed before he remembered that his wife's anger had always been a solitary thing, and that the worst was still brewing in her. Samuel considered this for a minute and, feeling nothing, knew that the hour of fear had passed. His hands tore out the stubborn roots, roots in this first land he'd managed to own. It was clear to him now, the true nature of Jacob's silence; his uncle had only meant to make a bigger gift of the house, giving as the last act of his love the unexpected. Samuel was grateful, regretting more than ever not having seen Jacob since his youth. He remembered a man mournfully amused with life, an intuitive leader fully aware of how futile power was, that to have it was to have only the illusion of it. "No man can truly rule another," he'd often said, especially during the roughest strains of Samuel's first job. "Not even slavery could do it. Remember that." And Samuel had. Whenever he'd heard his bosses' voices, whenever Maud gave him grief over problems she herself had created, the memory returned to him. Such simple wisdom.

The twins were at first so distracted that they wandered the rooms listlessly, as if reeling from bad news. It was as though they had never believed in their power and were disappointed that it had revealed itself in such a flippant decision. Ama suspected Chloe had only done it to sting her mother, who spoke to neither twin the whole day, except through Ama. Maud felt in full her humiliation, but she was not angry with the girls so much as with her own lack of strategy. While coaxing bugs from the rafters, she decided that she'd wanted to stay in the house, that she'd only asked the girls as a way to announce what she couldn't admit to Samuel. The house had been Maud's choice all along. Slowly her confidence returned, and when she began to whistle, the startled girls in the next room fell silent.

Ama spent her days trailing the twins, who were so eager to explore that they often forgot to eat. The hallways were lofty, with domed, pitted ceilings, and smelled of mothballs. They broke onto rooms as unique in character as the home's various owners: the room strewn with cane prayer mats and altars for the dead; a hall closet smelling of aged tobacco; the antiquated study; the kitchen, with its pockmarked cupboards, its fridge haunted by the three generations of fragrant food. The main hall ended in a living room, whose bay window had misted with age, like a huge cataract. Central to this room was the old, coughing fireplace, sensitive to strong winds. The upper floor held three bedrooms, and a molding bathroom smelling obscenely of urine. No one was brave enough to broach the root cellar. All of it amazed Ama. The entire house radiated not only another era, but another world.

The grounds, too, had a magic quality to them. Out front, mature firs shaded the yard. In the backyard, thrown into clear relief after Maud cleaned the window, a field of chin-high grass rolled in the wind. The nearest house, belonging to Saul Porter, who had apparently witnessed the will, stood a few acres away, only its decaying roof visible from the window.

Ignored by the twins, Ama often sat on the front stoop, watching the occasional person walk by behind the trees. Summer was beginning, with its fragile flowers. Ama ripped petals off their stems. Sensing someone's look, she turned. Behind her a pair of polyester legs stood, screened by the storm door. Her heart quickened: Mr. Tyne. She wondered how long he'd been watching her, and drew her knees up to her chest.

Mr. Tyne giggled nervously and opened the door. He smelled sweaty, of labor. Watching him navigate weeds to settle himself beside her, Ama was so startled that she did not rush away. His lack of balance, his sad wheezing at each step, didn't rouse her sympathy; they only emphasized the impropriety of his age. Terrified, she gave him a disdainful look, flinching as his eyes ran over her face.

"Sure is a beautiful day," he said. And with a kind of wonderment, he added, "Yes, yes, it certainly is a beautiful day." He frowned, as though at a loss to convince himself. He began to pick the lint off his pantlegs, and the gesture was suffused with such sadness that Ama relaxed a little.

"It is beautiful," she said. "The marigolds are already out."

Her voice seemed to surprise him, as though he'd forgotten she was there. "Marigolds . . . ?" He frowned, followed by a laugh at his own confusion. "Flowers, yes. Little girls do like flowers." He paused, bringing his rough hands together in his lap. "I myself have always preferred mathematics. Computing machines, such things."

Ama nodded, nervous. She didn't understand the mechanics of his conversation, and was on guard in case it took an uncomfortable turn.

A gust of wind shook the trees, and they tossed a few needles near Ama's and Samuel's feet. Ama watched the marigolds nod. She said, "I like how they look like fire, their colors." Ripping off a petal, she pinched it between her forefinger and thumb. Her gesture suddenly made her nervous, and she flicked the petal into the dirt.

Samuel toed it with his loafer. Watching people pass in the distance, he said, "'The greatest visionary could not achieve world peace, but a single demented zealot could cause dozens of cities to burn.'"

"Sorry?" said Ama, perplexed.

He grimaced, as though pained by his own idiosyncratic behavior. To Ama, he suddenly seemed nothing worse than a baffled old man, someone who'd had the misfortune to age before his time. She gave him a look of pity. "What were you saying about mathematics?"

Samuel assessed Ama uncertainly, as though making sure he had leave to speak about himself. Touching his bowler the way a beautiful woman reassures herself that every hair is in its place, he began to speak. "Well, I've always been a great lover of mathematics. From the first time I laid my eyes on figures—boof!—I was off like that. Numbers have always, always been my first love." He looked bashfully at Ama, who, knowing there was no suggestiveness in it, nevertheless blushed. Mr. Tyne seemed to take it as condolence. "If I may speak truthfully with you, it is my deepest wish to own an electronics store. Not only to be my own boss, although"—he chuckled—"that would be nice. But because I think I could build something important. A computing—" he broke off, frowning a little, and Ama understood he regretted telling her anything.

"Sounds great," she said.

"Does it?" he said, preoccupied.

His question was so sincere it touched Ama. It finally struck her that his attraction to her had nothing sexual in it; it had cleaner, sadder roots: estranged from his family, he was a deeply lonely man.

Ama looked compassionately at him. "You should really do it. It might seem impossible now, but my dad always says you won't succeed if you're too scared to try."

Samuel felt a little of the amused condescension adults get when children give them advice. He patted Ama's hair. "Well, let's go in to supper."

Feeling rebuffed, Ama trudged inside after him.

Ama dreaded dinnertime, because it made a show of allegiances.

Mr. and Mrs. Tyne, with the usual childishness that plagues cold marriages, used the gathering to rile up support for their polar causes. They were like politicians at the quick of their campaigns. Mrs. Tyne was obviously disatisfied with Aster, while Mr. Tyne had only praise. Samuel hadn't told his wife of his plans to set up his own electronics shop. Meanwhile, she continued to berate him at the dinner table while behind her back he sold off or secretly fetched the valuables left in the Calgary house. He lied and said he was trying to find work in Edmonton. He'd also been seeking out a storefront, and had seen a few possibilities. Ama's encouragement merely confirmed the importance of what he'd already put into action. Still, he knew he'd been a scoundrel. In the tiresome game of marriage, he hadn't played an honorable hand. But what could he do? His newfound confidence left him confused as to how to use it. He'd already given notice on the Calgary lease, making a clean break of it. Now he'd only to tell his family.

Aster, Mrs. Tyne insisted, was backward; even the outskirts. As she placed the beets and beef on the rickety table, she said, "*Sth*, that beef cuts much cleaner at home. There's not a decent knife to be found in this whole town, but . . . never mind. Like I say, it's only a fool who runs back to the bush when the city is brimming with oil."

And it was true, in the twenty years following the Leduc discoveries, oil had been spitting from every crack in Alberta. Every crack, that is, but in Aster. People rushed from farms and towns to share in the thirst, and it was a rare soul who left the city for something smaller. Like the Depression, the oil boom threatened to kill off the best towns. One couldn't look anywhere without seeing fire geysers, steel towers, mud endlessly tumbling into flare pits. The Americans were frantic for it.

Samuel ate his beets, giving the children careful looks. "Are these beets not remarkable?" He turned to his wife. "These beets are quite remarkable."

"Well, it's nothing to call the papers about, but I guess so," said Maud, not looking up from her plate. Her voice was thin, as if she were pinching the words back. "I read in the *Albertan* the Greeks had a good harvest. This might be from it."

Samuel smiled. "What an inspiring mix of people this town has, isn't it? The reports all prize the city's diversity, but the only diversity you'll find there is in its punishments." Again he appealed to the children, who gave him cautious looks.

Maud faced him coldly. "Only an idiot mistakes a mound of gold for manure. See things as they are beyond your nose—men are more forgiving when there's business happening all around, and more true in their brotherhood when they don't have the big social camera eye always on them." She began to eat methodically. "You mark it on the wall—village life in a white man's country is poison, even if the village used to be a black one. The city—that's the only going forward."

Samuel laid down his fork. "You speak as though man has the ability to walk through walls. And it is true, walls do go down—Aster itself has seen it. But until they go down, they are impassable. And if you have so much fog in your eyes that you cannot see it, well, that's when trouble comes." He tipped his glass against his lips, bitterly aware that only the thinnest drop of water crossed them. "The Greeks, the Italians, the Dutch, the Portuguese, even these few third-worlders, they have wiped the fog from their eyes. Calgary has left them empty-palmed. Edmonton has left them empty-palmed."

"Aster's nothing but a way station for the city-bound."

The room filled with the sounds of cutlery scraping plates, the lope of the ceiling fan cutting the heat in the room. These moments were familiar to Ama, and she grudgingly began (in fact, she suspected they waited for it) to banter casually with the twins on either side of her. Mostly she told anecdotes of no interest, jokes about nothing, but it had the effect of slackening a rope almost towed to threads. The whole family listened to her misfired wit in distracted agitation, and Ama went doggedly on, because there was nothing else to do.

In the midst of her chatter the doorbell rang. Its voice had dried over the years and now sounded like a dog's whimper. Samuel rose to answer it.

A couple stood on the porch. Their skin, and indeed their clothes, were so uniformly white they might have climbed from a salt mine.

This pallor, along with a well-fed corpulence, made the woman look much younger than she undoubtedly was. She had shrewd, vaguely blue eyes, her mouth filled with crooked teeth. She was so fat that even her smile looked like an immense effort under all that skin.

The man, for all his age, looked athletic. Less muscular than simply well built, his broad, heavily veined forearms ended in pink, delicate wrists. Despite his brawn there was something of the intellectual about him; a low-sitting pair of wire-rimmed glasses obscured his pupils, giving him an almost affected erudition. His speech seemed deliberately unadorned, as though he were used to giving others time to catch up with his ideas.

"Call the *Guinness Book*—we made it here in less than a month," laughed the man.

His wife glanced at him, then tapped the glass at Samuel's eye level, so that he was obliged to take a backward step. He opened the storm door.

"Raymond Frank," said the man, fingering the lid of a silver lighter in his fist. He gestured to his wife. "Eudora and Ray Frank. As second to the mayor on Aster's town council, I'd like to welcome you to the town. We thought we'd come and get a good look at you." Laughing, he thrust his substantial hand into Samuel's, all the while winking at his wife. "So far so good, eh?"

"Don't badger the poor man," said Eudora with a straight face, though Samuel sensed an undercurrent of comedy between them. "Will you look at this house?" Eudora glanced past Samuel, then brought her piercing eyes to rest on him. She shoved a foil-covered dish at him.

Eudora was a feminist, though her resulting behavior was more questionable than when she simply called herself a woman. She agreed with a woman's right to vote, but believed this the extent to which women should be involved in politics. She maintained that all women should have access to higher education, but if pressed enough she would admit it was unnatural. She believed that a marriage without children was no more than a pact between a rake and a hussy, yet she herself was barren. She was vice president of Aster's chapter of the

National Association for the Advancement of Women (NAAW), and yet she knew a woman's true duty was to her home. As a laywoman, she volunteered in homes for the mentally handicapped, helped to found Aster's first soup kitchen and could be persuaded on occasion to make one of her devastating custards for a good cause. At the helm of NAAW she wrote petitions to the municipalities of Calgary, Edmonton and even Aster to establish a special education course so that the "poor challenged dears" would be prevented from "compromising normal students." She proved herself a woman before her time by suggesting social awareness programs to crack down on prenatal alcoholism; but her reasons?—to stop filling cradles with "feeble-minded babies." In her crusader state of mind, the motives differed.

"Thank you kindly," said Samuel, taking the dish.

"It's a desert," she said, "but don't worry, I took out all the sand. No, really, it's a dessert torte, and by the dinner sounds in there I'd say our timing's just right." She looked beyond his shoulder.

"We have almost finished." Samuel smiled; a few seconds passed before her hint occurred to him. "Oh, will you not come and meet my family?"

The Franks shared a laugh between them, and Samuel stared, unable to discern the joke. Eudora reached for the pan in his hands and said, "I'll do the cutting."

In the kitchen, the meal had come to an end. Today, as on other occasions, Samuel noticed that the twins seemed to distrust their food in front of strangers. They set down their forks. Samuel laughed to distract attention from them and gestured to Maud, who, startled at the sudden company, tried to swallow as quickly as possible with a shy smile on her face. Before she could say anything, Eudora leaned between Ama and Yvette, as though her presence were the most natural thing in the world, and dropped the dessert in the center of the table.

Taking a backward step, she glanced at their plates. "Poor dears. Been cleaning so hard you haven't had a chance to go shopping. We'll take you, when you're ready."

In a look so quick Eudora might have missed it, Maud expressed her annoyance. "Don't trouble yourselves." Remembering herself, she wiped her hands on her thighs and rose to shake hands. "Whatever you've brought smells delicious. We're grateful for dessert when we can get it." She breathed a laugh. "It doesn't happen much around here."

"No, it wouldn't," said Eudora, looking from Ray to the ceiling draped in dust bunnies. Perplexed, Samuel and Maud watched Eudora begin to sort through their drawers. "Can't use that," she muttered to herself. "Or that." Maud glared at Samuel. When Eudora commented that they "obviously haven't done the drawers yet," Samuel thought Maud would implode with exasperation. Feeling that he should do something, Samuel appealed to Ray with his eyes to put an end to his wife's prying. The children sat paralyzed in their chairs, unwilling to raise their heads.

Ray looked blithely around him, oblivious. He only came alive when his wife glanced at him; then he laughed, and in a meaningless, childlike way.

Samuel was in awe. Here was a man thriving in his wife's shadow.

"Dora," Ray finally said, "get out of there."

"Coming, coming," she said, clearly disappointed with the knife she was obliged to take away with her. Skinning the foil from the dish, she leaned over a scowling Chloe to cut the fruit torte. Her eyes skimmed their plates again. "Ray's allergic to beets."

Here, at last, Samuel found a way into the conversation. "Codeine," he declared, then, clearing his throat at the general puzzlement, added, "codeine is my Achilles heel."

There was a silence, which Ray broke by saying, "Lot to dig through here, a jungle of a house." He paused, meditating on Samuel's face overtop of his glasses. "But you should be at home here."

Samuel smiled. "Yes, we have lost our children in the house—only Columbus and Hudson and Cartier show up for supper." He smiled at the children: Chloe and Yvette dropped their heads; Ama moved her lips timidly before looking away.

"Listen," said Eudora, in so commanding a voice that Samuel grew nervous. "Let's let the children do the torte-eating, the men do the washing up, and, Maud, you and I'll go talk in the backyard."

Maud passed air through her lips. Who was this woman to come into her home and start ordering them around? To Maud's astonishment, Samuel sprang to life and began in agitation to clear the dishes. Even with everyone staring at him he continued to stack each plate, like a boy fearing reprimand. Ray, with a dignity that made Samuel all the more ridiculous, gathered the utensils in a bored, easygoing way. Maud's face burned as she followed Eudora to the yard.

Drawing open the sliding bay window, which was still grimy even after a cleaning, Maud and Eudora stepped into the bristling wind. They stared out at the field of grass that was so tall and abundant it looked like water rolling on for leagues. Three birch trees rose at equal distance between them and the Porter house, of which only the rotting roof was visible.

"Will you look at this yard," breathed Eudora. "How can anyone live here?" She seemed to sense Maud's suppressed anger. "But you'll get it into shape, I know you will. We live in the country, so I know how hard it is to fight the wind from kicking dirt in the second you turn your back."

"Do you not live nearby?"

"Well, yes, but Stone Road divides us. This is still Aster, and we live on the other side of the road from you, so we live in the country."

"Ah," Maud nodded.

Eudora chinned toward the rundown house in the distance. "Met Porter yet?"

"Well, no," Maud flushed, knowing the lapse showed bad manners. She'd been badgering Samuel to call on him for the last week and a half. "What with all the cleaning, and Samuel looking for work in the city . . ."

Eudora stood in amused silence. Then she said, "Don't worry your head over it, dear. *He's* not going anywhere." She laughed, and they watched a magpie try to light on the shifting grass. "God knows I don't impose my views on anyone, Maud, but we do have an active church community, and you and your family are more than welcome to join it. Can I pick you up this week?" When she smiled, a single tooth jutted over her lip like the pale foot of a woman stepping onto a curb.

Maud fixated on this tooth. Eudora had hit her sore spot, for Maud wanted to bring more religion into her daughters' lives. She relented. "We would love to."

In the kitchen, Samuel stood at the sink washing dishes with Ray. Preoccupied at first, he didn't speak, handing the plates to Ray without much care. He knew he'd made a fool of himself, and he was trying to figure out why he feared displeasing others. He remembered his sisters as a malignant force, and, yes, perhaps Jacob had been a skilled disciplinarian, but at his age it seemed ludicrous to fear standing up for himself. He glanced hesitantly at Ray. Here was a man who might perhaps understand.

Looking over his shoulder at the children, Samuel lowered his voice. "What do you know about getting a bay in town?"

Ray smiled, slipping a dish into the plastic rack. "Not quite sure what you mean, Sam."

Samuel licked his lips. "What do you call it—eh, storefront property—for people to lease?"

"Oh, you mean a shop," mused Ray. "Yeah, I know a bunch. There's Skutton and Laidlaw . . . Brewster. Listen, I'll take you around this week. And don't think you're a burden—as your neighbor, and second to the mayor on town council, it's my duty. Here—" Throwing the soapy plate into the rack, he dug into his front pockets. Samuel turned off the tap, eyeing the children to determine if they'd heard. The twins kept eating, but Ama, never a good liar, gave Samuel little glances and smiled. He knew she believed herself responsible for his sudden resolve to find a shop, and felt a pang of guilt. Only when Ray had turned out his pockets, dumping a collection of lint and a lighter on the counter, did he find the pen and tissue he was looking for to scrawl down his number. Handing it to Samuel, he patted him on the shoulder. "Call me."

Just then Eudora reentered with Maud in tow. Maud checked to see that the children had not eaten too much of the torte (she'd always maintained sugar and children shouldn't mix), then followed Samuel to the stoop to see the Franks out. As the red truck drove off, Maud said under her breath, "Is every woman in this country just like Ella Bjornson?"

Samuel was aware of one thing: in Eudora Frank, Maud had met her match.

chapter SIX

S amuel had asked Ray to wait for him on the main road, and Ray
proved himself a man of his word. The red truck idled in the lit-
tered street. Samuel climbed into the enormous cab, which he
joked could easily house the whole of Togo. Ray nodded and, patting his
pockets, drew a cigarette to his flaked lips and asked for a light. Samuel
recalled Ray setting his silver lighter on the kitchen counter and guiltily
handed Ray the built-in one on the dash. The fug filled the cab; from the
corner of his eye Samuel watched Ray smoke in mild contemplation.
There was something different about him today, Samuel decided; Ray's
confidence was even more pronounced in his wife's absence. Samuel felt
envious.

"I was told some time ago that the boundary between Aster and
the country starts behind our house, and that in reality our home is in
the country," he said.

Ray smiled. "Fool's gold, Sam. You're practically in Aster proper."

"Oh, brother." Samuel knew he should be disappointed, but he
laughed instead. "Please do not tell my wife."

"Don't tell mine I smoke in here and you got a deal." Ray lowered his window and flicked the butt outside. "But a woman's bark is louder than her bite—first rule of marriage." He smiled. "Not done much exploring?"

Samuel understood the question as a general one. "Not really. I was born in Ghana and lived briefly in England, but somehow those countries were not so challenging as here."

"Life's one never-ending pain in the ass for you, isn't it?" Ray grinned, as if he'd told a good joke.

"Well." Samuel turned to look out the window. He couldn't understand these men for whom everything is a joke; he never knew where he stood with them. Outside, Sarcee Street stirred with early business. One by one, gates lifted from glass storefronts; hand-painted placards staggered the wooden walks; men in weathered suits wandered from doorways, a morning cigarette in their hands, their faces closed against the day.

"I gave up the suit for town life," said Samuel. He tapped his window, gesturing to the haggard men outside. "That is why."

"Don't know why these commuters don't just move to the city," muttered Ray. He cleared his throat. "So electronics is a new game for you?"

"My father was an entrepreneur of sorts. And so it was with my uncle. Cocoa. We had one plantation in Agona Swedru, one plantation in Otsenkoran. Huge, huge harvests, and not just cocoa—corn, maize, potatoes, yams, bananas, palm trees, oh, even them. Palm trees are very beautiful, and of the greatest function, too. The kernel gives a good pulp, and the top you skin for palm-nut oil, you know, you make soup, palm wine, whatever you want. It can even be used to condition the skin. We call it the most useful plant in Africa." Samuel's laugh was empty, and when he spoke again it was a little skeptically, as a man speaks when still on the cusp of some decision he's newly made. "I have always, even as a child, even during the hardest days of study, and the hardest days of starving, I have always had a great desire to own my own business." Samuel watched a man drop a coin and look wearily at it, as if deciding whether to spend the energy picking it up. "What you call 'rat race' is only a game of marbles—it begins quickly, but when it slows, and despite God's grace it does, you are lost." He looked cautiously at Ray.

Ray nodded. "I take your point. But it can't look good for you to go throwing away good jobs just like that. Think about it—you're an example. A role model. These highfalutin office jobs are hard for *any* man to come by." Glancing at Samuel's shocked face, Ray grew embarrassed. "But I admire you." He parked in an alley lined with blue trash bins. "We're on Glover, few down from Stone Road. We'll start here and make our way back to proper. What time you need to be back?"

"Before my wife discovers me missing." Samuel knew the joke wouldn't be lost on this man.

Ray wasn't listening. "If we're late enough, you might meet Clarish Clarke—he's my caretaker back at the farm. He comes in around this time sometimes—call him Jarvis, though. He's got a preacher's name, and it couldn't suit him less." Ray chuckled.

"Jarvis?"

"Who knows?" Ray jumped from the cab. "That's what he likes."

For two hours they toured every blank-faced shop within ten blocks of where they parked. Aster's layout was like a maze, with streets that changed into each other and few identifiable landmarks. Ray advised against Peahorn Street, but Samuel insisted on at least seeing it, so they wandered toward it. Derelict buildings lined the curbs, their windows blinded with rain-stained paper the color of moths. The few months of poverty Samuel had had to endure during his last school years in Gold Coast didn't assuage his discomfort at the desolate sight. Occasionally a man emerged from what looked to be an abandoned building.

Samuel and Ray returned to Glover Street. To lighten their spirits, Ray suggested they take lunch at the English diner, where bangers and mash were cheap. Eating seemed to relax them, and soon they made a game of naming the few strangers that passed by. Samuel asked Ray about his family, and Ray explained they were easterners who'd come west on the promise of work. "Most of them went straight back," Ray laughed. "Shit work is shit work whether you're east or west." Eudora had been the fiancée of an older cousin already living in Alberta whose father had died in the Great War when the Union government had gone back on its promise not to draft farmers' sons. "After five days I ended up with her and he ended up with my return fare to Ontario," said Ray. "You could say he lost all there was to lose in life." By default Ray had even managed to claim the age-old family farm. He'd toughed it out with Eudora, and now ran a parts business out of his garage part-time, though his true efforts went to upholding both the state of his farm and his stature in civic politics. Samuel spoke timidly of his own origins, which he sensed lacked the wholesomeness of Ray's beginnings. He hated to justify himself, holding back anything dubious, so that his story ended up being the one he'd often told the twins when they'd cared enough to ask about his life.

Trying for nonchalance, Samuel asked Ray about Jacob. "Exactly what sort of man did he become?"

"In these last years, a sighting of Jacob Tyne was as rare as a sunny month."

Samuel later came to believe that stopping for this lunch was what brought him his luck. Leaving the diner, they ran into one of Ray's longtime customers who knew of a little nook just down Glover Street, a choice property whose sudden availability had surprised everyone. He gave them directions, and as they walked there Samuel felt himself nearing the crux of all these hopeful months.

Not only clean and sizeable, the space was priced so low as to be suspicious. They called on the landlord, a stodgy, unlearned man, who led them through the musty space explaining that the price was the result of a dry low season. By then, Samuel had stopped listening. He might have been alone in that whitewashed haven, the home of his possible dream. "I'll take it," he said, killing the casual banter between Ray and the landlord.

"Oh, it's you who's looking?" The landlord looked skeptically at them. He motioned to Ray. "Thought you were taking it."

"I've got space enough between my ears without having to pay for it. This one's for Mr. Tyne." Ray smiled at the frowning man, and with their opposing looks they neutralized each other.

"Is there a problem?" said Samuel.

The landlord continued to look at Ray, then turned weary eyes on Samuel. "No, no. Follow me to my place and we'll sign the papers."

And so within minutes the dream had been bought. Ignore the questionable landlord, the distance from home, the fact that his wife was in utter darkness about this goal: Samuel Tyne had signed the lease on his own little piece of the world. After this, there could be no more doubts.

chapter SEVEN

Ama lay on her cot, prostrated with asthma. She looked from the window to the room, its charmless furniture barely distinct in the shadows. She knew the twins disliked this bedroom, the four ascetic beds pushed against each wall, but its austerity pleased Ama, especially on asthmatic days when she retired here and imagined herself a saint, her crucifix necklace resting coldly against her chest, looking to the window as if in the throes of divine enlightenment. What cleaning was to Maud, or secrets were to Samuel, this ritual was to Ama: a shameful, pleasurable vice.

Her parents had only called from France once. For a week she'd stored up complaints to tell them, but the happiness in their voices kept her from speaking. Instead, she agreed when her father said she sounded like she was having a good time, and retreated to her room to cry into her pillow. The goose down brought on an asthma attack. She turned on her back to look out the window.

The twins came in. They threw a lumpy burlap sack onto the floor.

Ama sat up, nervous. The filthy bag was covered with hairs and dead insects, and Ama thought she saw a live one crawl away. "What's in there?"

The twins behaved as though she hadn't spoken. Their stockings looked bizarre on their slender legs; obviously intended for larger, fairer women, they looked like sausage encasings that had boiled loose.

Dropping her arms to her sides, Chloe declared in a falsetto, "A crime has been committed in this house."

"We decree," said Yvette, "that no one should leave until such time as the case has been solved." Squinting and pursing her full lips, she suddenly dropped to her knees beside Ama's bed. "Are you sick, dearie?" she said in a high, twangy voice. Bewildered, Ama let Yvette push her back onto the bed, accepting the bedside cup of water Yvette held to her lips. "Aw, look at me, I'm sweet Florence Nightingale."

Ama was genuinely touched. Since the day of their arrival, when Yvette had suddenly taken Ama by the hand, she'd suspected tender feelings toward her. Yvette was merely too awkward, too shy, too afraid to express them in open company. Ama gave her an encouraging smile.

A dark emotion crossed Chloe's face, and in a second she, too, was on her knees, grabbing the cup from Yvette to have her turn. "You're farther from being Florence Nightingale than Ama is from being a genius. You're three-point-six inches too short and far too dark to come remotely close."

When Ama flinched and refused the cup, Chloe gloated. "Are you mad now?" she said. Craning her face alarmingly close, so that Ama could smell her gardenia pomade, she said, "Short of breath, but long on faith. A girl can't have everything, I guess." She rose to fetch a book on her bed. "We're out of the Bible, but here's something for you."

She handed the book to Ama, who took it from her, flinching. Ama read the title: *The Devils.*

Pacing the room in a goose step, Chloe recited, "Dostoevsky, Dickens, Disraeli." She gave Yvette a stern look.

Yvette rose and began to march behind her sister, snapping her legs up into an elastic step that seemed even more unnatural because she obviously did not want to do it. In a shrill voice that expressed precisely the opposite of the emotion on her face, she chanted, "D.H. Lawrence."

"Lawrence Durrell," yelled Chloe, taking another turn of the room.

"Gerald Durrell,"

"Fitzgerald, Scott."

"Zelda."

"Picasso."

"Gertrude Stein."

"Hemingway."

"Shotgun."

"Pills."

"Oven."

"Someone," Chloe finished, raising a brisk finger into the air, "will pay for these crimes." She lowered her voice to a hiss. "A crime has been committed in this house." And with that, she began to kick at the middle of the filthy bag, so that it not only spat objects from its opening, but broke apart at the center.

Frightened, Ama looked to Yvette. Yvette's face had completely transformed, her eyes dark and withdrawn, her chin rigid.

"Ladies and gentlemen," she bellowed, "the relics of the ranching age." Kicking the bag so hard it split entirely, she and Chloe fell to their knees and began to root through the junk.

These were no so-called relics of the ranching age. Wheezing, Ama watched from bed as they lined everything up. The objects were of foreign origin, with the occasional garish trinket that showed Jacob had had a sense of humor. There were cork sandals adorned with plastic rainbow beads; a torn dashiki; a figurine of Rex Anderson, M.D.; wooden ladles with animals carved in the handles; reams of bright, hand-sewn cloth dyed orange, green and puce; a mink stole filled with mealworms; a single baby's sandal; a heavy wooden bowl and its hourglass-shaped pestle; a crude pipe with a marble trapped inside; and finally, a slender wooden game board whose deep pits had been carved by hand.

They heard Mrs. Tyne's tired voice in the stairwell. "Breakfast," she called.

The twins became silent again. Ama tried to quiet her asthma, knowing Mrs. Tyne was so hot-tempered that she might get in trouble for it. All three were terrified at what the pile of junk would convict them of.

And certainly, Mrs. Tyne seemed to be in a mood, looking exhausted and a little short-fused. Upon seeing the mess, she set her mouth, and her shrewd, narrowed eyes made Ama anxious. But something defused her anger. She came forward to run a thoughtful finger across the board game.

"It's Oware," she said. "We used to play it as children." She ran her sleeve against it, fingering the notches as if checking the craftsmanship. Ama noticed a stripe of butter on her cheek, so negligent, so out of character for Mrs. Tyne, that its presence made her seem more vulnerable. Finally noticing their stares, she looked grimly at the children, and her voice tightened. "Well, no harm in you learning *some*thing today. Bring it down and I'll show you how to play."

In the center of the kitchen table sat a platter of toast in the shape of starfish. The sudden playfulness of this alarmed Ama, until Mrs. Tyne explained she'd only meant to test an old cookie cutter. Mrs. Tyne put the game on the wooden table with the delicacy of one laying glass. Lacking sea-beads, she dragged a crate of cherries from the fridge and placed it beside the board.

With a mischievous smile, she said, "Eat these cherries and spit the pits into this towel."

The girls looked at each other.

Mrs. Tyne laughed, and an elusive, old-fashioned beauty Ama had never seen before rose to her features. "It's all right," she said. "Go ahead."

Ama chose a dark cherry and, chewing it with a kind of dread, spat the pit onto the towel, awaiting reprimand. The twins watched, looking from Ama to their mother. Seeing no repercussions, they, too, began to eat, and before long all three girls brought forth dozens of tiny pits still red with pith.

Mrs. Tyne thumbed them clean under water, then returned them to the table in her knotted apron, where they'd dried. Gingerly, she dropped some into each notch. She laughed while explaining the rules, and her rare happiness made them playful and happy themselves.

Barely an hour had passed when they heard someone tapping at the door. Maud nudged Chloe to answer it, and in a second the sullen girl returned, followed by an exquisitely dressed Eudora Frank, who surveyed their game with annoyed surprise.

Maud put a hand to her mouth. "Church!"

With her raised brow and pursed lips, Eudora looked the very measure of condescension. Shaking the rain from her broad, magisterial shoulders, she glanced dismissively at the cherry pits, as if to say they were behaving like heathens when their minds should be on God.

Maud felt the blood rush to her face. "I don't know where my mind's at. First there was last night—I couldn't sleep with all that racket from the weathervane—and then when I saw this game, I—" She laughed and, gripping her daughters' shoulders, said, "Ten minutes! Give us ten minutes!"

"Oh, Maud, take your time. You know I'm no bully. We can as easily catch the eleven o'clock service." Her tone, and the rigid way she set her gray cloche on the table and remained standing, as if determined to wait in discomfort, were an obvious rebuke.

Mounting the stairs, they heard Eudora call: "Well, this is too gorgeous. Sam! Sammy! Please come here, let's talk about this weathervane."

Before they even reached the top, Samuel stood on the landing, the creases from his pillow etched into his cheek. "Did you call me, Maud?"

"Eudora did. She's in the kitchen." Maud bustled past, annoyed, and Samuel watched her merge into the shadows, taking the children with her.

He paused at the kitchen doorway, observing the forbidding figure of Eudora Frank as she fanned out her skirt and sat on a rickety chair with all the pomp of a queen. He watched her play with the feathers on her gray hat, mortified by his realization that he feared her. It was the fear he had of all forward women, a quality the young Maud had lacked, and half of why he'd come to love her. Laughing at himself, he entered the room just as Eudora screamed his name again.

"Oh, you're right there," she said, embarrassed. "We need you to take down this weathervane."

Her matter-of-factness seemed perverse to him. Who was she, after all, to come into a stranger's house and start dictating what needed to be done? He gave her a look of annoyance. She continued to stare at him, raising an imperious eyebrow and surveying his body as if to assess his worth.

He wanted to kick her out of his house, and yet he knew he wouldn't do it. The worst thing about her request was that, after his restless night, he'd been thinking of taking the weathervane down anyway. Frowning to show his displeasure, he said, "All right," and went out.

After berating himself in the shower, Samuel descended the stairs to an empty house. Only after calling for his family did he find the note on the fridge. Gone to church? It suddenly hit him that it would have been absurd for Eudora to get all dressed up just to boss him around, and yet at the time the thought had seemed natural. He stood with the paper in his fist, thinking. Was Maud seeking this woman's friendship to spite him? Samuel checked himself, feeling guilty at how these days he'd come to expect the worst in his wife. He drank a glass of tap water and, after sitting for a minute, went to search for a ladder.

Empty, the house echoed his every step. It was the first time he'd been alone in it. He walked through the rooms, searching the crawl-spaces and closets, thinking more and more of Jacob. In the room of prayer mats, Samuel imagined Jacob kneeling, slow with age, and wondered if he'd been the subject of any of those prayers. In the ancient study, where Samuel had taken to storing old wires in the drawers of the oak desk, he pictured the old man sitting down to write him a letter and being so respectful of Samuel's peace that he set the task aside with great moral resolve. In the root cellar, with its moist shadows broken up by light coming through the cracks, Samuel tried to fathom what his uncle had used this space for. Jacob hadn't left his imprint on this house. Even the furniture seemed impersonal, like a hotel's. Samuel didn't find a single ladder, and the only tools he managed to find were a blunt machete and two flat-head screwdrivers.

Outside, he assessed the weathervane from every angle, astonished so small a thing could make such noise. Craning up at it, he was suddenly struck by an odd feeling and turned to look at the house in the distance. He still hadn't seen Saul Porter; Maud had badgered him so badly about it that he'd made a point of putting it off. Now, he decided to go and ask about a ladder.

Wading through grass cold as lake water, Samuel studied the house. It looked derelict, with dirty shingles and a monumental roof that almost dwarfed it. The only hint that someone lived there was in the length of the grass, shorn by an exacting hand. With every footstep Samuel felt his trespass, and this made him nervous.

He knocked on the door. The yard was tidy, but quite impoverished, with rusty bicycle parts piled by the entranceway, and that pervasive smell of mothballs that also characterized the Tyne house. The porch had recently been swept, and from the eaves hung a quaint attempt at beauty: a handmade bird feeder. Knocking again, Samuel listened for sounds inside. Despite the stillness, he sensed someone was home. Sighing, he pulled a receipt from his pocket to make a note, but found he had no pen. He resolved to return later.

Samuel was drinking water in the kitchen, trying to decide what to do with his day, when he heard his family returning. Checking his watch, he walked to the door but didn't find anyone on the stoop. He opened the storm door and was about to return inside when something caught his eye.

A tall silver ladder leaned against the house. Samuel checked it for a note and found nothing. In the road were the same people he always saw, always with their distrustful looks, as if he might divulge their unemployment to their wives. He nodded and carried the ladder around to the backyard. Catching his breath, he squinted across at Porter's house; all he could see was that heaving roof, with its clicking shingles. How had Porter known he'd needed a ladder? He must have been watching Samuel all this time, but why hadn't he answered his door, or even bothered to ring Samuel's doorbell when bringing the ladder over? Feeling confused and affronted, Samuel lengthened the ladder, propping it against the house before going to find more tools. Besides the screwdrivers and the machete, the best he could do was an ice pick, a steel peg and a kitchen knife. By the time he returned outside, the wind had tipped the ladder into the grass, and stubbornly he knelt to pick it up with the screwdrivers and knife still in his mouth, the machete pinched between his knees. He knew he was tempting fate, but his luck held. He even managed to climb to the roof without nicking himself.

Up close, the weathervane was a pompous-looking thing, a peacock with a flaring tail of knives. Samuel didn't know where to begin; there seemed to be no strategy for how to handle it. When he held the head, the body swung away from him with a hellish squeal.

"Mother of God . . ." he muttered, pressing a palm to his ear to shut out the noise.

When he attempted to hold any other part, he came away with cuts so deep he feared for his agile hands. He began to sweat, feeling the wind would push him over, trying to overcome his sudden vertigo whenever he looked down. He damned himself for climbing up in the first place, reasoning that because he'd placed himself in harm's way, he should at least finish the job. He beat the steel with the machete, futile blows that sounded like a bell tolling. When he tried to unscrew it, it began to shriek in little fits. He grabbed it, poked it, even tried to break it off by hanging all his weight off the stem, but it wouldn't move. Admitting defeat, Samuel descended the ladder and went inside.

His hands bled, but he was too tired to bandage them. Searching the study's dark cabinets, he discovered a cask of palm wine among Jacob's empty bottles and, pouring himself a glass, sat to drink at the kitchen table.

When the women returned, they found Samuel in a state. Never in Maud's life had she seen him so drunk; even after cutting his hands on the glass he'd kept drinking.

Samuel belched against his fist, turning his weary face to them, as though challenging them to say something.

"Go upstairs, girls," Maud said. Hearing the strain in her voice, they fled without speaking.

Eudora wore that ruthless look Maud remembered from her friendship with Ella Bjornson. They did that, these women; pretended to console you while gathering enough facts to humiliate you at a Sunday luncheon.

"How dare you drink when there are children in the house? And midday, no less, and a Sunday?"

Samuel wasn't drunk, but had had enough to give his emotions an edge. His anger was so quick that he followed a tread behind it, and this lapse of feeling gave him the sense of not quite being in his skin. "Do not dare needle *me*, woman. These gashes were inflicted by *your* weathervane." He looked contemptuously from his wife to Eudora. "Look," he said, placing the glass on the table to show them his palms. "Look, look at this. I look like the stigmata."

"Samuel!" said Maud.

"What, *eih?*" he demanded, picking up his glass to resume drinking.

Mortified, Maud couldn't help but feel a little guilty. The weathervane business had been her fault, as she had complained bitterly for the last two weeks. She looked hesitantly at Eudora.

Eudora was a transformed woman. After the initial delight at finding a new topic to gossip about, she set her hat on the table and approached Samuel as if approaching something feral.

"Maud, I need a candle, a sewing needle, some gauze, if you have it, utility thread and bandages," she commanded.

Eudora cupped Samuel's hands in her own. "Looks pretty bad,

Sammy." As she made to touch the wounds, Samuel retracted his hands (though not without some embarrassment). Obviously shocked that he could defy her in any way, Eudora quickly recovered herself and rose to wash her hands at the sink.

Maud returned with everything but the gauze, and seeing her husband's reticence, she explained that Eudora had done some nursing during the war. "You're in good hands."

"The best," said Eudora, pulling her chair across from him, suppressing the creak it made under her weight by fanning her skirt. She rolled back her sleeves to reveal plump, hairless arms so pale the veins were visible. "We'll have you all fixed up in no time, don't worry." Her breath had an acrid smell, presumably from going too long without talking, thought Samuel. Eudora winked at him. "I know you've got to start setting up."

"'Setting up,'" Maud repeated in a cautious voice.

Curing the needle in the flame, Eudora said, "Ray said the shop's a beaut. Congratulations." She winked again.

Samuel flinched, and Eudora paused, thinking she was hurting him. "You all right?"

"Shop, yes, Samuel's little *shop*," said Maud. Though she had a staid, even flippant look on her face, Samuel knew she was furious.

Eudora laughed. "Oh, right. What do you guys call it—bay, right? A *bay*." Faking an indefinable accent, she made a demure face and said, "Congratulations, Samuel, on having obtained your *bay*." She laughed as though she'd told the world's funniest joke. "And watch, giving up that Calgary house will be the best decision you ever made. Why keep up rent at a place no one lives in anymore? At least with us we *own* both the farm and the house, so there's no money hassle." After a period in which no one spoke, Eudora patted Samuel's hand with pleasure. "You're a new man, Sam."

"He certainly is," said Maud. Avoiding Samuel's eye, she rose to see her guest out. Samuel heard Maud ascend the stairs, after pausing in the kitchen doorway to look at him.

Her face had had none of the accusation he'd expected. Only the look of some ancient fire finally dying out, the resignation of defeat. He'd finally outdone her. And the openness of her hurt was like some last appeal to his intimacy. Five weeks earlier it might have worked. Now he simply concluded he'd have to watch what he told Ray. Samuel regretted that she'd had to hear it from that woman, but what of it? It was done. He'd been saved the effort of having to explain himself.

That night, Maud waited for Samuel in bed. Despite its plastic cover, the mattress gave off an acrid smell at the least pressure. It was the smell of fevers and old age, and was probably the most telling relic of Jacob's last years. Still, Samuel and Maud slept on it, and if it bothered them, neither admitted it. In all truth, the idea had at first been so repulsive to Samuel that he'd ransacked the house for a replacement and, finding nothing, almost bribed the girls for their cots. But he was granted a moment of lucidity. The bed was his legacy, the only one he had. It allowed Samuel to surround himself with the last of Jacob's physical presence. And Jacob had not died in this room, so there was no need to fear it. Besides, Samuel had spent most of his savings on the move and on setting up shop, so only a rare dollar was left over for anything else.

As soon as he saw Maud he began to apologize. He lacked all passion, and digressed when the words seemed to have no effect on her. By the end even he was waiting for himself to finish.

"Very eloquent, Samuel," said Maud, "and your timing is, as usual, endearing. But I was only going to ask how your hands were."

Samuel paused, humiliated. "Fine," he said.

She turned out the light.

In the darkness, they listened to the wailing weathervane. Samuel moistened his lips and was about to speak, when Maud said, "Just go to sleep, all right?"

Samuel exhaled. "I barely knew either my father or my uncle. I'd only seen Jacob once before he came and offered to give up his chieftancy for me." At Maud's silence, he continued. "He did not speak of it, but it was family knowledge that he owed a great debt to my father's memory. I never discovered what it was—the whole time I knew Jacob, *sth,* nothing. And I was too young to remember *egya.* You know, I do not even know how he died, whether it was cancer, heart attack—you know Gold Coast. But I was young, so growing up I heard nothing but the highest praise for him. But I now know there was *something,* and Jacob would not tell me. Of course, there were rumors, myths. Some said the betrayal was over something as simple as love—that they'd competed for a village girl who played them against each other. Others said that Jacob had always felt himself the lesser brother, that my grandfather favored *egya,* so that Jacob did everything he could to thwart my father's success. That, ultimately, he was responsible for my father's death, because in *egya*'s times of sickness, Jacob taunted him to keep working. Some even went so far as to say my father wasn't sick at all, that something else—but that is tomfoolery. In the end, they were very close. They had slept in the same bed as boys, and once *egya* died Jacob began to sleep in that bed again. He accepted all *egya*'s duties, reared me like his own son. And even if he forgot it, I never did. I never did." His voice sounded vacant. "I know they both expected great things of me."

Taking her silence as indifference, Samuel turned over in bed. He felt a cold hand between his shoulder blades, then the motion of Maud rolling over. It was a fleeting, impersonal touch, but he felt all the emotion it was meant to convey. Frowning, he looked out the window.

chapter EIGHT

I n a three-day bout of work in which sleep became a hopeless goal, Samuel stocked his shop with all the tools of his trade. Scanning new catalogues with a thick-tipped pen, he'd noted the names of even newer catalogues he wanted to send away for. Possessed of a confidence shadowed by a fear it would leave him, Samuel laid the groundwork for his business in astute, genius (he considered) maneuvers. A lesser man might have sought the paperwork, bought the equipment locally and left himself guessing in the hands of God. Not Samuel. For nights now a single pure slogan had obsessed him: *Go global.* He didn't know if he'd heard it somewhere, or if it was his own, but for a man of his background in this mechanized world it seemed the appropriate motto on which to build his business. And so he sent requests to Taiwan and Germany for equipment catalogues, and made an inner note to send them business cards once he'd had them printed. He drove so often to Edmonton that Maud complained he'd wear the car to scrap iron. He used his old government contacts to convince potential clients of his deftness as an oil analyst, and received what he thought was a promising response. He brought back his hordes by night, and soon the shop was clotted with all that his craft demanded: fuse testers, transmitters, soldering irons, circuit boards, power supplies and, that apple of his eye, the oil-analysis machine, with its talent for measuring nitrogen, hydrogen and nitrate levels. The shop was soon so full he could barely fit his workbench. By the end he thought the dog's hours would cripple him. But nothing could match the satisfaction of having done the work by his own hand. A lesser man might have begged for help. Not Samuel. He'd gotten twelve hours of sleep in a three-day period, but his elation kept him lucid and agile. Another slogan came back to him, this one from his school years, and in his exhaustion it made him laugh a full ten minutes: *Dream it. Live it.* It had taken him half a lifetime, but he'd done it. Some, he ruminated, don't give themselves the chance to try.

The week before his opening, Samuel invited his family down to see the fruits of his labors. Grudgingly, Maud rounded up the girls, and the five of them drove to Glover Street in a tense silence.

So nervous it took him two minutes to find the proper key, Samuel unlocked the shop and let them wander inside. Under their scrutiny, he began to notice things he hadn't seen before. The ceiling leaked in one corner. Shadows like obstinate crows refused to scatter when touched by light. He looked hesitantly at the children and was pained by the pitying look Ama gave him. When they'd finished the tour, Maud paused, resting her arms on the counter.

"Well, Samuel," she said, "a greater man wouldn't have done any worse."

She herded the girls back to the car and, afterward, mentioned the shop as little as possible.

After two weeks, Samuel's spirits dampened. He no longer felt the grandeur of first ownership, and was given to watching the silent film of passersby on their lunch hours. Otherwise, people were a rare sight, and when one entered his shop he felt a sort of sick joy and mixed up his words in an impolitic move to make the quick sell. He began to pine after and dread customers, for before he opened his mouth he knew he had lost the sale. The shop became prone to deadbeats who came in to idle Samuel's time away with stories of the ridiculous. Felix, one such man, only left by threat of police. When the equipment Samuel ordered from abroad finally came, he found he had no money to pay the distributors and had to ask Maud's permission to dip into their shared savings.

"The self-made man condescends to ask me something," she said. "I thought you did as you pleased and paid no mind to anyone."

Nevertheless, she told him to take the money. He paid his bills and resolved never to admit he spent most of his day alone.

A peddler began to plague the shop. At first Samuel politely resisted, but his loneliness began to soften him, and with pity he permitted the man to at least finish his sales pitch. He was a coal-colored old gaffer in a pristine suit. Samuel took an immense interest in that suit. Unlike his own enormous suits, the peddler's looked like a leftover from adolescence. His cuffs and hems shrunk back to reveal slender wrists and ankles. His ginger Panama hat, like an afterthought on his large head, made his body seem even larger.

Gravely, the peddler placed three englassed candles of different heights and colors on the counter.

"Light of God," he said. "Multilingual." He pointed to the labels, on which the Lord's Prayer was printed in three different languages.

Samuel marveled at the man's accent, which was so filled with contradictions it was impossible to say from which country it originated. "Mule-tie-lin-gle," he'd said. Seeing that Samuel didn't resist him, he groped through his carton and placed three stuffed doves— "For the chil'ren"—and piles of watches and faux antique clocks— "What is a man without time?"—on the counter. As he continued, Samuel was haunted by a feeling he knew this man, though logically he was certain he'd never seen him before. He scrutinized the moist eyes, the hemp-like beard, the skin dark as a starless night. With the peddler's each movement, a tobacco smell emanated from his clothes.

Though the peddler averted his eyes, Samuel still somehow felt that the man was staring at him. And in this searching silence, as they assessed one another, each waiting for the other to speak, a feeling of fellowship rose between them. Samuel purchased two candles and a dove, and on the logic of that successful sale, the man came again.

Only some tragic past could produce such a man, Samuel decided. The peddler had the air of a learned man fallen on hard luck, and no one had more sympathy for that predicament than Samuel. On the next visit, he bought three new candles and a cheap watch to take apart and fix at will. Though it embarrassed him to think of giving this junk to his family, he felt he had to support the peddler in some way. He began to count on the visits to break the monotony of his day, and he thought the man, too, came to depend on his acquaintance. Not that they said much beyond trite sales pitches, a word or two about the weather. But they shared a common downfall: they were educated men cut astray by a world of circumstance, who were trying to find their footing. Or so Samuel liked to think of it. Every day after the stranger left, he spoke in confirmation to himself: "Yes, we are two doves in the same cage"; "You can lead us to the river, but you cannot make us drink"; and often, "The world sees us as problems, and all we want are the world's problems solved." In fact, Samuel, uneasy in a hermitry that wasn't self-imposed, had begun to talk to himself in lofty proverbs.

Cleaning the shop every afternoon, he tucked his newly purchased junk in a box under the counter, saying to himself all the while, "Baby steps, baby steps. It is with the aid of the tree that the tree-climber makes contact with the sky. Rome was not built in a day. It takes time for business to grow, to enhance itself. Samuel, do not despair. Success is inevitable. Slowness means that the base of the business has a chance to grow solid. It is hard to fell a tree that is leaning against a rock. One cannot fell a tree with one's hands tied behind one's back. And even if I am not an immediate success, what is wrong? One must struggle to enjoy his rewards. If man were to achieve everything at once, he would lose his mind."

With these sayings he was able for a time to believe that early defeat was the very best thing. For how indeed could a man feel any pride in an achievement merely handed to him? It was an initiation, a test of his staying power. He even began to take pride in his minor failures. It wasn't until he checked his accounts at the end of the two-week period and discovered his earnings well into the negatives that he got angry, throwing that anger at the likeliest source of his ruin—the mongrel peddler.

"A man can only take so much upon himself before his back collapses in foolishness," said Samuel to himself. "Does he think I am made of money, that he can keep coming in here and robbing a poor man blind? One hand washes the other, it is said. You scratch my back and I will scratch yours. And what has he done for me, eh? Has he brought me radios to fix? Record players? Has he even brought me his toaster? *Sth*. A time waster. Nothing but a big man after a poor man's bread." And it was as though this unkind reasoning was the eulogy of their friendship, for the peddler didn't return to the shop the next day.

"Good riddance," said Samuel. "Go and find some other millionaire to harass."

But when a second and then a third day passed in the peddler's absence, Samuel began to get antsy. He fell into such low spirits that he forgot his usual hasty speech to potential customers, and actually found himself with four contracts by the end of the week. And that is how, inadvertently, a peddler spurred Samuel's business. The peddler never returned, so it took some time for Samuel to connect his new success with that wayward man the color and scent of fresh ash. By the time Samuel thought to thank him, the peddler's existence seemed almost mythical. Samuel felt embarrassed to have directed his anger at this angel of goodwill, and mentally humiliated himself on that account all the time. As for his business, it carried on, and he quietly fixed things, continuing to mutter to himself. "It is an ass who bites the hand that feeds him. Noble men are fewer than jewels in this world."

"And it is an ass who keeps his business open during lunchtime, and talks to himself like a loon on day-leave from the crazy house," said Ray, laughing as he closed the door behind him. "I leave you alone for a week and you go batty on me. What gives, Samuel? Look so shitty I wouldn't know you from Adam."

Samuel laughed. "You old ass," he said, testing it out. Ray's smile permitted him to go on. "You fool. I grew this old and rundown waiting for you to visit."

"Well, salvation's come," laughed Ray. "Would've gotten here sooner, but I had a cold. You should have *seen* Eudora running her legs off, fetching me things. It's enough to make a man want a cold for as long as he can stand it, heh. So how's business?"

"If you break something, and do it quickly, I'll let you be my first customer. But, shhh, it's not legal yet."

"What, no license?"

"Just the seal of incorporation. I get the license next week."

Ray scratched the back of his neck. "I'll see what can't be done to speed it up a little."

"I'd appreciate it."

"You should," said Ray with a smile that didn't quite touch his eyes. Squinting his glasses into place, he began to assess the walls. "As a space, it's a beaut. You guys got all the luck." His eyes listed just above Samuel's shoulder, as though he was talking to a slightly taller man. "Well, brother, you've more than impressed me. I've just been sitting on my ass all day, reading paper after paper."

"What *is* happening in the world? I've been in here."

Ray lit a cigarette, exhaling with a distracted look. "Not much. Actually, lots. Let's see. The newest local thing is the library strike in Calgary. Down at the new university, if you can believe it. They want longer library hours. Now give me something of value, give me a fight for land or, hell, for something substantial. But *li*brary hours . . ." Ray chuckled. "And, who's it, the IAA just got the vote for status Indians." He drew on his cigarette, and it was difficult to interpret what he thought of the matter. "Oh, here's something for you—'affirmative action' just got instituted in the States, don't know the particulars, but it's supposed to help you guys. Can't say it'll do you any good up here, though. But now, what else, I feel like there's a story I wanted to tell—

oh, yes." Ray nearly collapsed in laughter, so that Samuel cringed when he accidentally dropped his cigarette on the carpet.

Weak with laughter, Ray reinserted it in his mouth. "Pearson lets the Yanks know Canada won't stand for the Vietnam War, right? Goes down to Philadelphia, petitions in hand, talking it up in true Canadian indignation style, right? Well, you know how President Johnson responds? You know what he says?" Ray could barely speak for his held-back laughter. Making an imperious face, he said, "He says, Johnson says, 'Lester, you peed on my carpet.' Ha. 'Lester, you . . . peed on my carpet'! Can you beat it?"

Samuel joined in Ray's laughter, but in truth, he only vaguely saw the humor in it. He was so apolitical, so cut off from the world, that the war, along with all other global conflict, seemed illusory.

"Hey, what's all this behind here?" Ray had wandered behind the screen Samuel had put up to privatize his actual workspace. Wires, plugs and circuit boards weighed down the workbench. Set to one side, underneath one of Maud's embroidered handkerchiefs, sat the project he worked on only when at his most confident.

Samuel hesitated, waving a weak hand. "Come on, that's my workspace. Get out of there." He tried to keep things casual by laughing.

Ray pulled the kerchief away. "What's this?" He stubbed his cigarette on the bench.

Samuel replaced the kerchief, his laugh nervous. "Nothing. Just a prototype I'm working on. Just a computing machine, an attempt, that is all."

Ray looked dubiously at him. As he shifted his glasses higher on his nose, Samuel was again aware of being just underneath his line of vision. Frowning, Ray began to speak but stopped himself. Instead, he said, "Well, I'll leave you to it. Only came by to see you were making out all right. Oh, and I wanted to invite you to my farm some time in the next week or two. I've got to go out and see it and thought you might want to tag along."

Relieved, Samuel said, "I would love to."

"Great, I'll stop by." Ray moved to the door. "Now what's all this?"

At the genuine perplexity in Ray's voice, Samuel raised his head. Outside, groups of people ran by. Ray leaned out the door, and cupping a hand over his eyes to see what could have attracted the crowd, he swore and then began to run himself.

Agitated, Samuel bumped his hip getting around the counter. He limped to the door to see Glover Street awash with people. The tense excitement in some faces and the dread in others convinced Samuel some catastrophe was happening. Having lost sight of Ray, Samuel ran not so much to find him, or even to know what was going on, as from an inner urgency.

The other shops along the street had been left unattended, some of the doors flung wide. But no one was interested in stealing. Everyone's attention was directed at the smoke gathering in the sky, a dark patch like a flaw in wood. It was so thick it looked like a solid object. Samuel felt as though everything had stopped, including himself, though he saw with detachment he was still moving. He turned the corner onto Dickson Street.

An enormous crowd stood before Thorpe's Diner. Urged back by the lay firemen, the crowd continued to surge forward, screaming above the dull roar of the fire. The smell of sulphur, usually so acute on warm afternoons, had given way to that stench only the burning of artificial things can produce. It clotted the nostrils and stuck in the throat, and Samuel found himself gasping. Others were choking, and a few men held the heads of wives who'd leaned over to throw up onto the nearby grass.

The flames became more violent under the water jets, simply shifting out of the way, before they began to sink. Each extinguished flame made a hissing noise and threw out a gale of black smoke that drew relieved sounds from the crowd. Once the fire was contained, Samuel was amazed to see how little of the building had actually burned. Brown water dripped from the singed awning, smoke spiraled off the roof, but the building's structural integrity was preserved. The fire ended suddenly, and exhausted, the local fire team dropped their hoses almost in unison, gripping their knees and catching their breath. But the crowd continued to stand there, their silence heavy with coughs and groans, staring at the diner as if the fire was still going.

"Fifty-five years," someone cried. "Fifty-five years."

". . . electrical wiring, and I said that's no wiring. We know, we . . ."

A crying woman, her sobs choked with asthma, threw her arms around a red-faced man.

Dazed, Samuel pushed through the crowd. Before he knew it he was standing among the damp people at the front, their pale, astonished faces looking at the smoke overcasting the sky. Studying the entranceway, which dripped with sooty water, Samuel realized he knew this place. Ray had brought him to this diner the day they'd found him the shop. Samuel started at the memory. Everything seemed connected in some dark and meaningful way.

He gave his head a shake. "Once you begin with the superstitions, you can kiss your rationality good-bye," he muttered.

Ray Frank appeared as from nowhere, and Samuel watched as he rolled up his sleeves to calmly direct the fire team. Beside him stood a fat, fussy-looking little man in a wrinkled black suit, also shouting orders, but in a less self-conscious way. Samuel walked up to them.

"Ray, did you see my wife? My children? I hope they were nowhere around."

Distracted, Ray barely acknowledged him. "No, no, didn't see . . ." He drew a hose toward him. "Oh, that's right, Eudora said she was having them in today. Should be safe and sound."

"Thank you, I appreciate that." Samuel realized that the obese little man was staring at him, and hesitating, he nodded. "Oh, hello there," he said, as if the man's height might indicate he was actually a child.

The man raised his eyebrows, and seeing his sudden interest in Samuel, Ray dropped everything to introduce them. "The Honorable Don Gould, this is Samuel Tyne. Sam, this here's the mayor."

Samuel shook hands, conscious that his were damp. He was dying to leave, to close up shop and see his wife and children, but he instinctively waited for some kind of dismissal. He nodded toward the diner. "I cannot believe this has happened."

The mayor assessed him with cold eyes. "I don't have time to stand around chatting about it. There'll be time enough to talk at next week's meeting." And he left to go direct things again.

Ray colored a little. "Well. I'll call on you, Samuel." He turned to follow the mayor.

Samuel felt dazed. Taking off his moist jacket, he slung it over his shoulder and walked back to his shop.

chapter NINE

T hat morning, before the fire began, Mrs. Tyne had badgered the girls into immaculate dresses and marched them over to the Franks'. Eudora came to the door in a tight dress, a white carnation tucked into her top buttonhole.

"Well, you girls certainly aren't the most polite neighbors I ever had, waiting so long to call on me," she joked. That jutting tooth made Ama nervous.

The Frank house displayed surprising good taste. Most of the furniture was beige, with the occasional colored chair, and Eudora hung only paintings, not prints, each chosen with a refined eye. Ama could tell by Mrs. Tyne's vague smile that it flustered her.

But Eudora's coarse joking soon gave way to restraint; she ran her hands down her clothes, fiddled with her satin cushions and responded to compliments by slightly lowering her eyelids. She set a kettle on the new gas stove, shoving a plate of cookies in Ama's hands before herding the girls downstairs to watch television.

In "Ray's Recreation Room"—"We call it the three Rs," said Eudora—sat a blond rug, a recliner, and a dinner tray holding a small television. "Ta-dah!" said Eudora, gesturing at it with her usual enthusiasm. As if remembering her earlier forbearance, she continued, "You may watch as much television as you please. I know you don't have one."

The girls sat rigid on the rug after Eudora left. Ama reached out and turned on the set, looking at the twins on either side of her to see if she'd done right. Chloe's face remained sober, but Yvette's reflected pleasure, and Ama smiled at her and sat back. She knew Yvette wanted to befriend her, but was merely too shy, or possibly too afraid of Chloe to try.

Without warning, Chloe stood and yelled, "I have to go to the bathroom."

Ama was appalled and, apparently, so was Mrs. Tyne. From the top floor her mortified voice called out, "Where are your manners? And how old are you?"

They could hear Eudora laughing. "Little door to the right of the washer down there." Her voice became demure. "We just had it installed."

When Chloe left, relief seemed to come over Yvette. She smiled strangely and, standing up, gestured for Ama to follow. Startled, Ama looked from the bathroom door to Yvette, who'd begun to creep up the stairs. When Yvette's expression darkened, and she mouthed the words *Come on,* Ama weakened.

Mrs. Tyne and Eudora took their tea in the kitchen. The girls tiptoed past, unhinged the storm door, and fell from the house into the streets.

It was a hot, fragrant day. Wild roses, marigolds and sunflowers finally awake, everything felt wonderfully alive. Even the sickly birches looked lustrous. The pavement radiated heat.

After running for a few minutes, the girls sat by the roadside to catch their breath.

"Why did we leave Chloe?" said Ama.

Yvette didn't answer. She drew up her knees and began to pick at a scab. Ama was surprised by how weak and thin her knees looked, like the knees of a three-year-old.

Fat purple dragonflies began to pester them, and frustrated, Yvette swatted them away.

"I can't stand these goddamn things," she said. Seeing she'd shocked Ama, Yvette laughed. She stood and wiped her hands roughly on her thighs. "Come on, let's go."

They explored the town for half an hour, barely speaking. Aster seemed an oasis, a small, isolated place amidst miles of nothing. Its streets were inconsistent, some changing their names every few blocks, so that tourists (the few who arrived each year) were often confused. Of those streets whose names remained consistent, half ended abruptly in wilderness. The commercial district was confined to three streets, the rest being either residential or derelict. The girls took Pine Creek Street to its end, and sat in a thicket of three-foot-high weeds.

Ama didn't understand why Yvette ignored her. Hadn't they run away from Chloe because they had wanted to be alone together? But Yvette only became interested when Ama stopped trying. Then Ama felt Yvette's huge eyes scrutinizing her. When Ama tried to engage her, Yvette looked away, only to begin the whole uncomfortable process again a few minutes later.

Yvette swore every time she killed an insect. And yet, when Ama asked her if she'd like to leave, she only scowled. The foliage was filled with slow-moving black-and-yellow grasshoppers, ants and maddening blackflies.

"Know what?" said Yvette. "You're just like these flies. Pesky."

Ama searched Yvette's smiling face. "You don't mean that," she said. When Yvette's smile grew even wider, Ama laughed nervously.

"Let's go!" Yvette rose to her feet and, hopping off on one leg, accidentally jumped onto a tall anthill. "Mother of Christ, get them off, get them off!" As Ama slapped the few red ants off Yvette's legs, Yvette began to twitch and dance and scream. And she was such a sight, so comic, that Ama laughed. A dark look crossed Yvette's face, but she seemed to realize her ridiculousness and began to laugh, too. Holding her hands to her mouth, she ran back to Pine Creek Street with Ama trailing behind.

Yvette came to a halt. Her face had hardened, erasing any trace of her earlier excitement. "I have to go to the bathroom," she said in a cold, unemotive voice.

Ama felt disconcerted. "All right."

"Let's go to Thorpe's," said Yvette. "Last one to cartwheel there is a rotten egg."

Yvette turned a series of cartwheels. Ama was perplexed that someone who supposedly had to go the bathroom was physically comfortable enough to strain herself this way. "Okay," screamed Yvette, as Ama continued to walk, "it's the walkers versus the cartwheelers." And she flipped the entire way to the diner.

When they entered, dressed in their Sunday best but with weeds in their hair, they were stared at so fiercely that Yvette walked out.

"I hate that," said Yvette, trembling. "Even though this town used to be all black, everywhere you go they stare at you."

"Well, we don't exactly look like queens." Ama pulled fluff from her hair.

Yvette gave Ama a sullen look. "It's a *diner*, Asthma."

Ama flinched. "Don't call me that. You don't mean it."

Rolling her eyes, Yvette grabbed Ama by the sleeve and led her to the diner across the street. Jackson's had that heavily varnished look that implies filth even when extremely clean. They took a booth by the back, the farthest from the washroom, and making a drama of clutching her gut, Yvette ran to use it.

Ama sat looking out the window. On one side of Aster, the roads sloped gently down to the river, so that Ama could almost see over the copses of spruce to the water. She drummed her knuckles on the table, glancing around. A man at the counter looked over his shoulder at her, smiling when their eyes met. Ama looked quickly away. Only two other booths were occupied, both by people sitting alone. In the farthest one sat a thin, amiable-looking man with a newspaper, whom everyone seemed to call "Cap'n Ron." He had the throat of a flute, whistling so luminously his range rivaled the weathervane.

"Listen to the old pipe," said the counterman.

In the middle booth sat a small Asian woman with the bones of a bird, her eyes downcast. She appeared to be arguing with someone who was no longer there. She ate her breakfast one item at a time.

Finally, Yvette returned from the bathroom. "Did you fall in?" teased Ama, instantly sorry she'd said it. Yvette gave her a dark look.

When the counterman came to take their order, Yvette stood to leave. Ama grabbed her hand. "No, no, it's okay, I've got money. Let's get two strawberry milkshakes, all right, Yvette?"

Yvette shrugged, crossing her arms against her chest. Instinctively, Ama felt there was something different about her. "Are you okay?" she asked. "Were you sick in there?"

Yvette laughed through her nose and gave Ama a haughty look.

Ama's face flushed. She didn't understand the hostility.

The counterman placed the milkshakes on their table. Sipping hers nervously, Ama studied the indifference on Yvette's face. Yvette guzzled hers down, as though she hadn't eaten in days. An idea occurred to Ama.

"Chloe?" she said, searching Yvette's face.

Yvette looked startled. "Chloe?" She laughed. "You're just as crazy as she is. You know she sees signs in everything? Like if the weatherman says it's going to rain and it stays sunny, then that's an omen. Or if rooms are painted dark colors, then they're sacred, and so are dogwoods, and the number six, too. But she can't count anything out loud. To her, counting something is like cursing it, and anyway, she seems to think everything in the world is connected so that there's really no point in telling things apart." Yvette scoffed. "Chloe thinks she was born so that the sun would have a reason to shine." Yvette pressed the back of her hand to her forehead and said in a falsetto, "Her life is one of awful responsibility."

Ama continued to drink, not knowing what to say.

"Just between you and me," said Yvette, winking, "she's completely insane."

Ama kept her eyes on the table. The girls drank in silence.

"Now *I* have to go to the bathroom," said Ama, sliding out of the booth. Once there, she feared Yvette would leave without her, but part of her wanted that to happen. Washing her hands, she took a deep breath and swung open the door.

Yvette had switched sides in the booth. Her face looked tired, almost sensitive, and sitting across from her, Ama felt a pang of guilt.

"Did you fall in?" said Yvette, and Ama smiled at the joke. "I couldn't sit there anymore. The sun was in my eyes."

Ama cupped the sun from her eyes and studied the face before her, convinced that it was Yvette who sat across from her. But for a moment she'd believed it was Chloe.

"You know," said Yvette, "Aster used to have what's called the Aster Family Picnic. Mr. Tyne told me. Even the Stampede couldn't beat it. They had greased-pig chases, taffy pulls and everything. Potato-sack races, horse races, dancing . . ."

Across the street people began to rush out of Thorpe's Diner. There was a blast, cracking the storefront, and voluptuous smoke poured from the windows.

"Thorpe's is on fire," said the counterman, dashing outside. An astonished murmur went through Jackson's. Dazed, everyone dropped their money on the table and ran out to see what was happening.

Ama couldn't believe it. The yellow awning fell across the storefront, edged in fire. Flames flew off the weakening roof, and a smell of burning plastic weighed down the air. Ama's chest seized up.

Yvette looked frightened, the light of the fire filling her eyes. Her lower eyelashes were wet.

"I need to go home," said Ama. "I'm choking to death."

They walked back in silence. No one was home at the Tyne house. With unexpected tenderness, Yvette put Ama to bed, giving her her medication and insisting on holding the cup for her as Ama drank. Ama lay prostrated, with delusions of sainthood, until an hour later, when they heard the door open downstairs.

It was Mr. and Mrs. Tyne. Reaching the girls' room, Mr. Tyne looked tired, and a little sheepish, his bowler crushed in his awkward hands. But Mrs. Tyne's outraged face looked like a stranger's, her cheeks puckering unnaturally, her eyes cold. Mr. Tyne lowered himself onto one of the cots while Mrs. Tyne paced the room, agitated, making strange movements with her hands.

"How dare you run away like that? How *dare* you!" Her voice rose an octave. "And without telling me, without even—how disrespectful! And now this fire—don't you know how terrified I was?" She gestured to her husband. "How terrified we both were? God, you just don't think! You're so selfish." Her whole face trembled, and as she turned to shield her face from the room, Ama was struck by the enormity of their actions. She began to cry.

The crying seemed to ground Mrs. Tyne. She ran a hand over her mouth and assessed them. Her voice sounded parched. "You've got asthma?"

Ama was too scared to answer.

"I gave her her medicine," said Yvette flatly.

Mrs. Tyne didn't look at her daughter. Turning to her husband, she asked, "Where's Chloe?" then she turned to Yvette. "Where's your sister?"

When Yvette shrugged, Mrs. Tyne looked as if she would throttle her. Ama spoke up. "She didn't come with us. We went without her."

"She's still out there?" said Mrs. Tyne. Her angular face made her eyes look huge and somber. Wearily, as if it pained him to waste the energy, Mr. Tyne rose from the bed and said he would go find her. "Finally, a little help," muttered Mrs. Tyne as he left. She berated Ama and Yvette for a solid hour.

Afterward, Yvette and Ama lay on their cots not talking, intermittently falling asleep and reading. At dinnertime, Mrs. Tyne called them down, and the three ate a silent meal of kenkey and spinach stew, which Ama hated but ate out of fear. They were ushered upstairs again, and around nine in the evening they heard the storm door click downstairs. Ama raised her head off the pillow, Yvette shut her book; holding their breath they sat looking at each other.

Only the intonations of Mr. Tyne's muffled voice could be heard. He sounded tired and a little defensive, and Ama concluded he hadn't found Chloe. But then they heard a higher, gruffer voice, unmistakably Chloe's. For once in her life she sounded reticent, even scared. Mrs. Tyne's voice continued to rise in pitch, culminating in a great scream: "I've had enough of this three-way mischief! You'll sleep in the spare room tonight."

"The Iron Lung," said Yvette.

"What?" said Ama.

Yvette turned her face to the wall.

A series of feet trod up the stairs, past the girls' room, to the small room the twins referred to as the "Iron Lung" because of its cold emptiness, its gray decor, its single frosted window. Behind the wall they heard Chloe pacing.

Ama lay awake in the dark. She thought of how strange the day had been, and wondered if anyone had gotten hurt in the fire. She wondered, too, if it really had been Yvette the whole time in that diner, or if she'd been the victim of one of the twins' jokes. What most disturbed her, though, was Mr. Tyne's reluctance to go and find his daughter; in fact, his reticence to enter family life at all. It seemed unnatural. But as soon as this vague thought occurred to her, she felt guilty; who was she to criticize her elders? She closed her eyes, then opened them again. In the dark she could feel Yvette staring at her. No, not so much staring. Listening to her breathe.

"Yvette?" she said, but no answer came.

The next morning, while Chloe showered and Ama helped Mrs. Tyne with the breakfast dishes, Yvette came in to beg her mother for new clothes.

Mrs. Tyne wiped her hands on her thighs. "After the stunt you pulled yesterday? What do you expect me to say to that?"

"But I'm tired of looking like Chloe, like some nondescript goof," said Yvette.

Mrs. Tyne seemed impressed by the use of the word "nondescript." "Give me a single good reason."

"I thought you wanted daughters. Don't you want me to dress more like a lady? More like her?" Yvette gestured to Ama, who felt a thrill of pleasure. Her cheeks reddened. "In our era it seems more necessary than ever to clearly define gender. Otherwise, you leave me open to censure and the prospect of unmarriageability. Who knows? I might be driven to throw myself on the pyre of parliament. I might actually thwart the divine comforts of housewife-hood and become prime minister. And where would that leave me?"

Mrs. Tyne looked at her daughter. She was too surprised by Yvette's sudden articulate outburst, her erudition and splendid vocabulary, to sense the insult in the girl's comment. "You're a piece of work. I'll think about it."

That evening, when the girls retired to their rooms, Yvette and Ama discovered a package on Yvette's bed. Tearing it open, Yvette sat back, astonished at the colorful, frilly dresses that fell from it. There were five in all, with matching underwear, and even a single, unadorned training bra. The bra mortified twelve-year-old Yvette.

Ama sat beside her on the bed, and whispered, "I've started wearing one, too."

Yvette gave her a look of such disgust that Ama went back to her side of the room. But Ama wasn't offended; she knew how insecure Yvette was. Yvette flung the bra on the floor, and stepping from her old clothes into the new, she sampled dress after dress, twisting in front of the dresser mirror. Ama rested her head against her knees and watched.

Mrs. Tyne appeared in the doorway, smiling. "Like them?"

Chloe coughed in the Iron Lung, and Yvette looked warily at the wall separating the rooms. Ama said, "They're beautiful."

Mrs. Tyne walked up and ruffled Ama's hair. "Gorgeous, aren't they? But you've got some just like them."

Ama nodded, enjoying Mrs. Tyne's attention. The older woman exuded that motherly smell of laundry and clean skin.

Even in striking reproductions, Chloe could never have embodied the grace these clothes gave to her sister. Like love, they called all Yvette's beauty to the surface. Mrs. Tyne even forgot herself for a moment and exclaimed, "You're as beautiful as Ama, now!" She'd used a good deal of what remained of her savings to buy them. Ama and Mrs. Tyne oohed and ahed so much that Yvette begged her mother to let her show them off outside.

"You want to go for a walk *now?*" Mrs. Tyne admonished, but anyone could see she was pleased to have finally done right in her daughter's eyes. "Okay, but just for a few minutes. I'll go get Chloe."

"No," said Yvette in a voice that darkened a little. "Just us three."

Mrs. Tyne shrugged. "All right." Gathering the dresses off the floor, she noticed the bra. "How about this?" she asked her daughter, almost shyly.

Yvette's face became cold. "I don't see what you're referring to."

"This. The bra."

"I'm sorry, I don't see anything. Let's just go."

Exasperated, but still in high spirits, Mrs. Tyne ushered them downstairs and into the streets. Despite dusk's descent, the pavement was still warm. Not a trace of that burning plastic smell remained in the air. They walked up and down MacDonald Street, almost vacant at this hour, returning home in a joking mood.

They entered the girls' bedroom to find the dresses cut to shreds on the floor.

Mrs. Tyne looked as though she would cry. Ama wasn't entirely surprised. Either truly upset, or because she could get away with it, Yvette screamed at the top of her lungs.

Mr. Tyne appeared in the doorway, breathless. He had obviously been napping, for the skin around his eyes swelled, and he looked bewildered. The buttons of his vest were wrongly fastened, as though he'd stopped to do it up. This detail surprised Ama.

Samuel looked once at the clothes on the floor, once at their faces, and shaking his head, he proclaimed: "Young Tragedy and Comedy are at it again." He left, thinking only, *Maud's been hiding money on me.*

Mrs. Tyne stormed out of the room. In the silence they could hear her confronting Chloe. Dragging her by the arm, she pushed her into the center of the girls' room and forced her to look at her scraps, as though disciplining a dog.

"Do you know how much this cost?" she said. Her anguish had no effect on Chloe, who stared indifferently at the pile. Mrs. Tyne grabbed Yvette's arm and drew the two together. "You two have to learn to get along." And nonsensically pushing both into bed, she turned out the light and shut the door with a slam.

No one spoke. The tension made Ama's skin itch. Nervous, she opened the door and went into the bathroom to get ready for bed. Sitting on the cracked toilet seat, she stared at the red bathmat. The Tyne house seemed crazy, full of conflict and hatred and things she couldn't understand. She checked her thoughts, feeling she was being judgmental. Certainly things here were odd, but wouldn't others make the same judgments about her own house? She washed her face and returned to the room.

It was moist and hot, and she could hear the twins breathing in the darkness. Slipping into her cot, she prayed they wouldn't attack her, or each other, or do any of the other drastic things she believed them capable of. Clenching her teeth, she fell asleep only to wake four hours later with a feeling of dread in her chest. The room was close and musky, but she felt no presence in the room.

"Yvette?" Ama turned on her bedside light.

On the floor lay the dress Yvette had worn on their walk. It had been severed, its pieces entangled with the white bra, which had also been destroyed. The twins' beds were empty.

chapter TEN

A ster's town hall sat on its outskirts like a kind of afterthought. Built with its back to the town, it loomed huge and vacant, surrounded by spruce and birch. Certain buildings have something human about them; attempts to revive the hall had only made it look older. The paint flaked away. The wood creaked. Woodlice devoured the foundations. Anthills rose like piles of sawdust around it. To the right of the doors sat two adjacent baseball diamonds, where the old legendary team used to play. The fields were derelict now, the grass a blond color, the fences sagging and rusted. Only a nearby grove of sweet-smelling cedars gave the area any beauty.

Under the building's eaves, a painted board proclaimed: ASTER CULTURAL CENTER. A Canadian flag gleamed underneath it, impervious to the rain and wind that had so aged the hall. Ray Frank parked abruptly behind a second red truck, fingering a cigarette in his chest pocket.

"It'll be a big one tonight," he said.

"You bet," said Eudora.

Maud sat between them. For the duration of the drive, Eudora had felt it necessary to lean across Maud's lap whenever she had anything to say to Ray. Not only that, but with Eudora being so obese, the cab was only large enough for three, so that Maud constantly turned in her seat to make sure the children, tossed around in the pickup's open back, weren't falling out.

When Ray helped the girls down, Maud rushed from the truck to check them for scratches.

"Oh, Maud, you're too much of a worrywart," said Eudora. "Kids are the most durable thing in the world."

Maud wished Samuel had come. He'd made excuses about being behind on his commissions, but Maud knew he just didn't care about anything beyond himself. To be fair, Samuel actually was behind on his business. But what he didn't tell Maud, what he didn't wish to, was that meeting the mayor had left him with a bad taste in his mouth. He'd taken the car and gone to his shop.

Inside, the hall was bright and almost modern, and someone had strung streamers across the stage, as though for a festive occasion. A long white table of sweet drinks and finger foods flanked the left side, while at the right a row of elderly women tended coffee and baked goods. Underneath the wonderful smells ran that scent of mothballs that haunted each building in Aster. An antique piano sat in shadow by the farthest entrance door. Maud was surprised at the sheer multitude of people.

Rows of bright-orange chairs had been set up, and the seats nearest the stage were taken. The Franks and the Tynes negotiated the crowd, Ray nodding at every few people, or Eudora stopping to say an enthusiastic hello. There were so many people that it was difficult to hear anything distinct. Maud kept looking behind her to make sure the children followed; only when they'd found seats did she feel at ease. Crowds had always been a challenge for her, especially the mix of crowds and children. Tying her sweater around her waist, she sat down.

"What are you doing?" said Eudora, smiling. "It's mingling time,

time to meet everyone, gossip a little." Her cheeks were red from the heat in the room. "How long have you lived in this town, and you don't know anyone?"

Ordering the girls to stay put, Maud followed Eudora, who whisked her into a group of three old women whose beige sweaters and faded features made them difficult to tell apart.

"Oh, hello." Nervous, Maud shook their hands. When she gave her name, none of them understood.

"Nah, Joanie, it's *Maud,*" said Eudora, her smile revealing her jutting tooth. "Maud Tyne," she enunciated.

"Oh, *Maud!*" said the woman on the end, whose sweater parted to reveal an almost concave chest. "Well, that's easy!"

"I've never been too good with accents," said the woman closest to Maud. Maud studied the good-natured face, the eyes colorless with age, the veins unconcealed by fragile skin. The woman was so obviously from a different era that Maud refused to take umbrage.

"I've heard about you," said the woman in the center. She wore a pair of telescopic glasses, which gave her an inquisitive air. "You're old Tyne's daughter. That Jacob who used to live out on Porter's land."

"Porter? No, it was Jacob's own. And I'm not his daughter—my husband's his nephew."

A surprised murmur passed between the three women.

"I'll be damned!" said the old one closest to Maud. "Learn something new every day."

Eudora seized Maud's hand. "I'm taking her off now, girls. We'll talk later."

When they'd gone a little ways, Maud said, "*Porter's* land?"

"Eloise is a bit senile."

Eudora dragged Maud to meet group after group, most also failing to understand her accent, which, in truth, she knew was hardly noticeable.

"Like Eloise said, not too many outsiders come in," said Eudora. "Oh, look, there's Ray." When Eudora waved, the skin under her arm swayed. Ray walked to the microphone, and a little too officiously, he insisted people take their seats.

Maud found the girls where she'd left them. "Any new discoveries since I left?" she said.

Ama shrugged, while the twins exchanged glances.

"Sorry," said Chloe in an imperious voice. "I can't understand your accent."

Maud was shocked. "Sometimes you two behave like two-year-olds!"

The look of hurt on the twins' faces made Maud angry with herself. Though generally a strict woman, she rarely belittled her children. Feeling guilty, she turned a little away from them in her seat. The woman on her right noticed this and used the opportunity to introduce herself.

"Tara Chodzicki," she smiled. "Said, 'Shud-it-sky,' but spelled C-H-O-D-Z-I-C-K-I. These Asterians have problems with my name, too. I've heard about you. So glad you could finally come out." And taking the thin, aristocratic hand, Maud felt relieved. She made small talk with the woman until Eudora reached across the children and seized her thigh.

Appalled, Maud moved her leg a little, smiling nervously.

Eudora set her lips. "I just wanted to tell you that Porter's wife is by the south doors." And without greeting Tara she faced the stage.

"His wife?" hissed Maud, and forgetting her own manners, she reached across the sullen children to touch Eudora's arm. "All this time he's had a wife? And she wasn't Christian enough to call on me?"

Eudora looked amused. "Well, she's *not* Christian. First one died, the man goes all the way to India for the second one. But *shh*, it's starting."

Maud craned her neck. A tall, well built woman stood at the rear doors, half of her face obscured by a kente kerchief. So she was from Gold Coast too! Seeing her skin, it was easy to see how Eudora had mistaken her for an Indian. She was the color of weak tea, slightly darker at the joints, with full, blood-colored lips. Maud strained to see the woman's eyes.

"Welcome, welcome everyone," boomed Ray's voice through the loudspeaker. He looked dwarfed by the huge stage. "You all know me, but I'll introduce myself to any newcomers." He paused at the few claps. "I'm Raymond Frank, second to the mayor, and allow me to introduce the other people up here tonight, who, if you don't know, you should. At the end we have Constable Robert Parry."

An apprehensive man stood up, blinking in every direction. Instinct told Maud he must be at least forty, but he had that look of preserved innocence women seek to protect and men take advantage of.

"Wilma Flint, on our security council."

Stocky and self-possessed, Ms. Flint waved with great condescension. She sat down long before the clapping came to an end.

"She acts like butter wouldn't melt in her mouth," muttered Eudora.

Ray went on to introduce two nondescript men before he got to the mayor. Maud couldn't believe her eyes. The mayor could not have stood any taller than five feet, and if the brusque way he moved was supposed to conjure height, it only made him look shorter. He had an old-plains mustache and richly pomaded hair. Maud imagined him smelling of fresh tobacco, maybe even lavender oil. He looked like a working-class man trying to play the aristocrat.

Ray lowered the microphone for him. The mayor beamed, his oily skin radiating warmth. "Great to see you this evening. As Asterians, we all have a right to know what's going on in our town, and to know that government is not in the hands of a few elect, but is everyone's business."

He paused for the ecstatic clapping and few appreciative calls. Maud looked around, startled.

"As you know, the most pressing matter of business is the fire at Thorpe's Diner. But as we expect this to take some time to discuss, we'd like to get other matters out of the way first. Let's start the open forum."

People from the crowd rose and, approaching the microphones, discussed everything from whether a building permit was needed to erect a fence to the unseemly number of stray cats lately plaguing Aster.

Next, parking regulations. When that order of business was settled, a coalition stood to lobby in favor of Article 9, which restricted people from making changes to any town property without consulting an elected Board for Historical Preservation. The minority coalition, who'd prepared notes, rose to state why such a thing was not only unfeasible, but bordered on immoral.

"No one should support this article," said a man with unnaturally large ears, craning so close to the microphone they could hear him breathe. "It's a load of crap."

Maud couldn't believe the energy people put into their arguments.

"All right, all right, enough discussion," said the mayor, at last fed up with everyone's pettiness. He cleared his throat. "Thorpe's was very dear to us all, and has been with us twenty-three years, a cherished, welcoming place."

Yvette shot Ama a look.

"We are extremely lucky no one was hurt. And Thorpe's will be restored, but we must think of our future." He gripped the podium. "This is our fourth fire in almost as many months. We must give this a long, hard looking-over. We cannot allow what happened in Athabasca in 1913 to happen here. We cannot allow our entire town, our businesses, our *lives*, to be destroyed by fire." Recovering his gentle voice, he said, "Please welcome Constable Parry."

People seemed confused over whether to clap or not. Stepping awkwardly from his seat, Constable Parry approached the microphone almost with fear. He tapped it, hesitating. "Thank you, Mayor Gould. Everything you've said is true—we cannot allow what happened in Athabasca to happen here. We must protect our businesses, our homes, our lives." He breathed a laugh. "Now, I can't discuss the specifics, obviously, except to warn you that these were not so-called acts of God. We do have a possible arsonist, that's unconfirmed, who may or may not be a townsperson, who may or may not even be an Albertan. What we *don't* need is . . . what, what we don't need . . ."

The constable raised his head, as did the entire audience, at the music filling the room. It was a whimsical aria, played on the high register of the antique piano, a variation with so many notes it was dizzying to listen to. The swift, piercing notes rose and fell over each other. The longer it went on, the more people strained in their chairs to see who was playing. Maud paused, stricken. Sitting on the piano bench was Chloe.

She hadn't even realized the girl had left her seat. More bewildering was that neither twin had taken a single piano lesson, neither Maud nor Samuel knew how to play, and yet Chloe's playing was so dexterous it seemed the product of years of study.

Tara Chodzicki nodded along with the music, tapping a finger on her knee. "Bach," she said to Maud, smiling.

Maud rose from her seat and walked to the piano. Placing a firm hand on Chloe's shoulder, Maud hesitated before the staring audience, whispering to the girl, "I think we should go back to our seats now." With complete indifference, Chloe closed the lid of the piano and followed Maud up the aisle back to their chairs. When Chloe was firmly seated between her sister and Ama, Maud nodded in general apology to the audience, bowing a little. From the back doors, Porter's wife stared at her, and Maud imagined she saw contempt. Blood rushed to her face.

People murmured to each other. Ray frowned, walking around on stage as though he did not know what to do with himself. The mayor nodded at the constable to continue, and clearing his voice, he said, "As I was saying, what we don't need in this town is a witch hunt."

A man in dungarees near the front stood up. "I heard this fire was different from the others. Like it started differently."

The mayor took the microphone from the startled constable. "Open forum is finished, Mr. Jennings. Please be seated."

Another wave of muttering went through the room, and Ray made no attempt to hide his anxiety. Maud was mortified. Even Eudora seemed to regard Chloe with apprehension.

Maud was aware of an aversion growing in her, an inability to even look at Chloe, and her guilt over it made her cheeks burn. "Sorry," she said in a soft voice, but to no one in particular.

"Oh, dear, we know." Tara Chodzicki placed a cold hand on Maud's arm. It was as though the woman had known embarrassment and grief, and gently sought to tell her so.

Eudora shot Maud a look. She turned and continued to listen to the constable's speech, which had weakened and digressed. He was so green a public speaker he couldn't overcome being interrupted. He sputtered, calling on the people to be vigilant, but not overly so, to report any "strange business," to "do their bit in the way of good Samaritans." When he finally stepped back from the microphone, his hands were so white from clutching it that those seated as far back as the twelfth row noticed they glowed like ice.

When the meeting ended, Maud rose to leave as quickly as possible. Tara Chodzicki, her earrings swinging like horseflies about her cheeks, touched Maud's shoulder.

"It's so rare to hear the piano played with such talent, especially Bach, and especially by one so young," she said, with a great deal of breath in her voice. "I don't mean to intrude, but I used to teach at a conservatory. I should very much like to have the chance, of course, providing she's not already in someone else's hands, to train that little girl. I know you were embarrassed, but really, she's quite astonishing."

Maud felt a mixture of pride and dread. "I don't know what to say." She glanced at Chloe.

"How about 'yes'?" laughed Tara Chodzicki.

Eudora took hold of Maud's wrist. With an artificial smile, she said, to Tara, "We got to get going."

Tara held up a slender pink finger. "Ah, one minute, Eudora."

"We're leaving," said Eudora. Her face flushed. "Chloe's too busy with housework and prepping for school next fall to have lessons."

"Eudora," admonished Maud. She felt appalled at having someone answer for her.

"Well," said Tara Chodzicki, clasping her heavily jewelled hands.

"At least do me the honor of having dinner with me? I live on the outskirts, near Athabasca."

"No," said Eudora. And gripping the bewildered Maud by the arm she tapped the children awake and led them away from Tara and into the crowd.

Maud was furious. "That's too much! That's just too much! I have never felt so rude in my life. What on earth is wrong with you?"

Eudora muttered something, but in the throng of people Maud couldn't hear her. "What on earth are you saying?"

Eudora craned her head back. "An untouchable. Chodsikey's off bounds. When she was married, she slept around with Eric Davids, *also* married. His wife had cancer, for God's sake, and even died. Her own husband died not much later, a *suicide!* No, Maud, don't bother with her."

Maud grew thoughtful. These were serious charges. She couldn't condone adultery, especially under such circumstances, and suicide was a sin. But the woman had shown her such kindness that it was difficult to wholly condemn her. And yet, the Tynes hadn't found their footing in Aster society, so Maud had to concede she'd been saved from a most unfortunate friendship.

Outside a thin moon softened the darkness, casting a sensitive glow on the foliage. The crisp air was a relief after the teeming crowds, and Maud breathed deeply. She shuffled the girls together and put her arms around them.

"You cold?" she asked, and they replied by nuzzling against her. She was pleasantly shocked at the comfort they took in her, and pulled them closer. Something occurred to her. "Hey, have you seen Porter's wife?" She looked around her.

"Over there," said Eudora, nodding toward the doors where the tall woman stood, her face now fully in the shade of her kerchief.

Maud began to disentangle herself from the children. "Will you take them? I'm just going to go over and speak to her."

"Isn't one narrow escape enough? Oh, here's Ray."

The red truck squealed to a stop before them, and Ray yelled out the window, "Last one in's a rotten fish."

Eudora laughed. "He's so good with children, isn't he?" Something painful entered her expression. "He would have made a brilliant father."

Maud wasn't listening. Across the field the last stragglers were getting into their cars. Porter's wife was nowhere to be seen. Frowning, Maud climbed after Eudora into the cab.

It was full dark when they reached home. Samuel had parked in the street, and in the veiled glow of lamps Maud observed just how shoddy their old Volvo looked. Ray and Eudora kissed the children good-bye and stayed in the road until they'd all entered the house.

Samuel sat at the kitchen table, dolefully picking lint from a handful of change.

"Is this business?" said Maud. "Is this why you didn't come?"

Samuel sucked his teeth, but didn't say anything.

After rushing the children up to bed, Maud went to the living room to relax in front of the fireplace. Though a fire was never set, she loved the wistful sound of wind in the chimney; it reminded her of the neem trees of Gold Coast. Settling into a creaking chair, Maud looked out the window, lamenting the fact that it already needed to be cleaned again. Drawing in a sudden breath, she got to her feet and pulled open the bay window.

The lawn had been cropped. Once so tall, Maud had feared losing the children in it, it now ran so smoothly into Porter's property that the most skilled eye would have trouble assessing where one property ended and the other began. The grass looked blue under the porch light. Staring at it gave Maud the impression that time had stopped, for without its usual movement, she felt like she was staring at stone, like she herself would freeze to stone by looking at it.

Maud returned to the kitchen, where, finished counting his change, Samuel had abandoned himself to daydreaming. Having peeled off his socks, he'd put his feet on the table and sat with a faraway look on his face. Seeing Maud in the doorway, he quickly lowered his heels.

Maud smiled. "You had me so fooled." Seeing Samuel hesitate, Maud laughed and kissed him on the head. "The yard looks wonderful, thank you."

When Samuel persisted in looking confused, Maud played along by pretending to be exasperated. "What, do you want me to kiss your feet?"

"Why should you do that?"

"Exactly—why *should* I do that?"

Samuel sucked his teeth again. "Maud, I am in no mood for tomfoolery."

Pursing her lips, Maud remained silent. At the sink she began to clean her nails with the dishrag.

Samuel rose from his seat and went into the living room. Maud heard the bay window slide on its oiled track, heard Samuel's exclamation—"Eih!"—and listened to it close again.

He entered the kitchen, fiddling with the bandages on his hands. "Did you cut the grass?"

The demanding way he said this fueled her annoyance. "Use your head. And here I thought you'd finally done something for your family, finally thought of us for once."

"So it was not you who cut it?" said Samuel.

Maud narrowed her eyes, scrutinizing her husband. He was a greater fool than even she could conceive of. Worse, he was a fool who let other men do the work for him.

"Samuel," she said, "sometimes I just don't know."

And the sadness in her voice, that note of reproach and utter disappointment, made him look away. She waited as he scraped the change from the table, and let out a deep breath when he left the room.

chapter ELEVEN

T he drive to the Frank farm was uncomfortable. Clouds had brought on an early dusk and a blunt rain brought up worms to die on the pavement. The front stoops of Aster, usually so dusty and crowded by drifters, looked white as gravestones away from the road. A sulphurous smell pervaded everything. Rocks popped under the truck's tires, and drenched shrubs made it slide all over the place. Only at the main road, where gutters coaxed the rain away, did the wheels grow steady. Samuel was glad of this, for every time the car slid he let out an effeminate giggle that mortified both men. Ray had grown morose, smoking unceasingly and gasping up phlegm into a red rag kept tucked in his breast pocket. He smelled of dust and onions, and frowned every time Samuel laughed. Samuel's attempts to break the mood met only reproachful looks and terse answers. Samuel felt like a fool; this was not the Ray Frank he had known for a month. And yet his hurt seemed so absurd that, again, he laughed nervously.

Ray scowled. Then, as if regretting it, he said, "God, Samuel, I'm sorry. I'm in a . . . funk, that's all. Lot on my mind. You know what that's like." His blue eyes looked weary.

"I do," said Samuel, his voice barely audible against the rain.

Ray chuckled. "You're priceless. You do know that, don't you? I guess you're not used to this rain."

Samuel laughed. "Well, where I'm from, we do get the monsoon. And I did live four years in England."

Ray nodded, but said nothing.

A half-hour passed in silence before Ray announced they had arrived. The rain had abated, but everything was trod raw and muddy. Ray pulled into a damp thicket, the only upshoot of green on his lot. He cut the engine and then reached over Samuel's legs to pull his sunglasses from the glovebox, slipping them into his rag pocket. Samuel heard his boots in the mud as he jumped from the cab. He descended after him.

They walked along an uneven arm of gravel in silence. It was a warm evening, despite the rain, the air peppered with horseflies. Dandelions rose three feet from the weakly colored grass, and the men trod them flat. Their shoes slipped over the rocks. Samuel knew they'd met the edge of the property without even seeing it, for the very air changed its texture, and the smell of rot wafted from the distance.

"What is that smell?" said Samuel.

Ray took his time answering. "Stock."

"This is an animal farm or it is a wheat acreage?"

Ray was weary. "Both. You coming?"

As they neared, the smell became unbearable. In his boyhood, Samuel had never been able to stomach those impoverished local farms in which hang-bone goats and chickens ran around in a useless attempt to thwart death. It sickened him. The smell of blood hung over everything. Samuel held his breath.

Ray suddenly softened. He put a hand on Samuel's shoulder. "Sam, it's all the same to me if you want to wait in the car. I just thought you might like to see something local. Farming, and *harvesting,* for that matter, are as old as Canada."

Samuel ambled out from under Ray's hand, a move he hoped didn't look thankless. "All is fine. We have farms of this type in Gold Coast." He smiled and waved a vague hand in front of his face. "But the smell."

"You get used to it. Come on."

Suddenly they confronted an enormous orange cat, whose vulgar, senile eyes were moist with age. Ray grabbed the creature by the nape and swung it onto his shoulder. "This here's Oliver Orange come to greet us," he said, patting it. "Father to almost all the cats out here, the bugger."

Samuel laughed politely. He made a gesture to pet the cat, only grazing the tips of its matted, lice-ravaged fur. If Ray noticed him recoil, he chose to ignore it. Before them rose a weatherworn barn hung with a frayed Union Jack and a Canadian flag. It had been renovated as living quarters; a yellow flower box hung under the single window (obviously Eudora's doing). A man sat out front, studying something in his hands. A pen of sheep bleated, the sound haunting. In the distance wheat teemed all over the earth. Heavy machinery slept in the fields. It wasn't long before Samuel realized that the "stock" part of the Frank farm had the magnitude of a hobby. The pens and hutches of plaintive animals were isolated to a very small slate of land, more than half a mile back from the wheat.

Impressed, Samuel was nevertheless distracted by the vicious insects, voracious after the rain. Black-and-yellow grasshoppers jumped at his pantlegs, and the shrewd blackflies tirelessly circling his head made him anxious. Without warning, Ray handed him Oliver Orange, a sluggish heartbeat in a bag of fur. Samuel carried the heavy animal like a tray before him and followed Ray to the barn door.

"Jarvis," said Ray. "How are things keeping?"

Jarvis continued to bite a sliver from his thumb. Ray waited for him to finish. Jarvis spat into the mud and licked a pin of blood from his flesh. He dropped the block of wood to his feet, and two kittens skittered from under his steel stool. He rose to greet Ray as though he'd only now noticed him.

"This is my neighbor, Samuel Tyne," Ray said. "Sam, this is Clarish

Kent the third, also known as the Butcher, Leatherface, Draft Dodger and the American Dream. Oh, and Jarvis."

"Christ," said Jarvis, his irritation obviously feigned, the appropriate reaction in their friendly comedy of manners. Jarvis, whose skin was indeed brown and parched, raised a luminous green eye at Samuel. That eye traveled the length of Samuel's body, paused for a moment on Oliver Orange, who, by now, was made bad-tempered by Samuel's grip, and finally found something to reckon with in the ragged bandages on Samuel's hands. He appraised them for a good while, as though the measure of a man's worth lay in the severity of his wounds. He flicked a strand of black hair from his face and met Samuel's eyes.

"Tyne," he said. An unimpressed smile made him look almost handsome. "Tyne. An Englishman?" His laugh sounded like hiccups. "I guess the cold's no bother to you. Lot of rain in England."

Even Ray laughed.

Samuel felt a little winded. With the awkward movements of one who knows he's being watched, he lowered Oliver Orange to the ground. When he stood, he ran his hands down his pantlegs and giggled. They had put him on guard, and he hated it.

"I'm teasing," said Jarvis, with a derisive smile. He motioned to Ray with his head and led him toward a pen of screeching fowl. Samuel followed grudgingly, a trail of ginger kittens at his heels. From behind, the men were opposites: Ray was tall and fair, and his outfit, though rumpled, was clean, while Jarvis had a puggish body, his posture called down by fat, his clothes roan with the blood of animals. Yet there was something similar about them.

"So, five of the fowl went, and McArthur came for the duck he wanted." Jarvis leaned on the wire. "Me and the cats cleaned up. Granger and his son are coming for the harvest on Thursday. You know he solved the bunt at the east edge, but you did lose some wheat, not much, though." Ray bit a hangnail, chewing it pensively as he listened.

Through their conversation, in which they made no attempt to engage him, Samuel learned that *bunt* was some kind of wheat fungus, that the *kudzu* vine guarded against soil erosion and that Ray was making a ludicrously huge capital off national wheat sales to Russia and China.

"I'd buy a goddamn castle with your profits," said Jarvis.

"You could buy a goddamn castle with what you carry away as caretaker of this place," Ray said.

Neither mentioned the controversy of the Russian/Chinese agreement, which had most North Americans grumbling that Canada was helping the Reds. They spoke of other business while Samuel watched clusters of kittens dissolve like smoke at some far-off noise. A blue car nosed through foliage and cut its engine.

"It's that Catholic Johnstone. Looking for cheap veal." Jarvis waved. "The hell." He walked over to the car, leaving Samuel and Ray alone.

Ray offered an apologetic look. "So, Sam, what do you think of my lot?" he asked.

Samuel was pleased Ray valued his opinion. "You have done very well for yourself."

Ray smiled and turned his back to the wind to light a cigarette. He tapped Samuel's shoulder and chinned toward the barn, where they walked in conscious silence. With his back to the yard, Ray undid his fly and began to urinate against the barn's weathered base. Samuel felt sickened. He walked a little away, and though Ray did his business soundlessly, Samuel still imagined he could hear it. A man should not piss on his own belongings, he decided, particularly not on his house. Ray, who hadn't noticed Samuel's discomfort or had chosen to ignore it, began to speak loudly to him. "Dora and I are quite proud of it, actually. This building here was nothing but a gray box when we first came." Samuel listened for his zipper before turning around. "Look, Jarvis is at it again."

To the center of the yard Jarvis had led a panicked calf with yellow ears; it resisted his attempts to restrain it. A family of three watched the scene as one would watch a clown's theatrics. A young child threw his hands to his face.

"If that bull doesn't stop in one minute, we're going to have to help."

Samuel kept his anxiety quiet; he even laughed a few times at the calf's fussier movements.

"You know what we're doing, me and Jarvis?" said Ray. He trod out his cigarette and spat. "We're trying to come up with the perfect blade of wheat. An indestructible one, one that outlasts bunt, outlasts drought, outlasts grasshoppers, outlasts people, even." He chuckled. "It's been proved by experimenting that if you grow one plot of just one kind of crop, and you grow another plot with all sorts of different crops, the one with different crops yields a bigger, stronger and healthier harvest. So the idea is to take the best of all wheat and try to grow just those together. After a while you get to know what the strongest kind is, and there's your formula."

Samuel frowned. "Genetics."

Ray looked impressed. "Yeah, good, Samuel. Will you look at that calf go?" He laughed. "So Jarvis wants to start by crossing peas or sugar beets or something—he read it in a book—but I think if it's wheat we're after, it's wheat we're after. But it's really his gig, he's the one with the fancy degree. So, I wanted to ask if you've—Chrissakes, he needs help."

The calf was spastic now, slack-jawed and running at the mouth. Ray walked toward the scene, and Samuel followed unwillingly, never in all his life having dealt with such an animal. The child laughed less now, and his parents had fallen to solemn words. Jarvis was barely coping, and his sweat and exhaustion made him look feverish. "What the hell took you so long?" he yelled. "I'm of a mind to shoot this son of a bitch." The calf had bullied him into such an awkward position that all he could do was knife it back a few paces before it gained on him and he had to backstep again. The struggle had the air of some bestial tango, a bullfight of small and comic proportions. The child had begun to whimper, to draw the bottom of his coat over his eyes, and in a move to mollify him, Samuel pinched a nearby kitten from the mud and handed it to him. At first, the boy transferred his fear from the calf to Samuel, who at once understood he was perhaps the first black man the child had ever seen. But his fear was overcome by the softness of the offering. He accepted the kitten timidly, and Samuel noted the parents' quiet reproach. They meant to teach their son something about death, and Samuel had diminished its urgency. These were cruel people, and in a dignified gesture meant more as an act of mockery, he took off his crumpled bowler and bowed theatrically before retreating. They saw no effrontery in the gesture and nodded back, though Samuel noted they let their son keep the cat.

"Samuel, get out here," called Ray. The strain made his voice barely audible. But Samuel persisted in submitting to authority, and he went where he was called.

The calf's pink-and-black nostrils filled with mucus. "Grab this joker by the chin, grab it!" said Ray, scowling at the sight of Samuel hesitating. He knew he seemed rather effete to Ray, but he could barely *look* at the animal. He wanted to object on the grounds of his injured hands, but in Ray's world that was no excuse at all. When Ray called his name a second time, now with exasperation, Samuel bridged his hands delicately under the calf's writhing chin.

For a sickening few minutes, Samuel felt every vein and tendon in that neck, the jerking of the jaws drawing open, the raw, blood-filled breath gusting up every time the calf moved. Samuel's hands trembled. He was desperate to let go, to back away, could barely contain his nausea, but he knew leaving would embarrass Ray. So he held on, even as Jarvis cut into the aorta. Samuel closed his eyes. But the hoarse, preternatural sound of the calf suffering for breath and the child's startled scream as the torso hit the ground made a grave picture in Samuel's mind. He opened his eyes to see the calf collapsed, slack and nearly dead, its eyes like two thimbles of milk in its haggard face.

"You want all parts, brains, gizzards, what?" said Jarvis. He would intermittently hit the animal, wiping the blood from his face, tired, humiliated. He negotiated with the family man while Ray retreated to the barn, perhaps to clean himself. Samuel, however, was spellbound. He watched Jarvis drag the dead calf to a shed, the man following behind him. Samuel waited with the wife and child, both of whom ignored him in their own way. The boy placed the kitten on the ground, still looking astonished. Samuel, moved by the boy's quivering, and by the way he'd stifled his crying, almost told the mother what he thought of her. But he kept quiet and the men returned, the father lifting high a bloodstained package in victory. Jarvis, too, carried a bloody gum of papers in his hands, grimly satisfied.

The man handed the package to his wife, who held it as if it were breakable. He laughed, and squatted to ruffle his son's hair. *You'll be a man yet*, his face seemed to say. The boy's smile was uncertain, as though he understood some rite of passage had taken place, but couldn't fully comprehend what it was.

Jarvis dropped his bloody sack in front of the boy's kitten. Ferocious, agile, it pounced on the sodden sack and broke it open. Even the boy's father stepped back as the thick-pulp innards slipped out. The smell of blood summoned the other cats, and in seconds even Oliver Orange had his own fresh tripe. The boy scuffled back from the amassing crowd of cats and began to cry. Samuel flinched.

"Stand up!" said the father, and the boy stumbled at once to his feet. His father assessed him, and the boy almost managed to stop crying. His mother tried to cup his chin.

The man moved in upon his son. Samuel was horrified, and ashamed at his inability to give words to what he felt. A dark blaze descended the boy's pants.

His mother's face reddened, and she lowered her eyes. His father continued to stand in front of him, and in his back one could see that he'd grown angrier, his spine straighter, his shoulders tautening. No one spoke. He turned and paid Jarvis, and motioned for his family to follow him back to the car.

"You want a towel for the ride home?" yelled Jarvis. His voice hung over the yard. He hiccuped, and only after the car drove away did Samuel recognize his laughter. He watched Jarvis count the money, muttering to himself, and was relieved to see the barn door glint open. Silhouetted, Ray trod out to meet them.

"Well, look at the professor." Ray nodded toward Samuel.

Samuel admitted he was deep in thought, aware that something like a sadness had been accomplished inside him. His stomach felt bloated, and the quietest sounds in the landscape began to disturb him. He was conscious of an out-of-body feeling, as though he were merely a sightseer in another man's flesh. For the first time, he assessed the blood on his hands.

Ray turned to Jarvis. "And what are you mugging at?"

Jarvis explained how he'd thrown down the sack of innards in front of the child. A hysteria in his voice not only implied delight, but challenged anyone to refute his actions.

"You do that one more time, Jarvis, and it might get in my mind to hire someone new."

Jarvis gave him a skeptical look. He said, "It's so dark Sam's almost missing. Though I reckon we'd see more of him if he actually made a go of talking."

"Sam and I are leaving." Ray's voice was resolute. "You get the profits tallied, and I'll call tomorrow to see how Granger's making out. And I *will* call early, so you better organize yourself for then." Ray motioned to Samuel, and in a stupor, Samuel followed. As he passed Jarvis, the caretaker gave him an exaggerated bow.

"Good night, *Sir* Tyne," he said, and hiccuped.

Ray scrutinized Jarvis. "Tomorrow morning."

Samuel followed Ray out to the truck. It was full dark by now, and moonlight sat like water on the foliage. The wind teased a dry sound from the wheat field, and with the cats' cries everything felt haunted. Ray paused on the gravel path to pull Oliver Orange, wheezing, from the weeds. He muttered to him, ripping burrs from his fur.

"You know, Samuel," he said, "I'm awfully sorry. If I'd known how sick all this would make you, I would've never asked you out here. But you've got to admit, though, it's a surprise; as a man coming from where you're from, this stuff should be a bit less traumatic, right?"

"It is a thing I should never get used to." Samuel looked at the blood on his hands. Certainly in his country they killed to eat, as everywhere. But there was something less barbaric in those old childhood slaughters (the ones he'd witnessed, anyway), and he recalled that it likely had something to do with ritual. He had seen nothing today but ridicule and cruelty.

Ray smiled. "Got to get used to it."

They clambered into the cab, and to Samuel's dismay, Ray brought Oliver Orange with them. He cocked the truck, and in a minute they'd found the main road.

Samuel felt sick when Oliver Orange began to lick himself. The raw, fetid smell of calf's blood rose from the cat's fur.

"Seen Porter lately?" said Ray. His left hand governed the wheel while the right one rested on the sullen cat. "I meant to ask you, in regards to what I was saying before, about the wheat. You probably don't know the crop story."

But Samuel was preoccupied. Due to the sudden cutting of his grass, he'd taken it upon himself to research Jacob's property lines. He'd spent a fruitless few days in Aster's library and archives, only to discover something just when he'd resolved to give up. In annals as recent as last year's, the Tyne property occupied not two, but *twelve* acres. Barring that Jacob had actually sold or bequeathed Porter land, which seemed unlikely, Porter had taken advantage of Samuel's ignorance to help himself.

Ray failed to sense his distraction. "It was the late thirties," he continued, "one of those really dry years when fires start of themselves. Only a couple houses stood where you're living now, and yours and Porter's were the best of them. Because there were so few homes, people had huge lots, acres and acres. Some grew wheat, but mostly, as you know, it's not so good for wheat as it is for roots. So one year—oh, it was awful—the worst plague you ever saw came to us. So it was said—I was still back east at the time, but this story's carried well through the years. The worst grasshopper plague they'd had in years. Thousands, no, millions of grasshoppers covered everything for a distance of miles. They say it was like black snow. It'd happened a few years before, too, so people were a little bit more *chapter* TWELVE

Maud and Eudora drank iced tea in the Tyne kitchen. The heat seemed to suspend time, the hours endless. When Eudora spoke, Maud found herself staring at the sweat on her hairline. The ceiling fan failed to cool the room.

"God, this heat," Eudora said, touching a napkin to the hollows behind her ears. She looked flushed, but the blush was oddly contained to her face and hands, throwing her pale arms and neck into greater relief. "I envy you," she said.

Maud shifted to avoid sticking to her seat. "Why?"

"Being used to this heat. Days like this paralyze me."

"Honey, no one functions in this kind of heat. Even people in hot countries."

Eudora said nothing.

"Can you believe that fire?" said Maud. "I pray they catch those jokers before someone gets hurt. What a time to move to Aster. Oh, and I'm so glad you saved me from that Chodzicki woman—who

knows what would have come of it?" As if remembering Chloe's unsettling piano playing, which she still hadn't mentioned to Samuel, Maud
fell quiet.

"Chloe certainly has a gift for the ivories," said Eudora, evidently
sensing Maud's thoughts. "Did you and Sam teach her, or was that all
instinct?"

"Chloe took lessons for years in Calgary." Maud's face became
impassive. Fixing cold eyes on Eudora, she sipped her tea. "You know,
the Porters cut our lawn last week. Just like that, without asking."

Eudora snorted. "Well, at least you know you got the professional
touch. The old fool gets a new John Deere and field after field goes
down. I'm surprised your *house* is still standing."

Maud tapped a listless finger on the oak table. "He never came, he
never called, and when Samuel went over there, he didn't answer
the door. You know, they have not even come to complain about the
weathervane."

"What kind of world do we live in that we *want* criticism? Porter's
a bit of a crab, so even when he's home he's not home. And she—"

"Oh, *she*," said Maud, rolling her eyes.

"—she's a hermit in her own right." Eudora frowned, her white
eyebrows pronounced against her red skin. "What's it said about
Mohammed and the mountain? Let's go."

Maud balked. "Without invitation?"

"What a memory you have. How do you suppose *we* met?"

Dragging themselves from their chairs, Maud and Eudora approached Porter's house from the backyard. Trying to find it from the
front had proved useless—it was so overgrown with foliage that it
would have been difficult to convince an outsider the house actually
existed. The backyard, though, seemed cleared for this purpose. The
house was run-down, its weathered paint like some gruesome,
human rash. One could almost hear the decay: the roof's mis-
matched shingles clicking in the wind, its joints creaking, a phantom sound of glass shattering. An old laundry pipe broke gray
wind. Only the stuttering windowpanes betrayed its inner activity.

Both women hesitated on the steps, which were so logged with mildew Maud feared their collapse, especially under Eudora's weight. The whole porch shook.

Eudora knocked on the weathered door. A sudden movement, followed by an implausibly drawn-out pause, made the presence of people obvious to all. Maud and Eudora were willing to be fooled—what kind of people, after all, would take their privacy to such perverse extremes?—but then someone inside dropped a heavy object and ended the game.

Maud glanced uneasily at Eudora, who, seeing Maud's discomfort, set her lips. The door shuddered off a film of dust as it opened.

A sway-backed child stood before them, no more than seven years old. He wore a pair of cut-off shorts, and through his threadbare T-shirt they could see his skin. His face had a pained, almost claustrophobic look, like a chronic worrier's, so baffled that his lips moved without sound.

Eudora narrowed her eyes at him. "Get on your best behavior and go call your mother."

A woman appeared behind the boy, the woman Maud had seen at town hall, though it was difficult now to recognize her. With her hair in loose tufts, with her skeptical expression, she seemed entirely child-like, and not at all pretty. Gold amulets adorned her neck, and she wore the impoverished clothes of Maud's early years. But she wore them with crisp dignity. Two tribal incisions stood out on each cheek. She flinched with recognition when she saw Maud.

She spoke admonishingly. "He never said you are Ghanaian." As though scolded by someone absent, she invited them grudgingly inside.

From what Maud could see, the house looked much the same as her own, except, where the Tyne house looked colossal from outside but felt cloistered within, the Porter house deceived with its armadilline smallness. Inside, its rooms were huge.

Mrs. Porter led them to a kitchen, where a table of ill-clad children chewed stalks of raw sugar cane. They were as surprised at their guests as Maud and Eudora were with their hosts, and eyeing the strangers they lingered in corners, sat on counters, one even busied herself at the stove. Strangely, the kitchen was a precise mirror of Mrs. Porter's dignified poverty, so that even in a line-up of poor housewives she would have stood out as its owner. The floor had been overlaid with wall-to-wall carpeting that shamelessly displayed its stains. Over the deep freezer hung a print of the Last Supper, Jesus and his black disciples robed in kente cloaks. It stood out amid the squalor, and Maud appreciated that in God's haste to make neighbors of Tynes and Porters, He'd settled neither beside outright heathens.

The children seemed to multiply before Maud's eyes, though reason told her she'd counted them twice. All had inherited their mother's large, wet eyes and her strained look of poverty, which gave them an air of distraction, of stifled desires.

"My God," Eudora muttered to Maud. "It's the middle-aged Old Woman Who Lived in a Shoe."

The smallest children, their shyness agonizing, fled past the women in the doorway without excusing themselves. Unfazed by their bad manners, Mrs. Porter even seemed proud of their audacity. She nodded her guests to the table.

Hesitating, Maud and Eudora sat in the abandoned seats. And it seemed that no matter how far away they backed from the table they felt winded. Maud tried to smile. With the heat, the rancid scent of cooking oil and incense turned oppressive.

"I grew up just outside Accra," Maud said. "Which part of Gold Coast were you from?"

"*Eih,* what is this Gold Coast business? 'Which part of Gold Coast?' she asks. Ahein . . ." Mrs. Porter sucked her teeth. "Did we not see independence? Must we still go by that name? Are we not ourselves? *Sth.* And what do you mean by 'were'? I *am* from Winneba. I *am* from Ghana. I am *not* from *Gold Coast.* You sign the paper and like that forget your heritage, isn't it?"

Maud flinched. Eudora raised an eyebrow.

"Now you are angry, eh? The farther you travel, the softer your skin gets." Mrs. Porter gave Maud a contemptuous smile. "What is it you want to drink?"

Maud wasn't angry; on the contrary. She'd saved her children from this life by a hair. Eudora spoke with obvious restraint. "Whatever you have is fine."

Mrs. Porter nodded sharply to the child at the stove, who stopped stirring a tin pot to grab mugs from the cupboard.

"Your husband has my ladder," said Mrs. Porter. "Does he intend to be buried with it?"

Maud smirked, as if to condescend. "My husband tried to return that ladder a number of days ago," she enunciated. "Apparently, no one was home."

Mrs. Porter looked at Maud as though she'd spoken Greek. "He was schooled abroad, isn't it? Some fancy-pants school in England?"

Unable to repress her pride, Maud nodded. The frightened girl placed two steaming mugs in front of the company. Much younger looking from a distance, she seemed to age with every nearing step. Her eyes were sunken.

Mrs. Porter lowered her voice. "A man who goes to the gods for fire and keeps it for himself gets burned alive." She raised her voice. "He should have been more indebted to the country that raised him and taken his knowledge back."

Mrs. Porter had touched on the very guilt that had troubled Samuel's early married years. His sister Ajoa had badgered him in a series of whiny letters, stating that only thirty percent of Ghana was literate, that the dearth of teachers was killing the country, that Ghana had exported its finest non-renewable resource—its sharpest students. Five thousand students that year were educated abroad, and the few who returned no longer shared a common culture with the people. It was a paradox: the necessary modern education was killing off traditional tribal life. Samuel had been torn over whether to return. But he'd been abroad so long, and had such fondness and gratitude for Jacob, who'd settled in nearby Aster, that the choice had made itself. Though some days Maud knew he still wondered about it.

"Sam Tyne has done extremely well for himself," said Eudora, "and for his family, which is more than some have the right to pass judgment on. His success is *model,* and if we had more like him, we'd be better off."

Mrs. Porter's face seemed to say, *Is that so?* She and Eudora had taken an honest dislike to each other. The more Maud considered it, the more sense it made: the classic case of a philosophy colliding with itself. Both Eudora and Mrs. Porter seemed women of limitless strength, both believed in the necessity of children and keeping a good home. Both were crusaders of a kind; Eudora within the National Association for the Advancement of Women, and Mrs. Porter within her home. Yet each saw in the other an enemy, as if their common cause was somehow muddied by the competition. Simply put, each thought herself better than the other.

Mrs. Porter hadn't finished. "Anyone who thinks himself above grieving has something wrong with him. Moving to a new country does not exempt you from a proper burial and the forty days' libation. Your uncle was a good, good man, deserving of his final rest. Do you think you are not bringing punishment upon yourselves? Do you think we sleep in comfort knowing he has not received his proper rest?"

"Has Samuel been here?" said Maud. How else would this woman know which sensitive spots to hit? Maud looked at Eudora, who was frowning at a silent child sucking a piece of sugar cane.

Mrs. Porter sucked her teeth, shaking her head. She studied Maud dubiously. She began to speak, then thought the better of it, and simply said, "Ahein." Glancing at Eudora, she turned her ironic smile on Maud again.

Maud's face grew hot. She understood the judgment: not only did she fail to keep up traditions whose neglect would bring certain ruin, but she kept company with a white woman, which Mrs. Porter seemed to view as immoral. Maud sat in blistering silence, trying to find the right words to berate this woman.

Eudora found them first. "Not only have you shown utter disrespect for the Tynes' loss, but you've done just about everything in the book to make enemies of your families. It's not whether Jacob got his due that should worry you, the grudge the dead have, all that. It's the grudge the living have you should be worried about. The mess you've made of it with the people who share your space."

Maud looked at Eudora in surprise. She'd underestimated her, and gratefully squeezed her hand under the table.

Mrs. Porter stood from the table and raised her voice. "Who are you to enter my doors and speak to me this way? You, especially, always playing the big woman, always—"

The sound of someone entering cut her short. Porter stood in the doorway, wearing a straight-cut suit too small for his thick pugilist's body. Propped atop his head like an abandoned birdcage was a sagging Panama hat, and he clutched a box of stuffed doves, candles and cheap electrical gear under his arm. The shoes at the door and the rising argument had betrayed the company, and yet he proved himself a man of class by appearing pleasantly surprised. His dark face was thrown into relief by his luminous white beard. His eyes shined like wet stones. An engagement in them, a look of intelligence, like that of the twins, led Maud to think him educated.

Porter put the box on the carpet and offered his hand. "Ah, Mrs. Tyne. We didn't forget you, just our manners. We been busy as beavers here. Who don't know but it's the little things in life that'll kill civilization, isn't it? One day we'll get done dusting and it'll be the end of the world."

Maud shared a look with Eudora. Porter seemed elegant and easy, and yet three weeks he'd kept his door closed to Samuel. And not only did his attire seem less than respectable, but as a man he was a bag of mixed maps. His voice had a strange texture, as though every place he'd ever traveled to, no matter how short the trip or how remotely in his past, had left an imprint on his speech.

Despite this, Maud found herself smiling at him. "Pleasure." Eudora gave her a questioning look, but followed her lead.

"No need for introductions, Mrs. Frank. Three decades have made good neighbors of us." Porter treated Eudora's grudging hand with delicacy. Even she seemed to warm with that.

Only later, and as no more than a topic of gossip, did Maud realize that despite his friendliness, despite his wittily chosen words, he never once made direct eye contact. More startlingly, his children stopped fidgeting and followed him with a cautious look. Even Mrs. Porter, for all her self-righteousness and indignation, receded into stiff civility.

Porter sat at the creaking table. "A moment ago you were raising the dead with your voices. What's the problem?" Maud began to explain, but his eyes rested on his wife's face. "Akosua, what's the problem here?"

In his wife's reaction lay the secret of his eyes. For as soon as he looked her way, she flinched. Her embarrassment grew as she spoke, as if suffering a public humiliation. Porter considered all she said, nodding, then asked her to explain her hand in it.

Mrs. Porter stopped short. Looking disconsolately from the company and the children to her husband, she said, "We were talking. I got upset, distastefully so."

Porter nodded gravely.

Akosua lowered her eyes and, in a dry little voice, said, "Ladies, please accept sincere and humble apologies on behalf of my family. It was far from our intent to give offense or do harm, and we hope you bear us no ill will."

Maud felt mortified for the woman. She studied Porter in a darker light. "We're as much to blame as anyone. Please forgive *our* . . ."

Eudora pinched Maud's arm. She was a woman who didn't make apologies she didn't mean. Maud understood this, and though pained, she stopped mid-sentence.

Thanking the Porters for their hospitality, Maud and Eudora left. Maud in a somber mood, Eudora in an annoyingly chatty one.

"See, *that's* what I mean," said Eudora. "*We* have practically no children, while *they*—liars, hypocrites, all of them. Can you believe her nagging you for not having a proper burial, and then behaving like that? I tell you, the only time they were right in there was when he said it's the end of the world."

"I've got a headache," said Maud.

They walked in silence.

While Maud and Eudora were making their fated visit to the Porters', the girls had spent the hot afternoon annoying each other. Ama sat on her cot, underlining likeable passages in *Alice in Wonderland* and watching the magpies in the spruce outside fight a family of sparrows from their nest. Her detachment no longer upset her. Every once in a while she would glance over at Yvette, who had thrown herself under the blankets, never to be seen again. The twins now refused to speak to each other. Though Ama hadn't seen their fight, she'd heard it, and judging from Yvette's face, it had been harsh.

Ama hadn't known what to say. She looked with apprehension at the lump under the torn blue blanket, and averted her eyes whenever she sensed Yvette listening. Since the night the twins had disappeared from their beds after destroying the last of Yvette's new clothes, Yvette hadn't really spoken to Ama. It was as if the day they'd gone for milk-shakes or their walk with Mrs. Tyne hadn't happened. Hurt, Ama nevertheless felt Yvette only needed to be shown patience, compassion, for her to come around.

Still, Ama averted her eyes. By the time Chloe walked in she'd begun to nod off.

Chloe looked stunned, as if she'd ended up where she'd least intended to be. She leaned against the wall, her trembling hands clutching at her frilly collar. Her fear seemed real, and yet cinematically excessive. Ama hesitated, waiting for Yvette to emerge from under the blanket. Yvette did so slowly, not once taking her eyes off her sister.

"What do you want?" she said.

Chloe clutched her collar oddly, as if choking. Ama and Yvette got off their beds to see if she was all right, but hesitated; fear hung like a repellent field around her. Ama, too, began to feel her dread, her hackles rising. Only Yvette remained reluctant.

"The cat." Chloe could barely speak.

Yvette frowned. "A carnivore of genus *Felis,* especially the domesticated kind or any of the smaller wild species."

Ama turned to Chloe. "What cat?"

Yvette sat, looking amused. "Tabby, Siamese, short-haired sphinx."

"It's crazy!" said Chloe.

"Cat-o'-nine-tails, cathood, catkin, catling, cattery, cattish, Kaddish."

Chloe frowned. "Shut up."

"Catamountain, cat burglar, catcall, catfish, cathead, cathouse."

Ama put her hands to her ears and shut her eyes. When she opened them again, both twins were looking blankly at her.

"Cat and mouse," said Yvette. She shrugged. "We don't have a cat."

"I don't know where it came from, but"—Chloe's lip began to tremble theatrically—"it was in the backyard, on the far side. I went outside to look, to see what the neighbors had done to the grass, and there was this cat, and he was crazy, with wild, wet hair, and his mouth had this stringy stuff hanging from it. He had this limp, draggy paw, and I started to run, but he was chasing me, all crazy, and I thought he'd bite me, and I didn't want to bring him back to the house, so I cornered him, oh, it was awful!"

"Calm down," said Yvette. "Where did you say it was?"

"I tricked him into that rusty shed at the edge of the yard. I locked him in there." Chloe's voice filled with wonder. "I shouldn't have locked him in there, should I?"

Ama flinched when Chloe looked at her.

"Show us," said Yvette. "You've got to show us."

"What are you going to do about it?"

"What do you think? Chase it away." Yvette left the room.

Ama heard the twins descend the stairs and, afraid of being left alone, she followed. Events in the twins' lives seemed to happen severely and without warning. She looked tensely at them.

Outside the heat was so strong it had already aged the more sensitive greenery. The grass, once a sea of luminous green whips, had been cut with military precision. All smelled of loam and resin, and there was a pervasive weight to the air that seemed to deaden the trees. Otherwise, the sky was a clean, piercing blue.

Chloe led them through the field, chattering away, pleased at being the center of attention. But she seemed to realize her sudden cheerfulness was inappropriate to the moment and stopped talking. Before too long they'd reached the edge of Porter's yard, which, despite its upkeep, felt shabby. They could hear the house creaking in the weak wind, and there was something infinitely sad about the way the rusted bicycles leaned against the siding. Chloe led them to a tin shed, its hinges red with rust, and the three paused outside of it, their breath quickening.

Yvette's hand trembled on the latch. Exhaling, she pulled the door ajar. Squinting into the darkness, she paused before swinging the door open fully and jumping back.

All three girls grabbed each other, ready to scream. But the shed was vacant save for a few crumpled paint cans, a sack of cement, and an ancient pair of gray-striped overalls.

"Nice joke, Chloe," said Yvette, narrowing her eyes.

Chloe looked closer. "It was here. Yvette, it was here."

Ama grew anxious. But all of a sudden and quite unexpectedly, Yvette turned and hugged her sister. Ama stood apart. No one dared again dispute the cat's existence.

chapter THIRTEEN

D espite the loosened tie and new lease on life, Samuel found himself incapable of that pride so attractive in a man on the verge of success. This came as a strange realization, for owning a house and a business had always been the great grail of his life. Now that he'd so easily achieved what he'd most wanted, he could not enjoy it, and only agonized over its possible loss. Nostalgia seized him; he'd spend cold nights at the belching fireplace, gazing at the ash and thinking of Calgary. He was like a man who blinds himself to hear better, and finds he cannot navigate by sound alone. It was ridiculous, and at the heart of it, Samuel blamed his corrupted sense of time for his troubles. In Gold Coast, when business was slow, a complaint held the same weight as a comment against the weather. Goods would wait, and people would come, and if there was a lapse in coordination, then God had ordained it. No cause for worry, business was a tide with both its highs and its lows, and only a fool didn't know that one followed the other. Everything had its season. Life in the tropics could not be wrestled into a schedule, and the people could live no other way. They did not rush to meetings in fear of being late, for without them, the meeting would not begin. They did not fear missing the bus, for without enough people, the bus would wait hours. Which made sense: without people, a meeting becomes an empty room; a bus becomes a metal husk without a destination. The Sabbath was made for the sake of man, not man for the sake of the Sabbath; thus the son of man is lord even of the Sabbath.

Here, time was immovable. Absolute. It ran on regardless of man or season, a tyrant who sees the face of a friend in the crowd and still issues the order to fire. It put Samuel on edge, left him constantly chasing the clock. It was this sense of time that Samuel struggled with, a web of scheduling that made him unable to enjoy his shop. For, in all truth, things were going wonderfully. He was making a fine living off his handiwork, and within a few slim weeks he'd established a solid client base by reputation alone. He was the man of miraculous hands who had the grace not to charge too much. An electronics prodigy. One man went so far as to jest that his son, in traction at the Edmonton General, would be dancing in a week at a touch from Samuel's hands. Samuel developed a virtuoso's assuredness in his work, even while doubting his choice to abandon his government job.

He was really like two men at this point, for no single life seemed right for him. He felt himself to be much more than what others gave him credit for, than what he gave himself credit for, than what life was letting him be. There was such feeling in him, in all of us, he thought, and what kind of God would tempt us with such potential and not give us the chance to fulfill it. He grew sick with this thought, sick on this success that he couldn't make matter to him, and he was so worried that one morning he woke spitting blood. "Stomach troubles," the doctor had admonished him on a sly visit to Edmonton, "You should quit your job and get an easier one." And Samuel had nodded, taken the prescription back to Aster and never said a word to his wife.

Ray dropped by the shop the week after Samuel visited his farm. He kept his truck idling outside, which hurt Samuel's feelings; Ray meant to use it to quicken his escape if the conversation turned sour.

"My own John Ware," said Ray. "How are you liking the cat?"

"Oh, he is a tiger, that one. Always trying to run away. Certainly the girls keep an eye on him, but one cannot always keep their eye on a cat."

Ray chuckled. "Old Oliver's got some kick in him yet."

The only kind of kick Samuel wished on Oliver was the kind that would send him miles from the Tyne house. He remembered the old cat's eyes. "Amen," he said. "Amen."

Ray explained he'd dropped by to ask Samuel and Maud to dinner to commemorate the four-week anniversary of the shop. "It's really just an excuse for a piss up," Ray laughed. "Got some homegrown pork for you."

The slaughter of the calf was ever-present in Samuel's mind, especially in those ponderous hours of repair. And though his beliefs (which he'd let lapse anyway) didn't forbid it, he'd always felt pork to be a disgrace to one's body. Swine were the filthiest of animals, and Samuel wondered what their worth would be if people hadn't claimed them as food. Samuel looked apprehensively at Ray, exhaling a perfect, girlish giggle. Ray frowned.

"Coming or not, Tyne?"

And whether it was because he felt he had embarrassed his friend by laughing, or whether deep inside him he wanted to settle his mixed feelings about Ray, Samuel agreed to go. The time was set for seven that evening, and after he'd called to let Maud know, Samuel sat down to his work with a sense of foreboding.

Maud was equally nervous as they parked in the Franks' driveway. It surprised Samuel; Maud behaved as though they were to dine with high-ranking officials. She fussed over Samuel's clothes, and asked with aggressive melancholy if she'd chosen the wrong clothes herself. Samuel snapped. "*Eh*, what, are your eyes broken?" He gestured at the Frank house. "Is it Buckingham Palace you see here, eh? Have we come to the high courts of Haile Selassie? Get a hold of yourself."

"Talk to me like that again and you'll see what I get a hold of," said Maud. Her look of anger, which she could hold longer than any woman Samuel had known in his life, silenced him. He often thought to himself, as he did now, that this look was her sole talent in life. The thought gave him both a vicious pleasure and a flare of guilt. They'd almost reached the door when Samuel saw the blinds crawling closed. Eudora must have been watching.

A cold greeting awaited them. It was clear from Eudora's face that she assumed Samuel's gesturing had been to punctuate some slur on her house. She took the Tynes' coats with apparent displeasure, indulging a childish anger, though Samuel couldn't help but feel guilty. But Maud understood; for Eudora Frank, a woman was her home. And Eudora's home was her creation, her only child, her thirty years' labor.

Ray rose through a doorway that led to the cellar-turned-den. All of his bristling distaste from that afternoon had left his features. He was in a jovial mood, even making faces behind Eudora's back when she set down their drinks. Eudora looked ill at ease in a gingham dress stressed at the seams, and Samuel was mildly alarmed at Ray's smirks and grimaces because he couldn't fathom that Ray actually meant to make fun of his own wife's weight. He diverted his eyes to the painting above Ray's head, which depicted a man on a dromedary scaling a sand dune. What an extraordinary animal, thought Samuel, and he could not resist picturing himself upon the splendid beast, a poncho blighting the cold, a thin cigarette pinched in his stern mouth. Samuel caught himself. He turned his attention back to the conversation, for one who dreams while awake is either prophet or madman. And there was nothing oracular about Samuel. Maud gave her husband a mystified look.

Ever fickle, Eudora's anger had lapsed. She fidgeted with new energy, and as she waited to respond to Maud, her hands moved like sparrows in her lap. This distracted Samuel, who marveled that even when silent Eudora drew attention to herself. In fact, he thought, glancing around the room, the furniture itself seemed subordinate to her, anticipating her commands. The beige love seat with buttons like sagging nipples seemed especially aghast, sighing under Eudora's weight. Beside it, a lamp cocked its prune shade at her face and listened with exaggerated respect. Samuel smiled.

Maud gave her husband a warning look, surrendering the conversation to Eudora, who obviously wanted to talk.

"And where are your Three Wise Men?" Eudora said.

"Wisely staying out of trouble, I hope," said Maud. "They wanted to stay home, and I decided they're getting to a trustworthy age."

Eudora made an incredulous face. "At twelve years old? My parents didn't ever leave me home alone until I was almost nineteen. Even then they were pretty scared, more scared, even—I was quite a looker, you know." She winked.

Maud smiled nervously, aware her judgment was being criticized. "All I know is that when I was growing up, I was left alone from earlier than I can remember. And not just left alone—left alone to take care of children even younger than myself." When she laughed, there was a great deal of breath in it.

"Different strokes for different folks," said Ray.

Maud made a dour face. She'd begun to find it rather imperious of the Franks, a childless couple, to comment on her parenting. "Anyways, it's been so long since the twins have gotten along that I thought this might help things."

"Squabblers are they?" said Ray.

"Oh, in the worst sense," said Eudora, turning to him with sudden excitement. "A week ago one cut up the other's clothes. Brand new, they were, and not even a scrap left to dust with!"

"Devils!" said Ray, sipping his beer. He had refused even a drop of the blood-colored wine, insisting that he couldn't betray his fifty-year relationship with malt brew for some cheap runner-up. Everyone had laughed, Eudora blushing furiously. So what the Franks were serving was little richer than vinegar. Maud quietly absorbed the insult; she was determined to enjoy herself.

"Don't worry, though," continued Ray. "You two are so *model,* your girls are bound to work themselves out. And Ama seems like good company. And"—Ray winked—"now they got—"

"What an angel she is," said Eudora, fiddling with a button at her chest that had somehow come undone.

Ray continued as though his wife hadn't spoken. "Now they got old Oliver Orange watching over them."

"Oliver Orange?" said Maud. She looked from Eudora to Ray with amused confusion on her face.

"You gave them Oliver Orange?" said Eudora in admonishment. "He was my favorite. Oh, well, I guess. Oh, well. I suppose those girls need the comfort of a pet more than I do."

Maud looked questioningly at Samuel, whose face tried to accomplish a look that would appease everybody. "The cat," he said, a curious waver in his voice. "Oliver Orange the cat. By now, though, he has possibly run away. The twins have never been good guardians for pets. Is it not so, Maud?"

Maud gave a gruff nod.

Samuel laughed nervously. "It is possible he has even escaped to Mr. Porter's yard, and possibly beyond it." His laugh grew dry. "First stop, Aster. Next stop, the world," he joked.

Ray broke the silence good-naturedly.

"Oliver Orange was always less a pet than a citizen of the world, it's true. And if he only got as far as Saul Porter's house, well, then, there are more than enough kids there to enjoy him. Hey, speak of the devil, I hear you just met the old codger the other day, Sam. You give him my message?"

"I *told* you—that was just Maud and me," said Eudora.

Now it was Samuel's turn to look incredulously at Maud. And here transpired one more of life's ironies: Maud was guilty of the very crime she'd suspected her husband of. With a dignity that surprised Maud, Samuel reached indifferently for his drink.

"But *she's* a piece of work," said Eudora. "The middle-aged Old Woman Who Lived in a Shoe. How's it go? Got so many children . . . ? Really, it was like being surrounded—oh, got to check on the roast."

Ray scrutinized his wife's hips, drinking his beer. "I tell you, we've got a policy to change in this country if we don't want to see another depression. Year after year, rules of entry just get laxer, and if we keep on like this, we don't risk just our culture, but bankrupting ourselves. What happened with ranching turn of last century could happen to any other cornerstone of our culture. People come over, need land, so the government sells off what it's been leasing to ranchers. All went to new farms."

"Aren't you a farmer?" said Maud. "How can you complain?"

"I know where my heart's at. And what happened to ranching could happen to farming, easy. Cities are growing like a cancer, and they have to, what with newcomers' demands, but pretty soon the whole of Alberta will be one big city. Sam was right to leave the city, he was right in helping to fend off the inevitable. I only hope there'll be more to turn the tide."

Maud frowned. Eudora returned and sat. "We eat in five minutes," she said. There was a second of silence. "Why so serious, everyone?"

"Look," said Ray, straining up in his seat, his glasses halfway down his nose so that the frames dissected his eyes. "I may not have a diploma to qualify my knowledge, but I read like no one I've seen, and I know my history. You get the Chinese who came up for the railroad last century, and God bless them for their excellent work, Mormons came in droves from Utah, bringing five, ten wives and who knows how many children. Russians, Hungarians, French Catholics, Jews— did nothing but starve once they got here. And you get ex-slaves— Porter himself. Now, tell me, where is there to put all these people? And don't mistake me. I'm talking from a perfectly practical standpoint."

"There was obviously space if all these people are still here," said Maud. She gave Samuel an uncertain look, but with Ray's eyes on him, Samuel only smiled.

Ray asked Eudora for another beer, licking the rim of the one he'd just finished. "I didn't mean to get you on the defense," said Ray in his soft voice. With his spectacles sloped to the end of his nose, he looked rather professorial. "It's not my intent to say these people shouldn't be here, or even don't have the right to be here. That's not for me to choose. I only mean to point out that if they're going to be here, they've got to accept not only the benefits but the responsibilities of being Canadian. A country's not just a piece of land. What makes a nation a nation is when a group of like-minded people decide to work toward common causes, common goals." He paused to ruminate on his empty bottle. "People who aren't interested in the concerns of language, religion, politics, all that, can't rightly call themselves *active* citizens. Really, now, think about it."

"You mean us," said Maud dryly.

"I don't mean you," said Ray. "I didn't say that at all." He took a sweating bottle from Eudora and thumbed off the cap.

"Hate to interrupt," said Eudora, "but won't you all move to the dining room? I've spread out a feast you wouldn't believe."

She hadn't lied. The low-ceilinged dining room, with its winking chandelier, was set with a buffet that would have depressed a glutton by the impossibility of eating it all. The meal consisted of a side of glazed ham with pineapples, a wizened duck and a roast that so strained its ropes that Samuel looked instinctively at Eudora in her dress. Bowls of rice, steaming vegetables and casks of wine also graced the table. The room smelled of cloves.

But the company had barely tasted the first dish when Ray resumed his conversation.

"Look at the Depression," he said. "Part of the reason North America fell off its feet was it was trying to support the new rush of people. Fact is, newcomers weigh hard on our social system. And I don't mean you—you two are *model.* But look at someone like Porter. No steady job, a wife who doesn't work, and look at his brood. She's barely off the boat before she pops out ten kids. And mark me when I say that twenty per cent of people in Canada are foreigners—well, those that declare themselves anyway, but fifty percent of our convicts are foreign-born, and no doubt others are the kids of foreigners."

Maud lowered her fork. "Aren't your ancestors foreigners, if you go way back? And what are these percentages you've thought up?" She gave Samuel a harassed look.

"Ray, please," said Eudora, "is this dinner conversation?"

"That's why the Farmers League is pushing to get a foot in politics," said Ray, as though he hadn't been interrupted. "They're about women's rights in the home and doctor-approved marriages and killing the influence of American morals on our country. They're about preventing preventative medicine and—"

"You're kidding," said Maud. "You can't not believe in preventative medicine."

"Actually, I don't believe in that either," said Eudora.

"I don't believe him when *he* says it. Don't expect me to believe it of you, Eudora."

Eudora furrowed her pale brow. "I don't believe in trying to change what's inevitable."

"To keep alive people who would've died in an older society, out of some ridiculous sentimentality," continued Ray, "is just bad government. Besides, what happened with this last *miraculous* heart transplant operation, the one done by this South African? They say the man won't live another week. And the one before that, last year's, they only managed to prolong that life an extra, what, eighteen days? It doesn't work, and it's a waste of money besides. These transplant surgeons are like vultures, just waiting for you to breathe your last so they can hack out your lungs and give them to some halfwit. No, ma'am, I don't go for that. All lives have their natural endings."

"But you *do* believe in trying to fight the inevitable growth of cities?" said Maud.

Ray smiled. "Urban planning and human unfitness are not the same thing."

"But, Eudora," said Maud, "you work with the handicapped."

"Exactly," said Eudora. "It's *because* I work with them that I feel this way. Maud, I really think you're misunderstanding us. I am—we *both* are—sympathetic to the mentally handicapped. They're good-natured as children, just really *good* people who, with good training, have the possibility to be, well, *good* workers. I see it every week with my own eyes. What they need most are trained people who'll help them know where they excel and where they don't. If you shelter them and nurture them from babyhood, there's the potential for them to keep that babyhood innocence. They need a kind of education, not mindless charity, which is like using a rag to stop a flood. But getting to the heart of the matter is a hard thing—in this way, you got to admit they can't be treated like normal people. They've got to live in special homes with special staff that have the talent of helping them figure out their gifts, homes where they're cut off from the temptations that lead to alcoholism, prostitution, hysteria, what have you. I think the government would save money running mandatory facilities, if you compare it with the cost of fixing these people's mistakes. But Ray doesn't agree."

"The government just can't afford it," said Ray. "They should nip it in the bud before we're overrun." Maud challenged Ray on what he thought was a decent solution. He stared at her, chewing on a wine cork. "Enough of this," he said. "It's Samuel's day. Let's toast to him."

Regarding each other distrustfully, they fumbled through a toast to Samuel's success. When their glasses had been drained, and the afterward pause accomplished, they continued to eat without pleasure. It seemed the prelude to a hellish evening, with tense feelings and restrained conversation. But there is magic left in life even among adults. Whether they'd succumbed to the alcohol, or whether each had decided that life was too short to be self-righteous, they began to laugh with the ease of old friends. Maud proved surprisingly witty, and she made a series of brisk jokes. Ray, too, proved himself the family ham, entertaining them with astute animal calls during an after-dinner round of port.

"What's this one?" he yelled, making staccato sounds from his throat.

"Rooster!" said Maud.

"I took that advice thirty-five years ago, and I still don't have any chicks!"

Their laughter was halted when Eudora went red in the face. Maud poured her water, but Eudora waved it away, and instead a low, almost equine sound emerged from her. A laugh. Forgetting herself, Maud began to giggle.

"Three guesses who's sleeping on the couch tonight, and the first two don't count!" Eudora said, and the rest of them fell into laughter.

When Samuel thought he'd sobered enough to drive, the Tynes left the Frank house, feeling a little nostalgic. There had been such amity among the two couples, such a surge of kindness, that Maud had felt as natural in their company as if they'd been family. (Or, in Maud's case, better than family.)

"What are you thinking about?" said Samuel.

He actually sounded interested, and Maud was bemused. "Why do you let Ray get away with saying such awful things?"

Confused by the humor in her voice, Samuel tried to answer with the same contradictions. "You don't understand Ray; he's from a different time. And largely uneducated, too. Give him time—we could be an example to him."

Maud wasn't listening. She watched the black trees moving by her window. "Why don't we go for rides anymore, Samuel, like we used to?" she said. When Samuel didn't answer, Maud faced him.

His brow was furrowed. "His were strange theories. You know, it was as if he had, as if they *both* had, misunderstood a book that nevertheless made a great impression on them. It was as though . . ." He drifted into thought.

"Samuel," Maud said tiredly.

"It was as though they did not believe that man also has in him the ability to change, to better himself. To adapt."

Maud sighed and faced the window. Approaching their home, they noticed a light was still on in one of the upper rooms. Samuel remarked that the twins were still awake, and Maud grunted in response. The return of her coldness reminded Samuel of her betrayal in visiting the Porters. Still, he hesitated to ask her anything because he had betrayed her, too, by not mentioning Oliver Orange, and he didn't feel like arguing about it. He admonished himself for not taking advantage of her good mood when he'd had the chance. But that was the nature of marriage, he thought solemnly, an argument that only ends with death.

The house was unconvincingly silent, as though the children, in the midst of some mischief, were holding their breath. Maud frowned at Samuel, then ascended the stairs to the twins' door. Their light was off, but Maud could hear them shifting inside like mice in a wall. Turning the knob, she hoped they'd do a convincing enough impression of sleep so she could leave without punishing them. The hall light outlined their sleeping forms. But Maud didn't see Ama anywhere. She opened the door all the way. Only two of four beds were filled.

"Girls?" said Maud. "Yvie, Chloe?" When they remained silent, Maud turned on the lights.

The twins rose with feigned drowsiness, blinking their eyes. "Mrs. Tyne," Yvette said with false awe, "you woke us."

"Where's Ama?"

Chloe gave Yvette an indistinct message with her eyes.

"What are you doing with your eyes?" said Maud, and Chloe dropped back down in bed.

"Ama's in the bathroom," said Yvette. "I don't know if her bladder's weak, or if she does time travel through the toilet, but you never saw a girl who was better friends with plumbing."

Maud was astonished. "How dare you be so rude?" She slapped off the lights and, turning to leave, heard:

"Call us Annalia."

Maud felt a shadow pass over her. She flipped on the lights. "Which one of you said that?"

The twins looked at her with startled eyes, but Maud suspected they were holding back laughter. She stared them down a good minute, and when neither relented, she threatened them with what the morning would bring and slammed the door behind her. Agitated, Maud moved toward the bathroom in a kind of stupor. She was more mystified than angry, not only because they had (again?) called themselves Annalia, but because until now they had never dared defy her authority. More startling was the vicious energy behind what they'd said, as though they'd planned the slight earlier and had spent these last hours savoring the outcome.

In the bathroom, the plumbing made trickling noises in the wall. Maud turned on the light, a naked bulb blistered with dead flies that, heated, gave off a burnt cork smell. Maud's search for Ama quickly became ridiculous. A perplexed onlooker might have thought she was looking for a cat, for no nook went unscoured. In truth, she was driven by her own need to believe her children, and only after she pulled from behind the radiator a pair of glasses blind with rust did she admit that the girl might not be there.

She grew uneasy. And yet, whether because the wine still clouded her thoughts or because fear was really very foreign to her, her unease, impossibly, vanished. With her usual stern poise, she walked to the landing and called Samuel's name. He appeared at the bottom of the stairs looking sleepy.

"I hate to wake you," she said, "but our third cadet's gone AWOL, and the twins aren't talking."

Samuel dismissed Maud with his hand. "Children's mischief."

Maud adorned each hip with a fist. "That is the second time today you've abused me. You just stay there and stand your lifetime away, and when I have to call in the authorities to find her you'll know what kind of man you are."

Samuel began the stairs. "Have you spoken with the twins?"

"I tried, but for children of an unlistening father it makes sense they're not talking." Maud looked as if she blamed him. And he recognized then that he was tired in ways he'd always seen as weaknesses in other men; disappointed that even he could find himself out of love with his wife.

Together, they confronted the twins. Maud approached the nearest bed, where Yvette sat looking indifferent.

"Where's Ama?"

"We don't know," said Chloe.

"I didn't ask *you*. Yvette, where's Ama?"

Chloe nodded to a pile of clothes in the corner.

"What, is she hiding under there?" said Maud with a pang of conscience. She hated to think she might have accused her children of mischief they were perhaps not responsible for. As she walked to the wall to sort through the colorful clothes, Yvette said:

"She only said she was going to the toilet."

"Eh, eh, enough." Samuel sucked his teeth. Sitting on Ama's cot, he said, "No more tomfoolery. I want a report of your every action this evening." He noticed the twins glancing at each other before either answered. Samuel almost couldn't contain his temper in the face of this brazen behavior, which gave him the feeling of being a peon in a ruthless childhood game. Neither seemed able to speak without the brief communion.

"What is wrong with your eyes?" he demanded.

Maud placed a hand on his arm, as if to say this was her jurisdiction. "So this is what we get for trusting you? We'd have done better to chain you to your beds."

Neither twin spoke, but Yvette lowered her eyes.

Young Tragedy and Comedy, thought Samuel, but he felt none of the warmth the nickname usually gave him. Crushing his bowler in his hands, he stood into a stretch. His voice was tired. "I will begin with the cellar and then ascend. If I discover nothing, then I will comb through every blade of grass. If I discover nothing, I will search all of Aster. And if I still discover nothing"—he pushed his wilted hat into place—"I will search the world."

They all three looked at him curiously. Maud scoffed and shook her head. "Don't get lost yourself."

Samuel hadn't intended to make such an august speech, or any speech at all for that matter, but he'd wanted to end the conversation. Besides, his agitation, and his inability to master it, left Samuel prone to absurd outbursts. He slunk to the cellar where, hanging his dinner coat on a rusty, white-tipped nail, he began what he already suspected would be a fruitless search. He wondered, not without guilt, why affection for Ama came so much more easily to him than it ever had for his twins, who displayed all the natural brilliance and mischief he'd so wanted in a child. He felt a sort of embittered pity toward them, and reproved himself for it.

The cellar's darkness calmed Samuel. Roots and moss thrived in the cracks where the caulking had aged loose, and soggy documents wilted from their piles to the floor, tricking the eye into seeing thatched tile. Had the air not been so musty Samuel might have felt at home. Instead, he sensed a broken pipe somewhere and made a mental note to call a professional in the morning. As he pried through the clutter, calling out Ama's name, he was struck by the uselessness of man in the face of adversity. He granted that a person's most-feared enemy, what stalks each life, is death, and that there isn't a man yet who has managed to outwit it. For this reason, men pretended to be at the helm of their lives, but they weren't, and could only feign navigation on a river predetermined for them.

Samuel wrestled these thoughts through the cellar, through the kitchen with its insistent flies, through the room where Jacob had strewn cane mats for his morning prayers, through the hall closet with its smell of smoke, through the living room with its spiteful fireplace that gasped ashes in Samuel's face when he passed it. Man cannot master death, he thought. Not even Jacob Tyne. Jacob of the Harsh Mouth and Stern Fist. Our Saint of Clandestine Sorrow. Samuel felt a kind of remorse for the man he could not mourn. Jacob had been as severe and distant as he'd been anxious to give his nephew a better life. Samuel didn't understand the man, and, as ever, was perplexed by what he was expected to feel for him. In a lot of ways Jacob wasn't worth the brooding, had been a millstone on Samuel's back, remembered only for the little cruelties, each drawn-out act of kindness more like a punishment. Jacob had cared for him with an undisguised sense of obligation. Samuel had never learned the true cause of his uncle's debt, and how can you mourn a man you don't know? What was left but to bury and forget him? Why hold the forty days' ceremony—what was the point in pouring libation so far from the country in which that act meant something, and with a crowd of stragglers unknown to the dead? What was the point in being the only person who could keep the deceased alive by remembering him if that person had not given you a shred of himself to be remembered by? There was no point. Let the dead bury their dead.

Samuel completed his search of the main floor without success. He had that drenched feeling only tiredness of mind can provoke, and wanted to finish his search as soon as possible to sooner call the authorities. Thinking of Ama suffering somewhere made him nervous, so he thought of other things. As he trudged through the girls' Iron Lung, a favorite obscurity occurred to him: all of life's ambitions were mere diversions. Politicians sought refuge in conflicts, the immoral sought it in sex, and many men just worked until they dropped. You did everything to keep yourself from seeing the futility of it. But Samuel had joined that class of men who, having attained a major goal, suddenly see the vanity in wanting it.

Samuel sat on his bed. He feared the worst for Ama. He thought of what that would mean about the twins, and forced it from his mind. Maud found him staring at a blank wall, muttering proverbs to himself.

She sounded exasperated. "I've called the Franks. Yvette broke down and told me they abandoned the poor girl somewhere along the Athabasca—I guess they built a raft out of garbage and the whole thing sunk. Ama's not the great swimmer the twins are. I can't believe they'd just leave her there and try to keep it a secret. Even then, Chloe was about to tear Yvette's eyes out for admitting anything."

The pain in Maud's voice gave Samuel a surge of pity. But he continued to sit on the bed. When he suggested they inform the authorities, Maud waved a dismissive hand. She seemed to fear that legal action would be taken against the twins despite their age.

"Ray Frank's got a rowboat and Eudora's got her nurse's licence, that should be enough," she said. "Besides, it'll take the authorities an hour to get here."

Samuel gave in. He rose to go down and wait on the stoop for Ray, but Maud detained him by grabbing hold of his shirt.

"*I'm* going with Ray," she said, pressing her lips firmly together. "You stay here with the twins."

glasses had fogged. "Poor thing was sitting on a barely floating raft of weeds. Hanging on for dear life. I had to jump from the boat to get her."

"Oh, God," said Maud. She felt dampened, as if all her stress had been alleviated too quickly. "Let's get her in the car."

Ray scooped the girl in his arms, putting her on Maud's lap in the cab. The women fussed over her the whole drive, and when they reached the Tyne house, Samuel ran out to greet them.

"You found the child—is she all right?" he said. Seeing his anguish, Maud felt guilty.

"Don't fuss, she's fine," Maud said. "How are the twins?"

"Silent." Samuel touched Ama's forehead with the back of his hand. He turned to Eudora. "She's like an oven."

"Well, let's take her inside, for a start."

Samuel was disturbed that Ama hadn't acknowledged him. She had a monk's composure, her eyes oddly calm. Yet it was obvious that breathing was painful to her, her body jerking up with each breath. She stank of smut from the river, sludge, the ferment of weeds. And those smells provoked a pity in Samuel, a feeling he would later elucidate as sadness, for without her usual nervous kindheartedness, the girl seemed entirely strange to him.

They carried her to the kitchen and, clearing the table, placed her on it. Here, under Ama's aloof gaze, they argued about how best to treat her.

"I haven't used mustard plaster in years," said Eudora, scoffing at Maud's suggestion. "I brought my black bag. Let's cup her."

"Why complicate things?" said Ray. He removed his glasses to wipe off the fog that had collected when he'd entered the warm room. "Just give her whatever medicine her folks sent along with her, then back off and let her rest."

Eudora looked at him as if to say, *What do you know?* Samuel slid away from the group and leaned against the gas stove. Taking his cue, Ray did the same, leaving things to the women. Maud gave the girl her usual medicine, while Eudora lit a candle to heat the glass cups that would suck the poison through Ama's back.

As the women argued, Ray told Samuel how difficult it had been to save Ama, how he'd thought that at sixty-three he'd seen his last, having had to plunge into a fast current. Samuel studied Ray's face, thinking of the slaughter of the calf, his savage opinions at dinner, his condescension.

Ray's quizzical look made him turn away. And for the first time Samuel seemed to be brought to his senses. Raising his voice, he said, "Why do we not take her to the hospital?"

It was as though he'd suggested they dismantle the oven to build a flying machine. Eudora at least seemed to consider it, her thoughts plainly etched on her face: her feminist's belief in progress fighting against her homemaker's practicality, her love of taking offense fighting against her logic. She looked at Maud, who regarded Samuel with reproach. But Ama herself spoke.

"Don't take me to the hospital. Please," she said, barely audible. She turned her face away.

"Don't bother her, Samuel, she doesn't want to go," said Maud, urging the girl onto her stomach and raising her shirt so they could cup her.

Samuel was disgusted with his wife. She worried about her daughters, didn't want to call attention to their culpability in this mess. He gave her a dark look, but said no more. To be fair, he knew Maud felt affection for Ama and would never wish harm on her. And yet, for her, nothing could overcome blood ties.

"Why did the twins leave you there?" said Eudora.

Ama frowned, and the coughs she'd been holding back wracked her body.

After cupping her, the group carried Ama upstairs to the Iron Lung. Exhausted but unable to breathe, Ama only fell asleep at dawn. Ray dozed in a dusty corner. The others, so tired their conversation was senseless, rested against the furniture.

Eudora smiled. A sleepless night had sharpened her tongue.

"If I ever saw the devil's work, it's what I saw tonight."

There was no reply.

chapter FOURTEEN

I t was one of those mornings when an immature frost seizes everything and yet the sun continues to shine. The older leaves bled on
their stems, and people unfamiliar with Alberta's moody weather
might have thought it was autumn.

Samuel fastened the curtains in the Iron Lung to let the sun in. On
the pockmarked dresser he set a simplistic arrangement of marigolds
with a single, luscious wild rose rising from the center.

"This one is you," he told Ama, pointing at the wild rose. "A raving
beauty rising like the siren's song above the others." Her giggle made
him feel appreciated. He patted his hat with an air of pride. "Never
mind this electronics business, I should be a poet. A black Homer for
modern times."

When Ama's laugh receded into coughing, he sat beside her on the
bed to pat her back. Two days of quarantine had cleared her chest,
bringing back some of her old personality. Even so, she treated the
Tynes like strangers, using the shy and rigid table talk of their earlier
days. Crushing as this was for Samuel, he couldn't lament progress.

Ama had improved by strides; only a blind man would dispute the color waking in her face.

"Mr. Tyne?" said Ama in a rusty voice, recovering from her cough. Samuel marveled at the wonderful grades of color in her hair, like burnished oak. He ran a hand down her head.

"What is it? Are you feeling sick again?"

Ama's eyes were wet, her flushed face trembled. "I want to go home."

"It is impossible. Your parents do not return until September, and you cannot live unsupervised."

"To Grandma Geneviève's. She lives just outside Morinville. If you call her, she'll come for me for sure."

Samuel looked at the floor. Part of him had suspected this was coming, what with Ama's evasiveness lately, her kind but marked distance. Still, it pained him so deeply he feared being unable to keep the emotion from his face. Drawing his woolen socks across the beige carpet, he meditated on the way brushing the carpet's grain could darken and lighten its color.

"Well," said Samuel, "you are not a captive here. If that is your wish, I will certainly fulfill it." Trying to smile, he looked at her. "Your wish is my command."

Ama flushed, but clasped her hands across the blanket, a formal gesture that seemed to close the matter. Patting her head, Samuel rose to his feet wheezing a little, and trod downstairs to tell his wife.

Maud behaved as though resigning herself to the loss, but her relief was obvious. Samuel went to his study and slammed the door. It was some time before he could bring himself to pick up the phone.

He called Geneviève Ouillet three times in quick succession, to no avail. After fiddling with a radio for an hour, he called three more times and still received no answer. It annoyed him. Where did old women go in the middle of the day, anyway? Two hours later, she finally answered.

But she didn't speak. Samuel only realized she'd answered by the tinny song in the background, sung in a sentimental, foreign, tear-drenched voice.

"Mrs. Ouillet? This is Samuel Tyne. I—"

"Time? What, is this a census? I don't have time, I don't have it," she said in her decrepit voice, aspirating her h's.

"No, no, I am not a census, do not hang up. I'm Samuel *Tyne*. I'm your granddaughter Ama's guardian for the summer."

"Oh. Yes, what is it?" The woman seemed to be smoking, and she spat and coughed throughout Samuel's explanation. "Mm, yes, all right, then," she said when he'd finished, though Samuel wasn't convinced she'd understood.

He gave her the Tynes' address, spelling out the street name. "Are you sure you wouldn't prefer me to drop her off?"

She hung up loudly in his ear. Samuel looked at the receiver a few seconds before replacing it on the cradle. When he went upstairs, Ama looked impressed.

"I expected to be here at least another week," she said. "Grandma doesn't like to use the phone—she hates all technology. Even technology she grew up with. She thinks everyone's wrong to believe in it."

Early the next morning, Samuel and Maud set Ama's carpetbag by the front door and sat with her in the family room to await her grandmother. The twins had woken early and gone outside. Though annoyed, Samuel understood their fear of being rebuked by one of Ama's relatives. Maud had spent the morning dusting, but by noon the ancient fireplace had gasped ash on everything. The room felt stifled, and their being dressed in their primmest, most respectable clothes didn't ease things. At the bay window, the sky was white with the absence of any kind of weather. Everything smelled of mothballs.

"You might think of getting your grandmother a watch for Christmas this year," said Maud. She laughed hesitantly. "What time did she say again, Samuel?"

Samuel waved the hat in his hands, then resumed picking lint off it.

Dwarfed in a rose-colored chair, Ama gave them an apologetic smile. She'd tucked the wild rose behind her ear, reminding Samuel of a young, paler Lady Day. "Grandma really doesn't like technology," she said, "so she's never on time."

Maud raised her eyebrows and turned to the window.

They continued to sit in silence. And this grieved Samuel, for more than anything he wanted to speak to the girl, to change her mind, to silence the anxiety he felt over her departure. At first he'd tried to catch Ama's eye, stealing glances at her and smiling, but after Maud reproached him with a look, he forced himself to stop. Now they barely looked at one another, only deepening the uneasiness.

When the doorbell sounded at a quarter past four, Maud forgot the customary pause—what would visitors think, after all, if they all ran around like chickens?—and strode out to answer it. Samuel glanced at Ama, who removed the flower from behind her ear with nervous fingers, a look of regret on her face. As if handling something breakable, she pressed the flower between the pages of *Alice In Wonderland*.

Some people carry a portrait of themselves in their voices; others have voices so incongruous that when we meet them we feel we've somehow been lied to. Samuel had expected, had *hoped,* that Mrs. Ouillet's voice would prove deceitful. Instead, he found her so like the crass, underweight matron in his mind's eye that his accuracy startled him.

When he held out his hand for her to shake, she looked past him. She had a ruddy face, with deep lines etched darkly under her eyes. Like Ama, her hair had different hues in it, from rust to the whitest gray, yet the older woman seemed to neglect hers, and it dropped in matte strands from her bun. Her lips were full and pink, their vibrancy almost vulgar on so worn-out a face. Her pale gray eyes refused to rest on anything, and she looked distractedly around her.

Nudging past Samuel, she began to fuss over Ama. She smelled of hot maple syrup and tobacco, a pleasant mixture.

"She is feeling much better," he said. "Very much on the mend."

Mrs. Ouillet didn't acknowledge he'd spoken, scrutinizing Ama's knees and cursing in French. The angularity of her body, her excess flesh, made Samuel guess she'd once been immense. Experience had taught him large women were a force to contend with.

Maud gave Samuel a look of dread.

"Won't you stay to tea?" she said.

"Grandmère, *voulez* stay for *thé*?" said Ama.

Without acknowledging the Tynes, who stood quite foolishly behind her, Mrs. Ouillet spoke to Ama in rapid French.

Ama's face colored, and she looked hesitant. "*Je ne comprends pas.*"

"'*Je ne comprends pas,*'" said Mrs. Ouillet, shaking her head. "*Ah, seigneur. Tu me tues.*"

Grabbing hold of Ama's sleeve, Mrs. Ouillet shoved the girl onto the creaking porch. When Samuel attempted to help her with the carpet-bag, Mrs. Ouillet slapped his hand away, saying, "Tut tut tut tut," in an ascending voice. "*Lâche-le.*"

Samuel stepped out after them, watching Mrs. Ouillet force Ama into a rusted-out white van. When the van drove out of sight, he turned to see his wife behind him. He studied her thin face for signs of remorse and, seeing none, pushed past her without speaking. Grabbing his keys, he went for a drive to clear his thoughts.

Always at the back of Samuel's mind these days was the burden of finding the twins a new school for September. Putting off the task had simply added to his misery. He'd been so distracted he'd selected a school that had burned down years ago for the twins to attend. Maud had rebuked him: "Guess again, Sherlock." For cultural reasons, he then selected the Aster General School, which had stood in Aster since 1913 and was now in its geriatric phase, slowly losing students to the city the way an old man loses his wits. Maud hadn't even answered that suggestion. He was now deliberating over a school in Edmonton, though in a perfect world they'd be able to attend the same school as Ama.

For all his abstraction, it rarely occurred to Samuel that he was involved in illicit dealings with his neighbor. The phone call that put him in possession of a house, the providential ladder, the mown lawn, the discovery of the actual property lines and his wife's recent lie about her visit all heightened his paranoia of what to expect next. What exactly did Porter want from him? Why did he not make good on whatever his subtle actions were trying to express? Samuel had waited a useless month for something to happen. But almost as soon as he allowed himself to forget it, he received two letters.

It was a cold day, and the mailbox was still full when he returned from work. Setting his toolbox down, Samuel sifted through the flyers and found the first note. His name had been labored over in huge hand-writing, the envelope opaque in places with grease stains. Intuiting who it was from, he crushed it into his pocket. He almost missed the second note because it was stuck to a flyer. A telegram from Gold Coast. He felt a pang of anxiety: Why hadn't he written back to Ajoa last month? Why was he so stingy with his money whenever his mother demanded it? Surely he could send her sums above the regular monthly check? He tore at the seal with bated breath. After reading, he raised his eyes to the yard, and its familiarity, its unchanged beauty, struck him as perverse. Dazed, he went inside, placing his hat and the telegram on the stand of false, dusty roses. He closed his eyes for a moment, exhaled and sat on the bottom step of the staircase. A crash stunned him from his stupor. At first he thought it had originated outside, but when he heard the commotion coming from the living room, he rose wearily to his feet.

In his decrepit years, imprisoned by arthritis and the knowledge that he'd soon die, Samuel would remember this scene. For a moment he'd stood in the doorway, unable to enter. He felt the terri-ble energy in the room, which set his nerves on edge and led him to expect the worst. The twins stood in the center, with their backs to the entrance. Only when Chloe turned her head was Samuel pro-pelled by his anxiety into the room. He'd been struck not so much by the distress on her face as by the feeling it was feigned. Overwhelmed, he pushed past her.

On the far edge of the carpet, beside the silver ladder, lay Maud. Her leg had buckled unnaturally under her, her face in awe of the pain. Her breathing was ragged. Samuel kneeled and raised her head onto his thigh. She seemed on the verge of fainting.

"My leg," she said in a damp voice.

Samuel touched a thumb to her lips to keep her from exhausting herself talking. Her whole body was moist. He scowled in the direction of the ladder. *Porter will not rest until he has killed this family.* The twins approached and stood over them. And the pained looks on their faces softened Samuel's anger a little.

"It's not their fault," said Maud in a strained voice. She was still able to give Samuel a look of rebuke. "They didn't do this. I set the ladder wrong."

Samuel set Maud's head on the carpet. It hadn't even entered his head to blame the twins, but hearing Maud's pleas, he was filled with a dreadful certainty they had done something. Avoiding their eyes, he left the room.

Maud sensed his intention. "Don't call the ambulance, Samuel, don't! I'm fine. Let's just drive there ourselves."

Samuel hung up the phone and brought the car around. They made the hour-long drive to Edmonton (rather than go to the local hospital, Maud insisted on the Edmonton General so the neighbors would not have to know) in silence. Samuel kept glancing at the twins in the rear-view mirror. Not a trace of emotion could be read on their faces.

At the hospital the girls stayed in the car. Maud was rushed into emergency, leaving Samuel to sit in the waiting room. The more he tried to suppress thoughts of his daughters, the worse they assailed him. He distracted himself by trying to guess what the other people in the waiting room were enduring. A fat man in a plaid shirt stared at an envelope in his hand, and Samuel realized that he had forgotten the letter he'd tucked in his pocket. Samuel went outside for privacy.

Though it was still sunny, a mean rain had started to fall, growing more violent by the minute. A devil's rainstorm. Samuel crouched under the awning, contemplating a drop of water on the brim of his hat. As he read the stained letter, an orderly called his name.

Maud's internal organs were just fine, but she had a hairline fracture in her tibia and the very tip of her toe bone had been crushed. "We just need a few hours to fit her with a cast, and then she's all yours," said the man.

Samuel grunted his consent.

"Now," continued the orderly, "you can have fifteen minutes with her before we begin the resetting. Tell a few jokes. Lift her spirits a little." He winked.

Samuel hated being the bearer of bad news. Shuffling into Maud's room, he was pained by the smile she greeted him with.

And yet, as soon as Samuel smiled back, she seemed to see something in it and herself stopped smiling. Suddenly, she looked withered and vulnerable on the white bed, and when he took her hand he was surprised to see how wrinkled it looked. Maud looked incurably old and, to her credit, wary.

"Maud," Samuel began.

"They tell you something they didn't tell me?" she said. "Using the husband to break it to me gently. Just give me the news. Did I rupture something?"

"Maud, your father is very ill. They say he is on his deathbed."

Maud looked perplexed.

"A telegram has come from one of his wives. They say he is on his deathbed and they want you to come. Or to send money."

There was a vague smile on Maud's face. "When?"

Samuel hesitated. "The telegram was for today, but it has been several weeks since he fell sick."

Maud nodded, as though it all seemed sensible to her. The vacant smile remained on her face. "Tell them I'm ready for my cast."

"Maud," said Samuel. He knew that despite her father's cruelty she grieved for him, but, for some reason, refused to share it. "What kind of talk is this?" he said.

"Tell them I'm ready," she said, sinking back into the pillows. She began to contemplate the ceiling.

Samuel stood in the doorway, waiting for anything, a gesture, that would let him share her anguish. After a minute of silence, he left to find the orderly.

chapter FIFTEEN

Who knows through what channels the town heard of the accident. People poured into Samuel's shop to offer condolences. The most memorably sincere person was a woman called Tara Chodzicki.

Samuel was impressed by her tact and wit. She brought butter cookies in tinfoil, opening the package with her agile, ringed fingers. "Give Maud my love. And tell her I've still got my eye on Chloe's hands."

Samuel smiled. "I give up. Why her hands?"

She tapped Samuel's wrist playfully. "She'll know what I mean." Winking, she left the store.

Samuel laughed, marveling at how everyone was winking at him lately.

When he brought the cookies and the message home to Maud, she rolled her eyes. "Never mind, Samuel, it's all nonsense." She was still too disgruntled by the spectacle of Chloe's playing to discuss it, least of all with Samuel, from whom she felt increasingly estranged. But she ate a few cookies, chewing thoughtfully.

Talk of Maud's misfortune somehow spurred rumors of the twins' possible hand in Ama's river accident. Ray did his best to curb the rumors, using his status as a representative of the town council as leverage. Samuel was grateful, though he suspected the gossip originated with Eudora.

"Dora?" Ray shook his head. "Naw. She's too busy knitting sweaters for Vietnamese kids—it's the new thing with the National Association for the Advancement of Women. Apparently, if the kids wear darker colors, they're harder for the snipers to see."

It's a little late for her to think of protecting children, thought Samuel. Though for all his criticism, even he had trouble facing the twins these days, viewing them with a new critical eye. The twins repelled him, and he couldn't help speaking distantly to them, feigning preoccupation. It was as though he had condemned them in his heart. Whenever they caught him drawing on his socks in the hallway, or muttering proverbs to himself as he left the bathroom, he felt all the warmth leave his features. He would pretend he hadn't seen them, or nod and keep going. He felt ashamed, but he couldn't stop himself. His neglect provoked little tricks from them: his best shoes filled with talcum powder, his favorite radio laryngitic with cut wires, the slow, sad unraveling of everything he took pleasure in. Again, he pretended not to notice. The vandalism soon stopped.

Samuel's disregard of his daughters held a strange pleasure for Maud. On those afternoons she was strong enough to get out of bed, she made a circuit of the house on her crutches, surveying the blindness that now passed for family love in her convalescence. She felt selfishly alive in their silence, though she admonished both parties for behaving like babies. The love lost between them seemed to heap more upon her, and she got along better with everyone now that they rarely spoke to each other. Not without feelings of guilt, she put off reconciling the three for the sake of her own elevation in their eyes. And in the wake of her father's sickness, which she refused to discuss, she needed more attention than ever. Her accident couldn't have been more compassionately timed. She felt how precarious the balance in the house was, and feared that a minor shift could change things at any minute. And so, she was greatly annoyed one afternoon to hear the doorbell ring.

Samuel reached the door first, and, intuiting more bad news, Maud tried to nudge him aside with one of her crutches.

Samuel was put off by how familiar the man seemed, though he was certain they had never met. Ignoring the woman at the man's side altogether, he stood studying him.

Maud limped forward, an anxious smile on her face. "Good to see you again," she said, trying to balance on one crutch so she could shake hands.

"Don't trouble yourself," said the man, glancing around the hallway. He looked hunched, deflated, but with hale, broad shoulders, like someone who'd prevailed through years of backbreaking labor only to be compromised by old age. At first it seemed that his eyes wandered out of some desire to be tactful, but it soon became obvious there was something calculated in it. His face was so dark it had the hue of an eggplant, and his refusal to meet eyes solidified Samuel's unease.

The man looked at him but quickly averted his eyes. "Mr. Samuel Tyne," he said in a hybrid accent, "Tyne Electronics." He closed his eyes as though ruminating upon something. "Six candles, two doves and a watch," he said.

Samuel flinched. "The peddler."

"Samuel!" said Maud.

"The peddler," Samuel repeated. Of course, the mongrel peddler.

The man's laugh sounded like a clearing of the throat. "I keep my *peddling* to the early days of the week, if you please, and the rest I spend trying to trick people into believing I'm a respectable man by dressing like one. Is it working, do you think?" Laughing at his own joke, he offered his hand, which Samuel rushed to catch as though a ball had been thrown at him. "Saul Porter. This is Akosua. She's Ghanaian, like you two. She's real sorry you all got off to a bad start the other day." Roused by his sideways glance, Akosua gave them a startled smile. When her husband persisted in looking at her, she started as though remembering something.

"Everywhere in the street your misfortune is spoken of. We have come to condole with you," she said in a rehearsed tone. She held out a foil-covered tray, which the Tynes instinctively regarded with suspicion. "Plantain and spinach stew," she said.

Porter shook his head. "For such a thing to've happened with my ladder."

"How is it you know it was your ladder?" said Samuel. Maud gave him an exasperated look.

Porter raised a hand in appeal. "I heard a ladder, and so I thought . . ."

"We're so rude!" said Maud, pained at her lack of social grace. "Let's all go into the kitchen." Maud took the lead, while Samuel, still recovering from his surprise, pressed against the hallway wall for the others to pass.

Akosua was an average-sized woman, sap-colored, with dainty, forgettable features. But Samuel couldn't wrap his head around Porter. He couldn't believe it was him, this small boar of a man who left letters in his mailbox and had hidden himself until now. This was him. Samuel felt unsettled, but also a little disappointed. Porter had undone the very different image Samuel had of him in his mind.

They spent the hour adjusting to each other's company. Almost as soon as the Porters were seated, a fusty, smoldering smell bled from their clothes, an intimate scent, which hung about them palpably. Samuel helped Maud lay out the casual tea they used for all their sudden company, but when they'd finished, the tabletop so frothy with doilies it would have made a spinster flinch, they realized that the Porters' poverty might lead them to think the Tynes were showing off. No one spoke as Samuel began to serve, but Akosua gave Maud a sulky look that made her ashamed. An uneasy mood filled the room, a leaden silence that fended off Saul Porter's attempts to pelt it with witticisms. Only when the twins entered in their pajamas, holding alternate volumes of *War and Peace,* did real animosity surface in the conversation.

Akosua regarded the twins with a smug look on her face. "Are these the two who have done you trouble?" she said, her pleasure obvious. She beckoned to Yvette, who took a bewildered step backward and glanced inquisitively at her sister. Akosua scoffed. "No discipline," she said, pretending to address herself, though her voice could have filled a theatre. "*Bra-ha.* I'm Auntie Akosua."

When the twins didn't respond, she laughed bitterly. "They do not understand the simplest order, or it is stubbornness? *Bra-ha.*" In a voice less interrogative than whiny, she questioned them in Twi. At their silence, she made a disgusted face. "Eh, even the littlest ones know it. Are you not Ashanti?"

Samuel was furious. But no sooner did he open his mouth than Akosua began to recite every known cliché in all the Ghanaian tongues she was fluent in. When the twins looked perplexed, she sucked her teeth and shook her head, though she couldn't keep the smugness from her face.

That gesture enraged Samuel. Frowning, he laughed, a laugh that called attention to its falseness. Sensing a breach of the etiquette the Tynes used in company to stop gossip from leaving their home, Maud motioned to the twins to refill the water carafe. It was an impolitic move, for as soon as they placed their books on the table, Akosua leaned across her husband to see what they were reading.

"Eh, they think they are big big? They think they are whites or what?"

Samuel looked in exasperation at Saul Porter. Throughout all Samuel's years of study in Gold Coast, he had been a symbol to the confused population of their country's ills. The British-imposed school system and its misguided graduates were killing the tradition of a country that had already lost so much. Yet, the students who never returned from abroad were even worse, because they left the country bereft of leaders. And so the educated could not win. Samuel was so sick of his guilt, so sick of the social stigmas that had crossed the ocean with him and the way they could be twisted to dismiss the brilliance of his daughters, that he violated the Tyne's etiquette with a satisfying outburst of sense.

"Since when," he said, "has literacy altered the color of one's skin?"

This roused Porter, and he looked at Samuel as though urging him to go on.

But what was there to expound on? Samuel had said all he meant to say. But having pierced the fog that had dulled Porter until now, he felt encouraged to keep speaking.

"Should a Ghanaian not be happy to see another Ghanaian educating himself? You say only big big man should concern himself with these things. But does this attitude not contribute to uneducation and poverty in our country? The state of things in the world is such that you must immerse yourself or perish. Even now I do not say it is the British system, but an inherited set of ideas, of customs we must somehow integrate better with our own traditions. Perhaps if I lived back home, at this time now, now that we have seen independence, I should never say these things. But I have always thought that a black can, and should, define himself beyond being black. Black, white, Chinese, Arabian—life is much more than that. Egyptian, Senegalese, French— never, never, never accept the limits another wants to give you."

"If you don't love another's limits, why love their education?" said Porter, whose authority drew everyone's attention. "Reading's made all the difference, at least for my part. It was not being able to read that kept the vote from us in Oklahoma, sent us north in the first place. We always been the bottom of the pecking order. No respect. Not once, in all those books you reading, are we presented as decent, intelligent men. We ain't *even* men. Minstrels, animals, but never upright men. And I'd know, I read all those things once I learned to—self-educated. Won't read them again. We're the absolute last in this world with nothing to be done of it but keep on living. I'm a black man, wouldn't want to be nothing else, and it makes me cry to see one who does."

Samuel winced, and his face became anxious. "You misunderstand me."

Porter shrugged. "I speak from my life. My family came up when I was eleven, twelve maybe, and we were healthy, moneyed, what have you. And this country, claiming it's all for human rights, claiming it's superior to the States and accepts everyone, didn't treat us no better than a common dog." Porter grimaced and coughed, reaching for the water that after sitting five minutes had attracted lint to its surface. When he'd emptied the glass he coughed against his fist.

"They came down with posters—what else? Called it 'Last Best West,' said they needed settlers for ranching, dairying, grain, fruit farming, that sort of thing. Now, we weren't ever ranchers, but my folks thought, what the hell, why not try at least, because we ain't getting nowhere here. Thirty years the Civil War had ended, *over* thirty years, and things weren't any easier. Good for nothing but barbers and bootblacks—if your luck was buttered, you became a porter. So you can imagine. My father, Harlan, was born in Georgia, and he went west after the war, living all round Kansas and Utah, Oklahoma, but he was always at blows with *some*one. One night he came home—I was helping get his supper—and he says to me, he says, 'Son, it's only a matter of time before I kill someone or get killed myself.' He was usually so irrational that when he talked sense it really made my bones cold. A week later, at his Masons' meeting, he talked to Jeff Snick, who said he's getting a group together to head north. Week after that we locked our front door for good. My mother always said it was the only decision Daddy ever took his time with. And he decided in a week, so you can imagine just how rational a man he was."

Porter went on to describe their mulish journey. Assailed by fatigue and boredom, the group of two hundred were quite dispirited when their train pulled into Edmonton. Young Saul had tired of his casual game of cards with Oscar Bishop, whom Cece (whose people had educated her) had dubbed "Othello" because he was jealous of everyone. Saul lay down to listen to yet another of Uncle Mack's stories of his days as a libertine youth in Utah (all of which he made up on request). Just as Uncle Mack was set to bound without his pants from the bed of a lady whose hunter husband had suddenly returned, the train belched to a halt. Nervous, but emboldened, the group stepped from the carriages and met the local amateur media. A prepubescent reporter for the *Journal*, smiling with fear, pestered them with the question everyone wanted answered. From Emerson to Winnipeg to this city, from the most refined genius to the city's worst wretch, people wanted to know how these pilgrims had come through the rigorous border check unscathed. And it was true; they'd come with riches and livestock and glorious health, so it had been impossible to detain them, though the authorities tried. Always one for pranks, Uncle Mack began to groan and sway in the middle of his explanation to the reporter, who save the chance of race and geography was young enough to be his son, and declared that he was so tired he could feel himself turning yellow. The young man's eyes widened. A slow wave of laughter went through the crowd.

Soon, over the next few months, there would be little enough humor in their lives. Even those used to the abuses of settlement were surprised at how brutal the land was. They chose the northern areas of Alberta left alone by earlier settlers, areas overcome with brush and ankle-twisting swamps. Their southern corn, wheat, barley and oats could not be prompted to grow in this pauper's soil; it seemed to be armored in a crust of rock. Unwilling to let the land control them, the pioneers tackled the task of clearing with vigor. Armed only with axes and grub hoes, they tore through putrid foliage and trunks of spruce so large that Saul and a friend could sit and circle their legs around them without their feet touching. In the sulky heat of summers so parched they threw dust in your face at every step, Aster was plagued by voracious bullflies, primitive drainage, a lack of doctors and the burden of no good roads to and from the cities. The rain produced mud so thick they swore the children would drown in it. Winters were even worse. Not only could flesh freeze in less than one minute, but the cold seized what few paths they had slashed clear. After a week spent pinning chickens at Canada Packers, Harlan Porter returned home freezing, utter defeat written on his face. With the regret that characterized all his decisions, he commented to Saul: "Any country where a man's got to wear three pairs of socks ain't fit to live in."

Little did Harlan know how precisely that argument would be used to keep his friends from following him north. No one wanted them for neighbors, blacks bringing with them a plague of racial problems. The government decreed immigration akin to suicide; Negroes simply could not adapt to the rigorous northern climate. No one was more supportive of that view than groups who were themselves marginalized in the province: various women's groups including Eudora's pet project and the Imperial Order of Daughters of the Empire, and the French of Morinville, all of whom put forth petitions to the federal government. The Edmonton Board of Trade finally declared a large-scale campaign, using the neutral grounds of banks and downtown hotels to stock their petitions. In a perverse tactic, the board canvassed door to door to stress the urgency of the crisis and get more signatures. The campaign was troubled when several black settlers took to harassing the canvassers, Harlan and Saul among the few but ruthless disrupters.

Their intrusion prompted the secretary of the board to admonish the protesters for not recognizing what was done for the good of their own people (the smaller the black community, the better the privileges), and the petition continued to collect a wealth of signatures. The blacks of Aster were slandered in the newspapers, which assured readers that every measure was being taken to stall their immigration.

And yet, despite hard social and climatic conditions, the settlers found much to love in their small piece of the West. It was lush with water and grass, never lacking for timber. Their isolation gave them the gift of a close-knit community. They built their own school of hand-hewn logs and wooden shingles. Some even supported their families through hours of construction or service in Edmonton. But when they heard of government tactics to thwart new black immigration (including the deployment of a black doctor to lecture on the horrors of Canadian life), they were weary. And when they heard the migration had ceased completely, they were weary. They watched their boys get rejected for war service, only to be accepted the second time around, and they were weary. They watched Harlan buy the horse that had supposedly killed cowboy John Ware, and watched it die trying to escape its pen. They watched the Depression devastate nearby small towns, and then their own. The farms collapsed. Saul Porter's family took great pains to survive, scouring fields for metal, bottles, anything of value. People left to be educated or employed in Edmonton, or returned to the States. The Second World War opened the town entirely, the line of its founders extinguished, and now it is the Aster of Samuel's time.

Porter ended his story with distaste, clearly mourning that ruined, irretrievable Aster whose hardships had roused purpose and fellowship in the community. For a minute he muttered to himself, glancing around with an intensity that set off a wave of nervous movement. He collected himself, smiling at no one in particular, and his wife looked at Maud and said, in an attempt to change the subject, "Which is the more painful—your broken leg or your father's illness?"

Akosua was of that clumsy, self-conscious sort who ends up offending when meaning to console. All in the same breath, she managed to condole with Maud about her father but still imply that Maud was in the wrong for not going to his sickbed. She also suggested that perhaps father Adu Darko was dying of grief for his absent daughter. Her assumptions about Maud's father were annoying and intrusive.

But Akosua soon appealed to Samuel's sense of humor, and he took pleasure in the crass and thoughtless insults tucked like trapdoors in all she said. The twins, too, seemed amused, every few minutes laughing out loud. Only when Maud mentioned the Porter children did things become outwardly funny.

"Lot of the children are from my first wife, who died," said Porter.

Akosua made a noise of incredulity. "Eh! You think it is all for me? Do I look so old? Believe it or not, the good Lord has been more merciful than the two of you have been today!" She gave a restrained laugh. "Have I lost my knees already, at my age?"

Samuel and Maud instinctively looked at each other, as much to say, *How old is this woman, anyway?* Chloe skulked toward the only empty chair. So casually the company missed it, she gave Yvette a guarded glance; dismayed, Samuel watched Yvette sit where Chloe's eyes positioned her.

Mrs. Porter, who, in Maud's eyes, had spent the whole visit tricking them into paying her attention, stuttered once her desires were realized. She licked her lips, and her laugh became dry and plaintive. She spoke as though she feared what her nervousness would prompt her to blurt out next and yet could not stop talking. Samuel liked her fidgety cricket's hands, and the way she acknowledged their attention, like a child at a recital. It astounded him that this woman, so accomplished in the cruel art of insults, was really just another washed-up housewife, nervous under her husband's eye. Samuel searched her face for irony, finding none. When she attempted to speak Twi with Samuel (who responded with boyish gusto), Maud put a stop to it.

Mrs. Porter retorted, "This is bad-o. When it is a woman herself who wants to kill her heritage, then the children have black days ahead."

Maud's surprise mingled with a singular dislike for this woman. She was livid, trying to think up a response, but Saul himself silenced his wife with one wield of the eye. Akosua flinched.

The conversation became a low-key exchange between Saul, Maud and the reluctant Samuel, who felt genuine remorse that his talk with Akosua had been cut short. Letting his eyes linger on her face, he rebuked himself for the haste with which he had first judged her. It was true, there was a fastidiousness in her features that was decidedly un–Gold Coast, but perhaps that gave her more appeal, for her beauty was an afterthought, acknowledged only by that brand of man who could willingly admit when he was wrong. And so those privy to her grace were more shaken than they would be had it been blatant. Only when she gave him a questioning look did Samuel realize he'd been staring at her. He shifted his eyes to see Yvette looking at him.

The men went outside while the women cleared the table. Among men, Samuel was a much more voracious speaker. He thanked Porter for cutting the grass and, despite weeks of distrust, even confessed to his success in business, thanking Porter again for the silent role he'd played. Porter nodded absently, as though scanning Samuel's chatter for something of worth. Samuel sensed his indifference and grew quiet, following Porter through the yard. As they walked, Porter kept his eyes on his house in the distance, which in the afternoon light looked so worn it might have been the detritus of a fire. Even from their position they heard the wind in its cracks. Porter skirted the ankle-high grass with little effort, while Samuel found he was winded by the time they reached Maud's laundry line at the edge of the property. Four pristine, damp sheets weighed the line down, and as the men ducked through they found them hard with the freak summer frost. Porter coughed, spat in the grass and pulled a crude, yellowed pipe from the pocket of his striped jacket. From a separate pocket he drew a tobacco pouch, and Samuel watched as with shaky hands he crushed the roots into the stem. The pipe was a primitive one, just like Jacob's from the early days, and the slow recognition of this put Samuel on guard. Porter indulged in the sweet fumes, his eyes closing ruminatively before he jerked the pipe at Samuel, who declined. For a time they stood in what appeared to be a moment of complicity, but Samuel intuited a prelude to graver business.

Porter chinned toward his house. "See that? For years that house and this one owned Aster. When they were both just log cabins with off-kitchens. Not one thing was decided without permission from one of these houses. This was before the others came and split it into districts and what have you. Aster was run *by* us and *for* us."

"You can find no greater admirer of the early Aster than myself. Never mind this nonsense about districts. I moved here because I thought nothing would have changed. Maud said to me, she said, 'One should not dream when he is awake,' but I brought them anyway." Samuel looked at Porter for approval.

Porter sucked on his pipe without the least sign of having heard. "These houses were the heart of Aster life, and my father built mine, Jeff Snick the other. Weren't much to look at back then, but look at them now. Snick was more of a handyman than Daddy, and so yours has the more attachments. But they're both good homes, and it broke my heart to see yours fall to pieces at the hands of bums. Sickening, stupid lodgers who didn't treat the house no better than if it were a way station on the way to a better slum. It was even a brothel, once, run by some harlot widow. I was damn glad when Jacob turned up—he looked just the man to right things, you know? And he was, he really was." The wonder in Porter's voice was genuine. He overturned his pipe and looked Samuel in the eye. "Your uncle was the best kind of man there was."

Samuel gave a hesitant laugh. Porter appraised him.

"Life's a low-down shame shouldn't happen to a dog. And your uncle's life ended worse than that. I was here, caring for him after the first stroke happened, then I cleaned his house some after the second stroke took him away."

Samuel started at his words. He wasn't aware Jacob had endured a first stroke that hadn't killed him, that there had been a window in which to make amends. He turned coldly to Porter. "So."

With provoking slowness, Porter thumbed the mouth of his pipe to crush out the last embers. He gave it a vigorous shake and returned it to the appropriate pocket. Only when Samuel reached the edge of his rage was Porter prompted to say something. "Did you get the quote I sent you for the property? A little low, I know, but your house ain't in the best shape, and now's a good time to sell."

"Eh! Do not fool with me." Samuel's voice cracked with suppressed anger. He resisted the urge to point a finger in Porter's face. "It's *you* who needs to give *me* land. You think you can stand here and make an ass of me? I have seen the records. Oh, I have seen them, brother. How dare you demand what you've already stolen?" Samuel walked a few steps away, then returned, shaking his finger. "Watch yourself, eh? You are my elder, but you watch yourself." Samuel began to walk away again when he was arrested by Porter's voice.

"Hear me out."

Brought almost to tears by his anger, Samuel walked back to Porter. He finally abandoned his vague notion that Porter was irreproachable, the naïve idea that people who've endured hardships are cured from causing harm themselves.

"Your uncle left me that land in his will." Porter spoke as though it was an irrefutable fact. "When I called you about your inheritance, I was referring to the house and the few acres around it."

"Is that so?" said Samuel, mockery in his voice. "Where is this so-called will?"

"I handed it over to the town officials. And, I know you ain't going to believe this, but when I requested to have it back so you and I could mull over it together, they told me they misplaced it among paper-work, and why don't I come back in a few days time. Well, I went back, but they still couldn't find it. Never tried again. But you don't believe me, do you?"

Samuel made an incredulous sound with his lips. Did this man think he was an imbecile? He brushed a fly from his cheek.

"Listen, that will kept them from turning your place into a heritage site. I turned it in for you. I did it because Jacob had so much integrity that it's a rare man who wouldn't die to bring about his last wishes."

Samuel felt this last phrase was calculated to sting him, he who had refused to view the body and dispensed with the forty days' ceremony. "So then why are you now trying to take the land and the house from me, if Jacob willed it so?"

Porter pursed his lips. "You have to admit you ain't done the soundest job of keeping up the place." He paused. "You'll be well com-pensated. You surprise me, Samuel. Your uncle had such integrity. Go to the authorities if you don't buy my story about the will. Or don't, what do I care? But to call me a thief? To call a thief the man who cared for your uncle as he died?"

"A man who had no right, *no right,* who didn't even call me after the first stroke, if indeed he hasn't made the whole thing up—"

"It's on *your* conscience, Tyne. It's on your conscience. That's all I got to say." Walking away, Porter paused. "But think about the quote. I'll by no means be as generous later."

Samuel restrained himself from calling the old man names. Watching Porter return to the house, *Samuel's* house, to continue the afternoon as though nothing had happened, Samuel grew furious.

Twiddling the bowler in his hands, he set his jaw. But trying to suppress his anger only worsened it, and he looked blindly around him for something to break. The sheets on the laundry line buckled in the wind, and in a lapse of feeling, as if watching another man act, he ripped down every single one. The thrumming sound of them falling pacified him a little, but it was only when he'd yanked down the line itself that he felt better.

But his relief didn't last long. Seeing the destruction he'd caused, Samuel felt astonished he could so lose control of himself. It also dawned on him how Maud would react, and this time her anger would be justified. The thought of quarreling with her made him anxious, and, in truth, he had no defense for actions he himself felt ashamed of. Gathering up the muddy sheets and the line, Samuel crept to the cellar and stuffed them behind a pile of old suitcases. He would deal with it later.

chapter SIXTEEN

I t didn't take long for Maud to notice Samuel's new blindness to
life. He seemed to navigate the days with indifference, and if he
sometimes grew irritable, he would catch himself and become
withdrawn again. Maud began to ignore him, and found in this way
she was able to tolerate his suspicions about her accident. One minute
she'd been standing on the shaky ladder, dusting, the next minute she
was on the floor with her daughters looking over her, too afraid to
touch her. But she would swear on the Bible her daughters had not
pushed her, and wondered what kind of a man Samuel could be not to
believe this.

Maud knew the twins felt his neglect, and she resolved to make up
for his lack of interest. She kept an eye on them, and when she discovered them drafting a letter to Ama, she offered to type it on the antique
machine exhumed from the attic. The girls were guarded at first, but
they accepted. Maud glowed with pleasure; taking after Eudora, Maud
had been running herself ragged in the need to be useful to other people. Besides helping the twins, Maud's greatest coup was doing for

Akosua Porter what she wished someone had done for her upon her arrival in Canada. Every day Maud could be found talking to Akosua in the Tyne kitchen, pontificating on the workings of Western society. Despite its rocky start, a lukewarm friendship had begun to develop between them. The alliance arose less from a mutual regard than from their shared lot as exiles, and on Maud's side it was even bolstered by a little pity. But they got along well enough. Maud told Akosua what to shop for, and donated some of her best clothes to the Porter cause, leaving herself a monk's wardrobe. When she attempted to raid the twins' closet so that the smallest Porters wouldn't go without, she was so badly rebuked that she went away guilty. She now offered to type their letter with such enthusiasm that it couldn't help but compensate for her earlier blunder.

Clearing a space on the huge oak table, Maud settled in behind the typewriter. She hated the way her leg felt in the cast, and the deadened sensation especially bothered her when she was sitting. Trying to ignore it, she focused on the task at hand, sipping tea as she leafed through the water-stained pages of the twins' letter.

It surprised her to find they were writing to Ama. And this was no small note of courtesy, but a missive already fifteen pages long, their exalted, almost religious prose written in both their handwriting. Maud's astonishment grew by the page. Leaving the typewriter idle, she read:

Objects seem to have a life of their own, they live and die like us, and have the power of motion. In a lot of ways, they are more decisive than people, who sit sit sit their lives away, and not in protest, but because they are in-ambitious and inert. This is a lesson. Our belongings keep moving by themselves. There is object will, and there is human will.

Frowning, Maud thumbed a few pages ahead.

We so wanted to go to the Stampede. We read a history of it last week and are writing one ourself. Here's a piece: One gargantuan spectacle, the Calgary Stampede was the brainchild of Guy Weadick, a young

New York–born cowboy with a knack for turning dust to diamonds.
With a mind overgrown with ideas, and a cash call so minutely tuned
it sprung the locks off all coffers within a ninety-mile radius, he
wheedled the infamous Big Four into putting up money to fund this
six-day odyssey.

    That's just our start, we're obsessed. What do you think?

And further down she read:

Doctors are too overrated in our day—who can cure the human geom-
etry? We have an obligation to it, it is our poetry and our undoing, too.
The fireplace breathes ash in our face and we call it lethal, a mirage to
replace the greatest beauty. Mimicry, that is beauty, too.

Reading the letter to the end, Maud sat in silence, fingering the pages. She didn't know what to think. She tried to recall her own childhood, her private thoughts at twelve, but couldn't remember anything. The twins' letter seemed strange. Was this poetry? Had they copied some of this from a book?

"Chloe, Yvette?" yelled Maud, and received no answer. Rising from her chair, she dispensed with the doctor's advice and made her way up the stairs, fumbling with her crutches. She reached their room only to find the twins had gone outside. The curtains were still untied, making the furniture in the room look overcast. But the beds were expertly made, so tight you could bounce a pin off the middles, and she felt proud at their tidiness. Maud hobbled to the window to draw the curtains and, by the light that trickled through the trees, made out papers on Ama's old bed.

The first juice-stained pages were earlier drafts of the letter Maud was typing downstairs. Brushing those aside, Maud read others. They were all drafts of the same letter, each a meticulous fifteen pages long, some with only a few edited sentences and others with entire pages inked out.

Their need for perfection almost brought Maud to tears. The twins had lost the only person they had ever made an effort to impress. Putting everything back in its place, Maud resolved not to mention her discovery. She believed it would only make Samuel more reticent.

To give Maud credit, Samuel *had* turned a blind eye to the Tyne misfortunes. He'd begun to spend his off time with Ray Frank. They would take long walks along the wheat field, and Samuel grew used to its roiling electricity on windy days, its dusty smell, the way it gave depth to everything around it.

"The sky is so large it is as if we move like pawns under it," said Samuel, leaning beside Ray on the wire that harnessed the property. He smiled. "Like the eye of God."

"Amen," said Ray, scratching the last of his tobacco from his threadbare shirt pocket. He thumbed some into his bottom lip; his speech thickened. "Asked Porter about my superplant yet?"

The question had become part of their routine. Samuel shook his head. He wanted to ask Ray about Jacob's will, but was afraid of sounding suspicious or accusatory.

Ray spat an amiable distance from where they stood. "What do I need with a witch doctor's recipe, right? I can find my own." They stared off into the monotony of the fields, talking little.

In truth, Samuel considered the will to be the lesser of two evils haunting him. So he asked about it to avoid having to speak of the other. "Porter has told me something—*two* things. He said he has given the town council Jacob's will and that they have lost it, and also that most of my land was left to him in the will."

"Now I don't know about that, Samuel." Ray spat. "I personally don't deal with those things, property lines, records and such. But to set you at ease I'll find out who does and get you the real story. Leave it to me."

Samuel felt grateful. "I appreciate it. Oh, and thank you so much for pushing my business license through."

"That's what I'm here for." Ray winked.

Yet another wink, thought Samuel. He felt as if he had stumbled upon a town of conspirators. He smiled. But he now felt so beholden to Ray that to mention his second concern seemed like a breach of boundaries. So he held his tongue, and resigned himself to suffering alone.

For he thought of it as suffering, this feeling like a plank in his chest, and recognized with bitter irony that of all the misfortunes of the last month he was bothered most by the one that mattered least. His analytic disposition allowed him to block out most problems. This is why it disillusioned him to acknowledge the vulgarity growing in him.

Since Maud had made a project of Akosua Porter, Samuel had had no rest. Akosua would appear at any hour, interrupting meals without apology, as if she herself had no boundaries and so didn't understand them in others. At first he'd felt exasperated, like one obliged to give up his seat to a lady on a train, but when it appeared that this was no temporary pet project, Samuel felt a rage that baffled even him.

He'd pace the cluttered bedroom, with Maud's vague eyes on him, yelling, "I do not go putting my mouth in other people's affairs, but can a man not own his own silence? Must he be overrun by the talk of women every hour of his peace!"

"You see their poverty and yet you worry for your peace," Maud would say. "Can you not see that a poor woman gives birth to ashes? That without God's grace, me, you and the children could have been just like the Porters? Shame on you!"

On testier nights, Samuel would mutter, "Either that woman goes or I do."

"Then you'd better have your shoes resoled, for if God is righteous, he will give you friends like yourself, and you will wander your life in the streets with no one to show you charity."

After a while, Samuel realized he enjoyed his anger. He took pleasure imagining scenarios before bedtime, staggering humiliations in which Akosua conceded his strength. But when he rose in the morning and saw her helping Saul groom their properties, Samuel felt a kind of fascination. Just the sight of Akosua in her field clothes, or in her colorful church dresses, gave him an irritable feeling of confusion. He found himself waiting for her hated visits. When she did appear, always just when he'd managed to forget her, he felt a rush of fear, followed by anger. Could she not see she wasn't wanted in his house?

In her tedious, sympathetic conversation, Akosua tried not to insult him, and at the few blunders she did recognize she made pained faces. In this way Samuel began to listen with an apprehensive pity, afraid more for her sake than his own that she would say something mortifying.

"Kwame, oh, he's backward," said Akosua, referring to her son. "You say, 'Don't pee there,' and he pees there. He's like a deaf man. You tell him one thing and he does another. You say, 'Don't walk in the fire,' he walks in the fire. If there's an accident, *sth*. Bet ten hundred cedis Kwame is there. And it is not as if he is bad, just misfortunate. He is one with whom misfortune is a friend."

"A good boy prone to misfortune," Samuel repeated safely.

Akosua scoffed. "Heh—you are all mouth and no ears. Is that not what I said?" Remembering herself, she flinched, as much apology as she could muster.

When she spoke about herself she did so with an enunciative caution that really seemed more like stifled pleasure. She was at her most natural then, and despite himself Samuel found even his thoughts slipping into the old vernacular. They spoke in a patois of English and Twi, lowering their voices and smiling to each other lest they be caught in the act. Saul was never mentioned. Neither wanted to spoil the delicacy of these moments by talk of what was, after all, only politics. Samuel felt ludicrous, flirting with this woman he despised, but he couldn't deny the odd pleasures it gave him. Before long he had to concede that Mrs. Porter was a charming little bird, despite her effrontery, and Samuel always felt a pang of regret when Maud interrupted.

When Akosua left the room, Samuel would go somber, feeling keenly disliked. He would sit and ruminate on what they'd said before concluding that Akosua was the most severe and illogical creature on earth. Then he would resolve to waste no more thoughts on her. Yet the more he tried to cure his mind of her, the worse he'd wake during his working hours to find he'd been thinking of her. It disturbed him. He began to attack his work with the zeal of his early days, but to no avail. He could not fend off thoughts of this woman any more than he could enjoy them without guilt. He often wondered that he had ever found her plain. Her pimples hadn't damaged her beauty; conversely, her blemishes alone kept too saintly a face human. Akosua soon distracted him from his only other obsessions: Jacob's will, glory and death. Her voice, her wrinkling little nose, everything aroused him. On the night of his greatest humiliation, he sat locked in his study long after the house had dimmed, touching himself until his shame grew so intense he went to bed unsatisfied. A history had passed since Maud had touched him. Turning to her now would be like asking for an unkind favor. So he slept unsated and woke in a state of agitation. This was the measure of his days. Akosua was a kind of awakening for him; he felt both stronger and weaker, sadder but simpler in his thoughts, until finally a burning image of her within him compelled people to treat him better. Or so he believed. For during this era of fever his business matured, townsfolk smiled at him in the road, and even Maud began to relax her testy silences.

He sensed the chaos in the house but was unable to engage in it. In a dirty singlet and a pair of terry shorts, he took to going to his study during the night. The shorts, tight on the buttocks but loose up front, shifted as he walked, rubbing him into such a state that some nights he barely made it to his study to undo them. Later, when he'd emerge cold from the ash of his fantasies, he would sit and bitterly curse the woman who had led him to this lechery. But even anger and guilt could not sever routine. Only when he thought he'd been discovered was he able to stop. That night, grown daring, he'd left his study door open. And just when he was getting somewhere, he felt a shock of fear and went dead in his hand. Holding his breath, he strained to see into the darkness of the hallway. Finally convinced he was alone, he'd nevertheless learned his lesson. But every act has its punishment: that night he dreamt he had mastur-bated in public, in broad daylight, as a crowd of people streamed through the intersection. He awoke as though slapped, his heart spastic. Maud slept undisturbed beside him. He rose to get a glass of water and the dim light under his daughters' door horrified him. His night-wandering ended.

The next morning, in a move that showed Samuel he was mistaken about the truce with his wife, Maud complained about the heat in the house.

"This is not the tropics—the heat isn't free," she said at the break-fast table, not meeting his eye. "Keep this up and when winter comes we'll be freezing, with the electric company coming around twice a week to break our kneecaps. To think it was so hot I couldn't *sleep.* That's *never* happened to me."

Samuel studied his wife. There didn't seem to be any innuendo in her tone, but the twins kept their eyes down. "Well, if you did not sleep, then you are a great actress. You snored so loud you kept the girls up." And he looked meaningfully their way.

Maud was pleased with this, for it gave her license to go on. Touching her halo of rollers, she said, "It's as if you're in your own pri-vate hell and you're trying to roast us with you."

Samuel at last understood his transparency, that perhaps what people were responding to was not his hidden love for Akosua, but his sad agitation. He glanced around the table, sensing an air of complic-ity that excluded him.

Maud finally vented what might have been occupying those three untouchable minds. "What, pray tell, has happened to our sheets and our clothesline?"

The synchrony of their heads turning toward him seemed re-hearsed. With a sense of wonder, Samuel told the most sedate lie of his life: "I do not know." And they seemed to believe him.

Minutes later Maud questioned him again, and he knew she hadn't been outwitted. But something in him couldn't admit to what he'd done, so ashamed was he of his boyish fit of anger. Maud already thought he'd lost his mind. And how to explain *why* he'd been angry without talking about his problem with Porter? So, contrary to all logic, he told an even more erratic lie.

"Did you ever think that perhaps the crows have sunk it? That the crows downed it and that the Porters cleared it from our yard for courtesy's sake? Why are you asking a man, anyway? When I need to change the spark plugs in the Volvo, do I run to you, a woman?" The longer he prattled, the more he convinced himself of his indignation, and only the subtle look between the twins silenced him. "What are you making eyes at, eh?" he spat in their direction. "Eh? Man suffers through woman, you mark it. Man suffers through woman." Immediately sorry at having implicated the twins, he picked at his eggs in agitation.

Maud's voice was even. "The Porters know nothing about it—I asked them. It was Akosua who suggested I ask you about it. Like maybe she'd seen you move it or something."

Samuel prickled at the mention of that name. He couldn't believe the hypocrisy of that hag; it showed a lack of dignity he was unused to in a woman. Derisively, he said, "I am sure poor trash makes for trustworthy neighbors."

"A spokesman for the Ray Frank campaign now, are you?"

"I am a spokesman for none but myself."

Maud gave him a sickened smile. The rest of the meal was painful with repressed anger, and more than once Samuel had to restrain himself from shouting at the secretive twins. Their eye game was trying his nerves.

When they reconvened for dinner, even the twins were talking. They recounted writing fifteen pages apiece on some new voluminous project. Maud looked uneasily at them, but declared that she'd given Akosua Porter an in-depth lesson on nutrition that afternoon. And Samuel was in such good spirits that even the mention of Akosua's name didn't bother him. A record player that had been making the route of Edmonton's repair shops had finally found its cure at Tyne Electronics. Its owner, an old widower of the ranching era, had taken to playing his dead wife's Mozart over the machine's golden ear. When the player had broken and refused to be fixed, the old man had suffered a grief no more navigable than his wife's death. Last week he'd made the dispirited drive to Aster and, seeing Samuel behind the counter, put down the machine with the finality of a skeptic. Samuel, pleased that his miraculous hands were being lauded as far as Edmonton, treated this project with extra diligence, and that very day he had the old apparatus singing again. The widower had cried when Samuel turned it on. He gave Samuel a historic tip, carrying the player out as if it were a newborn child.

The story delighted his family, and each twin ventured a failed description of what the old rancher must have looked like. Samuel laughed harder than he had to, to atone for his behavior that morning. Maud seemed pleased with his new attention. Things were going so amiably that Samuel left the table in the middle of the meal to avoid seeing it end badly.

In his study, Samuel ruminated over the last of Jacob's palm wine. He'd kept the bottle in his desk drawer underneath a nest of wires, and when he drank from it, he thought the alcohol tasted of metal. He sank into the cracked chair. To his mind, the man of the last few days, that lecher sick on desire and blunt to all the chaos of life, had vanished. His second adolescence had finally come to an end, and he felt in full the weight of his problems, which, like gracious war brides, had waited for his trauma to be over before throwing themselves upon him again. Samuel, resigned, toasted this last drink to an age that no longer suited him.

There was an apprehensive knock at the door, and he hesitated before calling out an answer. Maud slipped in, clutching the sides of her mauve dress in an anxious way. Her eyes had a quiet determination that put Samuel on guard. He feared a reprisal of their earlier conversation, and felt too tired to be evasive.

She sat on a pile of boxes near the bookshelf, and when she spoke her voice wavered. "How long," she said, "do you intend to ignore your family?"

Samuel was relieved. Having somewhat come to terms with his behavior of the last week, he was even eager to talk about it.

"Because I really think that this family is on the edge of some minor collapse."

Maud was burningly embarrassed, as though annoyed that her sophisticated feelings had been reduced to a cliché. Samuel found her vulnerability endearing, and let her go on.

"I hate this," she said, biting her lip. "I hate having to talk about them like this, behind their backs, but . . . you haven't seen those girls, Samuel. With all their letters. I think they're really hurting for our guidance, like we've been neglectful. And I think they're really suffering for a friend right now—they've got each other so tied in knots that it's not healthy. They need some air." She frowned. "I really think we should ask Ama back."

Samuel nearly choked. It was eons since he'd thought of the girl. "How long has she been gone?"

"Two weeks," said Maud. "How easily men forget what isn't right in their lap."

It occurred to Samuel that though Ama might be a good influence on his daughters, his daughters would not be so good for Ama. He didn't feel confident she would want to return, or even that she should. "They left her in the Athabasca. She might have died."

"I know, and that's terrible, Samuel, but they're children. They're troubled. And maybe we haven't been much good as models lately."

He accepted the slight in silence, brooding. Children, certainly, but unlike any children he'd known. He realized that their acumen and their advanced reading habits made him a more rigorous judge of their actions than he otherwise might have been. Still, he found it hard to reconcile the many accidents that seemed to happen in their presence. "They are children, but they are brighter than some adults."

Maud nodded. "It's this idleness and neglect that brings out the worst in them. They need companionship and guidance."

"They have each other. And they have had you."

"Maybe that's not enough." Maud's lip trembled. For a time they sat in silence. When Maud spoke again her voice had lost its confidential tone. "Let's call that Ouillet woman. Let's get Ama back."

Samuel frowned. As much as he disliked that grandmother, one did not have the right to take the child from her. "I do not know," he said.

"If you only knew, Samuel, how much they need her now." There was real pleading in Maud's voice; she had set aside all of her pride.

Samuel exhaled. He tapped his fingernail on the glass before him, shifting in his chair.

"All right," he said finally. "Just let me finish this drink."

chapter SEVENTEEN

If, as Eudora believed, a house is the direct reflection of its owner, then Mrs. Ouillet was an eccentric but innately beautiful woman. Driving up her narrow gravel drive, Samuel could not help but admire the gabled, towering house behind its veil of cedars. Painted a delicate blue, its turret was circled with damp, imported vines. Before it lay a stunning grove: glossy berries overhanging an elaborate trellis, rows of flowering cabbage.

Mrs. Ouillet had sounded curt, if not a little put out, on the telephone when Samuel called. It was all the same to her whether Ama stayed or not, she simply wanted them to choose one. "I can't take these comings and goings," she'd said. "At my age, you come to value your peace above all else."

Samuel helped Ama pack her belongings and carried the bag out to the car as she followed behind him. Though she didn't speak, Samuel could see she was apprehensive.

"You are certain you want to return?" he said.

"Oh, yes," she said, nodding. "I was getting so tired of being at

Grandmère's. She hates to speak in English and I only know a little French."

As they drove off, Samuel continued to reassure her. "I understand the twins have written you a mountain of letters. They have missed you so much."

Ama looked a little disbelieving.

"I must warn you, though," Samuel continued. "You will find Maud a little altered from when you left. No, no, do not worry, she has only broken her leg. But she is housebound, and what, what is it . . . cranky." He winked at her (it was catching, with all the winking in Aster). "So beware."

Ama gave him a wry smile, which Samuel intuited to mean that Maud seemed born cranky. He laughed and patted Ama on the shoulder.

To Ama's disappointment, the Tyne house was exactly as she'd left it. Not that it could change much in two weeks, that which had resisted true change for six decades.

The twins' welcome depressed her even more. They stood with their arms at their sides, defying her affection with wary looks. Their stillness reminded Ama of those strange, vagrant deer that wander into the city and petrify at the sight of men. Neither Mr. nor Mrs. Tyne noticed anything wrong.

But Ama was determined. Yvette, especially, seemed to be giving her pointed looks, convincing Ama she'd only to befriend Chloe to bring them both around. She followed them upstairs and, sitting on her bed to unpack, watched them with cautious eyes.

They seemed to have grown thinner, their angular cheeks giving them a severe, almost mean look. The thought occurred to her that perhaps their parents had starved them as punishment for trying to drown her, and Ama felt bad both on their behalf and for having such a thought in the first place.

The twins sat across from each other on Yvette's cot, twining their fingers with string to play cat's cradle. Chloe had her back to Ama, but Yvette's face was visible, and she gave Ama nervous, inviting looks. Ama stopped unpacking and sat on the floor beside their bed.

"My grandmother's crazy." Ama flushed, not knowing why she'd said this. Her father had cautioned her to be discreet with family matters, and she'd always taken great pains to keep the truth from her friends. The twins didn't acknowledge she'd spoken at all. Ashamed, Ama picked lint from the carpet. She stretched her long legs under the bed and, feeling paper with her feet, leaned over to see what it was. There were hundreds of letters.

So they did exist. Ama couldn't keep from sounding grateful. "Your dad told me you wrote me a million letters. Why didn't you send any? I was so lonely there."

Chloe turned to look at her, an unsettling smile on her face. "Oh, yes, we wrote a million letters, a billion letters, a trillion." Her smile deepened when she glanced at her sister.

Looking as though she would cry, Yvette said, "Oh, yes. We wrote you so many beautiful letters you could paper the Sistine Chapel with them. They're so beautiful Seneca would have wept. They're of such sublime artistry that if we'd sent them to Pontius Pilate, he would have had Barabbas crucified instead."

"They're so beautiful," continued Chloe, dropping the string in her lap, "they predate the Rosetta Stone. They're so beautiful that monks have wept, treacherous men have been slain, and fallen women became sirens in their next lives." Her voice rose in a falsetto. "They're so beautiful that . . . they're so beautiful . . ." Her theatrics made her forget what she'd intended to say. She shrugged. "They're just that beautiful."

Ama grew nervous; she hated their riddles. She turned to Yvette. "Can I read them?"

"No," said Chloe. She gave her sister a warning look. "We'd rather burn at the stake than put them into your philistine hands."

Ama tried her best not to look hurt. She was tired of being mistreated, though. "You know, you really can't keep t-treating me like this."

In stuttering, Ama made a fatal mistake.

Laughing, Chloe bit her lip and said, "P-p-p-puh-p-please accept our d-d-duh-d-d-deepest ap-p-pologies. W-w-wuh-we m-m-mean no h-h-ha-h-harm. Accept our d-d-d-duh-d-deepest con-c-cuh-condolences f-for y-y-yuh-y-your sp-speech p-problem."

Ama stood up. "Stop it! I'll tell on you."

Chloe made a face of mock horror. "T-t-t-tell on us? Y-you'll n-need a t-translator, the w-way you t-talk!"

Ama rushed from the room. In the dark, cloistered bathroom, she splashed water on her burning face. Why had she believed things with the twins would be different? Why had she made that assumption? Still, something in her believed Yvette was capable of friendship, something wouldn't condemn her entirely. Wiping her face, Ama went to read in the Iron Lung. There, she fell asleep, waking hours later to the sound of dinner. Rubbing her eyes, she went downstairs.

Mrs. Tyne rose to fetch Ama's plate from the oven. "The twins said you were sleeping. You looked so tired, I thought we shouldn't wake you."

Seeing how awkward she was on her crutches, Ama raced to help her. Mrs. Tyne handed her the plate and gave her a brusque pat on the arm. "Good to have you back," she said.

Mrs. Tyne lowered herself into her seat. She looked strange, half of her hair seared straight by a hot comb, the other half an Afro awaiting transformation. Her skin had a slight sheen on it, and she looked sad and a little harassed. She was arguing with her husband.

"They will master every future household," Mr. Tyne was saying, his bowler placed neatly in his lap as he ate. "Computers will reign so wholly no man will lift a finger again, even to scratch his ass."

"Your language," said Mrs. Tyne, nodding toward the children. "One should not dream when he is awake, Samuel."

Mr. Tyne made an exasperated noise. "If you women ran the world, we should never have escaped the Dark Ages."

"If progress is about being reckless, Samuel, then you're right."

Ama glanced at the twins. They ate in silence, not looking at anyone. Only when their parents began to speak of how to manage things in the fall, did Chloe enter the conversation.

"Wuh-w-we like your ch-ch-choice of the E-E-Ed-Edmonton s-school. We-we-we've h-heard g-g-great things about it."

Ama flushed. Chloe elaborated on her praise for the school in Edmonton, stuttering the whole time. Yvette watched her sister with a vague smile on her face. Mrs. Tyne flinched. But probably because the twins rarely spoke, she encouraged Chloe with little nods. Mr. Tyne, after listening for some time, asked his daughter just what was wrong with her voice.

"N-nuh-nothing," she said, as though his question was absurd.

Mr. Tyne scoffed and dropped his fork. He looked around him, astonished at being taken for a fool. But Mrs. Tyne gave him a look that said it was only a game, and he picked up his fork and resumed eating. Ama kept her head down for the remainder of the meal.

Over the next few days, she avoided the twins. Ama spent her days in the dulling sun, or, sometimes, in the duller company of Mrs. Tyne. They would sit in the dusty kitchen, cooking and baking, until the Porter woman arrived. On those days Mrs. Tyne would adopt a reverent voice and teach them something both already knew. Mrs. Porter sat rigid as a schoolgirl, and like a schoolgirl, she'd make faces behind Maud's back. Ama felt bad for Mrs. Tyne, and would have told her if she hadn't been taught not to interfere in the world of adults.

One day, as soon as Mrs. Porter had gone, Mrs. Tyne began to twitter on about the minor details of her life as if they mattered. Ama listened with a polite smile, waiting with a guilty conscience for any interruption. Hearing the postman arrive, Ama ran out to fetch the mail.

The only piece of mail was a small white card addressed to Maud Yaaba Adu Darko. Ama brought it into the kitchen.

"I think this is for you, but I'm not sure," said Ama, handing the card to Mrs. Tyne. Mrs. Tyne was thawing kenkey for the evening meal, unwrapping the cornmeal from long green leaves. She motioned for Ama to drop the mail on the table, but turning to glance at it, she asked the girl to bring it in to her. With clumsy hands she fumbled to open the card.

Even after scanning the news, Mrs. Tyne stood unmoved. Indeed, what was most strange in her face was not so much a single expression, but the many suggested by her calm.

Suddenly Mrs. Tyne's face softened, and she began to cry in the suppressed, ashamed way of hard women.

Out of fear, Ama began to cry, too.

"He's alive," said Mrs. Tyne in a parched voice. "My father was sick, but now he's alive."

She sounded relieved. But also mortified, as if realizing that these past weeks she'd been counting on him to die. There was no malice in this feeling. It was simply that he had already died for her. His sickness had made his death seem inevitable, logical, even desired. Her prayers for a swift and easy death meant she had finally forgiven him. She didn't want to go to his deathbed—she just wanted his death. After all these years, he owed her that favor. But he couldn't even do this for her, and so she saw his recovery not as one last incredible act of will, but as a final betrayal against her.

Maud smiled sadly at Ama. "My father was a hard man. A practical one," she conceded, "but a hard one." About to continue in this vein, she thought the better of it. "As a girl I was just as fierce and crafty as the twins. Me and Philomena Keteku used to go down to the river, which—and this is going to sound silly—well, it's so much more what water is supposed to be than any other water I've ever seen. You have your Athabasca, your Bow, your creeks, even the Pacific over the mountains—all nothing. Nothing is like our own rivers. Philomena had a brother, Eric—he and his friends would find a timber log and we'd all use it to float on the river.

"The four of us—Philomena, Eric, Kojo and I—we would all rush down when the turtles were out. Oh, you should have seen these creatures, at least ninety pounds, humongous. And it would take all four of us to tip one, but once it was tipped, that was it. You could stand two hours and watch it struggle to turn itself. Eh, we were mean-o. But you had to be careful—if one kicked you, you had a sore for a month. I know one boy who died when his sore didn't heal."

Mrs. Tyne spoke of being her mother's only daughter, but one of twenty-three of her father's, talked of her schoolgirl friends and of the flock of chickens she'd tended, who, as soon as they saw her coming over the hill would rush en masse to meet her. Each had such a distinct personality, she claimed, that she'd named them and groomed them according to their various tastes. She'd even organized a system to be followed in her absence, the robust ones carrying the burden of the tubercular, to trick her father from distinguishing the sick from the fit. But he still killed them.

"We couldn't go hungry," said Maud, "so that was the end of that."

And so it was, on that strange afternoon, that Ama and Maud began to truly like each other.

chapter EIGHTEEN

S amuel was the kind of scholar who learned best through elusion. School had taught only complicated problems, until lessons of common sense seemed insignificant. What distinguished genius was not only talent, but an ability to strike at the heart of a given thing, to see with the prophet's eye what has eluded others. In his Gold Coast years, Samuel earned the reputation of a savant. No one who spoke to him outside of class could reconcile this doting, shy boy to the computing genius of the classroom. Some were so skeptical that they made the long walk to the university to watch. On these days, his spiteful teacher couldn't help but relish his prodigy's talents, throwing the most difficult equations at Samuel and smirking as though responsible for the boy's brilliance. No one could keep up with Samuel, and when asked about the roots of his genius, Samuel would reply in a way that made people feel they were being made fun of: "I think of the simplest, most likely way to do something, and I then perform its opposite." He could solve no problems except those of intense difficulty; the easiest ones eluded him. Only when he was befuddled, almost painfully inundated, would the answer come to him like a slap, and he'd reel at the clarity of it. It was as though once he was humbled by his human limitations, God relented and gave him the answer. And so study abroad, seen as a great blessing since only the most rigorous school could challenge him, was also viewed as treachery, for once again what was best about the nation was being plundered.

Now, his youth over, feeling old, Samuel sat in his shop struggling with an oil meter and was struck by the magnitude of his failure. Sure, he had accomplished more than thought possible for a black man of his class, had even, in terms of his background, lived beyond his supposed potential, but he had always hated social constraints that told men what they could and could not do, and wondered now what had happened to his resolve. He hadn't worked on his rudimentary computer in days, low on confidence, unable even to look at it. He'd always fancied himself a modern Charles Babbage, the man who would put an autonomous, free-thinking machine in every home. Computers had already proved themselves useful: had the Allies not just won a war through technical accuracy? Computers had cracked codes in enemy communications, decrypting what passed between the Germans and the Japanese. Radar intercepted enemy aircraft. Guns were calibrated more accurately. And all of it made possible through the descendants of the Industrial Revolution.

What had happened to Samuel's ambitions? His desire to free people from tedious tasks, to leave their minds open for higher pursuits? Samuel suspected he knew what had happened: family. Maud thought so little of his idea, and made such fun of him, that he'd begun to despise it himself. He set the prototype aside and turned his eye to more practical matters: His correspondence course with the National Radio Institute.

So it seemed absurd when the next unit in his course was Computer-Building Basics. Over an agitated two nights, Samuel crafted a prototype of vacuum tubes and binary switches with the slow, methodical logic of a grandfather. For twenty-three hours he wrenched and rewired, singed his cuffs and toiled himself sick build-

"That's s-so adventurous!" said Chloe.

Samuel frowned. "Talk properly, girls."

"Our own Henry Ford," said Yvette.

Maud leaned back in her chair, a wry smile on her face. Samuel licked his lips. "What do you think, Maud? Ama?"

"What do *I* think?" said Maud, her smile widening.

Samuel felt so nervous he giggled. Had he known the state of her day, he would not have indulged his laughter. Indeed, if he were half as sensitive to human moods as to technology, he wouldn't have spoken at all. Even the children sensed her irritability.

That afternoon, Akosua Porter (more pupil than friend, it was true) had accused Maud of intolerable condescension, which was "without reason, coming from one who allows their house to suffer under the stupidity of its master and the evil of its children." Akosua had flinched at her own words. Seeing Maud's fury, she tried to appeal to their shared reverence for honesty: "Truth," said Akosua, "is stronger than an iron horse." But truth is not always the wisest course between those who don't consider themselves equals. Maud gave her a tongue-lashing so apt it might have been a written speech.

Still smoldering over her rebuke, she had only half heard what Samuel said, but the mention of risking their savings was enough to rile her. "Samuel, of all the stupid things you've done over the years, this is the worst tomfoolery you've ever dreamed up. God help you if you spend our money on this."

Samuel glanced around the table, at Ama, who made pathetic attempts to ignore his shame, at the laughing eyes of whatever twin sat just right of her. His girls were becoming harder to tell apart, but he didn't care one bit. He heaped spinach onto his plantain and, with an obvious lack of appetite, put it in his mouth. Dinner continued quietly for some time, neither adult addressing the other. Asking Yvette to pass the plantain, Samuel did something he regretted to his final days.

If only she hadn't stuttered. She used a napkin to select the least-burnt pieces, and handing them to him with her left hand, she said, "For the p-prince, Mr. Tyne."

Samuel looked at the frail arm holding the oily napkin above his plate, and jerked the plate out of the way just as she dropped the food. The girl looked confused, pulling back her arm as though afraid of being blamed for the mishap. She continued to stand, hesitating over her chair, until Chloe pulled her down into her seat.

"You sh-should get that sp-spastic arm looked after, Mr. Tyne," said Chloe.

Rising from his seat, Samuel leaned across the table and struck Yvette across the face.

The blow resounded like a deep silence. Samuel, self-conscious, glared from face to face, enraged. Maud looked shocked, as if to say, *Is that your idea of raising children?* She glanced possessively at Yvette, who was recovering more from disbelief than from pain. But it was Ama's look that hurt most; the fear on her face compounded his guilt.

Samuel sat down, fidgeting with his knife and fork. When he spoke he sounded strained. "Do not again dare to give me your left hand—you think I am a vagrant? Don't play the goat. Never will you *ever* show me, your *elder,* that left palm again. And never will you ever talk like that again." The hatred on his children's faces gave him a new kind of anger, this one righteous, smug. "Are you retarded children? No. Have your mother and I not educated you? Have you two not the privilege of good, sound brains? Why are you wasting what God gave you on some foolish retard talk? *Eih?* No child of mine will show himself a retard, or ever give his left hand to an elder again." At his last words, he looked as if he would cry. No one understood, least of all Samuel himself, that he spoke more to punish himself than to hurt his daughters.

Avoiding eye contact, Samuel left the table. He went to his study, but today it offered no refuge. Instead he went outdoors, where an early dusk had fallen because of a day-long rain. He noticed, from the cold slab of his short patio, that halfway through his property some- one had cut down a tree. Its stubbed trunk rose from the ground, and scattered around it were bright wood shavings. The paleness of the shavings on so gray a day made it seem as though the sun was shining over a single, charmed spot. Samuel looked at it, turning his face instinctively to the Porter house. He went back to his study.

That night Ama went to bed ashamed of Samuel. Everyone had their lapses, but it terrified her to think what he was capable of, despite his gentle nature. She slept terribly.

When she woke in the pale hours, the twins, resurrected in spirits, sat on Chloe's bed playing cards. Their happiness freed Ama from the burden of feeling sorry for them. She smiled. "Why are you two up so early?"

Chloe's face hardened and she took on a withdrawn look. Yvette didn't turn around. Neither spoke.

Ama asked them another question; again, silence. Exasperated, she left to take her bath. When she returned, the girls were gone, the collars of their cots so prim they looked artificial. Ama dressed and descended the stairs to find a busy Mrs. Tyne hopping about the kitchen in her walking cast, harassing herself with biblical proverbs under her breath. It was a sight to see, this jaunty, whip-thin woman who'd rolled pantyhose over her cast so that her leg looked hideously edematous. When she saw Ama, her face became girlish, and she beckoned to be helped to a chair. Ama crouched under her bent arm, and after seating her took up the chair across from hers.

"The twins will be thirteen next week," said Mrs. Tyne. "You're their age. What do you think they want?" When Ama looked uncertain, Maud realized the girl feared this was a test. "I only ask because I hope to make this a bit of an event, you know, because of Sa—because of yesterday."

Ama relaxed. Feeling mischievous, she answered, "A compass? It's cleaner than breadcrumbs for finding your way around this house."

Maud frowned, as though considering the appropriateness of the joke. A slow smile brightened her face. "I saw a book the other day— *How Not to Dominate Conversation.* How about that?"

Ama laughed. "How about a book of word games and riddles?"

"They *wrote* that one. How about *Letter Writing for Amateurs?*"

"*How to Start Making Sense in Ten Easy Steps.*"

"Oh, there's no romance in that," Maud laughed. "How about—" Something in the hallway caught her eye, and Maud glanced up to see Samuel lingering in the doorway, the ancient bowler pinched in his hands. The tactless hour of the day, the apologetic gestures, his stern, too-determined jaw—all of it did more to convict him than if he'd simply walked in admitting it. Maud gave him a vague clouded smile that let him know she understood. Relieved, Samuel avoided Ama's eyes and continued to his study. Maud looked at the empty doorway a minute longer, then turned her fragile smile on the girl. She didn't think, *My God, he's ruined us,* as any other wife might have done; rather, Maud was conscious of the stupidity of her smile, and marveled that she was more fascinated by it than by her husband's indiscretion.

That evening, at dinner, Maud attempted to speak to the children, who were so despondent she lost interest. Still, the twins' very silence, their expert control over their gestures so as not to be noticed, drew everyone's attention. Each twin seemed rigid and nervous, sharing little glances.

"What did you girls do today?" Maud said, upset, wanting to put them at ease.

The twins concentrated on their plates, chewing as though it strained them to do so. Ama raised her head and shrugged, for she'd spent the whole day cooking with Mrs. Tyne and didn't find it necessary to answer.

Samuel kept his eyes averted. Not only did he know the twins' silence was due to his having hit Yvette, but he suspected Maud doted on them now as a kind of apology. Glancing at his daughters, he felt a sense of awe. Without looking at each other, they brought their forks to their lips in perfect harmony. Their fingers trembling, they looked like a trick with mirrors. Samuel stared at them. Despite their spectacle, they seemed terrified of attention. Both Maud and Ama averted their eyes. Samuel stared, then did the same.

Something rattled against the linoleum. Samuel looked down and realized Chloe had dropped her fork. After a long silence, Maud hobbled down on her good knee to retrieve it. Just as Maud was setting the fork on the table, Yvette, with an anguished look on her face, then threw hers down. Sighing, Maud picked up that one, too.

Samuel, appalled, gave the twins an admonishing look and was about to speak when he found he didn't know what to say. Not only was he mortified his wife was being punished on his behalf, but he disappointed himself by not making the apology that would put all this to rest. For some reason, apologizing to Yvette seemed like admitting the stupidity of his grand dreams. The link was illogical, but firm in his mind. And besides, one did not apologize to a child. He finished his meal in silence.

That night was a restive one for Samuel and Maud; the bed felt too small to hold both them and their resentments. Each faked sleep, the only device left to them. The room was noisy with drowsy little sniffles, with timid coughs. But what consumed Maud had nothing to do with Samuel; instead, she thought of the laundry, of the blood-dark rust that collared the kitchen tap, of the endless decay that weighed on their space, making the rooms unbreathable. Her nausea at the dirt felt, at times, like insanity.

Maud rose from bed, sighing at the wistful, unconvincing coughs Samuel made to console himself, and entered the hall. Fumbling for the light switch, she thought she heard a sound and stopped to listen. Again, there it was, a noise like objects falling in a distant room, and navigating by touch she discovered its source. The clothes hamper's closet. Exasperated, she whipped off the latch, the automatic light blinking on to reveal Ama shrouded in white sheets, her eyes large with fear, breathing as if she'd run a race. Ama seemed both relieved at Mrs. Tyne's presence and ashamed at having been caught. She had sheets draped over her head.

"Hibernating?" said Maud, somewhat surly. "What are you doing in here?"

Ama averted her eyes in embarrassment. "The room was too quiet."

"'Too quiet?'" Maud struggled not to hurt the girl's feelings. "People in Toronto, in New York, in London, would pay ten dollars a minute for what you've got. When you grow up and move to a big city you'll remember this and cry. Now, come on."

Grasping Ama's hand, she led her back to the room she shared with the twins. It smelled of mulch and wet clothes, with a hot, close atmosphere that felt unsettling. The water heater clucked in the corner, wind made the eaves outside creak, but for all these noises the room felt densely silent, a calm like the eye of a storm. Maud's hackles rose. She searched for the light switch.

The twins had pushed their cots together, and lying side by side, they stared up at the ceiling. Maud approached them. Bodies rigid, their vague, glossy eyes stared up without judgment.

Maud's fear gave way to confusion. "Is this a game? Stop it! You scared your friend half to death."

They remained impassive. The white of the sheets set off the whites of their eyes.

"We'll talk about this tomorrow. Come on, Ama." As Maud led Ama away, she thought she saw a look on Yvette's face. "Yvette?"

But Yvette recovered her composure. Turning off the lights, Maud led Ama to the Iron Lung and tucked her to sleep in there.

Alone in bed, hesitating at every noise, Samuel groaned in delicious misery. He felt himself to be at the root of every family problem, and yet his anxiety and guilt were oddly fleeting. Yes, he had risked the family savings on an uncertain business venture; yes, his roles as a decent husband and father were on tenuous ground, but he refused to feel remorse. He felt worst about—and for a prodigy of self-flogging, even this was not severe—actually hitting one of his daughters, about the look on Ama's face. In fact, Ama's fear hurt him more than anything. His children at least had a reason to hate him. But Ama? He knew he should apologize, that his wife couldn't keep accounting for his actions, but he couldn't. He was in turmoil, wishing he could ask

Ray for advice, only to recall their fight, which had ended in spite so strong Samuel had sworn it would make a mandrake grow on his grave. Now he felt at a loss to locate the exact cause of their argument—Ray's intent seemed less offensive now that Samuel could see how he might have misinterpreted him. He lay confounded by worry, soothing himself with the thought that all problems were mere theory, and made a halfhearted game out of waiting for his wife to come back.

chapter NINETEEN

T he Franks showed up on the Tynes' doorstep, birthday cake
in hand. Samuel started at the sight of them, not only pained
because of recent enmity; their visit blighted the best hours
of his day, the morning. Unlatching the storm door, he was haunted by
the feeling of having performed this exact act weeks before. Again,
Eudora, pale and hasty-looking, with a foil-covered dish in her withered hands, and, again, a satisfied (if less blithe) Ray behind her, holding a crow of an umbrella over his wife's head.

"You may have been trying to forget us, but we haven't forgotten
you," said Eudora, in a voice somewhat too blunt to be humorous. "You
going to let us in, or you waiting for the hurricane to finish us off?"

With the docility Samuel despised in himself, he let them in,
accepting their wet jackets with servitude. When he gestured the way
to the kitchen, Eudora said, "It hasn't been that long, Sam. We were
older friends than that." Samuel tried to show his confusion at their
presence, so they'd know his friendship was not so easily re-earned.

Eudora evaded his eyes. "You should see what we brought. Your girls won't know this day from Christmas, right, Ray?"

Ray hesitated; he eyed his wife as though wondering at the appropriateness of going on without a formal apology. Still, he followed Eudora to the kitchen, where she pulled gold-wrapped gifts from a Hudson's Bay Company bag and arranged them at the far end of the table.

Samuel didn't know what to say. Maud came in behind him, despondent in an old bathrobe, running a pick-comb through her damp Afro and stopping blind upon seeing the company. She hadn't spoken to Eudora since the night of Ama's accident, when Eudora had made her comment about "devil's work." Without being seen, Maud backed out of the room.

Ama came into the kitchen, fidgeting in her pink dress, as though she longed to go to Samuel but didn't trust him. Then the twins entered, stone-like. Fact was, the Tynes had planned their own small party for that afternoon, and though Maud had been its sole organizer, Samuel had so taken an interest in the overheard details that he felt like a willing accomplice. Now, not only was the original plan being undermined by tactless guests, but the twins didn't show even remote excitement at having accidentally seen the preparation of festivities much more elaborate than those Maud had planned. Samuel kept an eye on his daughters, sad to have to acknowledge to himself that their silence had aged them. Not so much physically: they were awkward as ever. But there was a current in those cold eyes, a judgment that saw through human bustle and cheer. Perhaps that was it—they had the invalid's contempt for false joy.

Eudora almost lost her composure. "Will you look at the two of you," she said, her voice full of breath. "Only one year older and wearing it like it's twenty. Ray, will you look at them?"

Ray smiled, blind to the change. "Finer girls Aster has not seen." With his characteristic way of addressing the ghost above Samuel's shoulder, he looked apologetic, and said, "Yes." Though Samuel was uncertain how to read that gesture, he was happy to see in it an attempt to make amends, and reassured Ray with a smile. Ray nodded back. There was something endearing about that vulnerable nod, about the shaky, wire glasses that magnified Ray's eyes, giving him the look of a learned turtle.

But only on Maud's terms could wounds truly be mended. When she entered, in a black dress too funereal to be festive, the verdict of the party hung on her, and she knew it. She sat at the head of the table, making a spectacle of her annoyance, and Samuel thought he saw one of the twins roll her eyes.

Eudora ordered Samuel to find a good radio station as she unstacked the guestware from the high cupboard. Ama arranged the presents, hoping, perhaps, that the Franks had thought to bring a little something for her, and Maud lit the chessboard cake, its tiny black and white candles cast in the mold of game pieces.

"Where the devil did you get such a cake?" said Maud.

Ray nodded toward his wife. "Dora's hands. I knew they had to have some purpose beyond dialing the phone." He smiled, but looked preoccupied, touching his breast pocket.

"Oh, shush," said Eudora. "At least mine are active. But then I guess by keeping yours down your shorts you always know where to find them in case of emergency."

"Just the opposite—they're lost in there and I like it that way."

Eudora frowned. "Children, Ray."

Maud seated the twins at the head opposite her, and placed Ama and Samuel to their left and their right, facing each other. To spare them Samuel's conversation, Maud seated the Franks nearer her end.

"Oh, no you don't," said Maud, when Eudora started to lower herself into the seat beside Samuel. "You keep me company over here."

This also kept them from the twins, who surely dreaded the attention. But the twins sat in such silent, strained rigidity that it became impossible to look elsewhere. Maud kept trying to attract the company with loud, witless remarks, and watching her fail at this led Samuel to see how much she blamed herself for her girls' behavior. That Maud would risk ridicule to save her children from their natural speech; that she

would play the town ass to dissuade outsiders from seeing the very obvious truth; that her own self-respect meant less to her than the loss of her
daughters' good names in Aster: all of this gave Samuel a sort of detached
shame.

His bad mood passed as talk turned to politics—if the Farmers
League would ever regain its foot in Albertan politics, the delusion of
the women's movement, whether provincial-level reform of the penal
system was needed to properly punish the arsonist once they caught
the bastard. Lately, penal reform had been hotly debated in the Frank
house, leading to three hoarse quarrels, a slapped face, constant name-
calling and five painful nights on a couch no lusher than padding. The
Franks had finally agreed never to mention their wretched views again.
But Eudora broached it once more, aware all the while of her husband's benevolent smile weighing on her. She'd recently interned at a
facility in Edmonton.

"It's where they send the in-betweens, meaning people who committed some crime but are given a break based on mental instability.
And, you know, the longer I volunteer, the less convinced I am in the
value of rehabilitation." She began to cut the cake. "It's true some can't
help it. This one woman, Mary—ha, *woman*—child, more like it. An
epileptic. She took up with an older man who supposedly told her
that"—Eudora dropped her voice—"laying down with men for money
would cure her seizures. Simple as a cat, I tell you. Just as vicious, too,
sometimes. Anyway, she's more like a transient to the house—a traveling salesman, as Ray calls her." Eudora winked at her husband, a gesture that gave more weight to his wit than it deserved.

"It would appear that prostitution has some hard penalties," said
Samuel.

Eudora admonished Samuel with her eyes for daring such a word
in the company of young ears. He grew reticent, and stifled the nervous laugh he knew made him seem foolish.

"Day after day I go there, believing or trying to believe that these
facilities are a good thing. We shall reform, I think. It can be done. But
when I sit here, and really think about it, I just can't *stand* the

thought, can't bear it, that someone like this Aster Arsonist, who might even be an Asterian—"

"An Asterisk," said Samuel, with a hesitant laugh.

"An Asterian"—Eudora raised her voice—"going about his regular life in his regular clothes, has the power to take away our homes, to take away our businesses, maybe even to take away our lives, and that his only punishment might be to spend a few hours a week with me for a decade, and then get back all his privileges as though nothing's happened. That's not right."

"I don't know, Dora," said Ray. "A few hours a week with *you . . .*"

"There was a saying in my house," said Samuel, clearing his throat. "There was a saying, when this similar thing happened in my village: One who sets outward fires is burning within. Meaning that what that man likely needs is aid, though he should also be punished. And they found, when they caught that joker, that after a beating and some imprisonment, they could then begin his reformation. Now, I don't believe he should necessarily be beaten, but there is greater room in a man's heart for change than even he can be aware of."

"There was a saying in my house in Ontario, too, Samuel. Real men don't talk like jesters." Ray smiled, but his eyes were cold. His comment subdued the room.

"Go smoke, Ray, if you have to," said Eudora, flustered. "Going without makes you mean."

Ray rose as though the reprieve was late in coming. He left without speaking, disappointing Samuel by giving no sign they should meet outside. Samuel refused, once again, to believe Ray meant offense. Ray's era was less language-conscious, his learning unguided, his politics small-minded, even prejudiced. When more than common speech was required of him, he grew uneasy; and he had the autodidact's lack of humility when giving advice. But despite these faults, Ray had more of the human good in him than all the best-tempered men of Samuel's memory. Of this Samuel was convinced. The risking of his own life for Ama's could not be forgotten, wanting no gratitude for the act, even masking it from the public eye for the sake of the Tynes' reputation.

This reason alone filled Samuel with tolerance; and besides, only a small man couldn't laugh at his own cultural quirks. Moreover, Ray's comments seemed more insecure than mean-spirited. As a backwater, Ray felt challenged by Samuel's accomplishments—a sad position for anyone, so that Samuel resolved to set his pride aside.

He rose, motioning for the party to go on without him, as though such trifles weren't worth his time. Leaving, he recognized fully for the first time that the confidence he'd sought these last months was finally his. He was certainly still timid, with an empathy that doubled his own suffering in the world, but he had overcome his terror of being judged. And success, he felt, was close, absolute and irrefutable.

From the crumbling patio in the backyard, Samuel squinted around, nearsighted from years of detailed work. A quick glance around the yard revealed nothing but Porter's distant house, its brown shingles applauding in the wind. A few feet before it, a short, angular boy pushed a wheelbarrow, his baseball cap hesitating on his head like a bubble on water. He cut a sharp figure against the soft bulk of his house, and there was a funny sullenness in the way he jerked the empty barrow. Something in his black mood hinted at family anger, and, vaguely, Samuel began to walk toward him. It was a while before Porter's son noticed Samuel, but he halted when he did, folding his fists into his pockets and turning uncertainly toward the eaves of his house.

Samuel stopped. There, in the shadow of a rafter, stood Ray, his back to Samuel as he animated some hasty point to a complacent Saul Porter.

Samuel felt confused. He recalled Ray's wheat project, but the idea had seemed no more than a joke. Samuel was annoyed, uneasy, too, but beyond all, ashamed of his own possessiveness. Ray was entitled to befriend whom he liked, despite what could be said of his tastes. Samuel now worried he would be seen, and sidled away. The overturned wheelbarrow sat abandoned in the sun; the boy had disappeared. Samuel made his way back to the house.

The birthday party was listless, dying out despite Maud's wishes. Cake sat in untouched, glossy lumps in front of the twins. Ray entered, full of color and high spirits, but only as the Franks were leaving did Samuel get a moment alone with him. Affectionate as ever, Ray laid Samuel's worries to rest.

With his usual smirk, Ray said, "You made a fool of me out there, Tyne. Seems you never told Porter a thing about my questions." He chuckled. "He wouldn't tell me a thing about what he puts in his crops. It's looking like a two-man venture."

"Did he tell you anything about the will?" said Samuel.

Ray laughed. "So eager! You're going to have to give me a little more time with that. Besides, that's not Porter stuff, that's town stuff. Don't worry, I'll deal with it."

Samuel felt rather embarrassed after they'd left, and settling into his study, he glanced at the clock he'd set to Gold Coast time; it would be evening there. He recalled his sister's last letter, a reprimand for more money. She'd told him that if he persisted in not returning, he should at least have the decency to double their monthly checks. It was a common fallacy back home that all Westerners were wealthy; though Samuel supposed that comparatively he was. Every time Samuel received a letter from Ajoa—all of them livid and accusatory— Maud had to reassure him that they were entitled to their lifestyle, that it was long overdue and no great shucks by Western standards anyway. She explained that Ajoa wrote more because she missed him than to berate his lack of charity. And Samuel wondered at his inability to interpret people, often seeing in them the opposite of what they intended. But he wondered: When should a man anticipate others' befuddling feelings, striving to please and meet their needs, and when should he put them aside to fulfill his own?

Samuel brooded into lunch, only abandoning his thoughts when they grew scattered with hunger. The halls were dark and silent, and for the first time in weeks he was aware of the pitiful, scissor-like complaint of the weathervane. Strangely, they had neglected to call him to lunch, and the silence was odder still. He could hear his loose hem on the hardwood and the sibilance of a radio in a distant room. No, not a radio: tinny voices coming from the twins' room. Pinching up his pants to lighten the sound of his presence, he crept to the oak door and strained for clarity. He knew it was silly for a man to spy on his children, but they hadn't spoken in days, and he was relieved to know they at least talked to each other. *What* they spoke about he could only guess at. He leaned against the jamb, astounded to hear them nattering with the high-pitched fluency of squirrels. The rapid-fire staccato words sounded like a tape run backwards, rushed and guttural. Perhaps, Samuel thought, in their cleverness they have gone and learned another language. But despite his polyglot repertoire, Samuel couldn't discern it. Strangely inflected, whatever it was, they had both acquired enough to talk quite rigorously. Samuel placed his ear right to the cold wood, confounded. The talking seemed to halt mid-sentence, and he stood petrified, unable to leave in case they heard him step away. After a pause in which he was certain they heard him breathing, they turned on a radio and Samuel rushed away.

Later, Samuel would take a more tender approach. The next afternoon, Maud and Ama in town, Samuel shuffled into the twins' room. Removing his hat, he fiddled with it as he waited for his daughters to recover from their surprise. Crouched behind an empty bed, comparing their books, they had thrown them down in tandem as soon as he entered.

Clearing his throat, Samuel lowered himself onto Ama's cot and, giggling a little, made a conspicuous show of his own nervousness to put them at ease. "*The Idiot, Le Père Goriot,* yes, I myself read those ones in my youth. Quite delightful, quite delightful." He giggled. "Prince Myshkin and—who is it again?—Nastasya Filippovna, yes, yes. Eugène Rastignac. Quite delightful, quite delightful!"

His daughters' contemptuous looks silenced him. But just as he was about to speak, he realized he couldn't tell them apart, and so didn't know who to apologize to. He cleared his throat, hesitating. Looking from face to face, he said, "With my deepest regret, please accept my apology for having hit you."

The twin on the left seemed delighted by his indignity. She looked at her sister, who gave Samuel a cold look. He rose to his feet, disappointed, feeling he'd debased himself. Replacing his hat, he left the room.

chapter TWENTY

A ma felt drained. She'd taken to spending more time with Yvette and Chloe, only to find them sullen and evasive. Not only did they refuse to speak, but their gestures were restrained and mirrored. At first, Ama thought she had only to keep speaking to get a response. But they maintained their silence. Soon embarrassing herself, Ama would ambush them with constant talk. It wasn't long before she got the impression they were laughing at her, and, furious, she gave them a dose of her own silence. But she began to feel isolated, as in the darkest weeks of her mother's illness. Mrs. Ouillet had endured total paralysis, when no single word emerged from her lips. Ama remembered those lips: dry and opalescent, the muscle above them pulsing as she spooned food between them. Perhaps the twins, with their silent rigidity, were making fun of her mother. Ama began to treat the twins with spite.

No sooner had Ama given up on the twins than, lying in bed, unable to sleep in the hot, moist dark, she heard them whispering. Speaking gibberish, as if they knew she eavesdropped. But the fervor in their voices, and the occasional clear word, told Ama it wasn't staged. She held her breath and tried not to move.

One of the twins shifted in bed and spoke furiously. The response, also rapid, resounded with forced calm.

There was more shifting, and then Ama heard a high voice unlike either of theirs: "*You're* Chloe. *I'm* Yvette."

The other twin cleared her throat, said something in annoyance, and shifted in bed. A week of not speaking had ended to reveal frightened, fighting girls. Ama rolled on her side and tried to sleep.

In the morning, waiting until they'd gone outside, Ama rushed up to the bedroom and, shutting the door behind her, reached under Yvette's cot to read the letters they'd written her. Finding the space swept bare, she groped first under the extra cot and then under Chloe's. The letters were gone.

But from the head of Chloe's bed to its base, arranged in a strict, tidy row, she found two dozen hairbrushes. Some brass, some wooden, some of a plastic fashioned after gold. All lay with their handles at an exacting forty-five-degree angle. Their charms had been lost long ago, most of them broken or bent. Nevertheless, care had been taken with them, their handles glowing with polish, not a single hair to be found in their naked bristles.

It surprised Ama that Chloe could be so delicate with anything. Ama picked one up, fingering its engraved handle. Had these first belonged to Jacob? That idea seemed even stranger. Ama replaced the brush at the same angle as the others and quietly left the room, nervous that Chloe would somehow notice they'd been touched.

But when the twins returned home a few hours later, Ama knew Chloe was too flustered to notice. She seemed tousled these days, a little detached from her surroundings. Yvette did, too, but not as severely. Ama entered the bedroom mid-afternoon to find the twins stuffing something into a pillowcase. As if sensing Ama in the doorway, both twins turned to her.

Ama lost her fear of their synchrony. She saw how it was done: when one decided to move, she alerted her sister with her eyes, and lagging a little, one merely copied the other. Moving so slowly, it was easy to keep pace with each other.

Ama had just entered the room when Mrs. Tyne appeared in the doorway. She herself looked frazzled these days. She fiddled with the clasps on her vinyl raincoat. "Your father's lying down with a headache in the other room. I've got to rush out and pick up our dry cleaning before it closes." She checked her watch. "Oh, dear. Samuel's been begging for an aspirin. Do you think you can manage that for me?" Her question was directed at Ama, but it was Chloe who nodded. "Good. I'll be back in an hour or so."

The twins rose to get the aspirin. "I'll hold down the fort," Ama said. She picked up a book and sat on her cot.

As soon as the twins left the room, Ama lifted Chloe's pillowcase and reached her hand inside. She found a bundle of crumpled tissues. Something black and spindly was pressed between them, and mistaking this for a dead spider, Ama let out a little cry and dropped the tissue. But when she forced herself to open it, she discovered not an insect, but a small bale of coarse, black hair.

Ama stared at the hair for a moment. Then, as delicately as possible, she rewrapped it and placed it back where she'd found it in the pillowcase. In one smooth gesture, she tried to brush her imprint from the bed, wracking her mind to remember exactly how the sheet had been folded over the pillow. Fumbling, she made a double fold and, once in the hall, stopped to glance back at the bed with apprehension. When the twins appeared at the top of the stairs, she smiled guiltily at them, and excused herself to go to the Iron Lung, closing the door behind her.

Maud arrived home more than four hours late, held up by errands. She was conscious of a silence that shouldn't have existed with three teenage girls in the house. Draping Samuel's laundered blue suits on the banister, she called her daughters' names from the bottom of the stairs. Maud made her way to the kitchen, which was filled with austere light, and smelled of the marigolds rotting in a cloudy Mason jar. Maud whisked the jar off the table and tossed it in the garbage. Her eye fell on an open vial of pills on the counter.

Even as her pulse began to quicken, she continued to stand there, silent, unwilling to believe the faded label. Her anxiety hit her all at once, and dropping the bottle, she rushed for the stairs.

"Why did you do this?" said Maud, finding Ama on the landing.

Flushed and breathless, Ama stared, her large eyes confused.

Maud hurried to the master bedroom, with Ama following. Samuel lay on the bed, a dark distinct figure. He looked strange against the pink sheets, weightless; his body seemed to make no impression on the bed at all. Drawing a sharp breath, Maud lowered herself beside him.

"Samuel . . . *Samuel,* wake up."

Ignoring Ama's horrified look, Maud began to slap his cheeks. "Samuel, oh, good, get up. Yes, get up." Seeing him rouse a little, Maud slapped Samuel a little harder. When he began waking, Maud wiped her eyes on the cuff of her sleeve and turned to Ama. "Don't just stand there—get him some water."

Ama stumbled from the room. When she returned to give Maud the glass, her hands shook so much water ran down its sides.

Samuel was fully awake now. He seemed fine, perfectly like himself, excepting the absent bowler, which gave him a curious boyish look. Frowning at the glass forced to his mouth, he kept raising his hand to indicate he wanted to speak. He finished the water, gasping.

"Since when has a man's sleep attracted so many eyes?" said Samuel.

"How are you feeling?"

"Fine. The girls gave me two aspirins about five hours ago. I feel very much recovered."

Maud flinched. "My God, they *did* give it to you. But you look all right. How do you feel?"

Samuel smiled at Ama. "Oh, hello. I did not see you there."

"*Samuel,*" said Maud, "how do you feel?"

Samuel shrugged. "Just as I said. Fine. Recovered."

Maud wiped her eyes again. Samuel looked bewildered. Hesitating, he patted Maud's elbow.

"Get up and have a stretch around," she said. "Then we're going to the hospital."

Samuel started. "What? Wait, wait, wait. Is it one of the children?"

"You. *You're* going."

"Me? Don't play the goat, I'm fine. What is this hospital business?"

Mrs. Tyne drew a sharp breath. "When I went out, I realized I'd taken the last aspirin three days ago, so I bought a new package. Only I come home to find *this* sitting on the counter. It's codeine, Samuel. I didn't even realize Jacob had this in the house." Sniffling, she turned to Ama. "Where on earth did you even find this? And how could you give it to him when we all know how allergic he is?"

The look of terror on Ama's face made Maud relent. The girl had probably had nothing to do with it, but it pained Maud too much to confront the alternate possibility. She gave Ama an apologetic look. She examined Samuel for signs of illness.

He looked shaken. "I do not feel dead, so perhaps I have outgrown my allergy." He exhaled. "A little light-headed maybe, but I do not need any hospital."

Maud considered. "At least let me call Eudora."

"Oh, certainly, call her." Samuel laughed a little. "But if you choose to do so, know that you are forfeiting the rest of your night to inane conversation. The woman is tenacious as a tick. Besides, I will not let her near me."

"*Samuel.*"

"No, I mean it, call her. Just picture the headline for the next National Association of Petulant Bossy Women newsletter. 'Another Domestic Crime Story,' by Dora Frank. What news that would make."

Maud scoffed, but he had hit a nerve. "Tell you what. If you get up out of bed, do something active for the next few hours, and let me check on you, we don't have to go."

"Amen," said Samuel. He attempted to rise from the bed, but fell back, looking a little faint. "Just give me one minute."

"Ama," said Maud in a gentle voice. "Can we get your help?"

And with their help, one on each side of him, Samuel was lifted from the bed.

He did a little light gardening in the yard, cleared some sludge from the cellar, and by evening he felt strong enough to sit down to a broken television in his study. Maud and Ama kept an eye on him, checking for signs of his dying, and satisfied he wasn't, they retired to the family room to knit. During the whole tense day no one mentioned the twins, not even to call them down for dinner. They likewise remained hidden, the door of their bedroom only opening when no one was upstairs. Maud heard its hinges creak from the kitchen.

But by dusk she could no longer ignore them. Leaving Ama, she crept upstairs and stood at the threshold of her daughters' closed door. Raising a fist, she paused before knocking. There was no invitation to enter, but she did so anyway, frowning at the twins, who lay side by side on Chloe's cot, reading. When they looked at her, their faces made her feel ashamed of what she'd come to say. But she cleared her throat.

"You gave the wrong pills on purpose," she said, surprised at hearing these words instead of the speech she'd prepared. She was surprised, too, at the lack of conviction in her voice, a pleading sound. "You gave the wrong pills on purpose," she said again, this time more firmly. She realized she wanted them to defend themselves.

The twins regarded her in silence. A fleeting look of fear crossed Yvette's face. But she recovered quickly, her features filling with an indifferent, challenging look.

Maud felt an ache in her throat. Not knowing what to say, she left them to their reading.

chapter TWENTY-ONE

A naturally morose man, Samuel's thoughts turned morbid after the pill incident. He'd read in a book that human allergies were cyclical, shed and acquired every seven years. These changes had no precise demarcation; you only found out when exposed to new or neutralized dangers. Samuel felt grateful to have outgrown his allergy to codeine, which he'd discovered in his youth the day it had almost killed him.

It had happened during his flight from his old home to his new. Jacob slept beside him. To his left sat a dark-haired Englishwoman, fussy, nervous, who laughed every time he looked at her. Samuel at first thought he frightened her, but it soon became apparent she suffered from a general self-consciousness. Samuel concluded that her desire to appear ladylike was undermined by her vices. She ate snacks from her pocket, flushing with embarrassment. When her meal came, she ate with great relish, sopping up the sauce with a squalid bun.

When Samuel glanced at the tabloid she was reading, she laughed nervously. "I don't usually read such nonsense," she said, "but flights will do that to you, won't they? *That's* what I brought." She pointed to a pristine copy of Woolf's *To the Lighthouse,* stuffed into the seat pouch in front of her.

Samuel stared at her. Who did she think she was fooling? But he wouldn't have noticed had she not felt compelled to point out her weaknesses to strangers.

He should have known better than to accept this woman's advice. But Samuel's excitement had kept him awake for thirty hours straight, and Jacob looked so peaceful beside him.

"Well, it's not right for you to be left behind, is it?" she said, pointing to Jacob. She searched through her purse, retrieving an unmarked vial, and shook two pills onto her small, anemic hand. "It's codeine," she said. "You'll sleep like a lamb."

Sleep like a lamb he did, and almost didn't wake. He was only roused five hours later in an Algerian hospital. They'd had to ground the plane and take him there, so severe was his swelling, his toxic shock. When it became clear he would live, Jacob berated him for days: "Before this, I had never seen so old a brain on so young a body. Now it is the other way around."

Now, after having had no reaction to a second dose of codeine, Samuel wondered if the woman on the plane had given him codeine at all.

Samuel sat in his shop. No one came to offer condolences, and though glad no one knew of his accident, he couldn't help feeling somewhat disliked. Maud had gotten consolation for *her* accident. His mind was only taken off his childish bitterness by the arrival of Ray Frank, who'd run over on his lunch break from his parts shop.

Propping the door open with his foot, soot on his cheeks, Ray called, "Don't suppose you know much about tractor parts?"

Samuel shrugged. "Not really."

"You sure? You'd make good money. I'm doing the rest, but there's a part for the engine I just can't get from my distributors. Can you check with yours? I'll cut you fifteen percent."

"Oh, you do not have to do that," laughed Samuel. "Just find out about Jacob's will for me, and we can call things even."

Ray winked. "I appreciate it," he said, his eyes trailing a thin, haughty-looking woman pushing a stroller past the shop. Only when she'd passed did he focus again. "All right, Sam, take down this serial number." He recited it off the back of his hand.

"Wait, wait, let me get my book."

"Hurry, Samuel, I've got to motor."

Samuel fussed with the wires and papers strewn all over the counter, pressured by Ray's impatience. He found what he was looking for under his stool. "All right, give it to me again." But as soon as Ray began to speak, Samuel realized he had the wrong ledger. This one was filled with childish writing.

"Got that?" called Ray, already out the door.

Samuel flipped to a blank page. "Let me double check. Just say it one more time."

Ray made an exasperated noise, but recited it a final time, emphasizing each number as though speaking to an imbecile. He rushed out the door.

Samuel waited until he couldn't see Ray from the window any more to open the ledger. The twins often helped themselves to the empty green ledgers in his study, a hoard of thirty or so he'd permanently borrowed from the government office. Sure enough, on the front cover Chloe had inscribed her name.

Wed. July. 5. Y. stared at Asthma during dinner tonight—secret friendship? Thur. July. 13. Y. leaned over my soup when I went to bathroom—silica gel? Varnish? Did not finish soup. Y. alone in alcove with grape juice, seemed scared when I came in for cup. Did not drink juice. Mon. July. 17. 9:45 a.m. I go to bathroom. 9:48 a.m. Y. gets up to go to bathroom. 10:02 a.m. I yawn and roll on my right side. 10:03 a.m. Y. yawns and rolls on her right side. 11:55 a.m. I roll over to read—got my exact book in her hands, has just rolled over to read. Tue. July. 18. Y. stuttering. Saw a gleam in her eye at top of the stairs— moved out of way before she could push me. Wed. July. 19. Y. still blames me—detergent in my juice—didn't drink it.

The list filled half the pages of the notebook. Samuel closed it, sitting for a minute on his chair. He didn't know what to think; he refused to see anything in it, taking it for a game he would make sure the twins gave up. But he had a feeling. Not a mild feeling, like a hunch or even intuition. Dread.

To clear his mind, Samuel worked on his prototypes. All had been going just as planned, save the base costs, which were more demanding than he'd predicted and had begun to strain him a little. His friendship with Ray helped interest a few local investors, and having fronted him money, they merely waited to see what he came up with before giving him more. In all other matters he was his own man. He had proved himself, and felt vindicated. He was so close to justifying his life with a great work that it scared him to move too fast. And with Maud finally a little convinced of the plan's ingenuity, if not its practicality, he accepted the eventuality of fame and threw himself headlong into it.

But he couldn't keep his thoughts on the work, and closing early, he drove home.

The Tyne house was grainy with light that made the furniture look stark and severe. It was so quiet that Samuel could hear the water heaters ticking, the sound of wind in the grass out back. On the kitchen table Maud had placed a bouquet of fake roses in a horn-shaped brass vase, and Samuel felt for the first time all summer his uncle's presence in the house. Here was a part of himself Jacob hadn't managed to take with him to the grave. Seeing the vase, which Jacob had spent decades polishing, Samuel was reminded of the jealousy he'd felt toward it as a young man. How he had spat on it when ignored by his uncle, filled it with filth, and even, one time, attempted to throw it in a fire. But the vase survived, and he lived alongside it, despising it like a gifted sibling he was hopeless to outdo.

Samuel picked it up, running a finger along its nicks and scars. Someone else was home. A loud thud shook the house to its foundations, followed by silence, then a second thump. Still clutching the vase, Samuel left the kitchen and started upstairs. At the threshold of the twins' room, he paused for a minute before turning the doorknob.

In the center of the room, one twin sat on top of her sister, who lay on her back. The curtains were unfastened, and the shade made it difficult to see exactly what they were doing. Neither noticed their father. The one on the bottom whimpered, and in response, the other lifted her sister's head by the ears and threw it down with a resounding thud. When the girl cried out in pain, the twin on top grabbed her head again and slammed it on the hardwood. The whole thing seemed like some grotesque joke, a sickening scene they'd read somewhere and were re-enacting. The girl lying down began to moan, and her sister seized her by the head again.

Samuel yanked the girl off her sister. Stupefied, pained, his right eye began to spasm. The twins seemed so indistinguishable to him that his inability to tell the victim from the perpetrator only added to his distress. The girl who'd lain down stood up, dazed, and Samuel watched helplessly as, instead of gratitude or even fear, she gave him a look full of disgust, as though he'd humiliated her.

"What manner of game are you playing here?" he said, his voice cracking. "What manner of game is this?"

At the sound of his voice, the perpetrator ran from the room. Before he could stop her, the other ran after her, and he followed them down the stairs.

"You wait," he yelled, "you wait one second."

But they sped up, and in seconds they'd run through the house and out the bay door. Helpless, he watched their figures cross the grassy fields.

"What manner of game is this?" he muttered, sitting on the arm of a couch. He realized he was still holding the vase and, with an anguished noise, threw it on the floor. Had it all been a game, or had she intended to kill her sister? Was it some ritual he didn't understand, something they'd read in a book? Should their books be taken from them? When it occurred to Samuel his daughters might be possessed, he was astonished that the thought didn't resonate like it should have. Perhaps, unconsciously, he'd thought it before. He'd certainly seen cases of possession, and though he'd been a skeptic at the time, they remained remarkable to him. As a young man, he and his westernized classmates had taken a road trip to a tiny village where a public exorcism had drawn a crowd into a dusty compound. A man with an angular face sat on the ground at the center, wearing mudcloth. Someone called from deep in his throat, and the horde clapped and called back. The air was heavy with smoke. For a long time nothing happened, and Samuel and his friends grew bored. Finally, the young man's hands rose and trembled. His voice silenced the crowd, deep and prophetic, like the voice of a man already dead. The exorcist addressed him casually, as though they'd chanced to meet on a bus. But after a few minutes the afflicted interrupted and, in a way that would have humiliated him if he were sentient, began to scuttle in the dust like a land crab. The crowd taunted him, and he spat and banged his head on the concrete until knocked unconscious. Facing the crowd, the exorcist prayed over him and within minutes the afflicted had been restored to himself. When Samuel and his classmates broke through the crowd, the exorcist assured them the man had been fully cured and told them to go away. A hoax, Samuel and his mates agreed with smug, full-bellied looks.

Samuel attended two more exorcisms alone; one in which a woman was troubled by the spirit of a goat she'd reputedly poisoned, the other the case of an elder who'd negligently buried his only granddaughter. In both cases the same prayer technique was used, and both times Samuel carried away the same misgiving. Whether it was his scientific training or a more congenital skepticism, he refused to accept the authenticity of what he saw. It all seemed too comical, too dramatic, to have the depth of a miracle. He dismissed it as ambitious fraud, a dark industry from which the government profited as much as the average charlatan. The fraud often backfired on the "specialists," with everyone from farmers to politicians using them as scapegoats. In March of that year, even, the Tanzanian government had jailed five rainmakers for allegedly creating too much rain and destroying farmers' crops. Samuel found this ludicrous, the creation of rain so beyond the realm of man. But driving home from the last spectacle, he was depressed by an ancestral desire to believe, and lamented with bitter humor that too much schooling had made a white man of him. He never attended another event.

Jacob's grave was shallow and unblessed. Perhaps the old truths were right. Perhaps the twins' behavior was the dead talking through the living. Jacob was still wrestling his angel. And Samuel held the key to his peace and wouldn't use it. He hadn't bothered with a funeral and the time for libations was long gone; perhaps it was affecting his family more than he cared to admit.

The thought appalled him. Even if there were some truth to it, Jacob, though not kind, had never been vengeful. Lately Samuel had been wondering how Jacob could possibly have relied on Saul Porter for anything, never mind comfort in his staid old age. Samuel tried to reconcile the memory of one man to the reality of the other. Porter's ancestors had probably been money-doublers: that odious breed of *juju* men who convince dupes to leave money in agreed-upon places, promising that by some prayer-incited miracle the money will multiply, and arranging a date for it to be collected. Of course, the *juju* man collects it first, leaving rocks, empty boxes or sandbags to replace the stolen savings. Even professors and church pastors had fallen prey to his kind.

Samuel looked across the way at Porter's house. Last week, Porter had forcefully extended his property lines, cutting down trees on the Tyne side. Samuel was fed up. He'd rushed through the grass, surprised that Saul wasn't grooming the grounds. The Porter's rotting wood door gave Samuel a sliver, and spiders like ripe Spanish grapes draped the eaves. Samuel hadn't considered his speech beforehand, planning to let the force of his anger drive his words. He wiped wet dust from a window and tried to see past the treated glass; it felt like his whole life would pass before the door opened. He knocked again, and still no one answered. Backing away, he listened, trying to decipher human sounds. It appeared no one was home, but so it always did when the Porters kept indoors, and Samuel refused to be their fool a second time, to walk away while they watched his retreat from the shadows. Guarding his knuckles with his cuffs, he banged with the insistence of a landlord. Stillness responded, like a parody of silence, a held breath. Behind him, the heat slid off the green riding mower in trembling sheets.

"Will you come out," Samuel yelled, "or do we wait for this tedium to kill me and leave my body on your threshold as evidence of your malice?"

The fields echoed with his voice. This emboldened him, even while exposing the stupidity of his mission. Using both fists, he throttled the door as though it alone chose to keep him out, as though its closure was not the result of human will. He kept banging, because he knew that when he stopped he'd be sickened by his childishness. Finally dropping his fists, he backed away, trying to quell his humiliation by becoming more enraged. He headed home, turning now and again to scrutinize that house whose wood was so worn it had the dim, filthy look of sparrows' feathers. A troglodyte and a ragman, Samuel cursed. How was it this man could be so legendary and beloved when he was as tricky and untrustworthy as a thief? How could Porter be eternally in his fields, and yet eternally away from home? How is a man both everywhere and nowhere? The idea of two Porters occurred to Samuel despite its ludicrousness, one peddler, one gardener, both vagrant. Or no Porters, the man a figment of a bad dream. How easy life would be then.

Samuel went after his daughters. He searched all of Aster: Nothing. He returned home only when his stomach began to nag him.

Maud was in the kitchen, fixing the evening meal. She smiled when she saw him. "Am I ever glad to see another face. Poor Ama's just tuckered—we went all around town today."

Samuel frowned. "Why didn't you take the twins?"

Maud looked at him. "Where are those two, anyway? They usually stay indoors after six. And why aren't you in your study? Has everyone given up their habits around here?"

Samuel felt nervous at the prospect of explaining what he'd seen that afternoon; Maud would surely buckle under the news. She sensed his apprehension.

"What's wrong, Samuel? Tell me."

Sitting at the table, Samuel gave her the details, watching her worn face. She closed her eyes, gripping the back of a chair. When she spoke, she said the one thing he didn't expect.

"Leave them be. Let their anger run its course—they'll come back." Maud let out a breath, fidgeting. "I know them. For all of their hyper-activity and their fighting, I know them. They're scared, they're frightened, we've left them alone too long. We've been irresponsible. God, I wish we had just *said* something when this all began, this silence."

Samuel felt the intended guilt at her words. He knew he was responsible in all ways, for having hit Yvette, for being an indifferent father. During the meal he couldn't meet anyone's eye. Afterward, he retired to his study, so fatigued he fell asleep.

He was shocked awake by the sound of a shot. An awful musk pervaded the dark. Fully clothed, still clouded by sleep, he gripped the familiar leather of his armrests. He realized he was sitting in the dark like a dead man awaiting discovery, limp in his study chair, his head slack. He fumbled through rags and wires to the lights. Everything was in order, and his watch read ten-thirty. But the smell. It made every breath like an acrid spoon of medicine. Then he heard the cries, as though the light had made him sensitive to them, and he rushed to the window. A fire was raging across the field.

Shouting his wife's name, he ran out the bay door in confusion. A few field rocks broke his pace, but he was never aware of tripping, so fixed was he on the mass of people who'd gathered there, and the bellowing sirens surprisingly near. He felt tears in his eyes, pricked by the smoke and wild detritus from the bulk of Porter's burning house. Samuel thought first of his children, then of Porter's children, and then with guilt of Porter himself. It sickened him to think he'd loathed that man, and a new sense of fellowship entered him at the sight of this tragedy.

The fire filled the sky with an unnatural light. The flames rose and sank, giving off brown smoke. Every few minutes, with a low, doleful sound, like something issuing from the ground, a flaming beam collapsed, raining hot ash on the crowd. Flakes of golden ash smoldered in the grass around them, vibrant as fireflies. Just as the flames were dying, they would flare again, illuminating people's faces with a naked severity.

Samuel broke through the crowd, which cried out each time sparks shot high or a new child was dragged from the wreckage. Two firemen caught him by the arms and forced him back. The crowd, like a mound of moths, jostled Samuel aside to better see the fire. Ravaging flames ate at all sides of the house and the farthest wing had already scarred to ash. Samuel was shocked to see the very door he'd spent all summer knocking on torn free by a violent blast that roused screams from the crowd, who were beaten back by the firemen. A preternatural silence resounded between screams. The filthy smoke was choking, the showers of debris scattering people only to have them regroup in their morbidity to examine the burnt pieces.

Samuel ran, breathless, unsure of what he sought even while he screamed for people to move. The moon shone through gossamer smoke. The dark figures of firemen crossed back and forth past the flames. With great, voluble thunder the roof collapsed, spitting out a whip of fire.

Samuel wiped sweat from his eyes. Holding his breath, he watched them pull another child from the detritus, the poor thing screaming in fear. Samuel tried to get to the front of the crowd. But the harder he tried, the nearer he found himself to his own house. Yet when he resigned himself to the madness and propelled himself backward, the crowd responded by forcing him forward, and baffled, he found him-self just behind the line of firemen, a timid hand on his back.

It was Porter. For years Samuel would maintain he'd never seen so devastated a man. The top of his Panama hat was singed black, and his dreadful eyes were wet. He'd been restricted from going in after his family, and stood now with the impotence of a cripple, watching his life burn down.

"Tyne," he said with more emotion than Samuel had ever believed that man could feel. "Tyne, this is a bad case. Oh, it's a bad case. Oh, oh . . ."

Tears came to Samuel's eyes, and he went to put his arms around his neighbor. But the man resisted, as though not even this tragedy could make him forget their differences. Samuel withdrew, feeling a little hurt, and side by side they stood watching that spectacular mansion burn down, tired, aware of their enmity, but drawing a kind of solace from each other's company that they could not have found with any other man.

The fire lasted hours, until nothing was left to burn. Samuel stared at the embers. He watched the Porters reunite outside, amazed they'd all survived; there were considerably fewer children than he'd once thought. He took their survival not as sheer luck, or as human endurance, but as what it was: an act of God. Watching the children cower under police-issue blankets, nuzzling up to their parents, Samuel was filled with awe. He had witnessed a miracle. He felt disgusted for having thought ill of the Porters, and with a dry throat, with tears in his eyes, he waited for the police to finish with them so he could invite them into his house.

A hand touched his shoulder, and he turned to see Eudora, looking careworn, her face ancient with deep lines, her eyes rimmed red.

"Oh, God, Sam," she said. "Oh, God. Who knew this could happen?"

The ache in her voice made Samuel feel guilty. "This . . . this is a bad case."

She pressed his hand. "I've got to go. We'll talk later." And she walked off toward the Porters.

Now Ray had replaced the police and stood speaking with the Porters. The Franks seemed to receive the Porters like old friends. Samuel watched, then went home, where he found Maud waiting with a mug of coffee and some *toogbei*.

"Is everyone safe?" she said.

"Maud, a miracle has happened. Not one hair on one head was hurt. Can you believe it?" Maud looked like she'd lost weight overnight. Samuel worried.

"It's God's grace," said Maud, sitting exhausted at the table. "The twins came home."

"Oh," said Samuel. Their disappearance seemed to have happened a lifetime ago. "Where were they?"

"They won't say." Samuel noticed Maud's hands trembling. "But they're home now. That's what matters."

Samuel stirred his coffee with a forefinger. He sipped the drink, ruminating over the taste that recalled the ashy roots his family used to pry from their fields, which even boiled tasted of soil. He tried to collect his thoughts, but was too aware of his present wariness. A new, unwanted thought had come to him, and he sat in silence. Maud stared at him, and this, too, weighed on him. He left without dismissing himself, to stand with a kind of dark hopelessness before his daughters' unopened door. All was quiet, and raising his fist to knock he let it fall. Instead, he walked to his own room, where he collapsed onto the low bed.

He woke without sense of what day it was, a taste of ash in his mouth. Samuel stumbled downstairs, frustrated by the same foreboding. The house seemed stark, somber, the last of a lineage of great homes that, like their human equivalents, could not possibly deliver on an old glory. Its decay overwhelmed him, and he stepped outside, onto the front porch. Beyond the trees he saw the beginnings of fall. The crisp air rejuvenated him. He went inside, walking out to the patio, where the ground still smoldered before his feet. Porter's house looked like some huge, horrific, worm-ridden bird, its plumage blistered and discolored. He was still gazing at it when Maud brought him to earth with her voice.

Framed in the open bay door, she stood in a wrinkled beige frock, her hands nervous in her pockets. "The Franks are here."

Samuel nodded. He wanted to talk to Ray about the fire, to help the Porters however he could. He had suggestions for the town council on how to resettle them, what to do in the meantime, in organizing a drive to earn money to at least buy them a modest bungalow. Porter no longer had the money to pressure him to sell, and Samuel's sympathy ran strong. He went in.

The mood in the kitchen felt grave. The Franks wore the sober clothes of mourners, panicking Samuel with the thought that one of the Porters had succumbed to the fire after all. Eudora reassured him otherwise, and Maud asked everyone to sit, nodding at the fresh pot of coffee on the table. As Maud poured, Samuel expressed the Tynes' condolences, bumbling into an explanation of what could be done for the Porters. It was some time before he noticed the reluctance in Eudora's eyes, her periodic glances at her husband. He stopped talking.

"We're here precisely to talk about the Porters," said Ray, fixing Samuel with a look. "If I don't speak freely, I won't speak at all, Sam, you know that. So I won't mince words in saying that they feel, and *I* feel, that we have to look real deep into the causes of this fire." His glasses dissected his hard, clear eyes. "We have to get at the heart of this, and make amends wasting precious little time."

"We agree," said Samuel.

Ray scoffed, and Eudora gave him a guarded look, then confronted Samuel herself.

"Samuel . . ." she said. "The Porters say your daughters are responsible for the fire."

Maud made a noise of pained surprise. Samuel sat back. He felt a burning annoyance, but far worse was the idea's awful familiarity, the cause of his discomfort all day. But hearing it spoken aloud, the ludicrousness of it convinced him it wasn't true.

"Eh, is that so?" he said. "And how is that—they saw them?"

Eudora hesitated, glancing at her husband, who remained exasperated, but silent. "Well, no, she didn't see them. But she—"

"*She?* Who? Who, which '*she*'?"

Eudora's face darkened. Her voice became severe. "Akosua Porter. Now, she didn't *see* them, but she's certain they did it. If not physically, then—and we don't at all agree with this—through some magic or curse."

Maud made another pained noise. Grieved by his wife's anguish, Samuel grew angry. "Raymond Frank, a trustworthy man indeed," he said. "Brother, tell me. Did you not say these five weeks ago that Porter himself is known as Warlock Porter? Did you not tell me he burnt the pests from his fields? Or can I hear the wind?"

"She says you never had a proper burial for your uncle," said Eudora. "She says he's causing madness in your children because of it."

"*She* is the one who is mad. She left her common sense back home and brought her lunacy with her. What is this *magic,* what is this *curse*? Are we not in Canada? Did I turn my map upside down and end up right where I began?" He paused, then said, "Anyway, a curse would not function if the recipient was not guilty."

"She says they are evil." Maud watched Eudora with steady eyes. "She says they are evil, and you mind her."

"No one said 'evil,'" said Ray in a gentle voice. "You know no one here puts stock in that nonsense."

"What is this 'evil'?" said Samuel, his right eye twitching. "People are not evil, people are not good—they only behave in evil or good ways." The corners of his mouth had calcified with saliva. "We are what we are because of what we *do,* not do what we do because of what we *are.*"

Eudora pressed her lips into a bloodless line, trying to suppress her displeasure, as though the Tynes had withheld their true opinion all of these weeks, making a fool of her.

"Let's keep things reasonable here," said Ray, a little distressed. "Maybe, for all we know, it was an accident and they didn't mean to set the fire. But they've got to face up to that responsibility. And you've got to face up to the truth."

"*Truth,*" Samuel spat. "Don't tax your mouth with so heavy a word." Ray flushed, but said nothing.

"There was an arsonist before we moved here," said Maud.

"There were a few fires," Ray conceded. "But a few months ago, the man we suspected of being responsible, a Mr. John Rodale, left town for good. The fires stopped when he left. Besides, the ones at Thorpe's

Diner and the Porters' were different. I have no business telling you this, but it's a copycat, we're sure of it. Porter's was real significant because yesterday was August 15—the fifty-fifth anniversary of the fire that near burned down all Athabasca. The police are afraid it's a message, telling us there's more to come. All in all, the work of a clever person, of clever people."

"But the twins?" said Maud. "No one even saw them."

Ray cast a sidelong look at Eudora, settling back in his chair. He ran a nervous finger along the rim of his mug. "Now, this is the first anyone is hearing of this. I haven't even told the police, or you, Dora." He frowned in apology. "But the littlest Porter, Atoh, *did* see the twins. From his bedroom window. About two hours before the fire they came barrelling out your back door and across the field. He said he went down to talk to them and found them playing with a lighter, *my* lighter, the one I left here." Ray gave Samuel a searching look. "How much longer can we let these accidents go on, Samuel? Ama's near-drowning, Maud's leg, you, with the pills."

Samuel flinched. He glanced at Maud, who looked astonished.

"Who's next?" continued Ray, concern on his face. "I'm the first to admit your girls are brilliant, but it seems to me they're imbalanced. They don't have friends, they don't talk . . . they're not easy in society, especially one so close-knit as Aster. As your friend, and a council member, too, I recommend you get them professional help. Dora's done some work with the Red Deer Facility for Distressed Children, and we're sure that with her recommendation they could be in by next week."

"Eh, he is a doctor now, too?" said Samuel. "You will not fault me for asking to see your degree."

Ray controlled his words. "Whether you respect me or damn me doesn't matter. The twins can't stay in Aster. But I advise you, we *both* do, don't just take them back to the city with you. They can't cope in society, and by all means should be given a break from it. I know this is hard, but you have my word we'll give you a good price for your property."

The Tynes' prolonged silence made Eudora lower her eyes.

"Surely you wouldn't want to stay here?" said Ray, astonished. "Nobody blames you, but . . . you'd be uncomfortable."

"Property," said Samuel, frowning. When Eudora began to speak, he silenced her with a raised finger. "Ahein . . . so this is what you have made of my request for you to find the will. This, this *bargain*." He nodded grimly. "This stupidity with the wheat, this supercrop—it's no joke. You have wanted my land since the day Jacob breathed his last."

"That's unfair!" said Eudora, placing her pale, fat hands palm down on the table. "You make it sound like Ray's out to get you."

"No, no, I'll admit it," said Ray, his mouth down-turned. "This land is ideal for that kind of experimentation. I don't have even an acre of my own fields to spare for it. But I haven't been secretly plotting anything, sitting here rubbing my hands together and drooling, trying to plot your downfall. It's just circumstance, Samuel. The Porters need a home, and I have the money to give them one. If I profit by owning the surrounding land, then that's my business. Porter will, of course, be paying me back. Otherwise, where do you expect them to go?"

"Where do you expect *us* to go?" said Maud.

"*Your* children took *their* house. This is the one they want. Besides, you won't care who lives here when you're back in the city. The price I'm prepared to offer should be enough." Ray exhaled. "Look, Aster is close-knit—I know that's why you moved here. One man steals another man's horse, it's everyone's business, and that's the way it should be. We're not cold and uncaring like in the city. But crime's not as easy here, neither. Each man takes an interest and a responsibility in making sure the horse gets returned and the thief gets punished."

Samuel scoffed. "What is this village mentality you have? And what do you think—I can be convinced to deprive my family of our house and my wife of her only children?"

"I'm trying to do you a favor by not calling the authorities."

"*Call* the authorities! This is *my* house! *My* property! Do you understand me? Your municipality can have no clause on land I own or who lives on it!"

Ray looked sympathetic. "Generally, you're right. But if the municipality doesn't have the right to take a man's house from him, another man's children have no right in hell to take it from him, neither."

Samuel set his jaw, and his voice filled with disgust. "Land of opportunities, land of law and justice. Let me tell you, all I have learned in coming here is that nationalities don't matter—men are everywhere the same. When trouble comes, they never tire of looking for something to blame their misfortunes on. A child dies of malaria, and his mother nearly commits suicide trying to find out who sent the mosquito to *her* child. Always blame, blame, blame, as though there were no such thing as accidents. Let me tell you, my uncle, he took the blame of my family to such an extent that he let the conflicts of the past dictate and, quite frankly, belittle the rest of life. With such a mentality, what is the point in trying to live with each other?"

His words induced a silence more tired than thoughtful, and for some time the group sat dispossessed, wary of each other. Samuel kept glancing at Maud, for only the sight of her disillusionment was strong enough to revive his anger. The argument died into a silence both factions found hard to sit out. As the Franks rose to go, Samuel, relenting, said, "And if they tell you they did not do it?"

Ray exhaled with impatience. "They did it."

"But if they *tell* it to you?"

"We'll see."

As soon as Samuel had closed the door on the Franks, he heard his wife crying. He wanted to abolish what lay before them with a single, convincing phrase. But he felt tired, and didn't himself believe in a clean solution. They admitted the severity of their situation, and sat for a time without talking. He dropped his head to hide his twitching eye and spoke to his lap.

"Are the twins awake?"

Maud looked up, startled. "Samuel, please."

"No, *you* please," he said, but without aggression. "Are they?"

"Yes. Yes, I think so."

He rose without further speech. Maud followed him, the sound of her crying echoing up the stairwell. He put a finger to her lips as they reached the top. The door to the girls' room was open, and Samuel stepped through it, suppressing an urge to leave.

The twins sat on the cot nearest to the door, their cold eyes fixed behind him. He was filled with the terrible wonder of not being able to tell them apart. Also, there was their silence, and that stillness about them. The room smelled of stale water, of putrid smoke. Both girls looked frail and haggard, as though they, like Maud, had lost weight and gained age. They had bathed, but not thoroughly, and traces of dirt shaded their ears and other hollows. Samuel was saddened by the sight of what could be evidence, and unsettled at how each seemed like a reflection of the other. But studying them, he discerned a difference: he saw fear in one and hostility in the other. When he addressed them, Ama sprang up in the far bed, where she'd been pretending to sleep, and tried to say something with her eyes. Samuel and Maud glanced at each other, as though agreeing to get through the worst first, and ignoring Ama, Samuel asked his daughters where they had been.

The girl on the right flinched, giving her sister a quick look.

"Do your eyes have tongues? What is it you are saying that cannot be said to us?"

"*Samuel,*" said Maud.

Samuel crouched in front of the girl on the right. "Yvie, if it is you to whom I'm speaking, please tell me what is wrong. Your mother and I, we want for you only what you want for yourselves. If it is journalism, *be* journalists. If it is politics, *be* politicians. What we cannot condone is the two of you hurting each other, or hurting those around you." He paused with emotion. Chloe made an imperceptive eye gesture, and Yvette blinked. Samuel stood. "This has been a summer of accidents. Me, your mother, Ama. We accept them as misfortunes from God, and they are behind us." He crouched again, his face tense and serious. "What we need to know is if what happened next door—are we to take what has happened there as an act of God, as the doing of people far removed from us, or is there yet more to the story? Does that dirt on your hands mean anything but that you have fallen in mud?"

"*Samuel!*" said Maud. But Samuel could tell her objection arose from habit and fear.

"Yvie, Chloe," Maud said. "Just tell us you didn't set that fire. I— *we* know you didn't, but you're going to have to say it. First to us, then to Ray Frank. *Please.* We know you didn't."

"You are not responsible," said Samuel. "Of this we are certain. But given the circumstances—you ran out, you came back at the end . . ." Already annoyed, Samuel grew agitated when Maud started to cry again, and he stepped away from her to continue. "You go and you come back soot-covered, and—"

"With a lighter," screamed Ama, her voice so righteous she silenced the room. "They have a lighter, a fancy silver one. They were coughing when they came back and talking that gibberish, and the room stunk so bad with smoke it gave me asthma! It's those letters, those brushes! They're making them crazy. This house is making them crazy."

Samuel was pained to hear this from *her* mouth.

Ama began to cry. "Don't leave me here with them," she said. "Don't you leave me here! I can't live here anymore, I can't. Take me back to Grandmère. Don't you leave me here."

Samuel and Maud neared the door, solemn, but unable to leave without an answer. Maud was the first to go, leaving Samuel alone. He confronted the twins' cold, impassive faces.

"Will you not absolve yourselves?" he said.

They fixated on the dark hallway beyond him.

chapter TWENTY-TWO

The weather in the coming week heralded autumn. The leaves rusted almost overnight. Trees grew nude, baring arthritic sticks. The river aged to the color of lead, and the men of Peahorn Street, solemn, despondent, began to meet under the early streetlights to discuss the horror of another winter without work.

Samuel spent the days after the fire locked in his study. To avoid facing the window, which held a full view of the Porters' ruins, Samuel turned his desk. He'd sit for hours, staring at his shadow in the frame of sunlight on the wall. Raising his fist, he'd clasp and unclasp his fingers, marveling. Or he'd fuss through his papers, reorganize his drawers and, during the night, when his mind became strangely lucid, fix those very objects he'd once thought beyond repair. Anything to keep his mind from the life collapsing around him. Maud, too, had turned a blind eye to things, though he saw the worry in her stark face, her tense hands, her sensitivity to the weakest noises in the house. No one mentioned the fire, except in the abstract way people speak of misfortunes that have nothing to do with them. "What a shame," someone would mutter, to the general nod of heads. "A miracle, really, an act of God no one was hurt," another (usually Samuel) would say, and again, the nodding.

What Samuel truly thought of the arson, he would not admit even to himself. Not that he ignored it; but every time the thought that *they* might be responsible occurred to him, his mind grew dim and he felt incapable of going on. He rejected the idea, even while feeling there might be some truth in it. He avoided his family, and was glad when the twins stopped coming down for meals. He only allowed himself one regret: his turning away from Ama.

He didn't do it on purpose. Ama was sleeping in the Iron Lung until tomorrow morning, when Samuel would drop her off to spend the last two weeks of the summer with Grandma Ouillet. Somehow, he felt betrayed, as though Ama of all people should have stood by the twins, by the Tynes, by *him*. And though she was merely a child, unaware of her offense, Samuel still faulted her a little. But not consciously. He felt as ashamed as when he'd first turned from his daughters.

Driving up to the Ouillet house, Samuel glanced at Ama in the passenger seat, regretting how he'd treated her these last few days. He really did love the girl, but had begun to understand what Maud meant by "blood is thicker than water." On the doorstep, he swept Ama into a hug.

"You be good," he said.

Ama's mouth trembled. She was about to say something, when she thought the better of it and dropped the knocker.

When Samuel reached home, he found Ray Frank waiting for him, smoking. Samuel felt a dry fear as he stepped from the car, but collected himself.

"My house and my children are not enough for you?" he said. "You have come for my wife, my hat?"

Ray laughed. "Good to see you're keeping your sense of humor. How are you these days? Dora really misses Maud and says she wishes she'd call. Don't suppose you found that tractor part yet?" The longer Ray prattled on, the more amazed Samuel became. Did Ray take him for an imbecile? Did he truly believe things between them could stay the same? A summer of farming had reddened Ray's face so that Samuel thought he looked like a livid baby. When the older man jostled his glasses, wet red lines like welts appeared beneath his eyes. He was sweating so heavily that Samuel, drought-dry in his pewter suit, offered the red kerchief that garnished his breast pocket. Ray accepted it and, wiping his glasses, began to explain why he'd come.

"Me and Dora have been talking, and I realized a few things. So I have a proposal for you. I was thinking that after you send the girls away the Porters could come and live with you. I know that sounds nuts, but hear me out. You wouldn't have to move and would even make a little money." He cleared his throat. "I'm willing to do one of two things. Either I'll pay you a little rent on their behalf or buy the property outright from you, both providing I get to use the surrounding fields. I've already talked to the Porters about it, and they're willing."

Samuel remained silent. He inclined his head a little, as though trying to define a distant sound. "So this is it," he said. "The bitter heart destroys more than its owner."

Ray looked surprised. "Not bitter. Practical."

"Practical," said Samuel. Turning, he watched the nearby trees heave, their leaves dropping, the sun weighing on everything. He felt a deep-seated sadness.

"Aster has the worst village mentality I have ever seen. A troupe of big men trying to hide that they're still in diapers. This, as you see, is my house. These trees you see here are mine, this soil mine, these weeds *mine*. I decide who lives here and who doesn't, I decide when to leave and when to stay. Anything that happens here, *I* decide. *Me.*"

Ray grew more flushed. He handed Samuel's handkerchief back. "I've done nothing but look out for you. I sent you customers, I helped you get investors, I helped settle you in." He sounded sad to have to admonish him. "You figure things out for yourself. But you've got two days for your children to leave Aster before I'm forced to tell the authorities what I know. I'm sorry." He left without looking back.

Samuel set his jaw, his anger hardening. Not a single Tyne would leave Aster. Never, unless they themselves chose to. Samuel entered the house, sitting through a meal he was too preoccupied to eat. It was just he and Maud; the twins were refusing food. Out of guilt, Maud took three meals upstairs every day, carrying down the untouched trays at nightfall. She didn't want to tell Samuel about it, afraid he would force-feed them, but when he, too, didn't touch his food, she felt spiteful. She did nothing if not for her family. Her life was reduced to a few domestic routines: washing clothes (now drying above the fireplace); cooking meals no one ate; darning socks no one wore; and, though this was beyond enduring, trying not to ask questions. She was lost in the shadows of other people's secrecy, something she'd seen in other women but had never expected of herself. She avoided going outside unless she needed something without which they couldn't live. Aware of eyes on her, Maud became rigid and haughty, glaring back, though she knew that, once home, she'd buckle from the pressure. The whispering was the worst. In the shops, in the streets; she couldn't believe how she was being treated. Ray and Eudora had not only told the authorities about the twins, they had informed the whole town. With a bad conscience Maud remembered the way she'd treated Tara Chodzicki.

When Maud complained to Samuel, she was astonished to realize he hadn't noticed a thing. Nothing could touch his pride, and Maud felt both embittered and relieved to see him carrying on with dog-like disregard and simplicity.

"My prototypes are going so well," he said, "that to make adjustments now would be like putting on a suit when the tailor had only pinned in his intended alterations. Hey, I'm a poet. Yes . . . 'his intended alterations' . . . yes, yes. You move and it falls back to square one. Yes!"

Maud rolled her eyes. "We can't stay here, Samuel. We've got to go back to Calgary." She was too proud to tell him about the bag of burning fertilizer thrown at the front door, the desecration of their flower beds, the slurs from passing cars, the refusal of some shopkeepers to accept their money. Everything, in short, that the Porters had endured both in Oklahoma and in Aster's bordering towns and cities. Maud begged Samuel to accept Ray's offer and return to Calgary, or go anywhere else on the planet for that matter; anything that would allow her to salvage her dignity.

But how could he return? His house and business were his life; he wouldn't feel complete without them. He sensed his wife's despair, but closed himself off from it, shutting her from his study. What could a woman who'd led so narrow a life know about the wandering failure produced in a man? That, uprooted, he walked through the world without seeing and unseen, a nonbeing.

Now, when he'd finally discovered the work that would validate and immortalize him, they wanted to take it from him. He wouldn't let that happen. He could not return to his passive life in Calgary, an insensate wandering more like taking up space than existing. To give all that was sacred in him to the dogs, to cast his pearls before swine; he couldn't compel himself to do it.

So he unlocked his study, waved off his wife's pleas and made his way through Aster as though he were appropriate and even valued. Blind to all that wasn't work, the gossip, the stares, even the slurs, made a dim impression on him. The closest he came to noticing his mistreatment was when he went to Hayes' Drugs to buy his stomach medication.

The drugstore had that wonderful antiseptic smell Samuel associated with good health. Doctors' offices, banks and libraries also had this smell. He walked to the tall counter, greeting Hayes' son with a smile.

Hayes Jr. studied Samuel from behind the englassed counter. "We don't carry your medication anymore."

Samuel raised his brows. "I bought some here only last week. It is Napro—"

"I don't care if you bought it here in the last two minutes." Hayes grew grim about the mouth. "I'm telling you we don't stock it anymore."

"You must be mistaken." Samuel giggled. "Perhaps it has simply been misshelved. I have been buying it here for months now." He turned to see a line of people growing behind him. All wore that same expression, a grimness about their mouths, impassive.

"And," said Hayes Jr., "if you got any other prescriptions, you can take those to the city, too."

Samuel understood. He left the store.

Beyond that incident he saw nothing. Only on the day of Ray's deadline (on which nothing happened) did Samuel begin to see the shadow on the edge of his life. Everywhere he went, he was conscious of being watched, but would look up to confront nothing. This had continued for a week, this peripheral haunting, when at last he saw the cause of it. Porter lingered in the shadows across from his store, vanishing by the time Samuel had reached his feet to go and confront him. Porter hid in the foliage on Samuel's walks home, in the alley where Samuel tossed bad circuit boards, in the few loyal cafés that still served him. Taunting, leering, escaping confrontation. Had Samuel been less anesthetized by work he might have done something. Instead, he grew used to the apparition, barely raising his eyes.

One day his largest investor called him in for a meeting. Samuel walked to the man's office, dignified by a smart bowler and funereal suit, and was given a minute of Mr. Herbert Elliot's time.

Elliot, an aristocratic man, offered Samuel a Scotch before speaking. Samuel accepted. Sinking into the plush chair, he was unsure of how to begin and was glad when Elliot spoke first.

"I've got four and a half minutes, so I'll be brief," he said. Dwarfed by his sizeable desk, Elliot made up for his small stature with a grand, stentorian voice. "I realize there are times in men's lives where stress, and perhaps lack of money, incite them to terrible deeds. That standards of morality become dubious. But for you to have accepted money for what you know is a farce . . ."

Samuel was stirred into an awareness of his surroundings. "A farce?"

"I have spoken with people. People who, because of my rigid code of ethics, I have not the power, nor the right to name. Some people have no personal standards, but me, I was always taught to uphold a code of morality in keeping with my background." He sighed, wrinkling his huge brow. "In short, information's not sacred anymore, my boy. Your project isn't visionary—it's a practical joke. And you had me."

His severe look, the tenor of his voice, the words he used, all of it reminded Samuel of Dombey and Son from the government office.

Elliot became sympathetic. "I will not specify a repayment schedule—you have only your conscience for that. Besides, I know that somewhere in you is a man of integrity. I felt that, and my instincts are rarely wrong. So take your time, Samuel. But a warning—Wainright's not as fair."

Samuel had a terrible thirst. The glass in his hands was empty. Thanking Elliot for his time, he left the room consumed with the need to drink. The streets glistened from a recent cleaning. Samuel strode to the first convenience store, but was turned away even as he pleaded to pay five dollars for a bottle of pop. The next stores and bars also rejected him. He remembered the tap in his shop, three streets away.

The whole town seemed to grow silent. Passersby pretended not to watch him, but they couldn't quell the urge to stop in the streets, whole groups of people slowing as at the gravity of an accident. Samuel felt with each step he was entering a dream.

Someone had crushed the windows of Tyne Electronics, a fringe of glass like brittle ice framing the storm inside. A single window stood untouched, GO HOME FIRESTARTER sludged in paint against the pane. The vandals had urinated everywhere, so that the nauseating ammonia was potent even before Samuel entered. He gagged. His expensive European tools were broken and strewn among piles of mud. His ceiling had been blackened by an unsuccessful fire, his entire set of computer prototypes smashed. Graffiti ruined the walls, slurs of FIRESTARTER, ARSONIST. His workbench had been axed. His prototype diagrams and signed contracts were shred or burned to ash. A swarm of flies clotted the air. And in all this, Samuel salvaged the only thing he could find that had survived: the box of watches and candles he'd bought from Porter before he'd known who he was.

Gripping the wet box under his arm, he held back his vomit. But his reaction was only physical; at first sight of the destruction he'd felt such anguish that he'd had to toughen immediately or go wild with grief. He emerged calmly into the street while people pitied him or harassed him or simply looked askance. Not until he'd reached his own street did a terrible emotion well in him again, and he spat into the dust and cursed. Maud found him in the foyer, smelling like a toilet, and dragged him to the bath.

He lay in shock, unable or unwilling to tell her what was wrong. It wasn't until the RCMP came to the door that she learned what had happened.

Seeing the immaculate pants, the tall black boots, and the mustaches that gave their faces a severe, parochial look, Maud was beset with panic. She wiped her hands on her apron, trying to smile.

The policemen stood on the porch, chatting easily between themselves until they saw her.

"We're looking for Samuel Kwabena Tyne. Is he home?"

Maud's smile trembled. "Well, yes, yes. But he's really sick right now. Really, really sick. In fact, he's in a dead sleep right now." Her nerves made her run off at the mouth. "I was out shopping, and I came home to find him in an utter shock, just sitting there, staring at nothing. He smelled like a toilet, you know, like he'd . . ." She stammered.

A look passed between the policemen.

"We need to speak with him in regards to a property on Glover Street."

Maud clasped her hands. "Why, what's wrong with it?"

"You his wife?"

She nodded. They told her about the damage, asking her if she knew anything about it. At her negative response, they nodded. "Sheer vandalism. What is happening to this town?"

Maud went to see the damage herself. Grim, she assessed the frantic insects, the pungent smell, the slogans confirming the mess as a gesture of justice. A neighbor had done this, this act more lacking in humanity than anything she'd faced these forty-three years. Kneeling, she retrieved a few tools from the debris and, finding them broken, threw them down again. She tried to drive the mud out with a shovel, but the handle buckled in half where it had been burnt, cutting her hand. Glass, urine, an earnest finality to it all weakened her will to clean. Exhausted and disillusioned, she rose to her feet and walked the mile home with a pronounced dignity.

Samuel was sitting at the table when she entered. He was putting on a ragged pair of socks, lowering his foot when he noticed her, as though caught in some small but private ritual. He wore a singlet and black pants loose at the waist, and Maud was surprised by how much he resembled those jobless drifters of the Peahorn district. Sitting beside him, she gripped his rough, callused hands and began to cry. His hands sat unanimated in hers, and glancing at him she was struck by how resigned his eyes looked. In defacing his property, the vandals had beaten the will from his body. He looked dispassionately around him. His skin was toneless, gone ashen, and the new lack of direction in his voice made his words sound weighty and insignificant at the same time.

"You have seen a sight there was no excuse to witness," he said. "An indecency beyond anything." His voice was metallic, undemanding. "Men do anything to keep other men mediocre, they find any reason. God's inequalities . . . this is how they're overcome."

Maud snapped. "Samuel, this is about the twins, not some assault to your, your *genius.*"

"We are giving them up," he said. "We are giving them up."

Maud took her hands from his. "Ego! How dare you? How dare you. This is not about you—you're no genius! You are a small, simple, black man—you're no inventor. How dare you?"

He took her hand out of instinct. "Do you not see that they are already lost? They are not even eating. They beat each other. Do you not see it? I have been sitting here hours, *hours,* trying to figure out at what point they were lost. And you know it is impossible. Impossible. They have been lost so long it is beyond remembering."

Maud stood up, trying to regain her composure, but letting out a sob every time she looked at Samuel. Samuel gazed at her, as though her grief had no meaning for him. He knew she recognized the truth in what he said. He knew it.

"On Monday I will drive the girls to the facility for distressed children. You will come along, or stay home—it doesn't matter. They are too sick for us to be of any use to them."

Maud began to nod, shaking a little. "We neglected them terribly. Who are we to give them up now?"

"We do not have the means to cure them."

Maud continued to nod, turning her face to the wall. "And take Ray's money and move back to the city, just like that. Move back and start again as though we'd never had children at all."

"We are not moving back." He sounded passive, but irrefutable. "We are staying right here. We are staying here, and the Porters will move in with us."

Maud looked horrified.

"We will live side by side. Friend, enemy, they are no different in this life. Let them come—we will starve together."

"You're mad," said Maud.

"Perhaps I passed it to our daughters. I know *you* think I did. Whether it is the case or not, I will spend the rest of my life answering for it. It is on this day I finally come to understand Jacob. For what you cannot change, you make amends. You make amends."

Maud lowered her voice. "You won't do this."

"Will you have your daughters sick for the rest of their lives? Would you deny them normality, normal husbands, normal children, because of your selfishness? Let them go. They will remember the kindness at our age."

Samuel knew he'd touched a nerve. There was a long silence.

Finally, Maud said, "Why should *they* move in? They lost their home, but . . ."

"At our daughters' hands, which is as good as if we ourselves had done it. They lost their home, and we must account for that. We cannot go back to Calgary even if we wanted to. We are bankrupt, absolutely bankrupt. I will use Ray's money to begin paying back my investors. I owe great sums to two men, and will work out of the study. The Porters can help us with the upkeep. And it will stop all their tomfoolery—they will be indebted."

"You won't do it."

"We will," he said. "We will." And he left the house and wouldn't say where he'd been when he returned at nightfall. Maud had calmed down, but she gave Samuel indignant glances as if this would change his mind. He didn't notice.

Neither spoke nor saw the other until bedtime, when at their routine hour they met in the room, sensitive to each other's presence but silent. They lay apart, awake and listening to the darkness for hours. Samuel fell asleep only to be woken by his wife's crying.

"You won't do it," she said. "You won't do it, you won't, you won't." Her voice was full of breath, but there was a note of resignation in it that told Samuel this was the last of her resistance. Tired, he pulled Maud to his chest, an empty gesture she accepted as genuine. Her face was moist. He held her until she exhausted herself, slackening as she fell asleep. As he held her, he meditated on how pointless it was that sunrise was so beautiful when so few men actually saw it anyway.

As Monday approached, Maud worried herself sick trying to tell the twins. She continued to bring them trays of food three times a day, and each time found them playing dead when she entered, their dim eyes fixed on the ceiling. It had been five days since they'd eaten more than bread, and trying to force-feed them left Maud exhausted. Instead of leaving after collecting Saturday's supper tray, Maud sat on the bed vacated by Ama.

"It's been a long time since you girls have been well. Your dad and I, we, we don't know what to do." Tears entered her voice, and she was unable to regain her composure. "I'm sorry. I am so sorry." She picked up the dinner tray and rushed out.

On Sunday, Maud packed the twins' clothes under the scrutiny of their dim eyes. She was careful to pack both cases at once, folding the identical outfits in beside each other, a tight pain in her throat. Neither girl acknowledged her, and finishing she snapped the cases shut, placing them near the door. Before leaving, Maud walked between the beds and leaned over both girls. The girl on the left kept her head averted, her brown eyes vacant, the girl on the right's lip trembled. And for the first time in days, Maud addressed one separately. "Yvie," she said, "what happened?" After yet more silence she stroked her head, then left the room.

On Monday morning, Maud repacked the twins' clothes into garbage bags, for during the night they had destroyed the cases. Maud hid the remnants under the bed (they were Samuel's cases from his scholar years), and ran a comb through the girls' hair while Samuel loaded the trunk outside.

There were still no tears as the car neared the facility's gates. Leaning out his window to punch in the pass code he'd been given, Samuel's mind wandered as the wrought-iron gates parted.

He was remembering a conversation he'd once overheard in the government office. Through the foam partition dividing their desks, Sally Mather, his co-worker, had been crying softly into the phone. Samuel didn't mean to eavesdrop, but her stage whisper left him no choice. She spoke of not being able to pinpoint the exact moment her life had changed. As if things had simply shifted overnight—the marriage over, the ambition gone, everything lost. When she thought about it, the signs leading to it were clear. But she hadn't seen them until all was over.

Samuel hadn't made much of this at the time. But he wondered now, what about those times when the exact moment of impact is sharply felt, yet seems to have absolutely no meaning? What about when the clues leading up to it lack all sense, and amount to something inconceivable?

Samuel's hands trembled on the steering wheel; beside him Maud coughed weakly. In the backseat the twins sat dry-eyed, clutching hands. Gulls flew overhead, their dark shadows darting across the hood.

Samuel cut the engine. All was silent but for the gulls' crying and Maud sniffling as she turned her face to the window. The lot was empty at this hour, and the absence of witnesses almost made Samuel want to turn back—to start the engine, leave the grounds, and make the long drive back to Aster, as if by painstakingly reversing his actions he could somehow undo the whole summer, undo its every disastrous turn. But that would be impossible, and wrong. The twins needed to be here. And though he'd never understand their abnormality—the fits of dark brilliance that were their best and worst trait—neither could he let it continue.

Samuel and Maud stepped from the car. The sun dropped a thin layer of warmth over the cold pavement. They led their children into the brick building.

chapter TWENTY-THREE

It is a little-known truth that enemies make for discreet room-mates. Avoidance in a household, even when vengeful, is far more pleasant than too deep an intimacy. So it was when the Porter family moved in, bringing with it smells, unnecessary yelling and a resentful and suspicious gratitude. They took a full Tuesday to move in, dallying more out of spite than because much had survived the fire. Samuel watched them carry their belongings across the dead field. The six children made a game of it, propping as much as they could manage on their heads and laughing when it all fell off. Porter yelled for them to stop acting like asses, and the whole crew settled around the pot of hot palm-nut soup and fufu Maud made for them. It was the only meal the two families ever shared, later dividing more for privacy's sake than from disliking each other's company. Maud and Akosua still continued to cook together, Akosua finally forcing Maud to speak Fante, despite Maud having made a vow almost two decades earlier to forget the tongue of her birth.

So again, as in history, the Tyne house became a boardinghouse.

But things were not as bad as Samuel had imagined. Within a week he found himself living a kind of bachelor's existence, working in his study uninterrupted, socializing if he liked. He told himself all had turned out well, considering. The fires had stopped when the twins left. Seeing their absence and the recovery of general safety, the people of Aster stopped abusing the Tynes, judging their new poverty as penance, and even began to ask after their health again. Strange as that was, Samuel accepted it, pleased to be a part of something again, to wander about without being watched, to have children overrun his house without having to discipline them when they broke something. And no one bothered him in his study, so when the chaos overwhelmed him, Maud knew where to look. He used Ray's money to repay most of his debts, and worked hard to make up the difference. He was obliged to do work he'd formerly turned down; radios, kitchen appliances, any wired gadget with burnt nerves. The pay was paltry and the housecalls humiliating, but he otherwise enjoyed working from his study. Saul Porter kept up his ventures, peddling on the side to repay *his* debts. The arrangement, considering its nature, could not have run more smoothly.

Though Maud and Akosua often laughed together, behind closed doors Maud criticized the woman with such passion Samuel feared the Porters would hear her through the walls. Her anxiety exhausted him. She obsessed over the updates from the facility; Samuel would sometimes wake at some crazy hour of the night to find her running the paper against a light bulb, as though the watermark might tell her more. Samuel feared for her.

"Please be reasonable, Maud," he pleaded.

"What, so I won't ruin our good name in Aster? Don't think I don't see you eyeing me. Don't think I don't know you've got designs to put me away, too."

For a while he bore her blame, but it soon overwhelmed him. He began to answer her by saying, "If your hand makes you go amiss, you cut it off."

His own anxiety couldn't be suppressed much longer. To calm

himself, he took to cultivating a cocoa yam plant in the sunlit kitchen. Hayes' Drugs began stocking his stomach medication again, but he often woke spitting blood.

When Maud demanded, "Who will care for us in our old age?" Samuel would reply: "Old age means death, and death will be a pleasure after all this. I hope they throw us in a ditch and refuse to let our children remember us."

Samuel fluctuated between indifference and guilt. He'd begun to suspect he'd acted out of spite. He hated to admit he'd made disastrous choices, and had been making them since he'd been sentient enough to choose. And to use his faulty judgment to decide others' lives ... no, he had been right to do so. They needed help. But to accept their "psychosis"—he forced such thoughts from his mind. It was more comforting to think of where he'd gone wrong in other spheres of his life, such as coming to Aster. The whole thing had been a fool's dream, this ridiculous belief in the living perfection of the past. There is no place in the world untouched by time.

The days passed, and Samuel considered visiting the twins. The need to see them worsened by mid-September, when a yellow bus began to whisk the children of Aster to Edmonton schools. Samuel thought of Ama, whom he'd called to make sure her parents had returned safely. André and Elizabeth Ouillet were barely civil, and Samuel wondered what Ama had told them. To know she thought ill of him bothered him, but as with life's other pains, he weathered it.

Every few weeks Maud would make a dramatic proposal to go and visit the twins.

"They're not broken toasters, you know," she'd say, the humor always off-kilter. "You can't just shuffle them off for someone else to fix. You can't dispose of them."

Silent, Samuel would watch her lay out her Sunday clothes on the bed, her fingers trembling as she straightened their hems and wiped the lint from them. Her pain was most acute at these moments, and often he'd leave the room to avoid a confrontation. Sometimes he wouldn't make it to the door before, greatly irritated, she'd say, "Oh, stop eyeing me like that! You have no right. You have no right to scrutinize me like that."

He'd leave, only to find her in the same room hours later, the dresses put away, absorbed in darning his socks.

"Not this Saturday," she'd say, though he wouldn't have spoken. "We'll visit them next week. I'll send a letter for now, and a package with all their favorite food."

It was obvious that Maud would never be able to bring herself to visit. Samuel understood. It would simply be too much for her. She couldn't bring herself to see what she had done to them. And even if she were to undo it all, to bring the twins home and start all over, nothing that passed between them could ever absolve her.

For Samuel's part, he didn't mention visiting them, but resolved to go if she could ever bring herself to do so.

Despite the chaos in his life, or perhaps because of it, he found himself drawn to Akosua Porter. Less haughty out of her element, she maintained a dignity he thought bewitching at the most inappropriate of times. He thought of her as he worked, as he paused from work, and after months of abstaining he masturbated to distraction. She was full-breasted, a lovely beige color, and her blemishes were like freckles on that ageless face. He thought he would die the day she stepped from the shower in a red terry robe, smelling of lavender. She paused, giving him an annoyed look, and with the boxes clogging the hallway, she had to gyrate past him to get by. In an impulse that frightened both of them, he put a hand on her hip and pressed against her. He hardly knew where the lust had come from, was as terrified by his actions as she was, but watching her rush away he only feared she'd tell his wife. After days of panic, trying to figure out if Maud knew, he decided she didn't. And seeing how easy lust was to get away with, he started to put himself in situations where he could indulge it. The day Akosua responded, throwing open the door of her bedroom, Samuel collapsed on top of her, wriggling out of his pants. It was over as soon as it had begun; unsatisfied, they writhed away from each other as though they could hardly believe themselves. It was awful. The wrinkled thinness of their legs, the asthmatic panting, the briefness of it; all of this made them conscious of their age, and the indignity in this adolescent behavior. Pulling up his slacks, Samuel wondered how to ask her not to say anything to his wife, but Akosua spoke first: "Tell someone," she said, "and I will castrate you."

Samuel recovered quickly, not feeling too guilty. In putting away his daughters he'd performed the greatest evil of which he was capable; all other indecencies paled in comparison. He returned to his work clear-minded, tended his cocoa yam plant; his desire for Akosua defused. Like everything else in his life, he soon suppressed the urge for sex, and was able to meet her in all parts of the house without feeling anything. He grew fascinated by his own lack of feeling, to the point that he imagined killing a man wouldn't faze him. Then he'd remember his daughters. He'd repress his thoughts and get back to work.

The day Saul removed the weathervane from the roof, Maud got a telegram that knocked the last of her wits from her. The Tynes had grown so insensate to the vane's screeching that the excruciating silence left by its absence startled them. The telegram, a bad omen as only telegrams are, was nervously unsealed. Maud's father had died in Gold Coast two weeks before, and they needed her to come home and bring two thousand dollars for his burial. She suffocated with the news. She cried in Samuel's arms.

"Will the money drop from the sky?" she said. "We can't even afford to put gum in the holes in our shoes."

Samuel began to cry, too. Maud sat in surprised silence.

"Not one nail to hang our boots on," said Samuel composing himself. "No daughter to care for us in old age."

"Who mentioned them?" Taking her head from his lap, Maud prostrated herself on the bed and wept. Samuel left her to exhaust herself.

There were other voices in the house. Samuel was curious, for the Porters never had guests and he himself met his clients elsewhere, both families only too aware of their embarrassing living arrangements. Samuel stopped in the doorway of the kitchen. There at his table, without shame, amiable even, sat Ray and Eudora Frank talking to Akosua, who was recounting the story of her parents' goat, whose penchant for walking backward after being lamed in a fire had brought brief fame to her home. Eudora's laugh was soft, distracted, but Ray responded in his robust way, interrupting with jokes.

After all of the pain the Franks had caused the Tynes, after all of the secrecy, the false intimacy, they were spiteful enough to return to a house of ruin and belittle what remained of its dignity. Samuel was so stricken by the sight of them that he stood a full minute without hearing what they said.

Ray stood, a sad smile on his face. "We heard about Maud's father, Samuel. We come with condolences."

Samuel shot a sharp look at Porter, who crossed his broad arms. Akosua looked away.

"We brought a dessert torte," said Eudora, a little too eager. "Rhubarb and Saskatoon berry. They're at their best this time of year."

Samuel wanted to hit her. Not speaking, he turned to leave.

"Samuel." Eudora clutched the back of a chair for support, the magnitude of her weight making it groan. She looked half-dead, her skin the pallor of teeth, a green hue to the gray of her hair. She breathed audibly, and though her eyes were still sharp, they had lost their edge of criticism and instead looked desperate, nervous.

"Samuel," she said again, and a strange emotion crossed her face too fast for Samuel to understand it. "Tell Maud I'm sorry."

Samuel stared at her. He left without reply.

After checking on Maud, Samuel retreated to his study. He ignited his soldering iron to tinker with Wainright's old toaster. The job didn't pay money, but went toward closing his debt to that impatient businessman, who kept a tally of Samuel's finished jobs like a child's game on a cardboard slat in his office. Sometimes Samuel marveled, with a kind of detachment, that he was again at the mercy of two bureaucratic men: Elliot was like Dombey, Wainright like Son. But most of the time he tried not to think of this.

As Samuel worked, waiting for the Franks to leave, it finally struck him. The house was no longer his. And as boarders, he and Maud had no control over who entered. He extinguished his soldering iron and sat staring at the wall.

Late afternoon found him in one of his best suits, driving up the road to the gates of the facility. He parked and keyed in the code. The path was on an incline, and by the time he reached the grounds he was out of breath. He did not know exactly what he had come to do, only that he felt he should do something. Though he tried to suppress it, Samuel couldn't help but feel he'd been a painful failure as a parent, worse than a failure—that he had damaged his children in some preventable way. He picked a few marigolds and entered the building, greeting the desk attendant with a tense smile.

"These aren't visiting hours," was her surly response. She was a short, stocky woman who'd adorned her plain face with rhinestone glasses. "Besides, we can only hold so many people at once on the wards. Takes about a week's advance booking to see anyone."

Samuel giggled. "With that kind of wait one might think I have come to see the queen." He tried his hand at a joke. "I hope at least they are receiving royal treatment."

The woman looked harassed. "Name and number and I'll book you for next week."

She was immovable. Samuel gave his name and with a schoolgirl's deliberation she penned it into her schedule. But when he next returned, this time with Maud, who was talked into coming by the promise it would ease her nerves, they were denied admittance. An altogether different attendant eyed them.

"Eh," said Samuel, "last time I came here I signed up. Check your calendar."

The tiny woman's voice trembled. "Sir, you didn't sign up with me. We all keep our own schedule." When he began a tirade, she summoned her boss, a man of metal temper with a single thick eyebrow like a hyphen above disarmingly generous eyes. He made little noises of awe as he sought their names in the girl's new register, then, frowning, transcribed something in his own notebook and, promising nothing, saw them to their car.

Samuel tried three more times to see his daughters. Upon each visit he was thwarted by a different attendant with a different schedule, none of which corresponded. Dr. Stephenson responded to Samuel's concerns by restating the visiting days and promising to clarify things with the front counter so that the situation would not be repeated. And Samuel would return the next week only to be denied again. He couldn't believe the absurdity of this bureaucracy. He considered involving the authorities, and was disheartened when a lawyer, whom he couldn't afford anyway, told him that if he'd signed any paper making his children wards of the state he'd killed the case at the roots. Samuel couldn't remember *what* he'd signed. For days he searched his study for the contracts. It took time for him to realize that, though upset, he felt relieved each day the papers remained unfound. What would he do if he found them—force them to grant him visits he didn't know if he could stand? He realized with a kind of detachment that he fought mostly from a hatred of bureaucracy, rather than from a stinging need to see his children. In truth, his search had weakened his courage to see them. And so, Samuel stopped fighting. He found that he could bear it. Life continued as it was, and he waited for the coming of winter, for that simple change.

In early November, the foliage bloomed in a final gasp, the leaves rusting and falling. The trees grew angular. In a rare calm mood, Maud sat on the front stoop, her legs tucked under her like a schoolgirl, watching steam rise over the fields in the distance. Samuel stood behind her in the doorway. Seeing Maud like that, he felt a growing tenderness. He walked quietly to the kitchen to brew some tea, and with a steaming mug in each hand, stepped out to join her on the stoop.

Maud turned to him without her usual suspicion. She accepted the mug, pressing a gentle hand to the back of his wrist.

Samuel was touched by the gesture. Setting his own mug on the top step, he bent to stroke Maud's head.

She ducked, slapping his hand away. "Oh, stop your foolishness." As soon as she'd spoken she looked sheepish.

"That mist's really thickening over the fields," she said, wincing when the tea burned her tongue. "They say it'll be a hard winter."

Samuel sat beside her. He looked into her worn face, pained by how quickly she'd aged. "Perhaps," he said.

They sat on the stoop until sunset, watching the trees darken.

When Samuel could no longer see his hand in front of his face, he rose to his feet. "I am going inside. Are you coming?"

"Later."

Samuel collected their empty mugs. As he turned from Maud, she called his name.

"Yes?" said Samuel.

There was a deep silence in which he sensed her struggling to say something. The air between them was filled with the sound of crickets, rustling leaves, their dark heavy breathing. It seemed like minutes passed before he finally heard her meek voice.

"Thanks. For the tea."

Samuel smiled, then turned and entered the dark house.

Years passed. Not only the Tynes were touched by chaos; oil made Alberta a staggering fortune, until the mountains were walled like a beautiful daughter behind a concrete fortress of highrises. Cities flared in size, and in an embittering twist for Samuel, Calgary became a Canadian center for computer development. Aster widened its borders. Public favor divided, people shook up town meetings with reasons why it would pay to become a mere district of a richer town. In the end, despite lively backstabbing and a rash of threats so indecent even the mean-hearted were disgusted, a motion decided against it, and Aster stayed autonomous until years later, when the next generation abandoned its land. Alberta's new prosperity had attracted so many newcomers that a shift to the cities was inevitable. West Indians, Vietnamese, Koreans, Africans; the variety of faces even in Aster amazed Samuel. Most had come for the usual reasons: social gain, prosperity and the like. But some were refugees: six thousand Chileans fled after Allende was overthrown, Ismaili Muslims were cast out of Uganda, the Lebanese fled civil war. Instead of making friends with the newcomers, Samuel and Maud felt no affinity whatsoever with them. Their reasons for arriving had been so different, their payment for staying so out of touch with the clean hope of greenhorns, that they kept to themselves.

But even isolated from the world, Samuel and Maud felt its changes. They watched as loaders razed the remains of Porter's house to the ground and began construction on a posh-looking, alien replacement that, even given two lifetimes, neither the Tynes nor the Porters could never afford. And though Samuel knew the land was his, he was too tired to feel the kind of outrage it would take to put a stop to all this. He and Maud watched the town shift, the outer areas demolished to make room for the interests of farming and oil. And they watched, without relish, as Ray Frank fell on hard times and didn't recover. World grain sales sagged, and despite the Wheat Board's federal agency status, Trudeau refused to pull farmers from their rut. On government advice, Ray and his compatriots sized down their acreages, even stalling production on some fields. But this very measure brought ruin: just then China and Russia's crops failed, and the market soared again, bringing wealth to those stoics who'd toughed things out, and bankrupting the hasty. Ray, ruined, in the delusion of his last years, developed so bitter a hatred for Trudeau that had he been younger and prone to acting on his principles, his thoughts of assassination might have become an actual attempt. Instead, he had Eudora write hostile letters to the editor in which the phrase "federal shenanigans" was used no less than twice in each one, and in which he called for a Western revolt against Central Canada's policies. He adorned his truck with a bumper sticker that read THIS CAR DOESN'T BRAKE FOR LIBERALS, and led the Farmers League into its final evolution as a right-wing separatist party. Its members declared that the Trudeau government used the pretence of constitutional reform to bamboozle westerners out of their oil and property to use in the formation of a communist state. The Farmers League drew spectators to their monthly "debates" (usually drunken public forums for nonsensical Ottawa-bashing), at which Ray rose to decree that Alberta had not been part of Canada constitutionally since 1913. The party was anti-French and lobbied against the institution of immersion programs in grammar schools. Ray believed they could have made some headway were it not for all the infighting, and what might have been a peaceful death, one year later, was ruined by an incurable hatred for his colleagues, who had made rags of his final effort to bring about social change.

Eudora was inconsolable. Samuel and Maud drove the elder Porters to the outdoor funeral, surprised at the slight show of mourning at what should have been a crowded and venerated event. Ray had done much for Aster in his capacity as the mayor's second, and it grieved Samuel to see that a single wrong turn at the end of a life could cancel the memory of good acts. Fifteen mourners, four of whom were Porters, stood under the boughs of a poplar. Samuel and Maud watched the initial proceedings from the car, then left. Samuel had to finish restoring an electric kettle.

As Samuel was taking a break in his yard two hours later, a truck pulled into his drive. Seeing Eudora at its wheel, Samuel felt anxious and tried to go inside. But age was slowing him, and he'd barely made it to the steps before the Porters poured out and Eudora called his name.

She limped through the grass and tall dandelions, a brass-handled gentleman's cane in her hand. Her breath was audible, a sound like shifting paper, and she'd grown immense. Samuel's dread became a kind of angry fear.

She was an arresting sight in her mourning. Eudora wore a lush puce gown dignified by a broach at the throat, and the whiteness of her surrounding skin made her look dusted in ash. Her leathery, puckered neck shocked Samuel. Her decrepitude made him conscious of his own decline, so that the rift caused by old betrayals seemed more deep and futile than ever.

"Don't bother to get Maud," she said, her voice lacking its past strength. "I just wanted to say good-bye. Without Ray . . . I've sold what's left of the farms, the house, too. But don't worry, not this one. This one's for your families. I'll be in a nursing home come Tuesday.

Seventy's no better than sixty, Ray said it himself." She glanced around the yard.

Samuel stood clutching his hat. He placed it on his head, and said, "I am sorry for your loss."

Eudora gave him a desperate look, as though she'd been waiting for that gesture. "And I'm sorry for yours," she said, taking a gentle step forward. "I'm sorry for yours."

They stood looking at each other. Only when Eudora touched her eyes did he see she was crying, and without talking he watched her walk to the truck. He could feel her eyes on him as she revved the engine, saw the pleading in them. He went into the house without waving.

Samuel never told Maud; he couldn't risk upsetting her nerves. She spent her afternoons pretending to solve crosswords and watching game shows on the battered television Samuel had salvaged from the alley behind his old shop. The shop itself had been boarded with planks that swelled in all weather and were defaced by silly free-love graffiti that belied the horror of what had happened there. The landlord hadn't had insurance and, after initially threatening to sue Samuel, had merely swallowed his losses. Samuel tried not to pass by the shop at all, because when he did he was sickened by the deceit of what looked like a civilized business run aground by bad accounting. The farce this made of his economics degree, and the hypocrisy of the townspeople, exacerbated his neuralgia so badly he couldn't eat for a week. It had also become impossible to leave Maud for long periods; the Porters were either out or kept largely to themselves, and Maud was prone to disorienting panic attacks.

On a particularly stressful night, he returned from town to find her sitting on the foyer stairs. She was so terrified she didn't recognize him. She'd twisted the rings on her fingers with such violence that they'd cut her.

"We never abused them," she muttered. "We never hurt them."

Samuel took her arm. "I know, Maud."

"We should have stayed in Calgary."

"I know, Maud."

At first put off by these scenes, Samuel had soon realized she didn't really want her daughters back. The idea of their return frightened her. Her griping came not from the anguish of having put them away, but from her guilt at not wanting them back. She could not, of course, admit this; in fact, Samuel would have been surprised if she even suspected it of herself. But she'd stopped reading the progress reports from the facility entirely.

She strolled the grounds, cultivating a garden of equatorial fruit that had no possible hope of surviving the winter. When everything withered with the first frosts and the television failed to entertain her, Maud seemed to do nothing at all, so that to an outsider it might seem she had reached a kind of peace.

She would lie on the grimy chesterfield, one of the twins' blue sweaters supporting her nape, a water-worn romance novel blocking the sun from her face. She'd snore lightly, and Samuel would ease the book away so she could breathe better. Such was the case on that final Sunday in March of 1975, when Samuel entered the dusty, sun-filled living room, with its age-worn decor and its sad aloe veras leaking fragrantly. Maud's hair wreathed the buckling paperback, her hands relaxed on her thighs. Taking the book from her face, Samuel paused. Her eyes were closed, the moth-like eyelids ashen and fragile as ever. But her face had altered, so that she re-achieved the look of the obscure girl he'd courted at the church doors and married with a haste unusual for him. And he kneeled at the couch, feeling as if he himself had died, not anguished but at peace, because he'd finally seen the end of it.

They told him coronary thrombosis, though he knew with certainty that Maud, only fifty, had died of grief. He buried her beside Jacob in Dalewood Cemetery outside Aster, alone and without a tear in his eye. Their citizenship had been finalized; their flesh, his kin, cold in the ground, were now inseverable from Alberta.

When the final dirt was thrown he went home, and ignoring the Porters' pity, he climbed astride the rusted John Deere to mow a lawn now more ash than grass. He was aware of being watched from the bay window, but he had that hard feeling of being a spectator himself, as though he were traveling deep in his own body and could not resurface. He thought of Maud in her coffin, how a cut she'd given herself the morning of her death had scarred over. And it seemed the most undignified thing in the world to him that even in death the body continued to heal. He had them close the coffin.

On the first night of his insomnia, the night of her funeral, Samuel rose and made an altar of the disused fireplace. He placed on the mantel stray flowers from her wreaths, a piece of hair he'd clipped from her nape, pictures of distant happiness and recent ones, too. He hunted the house for Jacob's rotting albums, and placed chipped, worn-out photographs of all the dead relatives beside Maud's. He put a dried rose under an image of young Jacob, caught in a rare, apologetic smile. Beside this picture he placed Jacob's favorite brass vase. Samuel made offerings of yams and whisky to God, with prayers for the well-being of the dead who were at the mercy of being forgotten. He retreated to the vacant bed, dry-eyed and in a painful stupor, and at the first light of day he dressed in his cleanest blue suit to drive to the facility to tell his daughters.

Death, it seemed, was the only matter the facility thought worthwhile enough to require a visit. When he arrived, he was obliged to sit in a beige, windowless room smelling of vomit until they brought in Yvette. Samuel almost collapsed at the sight of her. Rather than twenty, she looked middle-aged. An orderly stood in a corner to oversee the visit, and when Samuel asked after Chloe he was told she was on a different, unvisitable ward. When Samuel expressed concern over how much worse she must be than her sister, the orderly assured him Chloe was fine.

"She likes to act up every once in a while," said the orderly. "I'll be happy to pass on whatever news you have for her, though."

Frowning, Samuel focused on Yvette, whose face was bloated with medication, and whose agitated hands made meaningless gestures as he spoke. Her hair was shorn to the scalp, and she exaggerated the movements of her mouth in her single-word answers. Her first words startled Samuel, who realized without being conscious of it that over seven years had passed since he'd heard that voice. Though its golden inflections were lost, it was largely the same.

Samuel felt a cramp in his heart. Clearing his throat, he said, "Yvie. Yvette. Your mother passed away last week."

She seemed not to understand. Samuel began to repeat the news when he was admonished by the orderly: "Don't overexcite her."

The only sign Yvette had heard Samuel at all was a trembling of the mouth. Samuel knew then that he and Maud were at fault for the twins' state; not only for having abandoned them, but for something blood-deep: *from their fruits you will know them.* Samuel took her tiny, rough hand in his own. They sat in this way until visitors' hours ended and Samuel was told to leave.

At home, the Porters didn't know how to behave toward him. Akosua treated him with a pity that aggravated him. The children went on with their lives, and Saul was his same cryptic self. Forty days later all eight of them crowded into the backyard as Samuel went through the necessary ceremonial gestures, pouring a whisky libation for Maud and belatedly for Jacob, asking the ancestors to put them to peaceful rest. Jacob could finally stop wrestling and be blessed by his angel.

Samuel gathered the courage to finish the letter to Maud's family, and the Adu Darkos' response shocked him into seeing how exiled he was from the culture of his birth. Instead of grief, Maud's uncle, Kojo Adu Darko, expressed brief condolences and insisted that Samuel marry one of Maud's sisters so that he would remain a relation. Samuel sent a letter declining the offer.

He tried to climb back into his life. Both men he was indebted to died. Elliot's will had forgiven Samuel's debts, but Wainright's hadn't, and so that angular man's son took the leash, and Samuel worked methodically, indifferent to the lifetime sentence. He had made the mistake of borrowing much more than he needed, of sparing no expense, as if the wealth was his own and without limits, and now he wass paying for it.

Samuel watched the Porter children one by one abandon town for city, and felt a kind of vicarious pride when Teteh, the second oldest son, was accepted for study at the University of Alberta. The eldest daughters married, Samuel a background shadow at these festive occasions. He pretended when he had to that he liked his second bachelorhood, though anyone could see he suffered.

With so little to distract him now, as he aged, he became hypersensitive to his changing body. Sweaty feet, acrid breath, a sort of sullen endurance to his heartbeat. Though obsessed, in an abstract way, with what happened after death, he also wanted to be able to say he'd taken as much as possible from life. He watched his body for signs of dying, and found them: the taste of lead in his mouth, a knot in his stomach that often stopped him from eating, a kind of drifting feeling that was like grief but didn't keep him up at night. An untraceable but definite illness was taking hold of him.

Thoughts of sickness consumed him. Only when misfortune struck the house could he train his thoughts away from it. He thrived on chaos; the greater the tumult, the more he could throw himself into life and forget for a time the stale, rotting sickness within him. Often he wondered how he could be so crazy—his illness was a phantom, a kind of physical grief at his wife's death. But the Porters' scrutiny of his lack of appetite made him eat even less.

Akosua, with her mother's intuition, sensed his sickness and began to treat Samuel like an invalid. She cleaned up after him, and watched him on the stairs to make sure he didn't fall, but when she began to cut Samuel's meat, he slapped her hand.

"Do you think I have grown so weak as not to have the strength to cut my own meat?" he cried. Akosua mumbled under her breath, but like an overbearing parent she continued to do these things for him. The kinder her actions, the more infuriated Samuel became. But she could not be put off, and he grudgingly accepted her help.

Samuel grew argumentative and disoriented. His work, even the most basic tinkering, became impossible. He began to view his illness as yet another weakness, something a greater man could cure by will, with diet and exercise. To *see* the change, you had to *be* the change, and Samuel riled his appetite and took short walks to cure this thing.

Every day that he failed to recuperate proved his bad character, and seeing his own limits hurt him more than the pain that had begun to plague his nights. During these midnight torments, disoriented, he began to associate the pain with the house and his loss of it. And as if to cure it, he began to take religious care of the front grounds, pulling out weeds with failing strength. Samuel cleaned up a little, discovering books of philosophy he hadn't read since youth, and in the weeks of insomnia he perused them. The more he read, the more he realized that the wise tended toward simplicity. Not that their ideas were simple, but that they delivered them with the clarity of a prayer so that their wisdom could be grasped by every man. He became suspicious of sophistication, for it seemed only those who didn't know what they were talking about needed to be brocade, as if to hide their ignorance. And he scoffed at how he'd complicated his own life.

When a few weeks of cleaning still brought him no peace, Samuel began to despair. Everything lacked tangibility, so that only the pain seemed real, reliable. It was a kind of stability, he supposed, but the worst kind. Noises in the house agitated him, and he hated the happy sound of Porter's children beyond the door of his study. The only consolation he took from their twittering nonsense was that they, too, would know the pain and solitude of sickness one day, and when that day came, there would be precious little to laugh about. Then he would suddenly see the barbarity of this thought, and rebuke himself for it. Only a sick man would begrudge children. Then he'd remember the twins, and sit brooding.

In truth, his sickness was like a second childhood. He found himself unable to comprehend what was taking place inside him, and grew indifferent to everything, watching his life from behind a window, uncomfortable everywhere. Most devastating was the constant exhaustion; it made him feel useless. His futility disturbed him; he botched six out of nine repairs for Wainright Junior and had to redo them. A vicious circle, because sometimes undoing the mistakes made them worse. He had never felt so worthless. And this, worsened by a decade of loss, made him irate and unbearable, until even he knew his tongue was more severe than the Porters deserved. But they withstood it, the children following their father's example by ignoring Samuel, and Akosua laboring to protect the last of his health. Samuel did not know which was worse. He continued to express his fear in bad behavior, and was surprised at the relief he felt when Saul began to bring him mugs of bitter tea on the evenings Samuel sat on the ledge of the bay window.

Porter approached with the cautious movements of a beetle, wearing polyester trousers and smelling of the lanolin he used for arthritis. The years had solidified him, so that he had that thickened, invincible look of a bull in its prime. He thrust the pink mug at Samuel, never meeting his eye, then sat beside him without being invited. Porter's old age was extraordinary: his beard was now shale-colored, its thick coils grouped by a blue elastic band; his right eye listed with a blindness Akosua told Samuel had begun in his sleep; and his immense brow sagged, as though worn out by a lifetime of thought. Sitting beside him, Samuel felt dwarfed, saddened that his sickness would make him even thinner. The two sat in silence, sipping their bitter roots, watching the sunset light up the ash. It became their ritual. In the years after Porter died (for he was closer to it than anyone knew), these shared nights became Samuel's foremost memory of his enemy. Saul seemed the only one willing to view Samuel's sickness with honesty, as the unchangeable fact that it was, and Samuel appreciated his practicality and lack of pity. When Saul died of old age two years later, Samuel presided at his funeral with this same nuts-and-bolts approach. Only days later did Samuel realize that he *did* feel something: sadness, relief, even an embarrassing sort of triumph at having outlived both him and Ray. But all this death made his own mortality more of a reality, so that his triumph was a small thing.

Samuel's sickness, unlocatable, incurable, dragged on for another twenty-one years. During this time he helped Akosua raise the last two children as his own, and in the unbearable vacancy left by Maud and Saul, they began to share a conjugal bed. The bed-sharing didn't last long though, for beyond Samuel's sickness and Akosua's unshakable distaste for him, they were conscious of betraying their spouses in a way that hadn't existed while they'd lived. The children grew. One moved to Edmonton to study law, and Akosua, having scrimped and saved her widow's pension, decided to take her last child back to Ghana.

The day of her departure, Samuel waited on the porch with her for the taxi to the airport. When it arrived, Samuel handed the driver money, embarrassed about being too weak to help with the bags.

Akosua touched Samuel's face. "I will be praying for you, old man. May God give you another fifty years."

"Of this life? Eh, never. Not for all the gold in heaven."

Samuel gave her a little money to take to his sister and his ailing mother, who by some Methuselan miracle, was still alive at the age of one hundred and seven. He himself could not return. His dead were in the ground. The house belonged to him again.

On the last day of summer, after years of prolonged solitude, Samuel received his first shock. He'd begun to wander the yard, as Maud once had, listless and apparition-like in the dark suits he'd wear to his death. A woman stood beyond the leaves of a far tree, looking at him with familiar astonishment. He backed from the tree, his hands fingering an invisible hat brim. It was one of the twins.

"Don't be afraid," she said, though she herself felt alarmed. He looked senile in his huge faded suit, like a child playing dress-up. "It's Ama, Ama Ouillet. The twins' friend." Samuel looked confused, and Ama approached him as though she feared he'd run away. She was amazed at how cruel the years had been to him. His hair had gone full salt, his nostrils and ears were comically large, his body like a blade in his humongous, outdated clothes. The only thing not ravaged by time was his radiant skin, still elastic, unlined as an infant's. She tried to smile; he seemed to recognize that weak attempt better than her genuine one, and let her guide him into the house.

Ama had bumped into Teteh Porter on the university campus. Now a dapper and swaggering man in his late twenties, he recognized Ama, and pulled her aside to tell her all that had happened since that summer.

"I think old Samuel's still living out there," he concluded. "He's a strong old codger. Heard he's been sick for years."

Ama worked the night shift on the Larkspur and Primrose wings of the Granada Nursing Home. Her ambitions to be a doctor had been cured by a violent love affair in which, miraculously, the only thing killed was her self-esteem. She drifted for years in and out of bad love until her sudden, self-willed recovery. The age of awakening having come late, she satisfied herself with the shorter training of nursing school. But it suited her, and was in so many ways more varied than the predictable prestige of being a doctor. Not a morning passed that she didn't collapse into sleep from overwork. She was skinny as an urchin, and the erratic hours had destroyed her beauty, but she preferred it that way.

The house astounded her; it had remained unchanged these thirty years right down to the bowl of false orange roses at the entrance. Clothes had stiffened on hangers, and the muddy children's tracks on the Venetian carpet could easily have been hers. When she entered the twins' room, with its burlap curtains and the child-sized cots she was gaunt enough to still fit in, she felt overwhelmed. She realized she'd put off returning because staying was inevitable. Aster felt frozen in time, though it had in fact seen more changes than any other place in Alberta. Ama recalled that summer here more clearly than any other era of her life, still confused about what had happened. Though she'd continued to wear her crucifix, pray daily and attend church, she'd stopped asking herself the meaning of these acts, or what comfort they offered. It took seeing the Tyne house again for her to feel, as if for the first time, the guilt she had let destroy her life.

She moved in, keeping her city apartment as a refuge. It was hard to reconcile the blundering, likeable Samuel of the past to this disconsolate wretch. At first Ama felt each sting of his bitter tongue, but within a week she realized he meant none of it. His slander was his way of saying he was afraid. When she tried to subdue him, he screamed that he was no goddamn animal, and that she could go to hell if she was there to make an invalid of him. So she became brusque, even rude, and he began to trust her, asking her to do things he was more than capable of. She became a sort of unpaid servant, so overworked she grew haggard. To change things she left him to his own devices for three days, so that by the time she returned he'd regained his self-sufficiency. In fact, his illness had become a painful embarrassment to him; sudden attacks of vomiting and diarrhea so hurt his dignity, left him so helpless, that Ama was careful to keep a steady face while cleaning up. Not that it bothered her: having watched her father care for her mother and having herself nursed her father, she beyond anyone understood that the body's misfortunes were not failings of character, had nothing to do with the beauty of the soul.

Then Ama discovered a thickened, hard growth in Samuel's abdomen. She wanted it to be a hernia, but begged Samuel to go to the hospital. When he refused, she arranged for Dr. Balsam to come in from Granada. A short, thick Englishman lauded for his drawn-out but accurate diagnoses, Dr. Balsam astounded Ama by the finality of his pronouncement, which only took ten minutes.

"Cancer, unquestionably," he said, frowning. "Don't know how many years in the making. Probably inoperable, but get him to hospital, won't you? At least then he'll die in two weeks, rather than one."

Ama felt stricken. She had waited too long to come back. She pleaded with him to go to the hospital and again he refused. They argued for hours, a spiteful clash that ended in him declaring that she would have to break every bone in his body to drag him there. It took her a day to see that for him it was already over, and she was ashamed at denying a seventy-year-old man the dignity of dying at home.

She secured morphine from the nursing home. From that time on Samuel was rarely lucid, but when he felt strong he would leave bed to roam the house, throwing on all of the lights, even in the daytime, so that later Ama would recall this period with a violent clarity. As though his inner darkness might be eased out with light.

He remembered telling Maud, on one of her worst days of worrying for the twins, "People can adapt to most anything—that is the nature of being a man." Faced now with the brief eternity before him, he saw how flippant, how cruel, that adage was. The ability to do something didn't make it less painful to do. To go on in the face of everyday banality was a kind of heroism. That he carried on, without the consolation of a possible change in his situation, was the triumph to which Samuel attached the last of his dignity. Living is an abstraction for all of us. For Samuel, it became an entity to torment and to be tormented by, a dog he bitterly prayed would misbehave so he could kick it. His living was more a fighting with life. He hung on as though affronting someone.

Samuel sat in a living-room chair, gazing into the vacant fireplace. Though it threw ash in his face, he continued to sit as if he didn't notice it. He was transported, for a moment, back to his adolescence, standing at a blackboard trying to solve a problem of horrific difficulty. And as he stood there, sweating, ready to give up, the answer came to him like a slap and he stood from the chair, leaning breathlessly against the old fireplace. He felt he'd had some kind of epiphany, but his mind was too restless and cloudy with drugs for him to grasp it. Only when he lay in bed with his usual night pains, did twenty years of agony become clear.

Between Samuel and Jacob there had been a silent agreement that neither would return to Gold Coast. Exile is hard to overcome. Aster, with its black origins, became a surrogate homeland, a way of returning without returning. But Samuel had never figured out why Jacob stayed. It made sense now. The betrayal between Jacob and Samuel's father didn't matter—Jacob had made amends. But the need to escape, Samuel understood better than anyone: that sudden desire to turn from anything you're obligated to, from anything that felt like duty. Samuel himself had turned from his family, his government job, from anything that had asked something of his life. Not on purpose; instinctively. The older men get, the harder they try to guard against unwanted demands on a life made suddenly precious by impending mortality.

Samuel remembered Jacob chastising him for a school essay he'd written but hadn't yet turned in.

"When your work is done, set it aside and forget it. Only a fool cracks a statue by continuing to carve."

And Jacob lived by his word. He'd stayed in Aster to have his own life before dying. He'd stayed because Aster was not so much a town he'd moved to, as a place that had happened to him. A new life begins, the past can never be recovered.

Samuel didn't sleep that night.

Ama began to clean the house. It turned out that filth and disarray were part of the home's foundations. Ama wondered that the Tynes had managed to live here for so many years. She fell sick with asthma. But she persisted, piling the clothes of the dead in the room she'd shared with the twins. She fastened the fragile curtains, and restored the living room to its stately but cheap character. She whitewashed the cellar, with its stink of rotting tuber and its larvae, and she poisoned the woodlice from the undersides of tables and banisters. The decay kept reclaiming its territory, but she refused to give in, recleaning what had been scrubbed an hour earlier. She swept the relics on the mantel, gashed at the ash in the fireplace solidified like tar. She straddled the shaky ladder of Maud's accident to wipe cobwebs from the water-stained ceilings.

But when she decided to prune the cocoa yam plant Samuel had been cultivating in the kitchen, her ferocious cleaning came to an end. The full plant stifled all the sunlight from the room. Ama made the morning drive from Edmonton in the dark, and found that having to sit in a kitchen where the sun never rose depressed her. She bought a paring knife from the drugstore, and at the first chance began to carve off thick, waxen leaves. Covered in green juice, she marveled at the white light filling the room. Samuel felt well enough to walk that day, and she brought him down to see the results.

His reaction could not have been worse. This man who so feared darkness, who couldn't stand a room darker than the beginning of dusk, made an anguished sound. He gathered the huge clipped leaves around him, arranging and rearranging them like a grieved child with the broken pieces of a toy. "If you cut it," he said, "it dies."

He stood looking at the slaughter around him. When she gathered the courage to go to him, he accepted her help, too grieved to feel embarrassed that he was now light enough to be carried on her thin back up the stairs.

For half an hour he wouldn't speak to her. She was about to leave the room when he said, "Ama. It is . . ." His throat was parched, and she held a glass to his lips. "It is only a plant. It is only a plant."

Ama gripped his hand.

He smiled, looking around as though to make sense of the room. "Can we not go outside?"

He had not been outdoors since his illness had become serious, and was amazed to see a stately farmhouse in place of Porter's ruins, the ash regenerated into a lawn so green and vibrant it looked fake. Barefoot, Samuel wandered the grounds, frowning against the radiant sun that hadn't touched him since the last devil's rainstorm of the previous May. After watching over him for a while, Ama was walking toward the house when he called her name.

He had found something, and gestured for her to approach. At first she could not make sense of what she was looking at. Only when she crouched could she see the strangeness of what lay in the ground. In a patch of the field where the grass had refused to take lay a small cat's skeleton, embedded in the dirt. The intricate skull and teeth were still intact, as were the rest of its bones: the only things missing were the bones of one paw.

"Amazing," breathed Ama. Samuel asked to be taken inside. The cat seemed to pacify him; he slept well that night.

It was his last walk outside. The backyard held nothing but the expensive house, and in the front the sounds of passersby behind the trees bothered him.

Samuel began to speak about his life as though the choices weren't over, as though what looked like death in him was a natural, and even necessary sickness. He began to say that once he'd overcome it, he would relocate to the kinder winters of British Columbia, rebuild his dream there. That he would take another wife, buy a suitable house and send for the twins to live with them. That if he could just hold on to his health long enough, he could reinvent the bachelor he'd been, with his arrogance and his hope. Ama didn't know how much he believed himself, or if he even believed himself at all, and so she nodded in a way that said she understood, but discouraged him from going on.

Samuel dropped his head back on the pillows. "I feel parched and stiff all over. My skin, my entire body, is turning into a desert."

Ama smiled. "It's the morphine, Samuel. That's one of the side effects."

"No no no no. It is because I have been away from the ocean too long. Every hour away from it turns my body to ash."

Ama turned him on his side. "You've become a poet now, have you? That's *not* one of the side effects of morphine. What did you used to say? 'A black Homer for modern times'?"

Samuel laughed, wincing. He looked faint. "If I live to see eighty, I will pilgrimage to the coast, walk into the ocean and never come out."

"Oh, stop being so morbid. Now, let's put some balm on the other side."

When she returned to check on him an hour later, his sleep looked too peaceful. Anxious, she leaned over his bed and saw him breathing. She was astounded at how the sickness had aged him. His skull had grown pronounced, his tribal marks looked like fresh incisions in his sunken cheeks. He smelled of sugar beets and sweet milk, and a darker smell she couldn't characterize. All signs she'd seen before.

When she returned again hours later, she found him almost sitting up, a stricken look on his face. She forced him to lie down, talking softly as he wept and sputtered under a pain she couldn't imagine. He began to speak in great outbursts of sound. Ama realized he was using actual words, probably from his ancestral language, and though it was impossible, she tried to understand. The whites of his eyes were bloodshot, and he seemed to lose control of his senses, belting out words, his eyes pleading to be understood. Finally he relaxed. Ama did not know if it was in his native language, or in English, but in the hour of his death, Samuel spoke only one phrase: "Let me wake up, the pain has seen night."

He died open-eyed at nine in the evening. Crying, Ama washed the body and laid it out in his best suit. There were no mourners, no one left of his loved ones for a viewing. She called the hospital and, while making funeral arrangements, tried to contact the twins at the facility, though after thirty years she was unsure if they were still confined. Her attempts were fruitless. Not even death held any clout with the facility anymore. After five days of waiting for the facility authorities to answer her inquiry, Ama had Samuel buried in a traditional kente robe in a plot beside Maud's and Jacob's. She and Teteh Porter were the only mourners, and afterward she drove back to Aster and sat on the ledge of the bay window, watching people in the distance without really seeing them.

It had been a beautiful day for an outdoor ceremony, with the kind of lucid weather she hoped to have at her own funeral. She thought often of her own death, but without fear, loss having been her only belonging in this life. For years, acceptance had been her only means of survival. She knew that no matter how miserable or wretched life became, all she could do with her meek piece of time was sustain it. Decades of guilt, lost faith, the betrayal by those few people she'd let herself love—it was worth enduring these things, if only for the gift of a single, exalted moment. And such moments happened, even frequently, in the lives of people wise enough to see them.

The day would come when a distant house would fall and take its neighbors with it; when Aster would be razed and sold off in plots to new farmers from far lands. She could see it crumbling already, the people with their petty grudges against one another, the children leaving for the city, richer towns growing like brushfire on both sides, abandoned land bought up with the frivolity of something cheap. But there would be time enough for those deaths, time after the lone twin returned to reclaim the home where all had changed for her. A time when, days, weeks, years later, she walks the weed-strewn path to the old house to find it so identical to her memory of it that already it is changing. That, burdened with her past and the dead sister she carries like a conscience inside of her, she sits where Ama sat, trying to endure her first night of freedom, waiting for the sight of dawn to believe she is strong enough to begin again. To know there is meaning in being alone. Devastated to have outlived everything, to have outgrown even her own madness, her solitude is only one of many new struggles she will have to overcome, the worst of which is knowing this. It will not be an easy road, but many have worse, and her only obligation amidst all the pain and occasional pleasure is to live in the best way she is capable of. That is all we have.

acknowledgments

I wish to offer my gratitude to the following:

Jordi MacDonald, Jack Hodgins, and Stephen Dixon for their varied
and endless support; Jackie Baker and Jeff Mireau for their critical
acumen on earlier drafts; Anne McDermid, Dawn Davis at Amistad/
HarperCollins, Diane Martin and everyone at Knopf Canada for their
expertise; Kweku Edugyan, Peggy Price and Bob Price for their patience,
guidance and support; The Canada Council for the Arts, the Fine Arts
Work Center in Provincetown and the British Columbia Arts Council
for invaluable funding; Steven Price, without whose encouragement,
critical eye and dogged faith this work would not have been possible.

A graduate of Johns Hopkins University and the University of Victoria, ESI EDUGYAN was raised in Calgary. She has completed a fiction fellowship at the Fine Arts Work Center in Provincetown, Massachusetts. Her previous work has appeared in *Best New American Voices 2003*, edited by Joyce Carol Oates. She lives in Victoria, Canada.